To Susan, for everything

THE UNMOORING

BOOK ONE

Chapter One
—New Frontier—

January 1961

1: Bird's Eye View

The snow began falling before midnight, swept across Washington by a stiff northwest wind. The skies cleared by sunrise, but then the gale picked up. It whipped the snow into high drifts across the city's broad avenues and plazas, like the one facing the Capitol, where a crowd was already gathering for the inauguration of the new president at noon. As the temperature plunged and the wind rose, many in the plaza huddled together and shivered as they waited.

Michael McMaster wasn't shivering. He was young, and he was dressed for the weather. And he was aglow inside, warmed by enthusiasm for John F. Kennedy and the new administration this energetic young leader was about to launch. Michael had cut classes at Columbia last fall to campaign for Kennedy, swept up in the candidate's eloquence, youthful good looks and air of romantic possibility. He'd eagerly done the campaign's scutwork, from stuffing envelopes to staffing phone banks. He spent election eve of 1960 at the subway entrance at 72nd Street and Broadway, handing out Kennedy flyers and trading barbs with Nixon backers. Today was the payoff for all the hopes and hard work.

Michael was also adventurous. By 10 o'clock he had climbed one of the bare trees bordering the plaza and found a precarious perch in the crook of a limb, accepting greater wind exposure for a better look at the spectacle.

Looking down, he waved to one of his journalism school friends, Marta Hauser. She was looking up with a mixture of eagerness and apprehension.

"Aren't you freezing? It's bad enough down here, but the wind must be really fierce up there."

"It's worth it. The view's incredible. Come on up, there's room. I'll help you."

"I don't need any help, thank you very much." Marta hesitated for a moment, then started up the tree, climbing nimbly. He moved over, and they nestled together companionably. Marta pulled her knit hat down over her long dark hair and looked out over the plaza.

"You're right, this view is amazing. And we'll probably hear better up here."

"I hope so," Michael said. "Robert Frost is supposed to recite a new poem. And then Kennedy. This will be a day to remember."

A Capitol Police officer interrupted them. "You two got to come down," he called to them. "You're making the Secret Service nervous."

"Cops," Marta muttered as she swung herself off the limb and started down. "Always on hand to ruin a good moment."

"Nothing's gonna ruin this for me," Michael said. "We'll be telling our grandkids we were here today, that we witnessed the start of a new era in American history."

"You sound like a newsreel," Marta said as they reached the ground. "I was for him, too, but let him do something before we proclaim any new eras."

Michael pointed at the platform. "Look at those old men sitting there in their ridiculous top hats. Eisenhower. Truman. Lyndon Johnson. Sam Rayburn. Everett Dirksen. There's a whole generation of fossils up there with only one thought: to freeze things the way they are and then invent reasons for why it has to be that way. What they've given us is a country that's entirely too pleased with itself, that's drugged on prosperity and consumerism. It needs shaking up, and Kennedy is just the leader to do it."

"Now you sound like a campaign ad," Marta said. "Did you miss Professor Fuller's lecture about how the press shilled for Kennedy during the campaign? He didn't mean it as a compliment."

Michael started to respond, then fell silent. In truth, what he saw in Jack Kennedy was sometimes difficult to put into words. In his more reflective moments, he recognized that much of it was atmospherics, the elaborate theatrics of youth, vigor and rhetorical polish that Kennedy and his entourage went to such great lengths to project.

Michael's elders had warned him against putting too much trust in the images politicians conjured for their own purposes. But Michael thought he sensed something about Kennedy that transcended campaign stagecraft: a restless intelligence and an instinctive impulse to disrupt, to stir a stagnant pot. Kennedy represented a challenge to the status quo by his very nature. The contrast between him and the outgoing president—the grandfatherly, tongue-tied, septuagenarian Eisenhower—could not have been starker. That symbolism, alone, might be enough to jolt the country into motion.

This prospect resonated deeply with Michael in his present state of mind, which had taken a restive, rebellious turn. Four years of college and two in the Army had sharpened his view of the world and of his country, and he didn't like what he saw. He had come to regard mainstream America as smug, lazy, and heedless—heedless of the suffering in the shadows that the postwar prosperity obscured, and just as heedless of its untapped potential.

His rebelliousness wasn't new; as a teenager, he had rejected his father's alma mater, Georgetown, and chosen to go away to New York and Columbia for college. This hadn't pleased his parents, but that was part of the attraction. And he much preferred New York's energy and elan to Washington's staid predictability. He fell in love with the eclectic stew of the Greenwich Village scene, and soon was taking long subway rides down from Morningside Heights to marinate in the mélange of avant-garde poets, jazz and folk musicians, and activists promoting any number of causes.

One cause above all fired his imagination, and symbolized his hopes for a new beginning in America: the civil rights movement's challenge to the strictures of racial discrimination that still scarred the South, more than six years after the Supreme Court had declared that segregation was unconstitutional. Just a year ago, four black college students had walked up to a lunch counter in Greensboro, N.C., sat down, and defied local law and custom by the simple act of asking to be served. They touched off a wave of protests that swept across the South and then spread to northern cities—and resonated deeply with Michael.

He saw it in the stark, uncomplicated terms of youth. Racial bias was wrong, a moral outrage, an ugly stain of shame on a country that called itself an avatar of freedom. There could be no compromise with this festering evil.

Michael had grown up in a white and rather rarified world, but the issue wasn't altogether abstract for him. The school he'd attended as a child and teenager was integrated, and not by chance. His own parents and other like-minded people had created it in the 1940s because they could not abide sending their children to Washington's officially segregated public schools. During his obligatory two years of military service after undergrad school, his units had been nominally integrated. Yet during training rotations in Georgia and Texas, he had seen the unequal treatment that black soldiers suffered when they went off-base, and how the Army brass did little to change that treatment. Michael had disliked the Army for many reasons, but that one ranked near the top of his list.

Yet even as Michael embraced his rebellious spirit, he knew that it had created an unresolved inner conflict, one that was worrying him more and more. He was determined to launch a career as a journalist. He was good at his craft, already writing for local publications, eager to land a job and hone his skills. More than once, however, he had been warned that his professional aspirations and his political instincts were on a collision course, that he would have to choose between journalism and activism.

He understood the warning, but he thought he could resolve the conflict. The best journalists, he thought, were those who embraced the idea of using their craft to hold power accountable—to heed the old precept that a journalist's job was to comfort the afflicted and afflict the comfortable. If he could honor that precept, he thought, he could also honor both sides of his inner duality.

And so Michael looked across the plaza at the inaugural platform, filling up with dignitaries in somber suits and full-dress uniforms, and saw it as the set of a play just before curtain time—a stage full of secondary figures frozen in place, awaiting the star, the sole character who could set the drama in motion.

2: On the Platform

Michael's recitation to Marta of the powerful ancients on the inaugural platform had omitted two people: his own parents. He was a child of privilege, a fact he habitually concealed because it caused him considerable embarrassment. For all his affection for his family, his parents were part of the generational elite that had made America what it was—and if Michael was unhappy with what it was, he thought he knew where the responsibility rested.

While Michael was scaling his elm, his mother was finding her seat on the platform, just four rows from the podium. It was a favored place, but Anna Arden's mood was far from complacent. For her, today's ritual was a welcome end to eight years of Republican rule—but also a source of apprehension. Unlike her son, she regarded Jack Kennedy as something of a blank slate, and she was anxious to hear how he would begin to fill it. Yet she couldn't quite shake the fear that she and her fellow liberals would be as frustrated by this new administration as they had been by the departing one.

As she settled in her chair, she accepted an awkward peck on the cheek from the man next to her, the economist John Kenneth Galbraith. The moment had its comic aspect; Anna was a small woman, and Galbraith was a gawky 6 feet 8, forcing him to rise for leverage and then bend almost double to deliver his greeting.

Anna and Ken Galbraith had traveled many roads together, from co-founding the liberal lobbying group Americans for Democratic Action to working on Adlai Stevenson's doomed presidential campaigns and then Kennedy's winning one. Now, Galbraith was back in government—but in a curious way, Anna thought.

"Ken, I hear you're ticketed for India. That's exciting, but I didn't know you had aspirations to be an ambassador."

Galbraith's long, expressive face twisted in a half-smile, half-grimace. "Jack is very happy to have me at hand—just not too close at hand," he said. "One might think a new president would ask an economist for advice on, well, the economy. The American economy."

"Did you and he have a problem?"

"The problem is that I advised Adlai before I advised Jack. I don't think he'll ever fully trust anyone who falls into that category. Take care, my dear. For Jack Kennedy, people like us may be useful at times, but we're to be kept at a distance. In my case, a distance of about 7,000 miles."

"Well, Ken, I know you'll be half a world away hobnobbing with Nehru, but I hope you'll think of us back here, and lend us your influence. We're going to need all the help we can muster to fight for our issues."

They both understood the precariousness of the liberal agenda at the start of this new administration. What they wanted was clear enough: action on civil rights, a government health care program for elderly Americans, federal aid to public schools—perhaps even finding a way to lessen the ominous Cold War tensions with the

Soviets. Kennedy had campaigned on some of those issues—sort of—but Anna believed he would need a lot of reminders that liberals expected results.

Anna had long harbored feelings of ambivalence about Kennedy. As the 1960 campaign season began and Kennedy launched his candidacy, she had distrusted him, recalling with distaste his tolerance of Joe McCarthy's red-scare demagoguery and his brother Bobby's work as a lawyer for McCarthy's committee. She'd cherished the hope that the party would give her old friend Stevenson a third shot at the presidency, and she resented Kennedy as an interloper when he snatched away the nomination.

If Stevenson was the liberals' great lost cause, however, Richard Nixon was their abiding nightmare. Once the Republicans nominated Nixon, Anna put aside her qualms and campaigned wholeheartedly for Kennedy. During the wilderness years of the 1950s, liberals had created a web of citizens' groups that spanned the nation, from the California Democratic Council to New York's Reform Democrat clubs. Anna became one of Kennedy's most effective emissaries to these activists, and to a network of women's groups.

Anna had experienced the capricious dynamics of power from both sides. She came from a family of New England social reformers—an abolitionist grandfather, a mother who campaigned for temperance and women's suffrage, a Unitarian minister father who sometimes angered his congregation with sermons criticizing Gilded Age greed. Anna was taught from an early age that her family's relatively comfortable circumstances amid America's great disparities of wealth created an imperative to act on behalf of those who were not so favored. She soon outgrew her family's genteel *noblesse oblige*, however, coming to believe that the iniquities of a systemically unjust society could only end through systemic change.

She first made her mark in life as a writer, crafting keenly observed pieces about the struggles of women working arduous jobs in textile mills, miners battling rapacious absentee owners, sharply drawn satirical sketches of life in Hitler's Germany in the 1930s, and a breakthrough novel about Americans made destitute by the Depression. Throughout most of those years, she was an outsider, a Cassandra trying to prod through the force of her prose. She was fiercely proud of this lonely, often unrequited role. A relative had once pronounced a judgment that she thought was exceptionally apt: "Anna, you're just a natural stranger."

But through her socially committed writing, she came to know Eleanor Roosevelt, and through the first lady, she became active in political life. She maintained her writing career after she married Alan McMaster and became a mother, but over time, the prospect of being able to do more than merely goad from afar became irresistible. By the 1950s, she had become a formidable political figure. She helped nurture the ADA into one of the nation's most influential liberal organizations and became a member of the Democratic National Committee.

Both Anna and Ken Galbraith had played outsized roles in the Democratic campaign last fall. Galbraith's work as an economic adviser to Kennedy became so prominent that Nixon paid him the ultimate compliment of castigating him as a malign influence on Kennedy. Now, though, the question was whether Galbraith, Anna and their fellow liberals would have much influence at all as the new president, elected by the narrowest of margins, maneuvered to broaden his appeal.

"You're really suggesting to me that he'll need a reminder about who got him to the White House?" Galbraith deadpanned. "Anna, you're becoming such a cynic."

Anna smiled wanly as she tightened her scarf against the cold. "Every politician needs reminding about that from time to time. But he may need it more than most."

3: Cold Warrior

As his wife on the platform and his son on the plaza awaited the advent of what Jack Kennedy had christened the New Frontier, Alan McMaster was inside the Capitol. He was sitting down in one of its small hideaway rooms for coffee with the president-elect, brother Bobby and a few close aides, summoned to offer his advice on a pressing foreign policy issue.

Alan was well practiced in this role. He was a first-generation Cold Warrior, and proud of it. When Kennedy during the campaign had flayed Eisenhower and Nixon for allowing a "missile gap" with the Soviets, Anna had been distraught by his militant rhetoric. Alan couldn't have been happier. He viewed Kennedy's promise to expand the U.S. nuclear arsenal as a comforting sign that Kennedy grasped the existential threat posed by Soviet Communism—even though Alan knew the missile gap didn't exist. He knew that—knew to a certainty that the U.S. had far more nuclear weapons than the Soviets—because he was one of a small group who, in his view, had a right to know such things. And a right, as well as a responsibility, to put that knowledge to use by offering sage advice to presidents and their inner circles.

Alan's membership in this exclusive club of foreign policy mandarins dated to before World War II—or, as Alan and his generation would always call it, The War. Like his wife, he had possessed a Roosevelt connection—but his was to the president.

Alan had caught Franklin Roosevelt's attention as a young diplomat posted in Berlin in the 1930s. His reports back to Washington warning about the rising menace of Nazi Germany had upset his State Department superiors, who shared the prevailing consensus in elite western circles that Hitler was mostly talk and no action, and vastly preferable to Stalin. But they reached Roosevelt's desk through a circuitous back channel and found a welcome audience in a president who shared Alan's dark view of the Nazis.

Alan was soon co-opted into FDR's circle of unofficial advisors, informants and idea generators. He stood out in this crowd because he had traveled widely in Europe and developed an extensive network of contacts, from politicians to intellectuals and artists, and the occasional spy. As the tormented continent spiraled toward catastrophe, Alan became increasingly useful to the president. Once the war started, he became an emissary and intelligence-gatherer for FDR, carrying out sensitive missions in Britain, North Africa and Russia. He also made himself useful to the OSS, the spy agency that was being built from a standing start to compete with the intelligence services of enemies and allies alike. When the hot war ended and the Cold War began, he continued on both tracks for the new president, Harry Truman, and the new spy service, the CIA.

While McCarthy was riding high, Alan had more than a little difficulty because of his early left-wing sympathies—he'd once tried to talk FDR into aiding the Spanish loyalists in their doomed fight against the fascists—but by the late 1940s, perhaps in overcompensation, he was stridently anti-Soviet. Stalin's takeover of Eastern Europe convinced him that the Soviets had to be resisted, and the United States was the only force capable of accomplishing that essential task.

So for Alan it was always simply The War, and it had never really ended. And now, after eight years on the sidelines during the Republican ascendancy, he had an opportunity to impress that view on a new president, one he saw as inexperienced but educable. He was part of a coterie of elders whom Kennedy, aware of his youth and his need to build bridges to the foreign policy establishment, was turning to for advice on how to navigate the deep and perilous waters of the Cold War and the equally treacherous shoals of the government bureaucracies.

Kennedy was also acutely aware that he was inheriting a world full of troubles and tensions. And at this moment, none was more pressing than Cuba. In less than an hour, Kennedy would emerge into the frigid sunlight to begin his presidency, but first he wanted a quiet word about how to handle Fidel Castro, the hot-blooded Cuban revolutionary, and his noisy challenges to American power.

Some of Michael's Columbia friends had decorated their apartments with matching posters of Castro and Kennedy, out of a naïve sense that they were fellow avatars of a revolutionary future. For Kennedy, Castro was nothing but trouble. Fidel was putting his enemies in front of firing squads, seizing American companies' assets and cozying up to the Soviets. He was making the U.S. look weak and impotent in its own backyard, and doing it with an insouciance that bathed him in an aura of youthful romance. That was Kennedy's trademark, and he wanted no competitors.

Just days ago, Washington had severed diplomatic relations with Havana, creating an atmosphere of mounting crisis. The air was full of rumors about a U.S. invasion. So the incoming president urgently needed ideas on how to deal with Castro, and, just as important, how to navigate the domestic politics of the situation. Kennedy needed no reminder of the political damage his party had suffered a decade ago after the Communist takeover in China, and no desire to begin his administration facing Republican demands to answer the question "Who lost Cuba?" On both fronts, Alan was prepared to offer advice.

"Mr. President—time to start calling you that, I think—we need to toughen our policy. I would consider a total economic embargo. If we really cripple Castro's economy, or what passes for an economy, the Cuban people aren't going to like that very much. It'll soften him up, make him ripe for the plucking by the next caudillo who comes along, and that man will profit from the example and be a lot friendlier to us.

"As for the Republicans, that will take care of itself if we're going full bore to bring Castro down. And they have the liability of his having come to power on their watch."

Bobby Kennedy, typically, was the first to respond, and just as typically, was full of enthusiasm for vigorous action. "That's terrific.

Castro can't last long if we squeeze him hard. And we've got ways to do it."

His brother, just as typically, was skeptical and questioning. "Well, yes, but if we do that, what's the next move? Won't that just drive him closer to the Russians? Won't Khrushchev call our bet by pouring in money to keep him afloat? And what's our counter to that?"

Alan shook his head. "The Russians don't want an expensive client state in a region that's so peripheral to their core interests. They won't get into a bidding war over a mercurial figure like Fidel. Khrushchev cares about Berlin, cares a great deal about Berlin, and Germany in general. He understands that's where this game will be won and lost. Latin America is important to us. It's not really important to the Soviets."

It was Jack Kennedy's turn to shake his head. "It could be more complicated than that," he said. "The fact that Berlin is at the center of the chessboard doesn't mean the Russians can't use pieces on other parts of the board to exert pressure. Or try to, at least."

Alan pressed on, trying to reassure Kennedy that there would be little cost in squeezing Castro. Kennedy listened intently but impassively and was silent for several moments before he spoke.

"Well, we'll think about it, and talk more later. Right now, I believe I've got an oath to take and a speech to give in less than an hour, and a few congressional backs to slap before then. Thank you for your help, Alan. It's always appreciated. We've certainly got to do something about Cuba"—Kennedy's Boston accent converted it to "Cub-ur"—"and we certainly will."

Alan started to speak again, then decided to take the hint, and take his leave. He'd been about to ask about something that hovered over any insider discussion of Cuba these days: the rumors about a CIA-sponsored band of Cuban exiles who were training in secret for some sort of anti-Castro mission. Speculation about the nature of the mission ranged from a series of hit-and-run sabotage raids to a full-on invasion aimed at overthrowing Fidel. When Alan had asked some old CIA friends about it, he'd hit a brick wall, even after the lubrication of several drinks.

The uncertainty over what to do about Castro—and the fact that a new president was even spending valuable time discussing a bearded, loud-mouthed upstart—perfectly symbolized the evolution of the Cold War in its second decade. The nuclear stalemate between the two global powers made direct military conflict unthinkable, and forced them to conduct their rivalry through proxies. Perversely, it gave the proxies inordinate leverage over their nominal masters.

And it spawned a shadow world of doubt and confusion, as each side tried to guess what the other's next move might be. Alan knew that Kennedy, as president-elect, had received extensive intelligence briefings on every issue of any significance. How useful or accurate that intelligence might be on a puzzle like Cuba was just one part of the uncertainty. High-level advisors were expected to be full of conviction and free from doubt, and Alan had fulfilled the role, confidently telling Kennedy that the Soviets wouldn't respond if the U.S. went after Castro. Yet, in the back of his mind, he understood that no one in Washington really knew for sure.

4: Trumpet Call

Alan walked out of the Capitol and into the sunlight, almost blinded by the glare. As he made his way to his seat on the platform next to his wife, he found himself wondering, as he often did after such conversations, just how much of what he said had registered. Kennedy was a puzzling blend of intelligence, charm, and glibness. He had a politician's knack of absorbing advice without fully accepting or rejecting it, keeping advisors within his orbit but never completely secure about their place in it.

For Alan, this was an old story; he had seen FDR work this magic trick many times. By long training, Alan had a sharp ear for language and a keen appreciation of its nuances; as he sat down next to Anna, he reflected that Kennedy had said he appreciated Alan's advice—but hadn't said he'd been persuaded by it.

Anna was huddled in a thick fur coat, her neck and ears swaddled in a woolen scarf to ward off the chill. She was hatless, her still-brown hair cut short on the sides and fuller on top. She turned and greeted her husband with a quick kiss. "And how is our Hotspur today? Ready for his Shrewsbury?"

"Let's hope your metaphor is inapt. I'm sure you recall who won that battle, and it wasn't Hotspur. Anyway, he's more of a Prince Hal, more interested in the wenching than the fighting. Oh, he's his typical self, eager to get advice, then full of questions when he gets it. But he's also full of confidence, ready for his moment."

"What did you talk about?"

"Cuba, mostly. He takes the problem seriously, which is good. He takes the Soviets seriously, too, which is also good. But he may be overrating their capabilities in this hemisphere."

Anna turned away with a frown. "That was it? Nothing about the domestic agenda? Education? Civil rights? Congressional reform? Sounds like a wasted opportunity."

"It was his meeting, and he wanted to discuss Castro," Alan replied, squinting into the midday sun as he looked out at the crowd filling up the plaza. "I'm sure he'll tell us plenty about domestic policies in the speech."

Kennedy didn't speak about policies of any kind. Standing coatless and hatless in defiance of the 20-degree temperature, Kennedy announced his arrival into the presidency with a medley of rhetorical flourishes that delighted the ear, if not the mind.

The first salvo came barely 90 seconds in: "Let the word go forth, from this time and place, to friend and foe alike, that the torch has been passed to a new generation of Americans ... tempered by war, disciplined by a hard and bitter peace, proud of our ancient heritage, and unwilling to witness or permit the slow undoing of those human rights to which this nation has always been committed."

And he was off at a gallop. First, a note of pure Cold War militance: "Let every nation know, whether it wishes us well or ill, that we shall pay any price, bear any burden, meet any hardship, support any friend, oppose any foe to assure the survival and the success of liberty."

Even as those words made Alan smile and Anna shift uncomfortably in her seat, Kennedy pivoted into a bow to the soft power of economic development: "If a free society cannot help the many who are poor, it cannot save the few who are rich." He coupled this with a declaration of his willingness to sit down with the Soviets: "Let us never negotiate out of fear. But let us never fear to negotiate."

Each generation of Americans, he declared, had been called to bear witness to its loyalty, often at great sacrifice. "Now the trumpet summons us again, not as a call to bear arms...but a call to bear the burden of a long twilight struggle." This was a battle, he said, to be waged not against a single opponent but against humanity's common enemies: "tyranny, poverty, disease and war itself."

Finally, the money quote, the one intended to be remembered long after lesser lines had faded. "And so, my fellow Americans: ask not what your country can do for you—ask what you can do for your country."

Kennedy struck a chord in each member of the McMaster family. Alan was impressed with the new president's hard-edged enunciation of Cold War resolve. Anna, a writer at heart, was taken by Kennedy's ringing phrases, and his overtures to the Third World and tension-easing diplomacy lessened her qualms about his commitment to liberal values. The couple walked into the Capitol, smiling in satisfaction.

As for Michael, the fine detail of the speech was far less important than its emotional resonance. What he heard was a young leader telling an older generation to stand aside, and living the part with his elegant good looks and—there was no better word for it—his unshakeable cool. That was it; John F. Kennedy was cool, in every way possible.

Michael was still glowing when he joined his parents in a high-ceilinged reception room off the House chamber. It was filled with cheerful Democrats thawing out in the welcome warmth, sipping punch and champagne, nibbling hors d'œuvres, and gossiping happily. He found Anna and Alan chatting with a couple of liberal activists from California. Anna looked earnest; Alan looked bored.

"Well, how was the view from the boondocks?" his father asked. "You know, I might've gotten you onto the platform, one way or the other, if you'd let me. Wouldn't have been any warmer, but you would have seen and heard a lot more. Better material for your piece for the Village Voice."

"I wanted to experience it in a different way," Michael said. "I'm not interested in how Ike or Rayburn reacted to Kennedy. I *am* interested in how ordinary folks—what your generation used to call the common man—thought of him. They're the ones who're going to determine whether Kennedy succeeds or fails. And, I'll tell you, they loved it. Freezing their tails off, but they shouted and clapped and ate it up. I've got a notebook full of quotes to prove it."

"Of course they shouted and clapped," Alan said. "Only way they could warm up. Let's see if they're still jumping for Jack when it's 90 degrees and muggy as a swamp."

"Always playing the cynic," Anna interjected. "I know better, but you won't show your other face, especially when our son's around. God forbid he should see that his father actually believes in something."

"He knows I believe in something. He just doesn't always agree with it. That's because he listens to you too much."

"You two done auditioning for the next Edward Albee play?" Michael said. "In case you forgot, I'm standing right here next to you. No need to speak about me in the third person."

"Of course. I'm sorry," Anna said simply. As an apology, she enveloped him in a sable-scented hug, which both pleased and embarrassed him.

"Okay, enough, I love you too. But I'm serious; he lit people up out there. We're so used to these pols droning on in monosyllables about God's favored land, and then this guy comes out of nowhere and talks about sounding trumpets and passing torches and asking what you can give to your country, not what you can take. Everything about him is a challenge to the way things are."

"He didn't come out of nowhere, he came out of Massachusetts, by way of a rich right-wing father who made his money on Wall Street," Alan said. "I hope you're right about him—well, mostly I do—but there's an unformed quality about him that makes me wonder, and sometimes makes me worry. And you can call that cynical if you want," he added, turning to his wife, "but you know what I'm talking about."

Anna nodded slowly, and the worried look that had been on her face before the speech returned. For Michael, in his youthful enthusiasm, a day of ringing rhetoric was enough to buttress his hopes that Kennedy would fulfill the promise of leading his country across a new frontier of discovery and adventure. For Anna and Alan, past was prologue, a cautionary tale to trust not in princes, fallible figures who are bound to disappoint eventually, no matter how boldly their trumpets call out in the bright dawn of their reigns.

Chapter Two
—Freedom Ride—

May 1961

1: Song and Verse

The sound of the singing reached Michael as he hit the top step of the subway stairs, even though he was still a block away. He'd heard these anthems before, on records and at campus rallies. But to hear them at a demonstration was different. It lifted his heart and quickened his step as he headed across City Hall Park toward the federal courthouse on Foley Square.

"We shall not, we shall not be moved. We shall not, we shall not be moved. Just like a tree that's standing by the water, we shall not be moved."

In front of the courthouse, about 100 people walked in a semicircle, chanting and singing. Their picket signs were simple and direct: "We Support Freedom Riders." "End Segregation Now." "Mr. President: Enforce The Law."

Behind and in front of the picketers, two lines of New York City cops stood silently, billy clubs in hand, looking bored. As another song started up, the voices of the picketers echoed off the courthouse tower and the surrounding buildings.

"Oh, freedom. Oh, freedom. Oh, freedom, over me, over me. And before I'll be a slave, I'll be buried in my grave, and go home to my Lord, and be free."

One voice stood out distinctly from the others. It belonged to a tall young black woman in a denim jacket and matching jeans, her long hair tossing lightly in the wind. Her voice is as striking as she is, Michael thought, as he walked up to her, feeling overdressed and a bit foolish in his standard-issue Ivy League blazer and dress shirt. Almost unconsciously, he pulled off his glasses and tucked them in a pocket.

"Hello, can I talk to you for a minute? My name's Michael McMaster, and I'm writing a piece for the Village Voice about your demonstration, for a package we're doing on the freedom rides."

The woman looked Michael up and down with a mixture of skepticism and curiosity. Her gaze made him feel even more self-conscious about his gangly frame and newly grown beard, which still itched mercilessly. Then she stepped out of the line. "Okay, what would you like to know?"

"Well, for starters, what's your name, and what brings you here today?"

"It's Riva Daniels, and I'm here because—well, the answer to that question is really pretty simple. I'm here because I'm going to spend my whole life in this skin, and I can't sit around and wait for someone to make things better for us. I've got to do for myself. *We've* got to do it for ourselves. That's what the freedom riders are saying, that's what all of us here believe. No more waiting, no more talk. Time to act, time to change things. Now."

As she was speaking, the singing marchers, as if to punctuate her point, changed from movement anthems to a satirical verse sung to the tune of "Frere Jacques."

Are you sleeping, are you sleeping, Brother Bob, Brother Bob? Freedom riders waiting, freedom riders waiting, enforce the law, enforce the law.

Michael jotted down the lyrics in his notebook, fully aware of what they reflected: a growing disenchantment with the new administration. For all his trademark talk about vigor and action, Kennedy seemed to be failing one of his first tests of leadership.

Earlier in the month, an interracial group of 13 civil rights activists had boarded buses in Washington for a journey through the South, determined to challenge the region's strict racial segregation in interstate travel. The reaction was swift—and brutal.

In South Carolina, one rider, John Lewis, who tried to enter a whites-only waiting room, was beaten up and left bleeding on the sidewalk. When the buses reached Alabama, a mob in the town of Anniston set one ablaze, tried to trap the riders inside and then systematically beat them when they escaped. When a second bus reached Birmingham, an even larger mob of Ku Klux Klansmen set upon the riders with baseball bats, iron pipes, and bicycle chains. Birmingham's segregationist police chief, Bull Connor, had promised the Klansmen 15 minutes to pummel the riders with impunity before his men showed up.

In Washington, the president and his brother Robert, who was now the attorney general, reacted as if the freedom ride was a personal affront. The president angrily ordered an aide to try to squelch it. Both brothers complained that the activists were embarrassing the country—and them—just as the president was about to embark on a round of Cold War diplomacy. All of this made it into the press.

In reality, the attorney general was working quietly behind the scenes to try to protect the riders. But the administration's public face was one of chilly indifference to a group of people who were being subjected to potentially lethal violence for peacefully exercising their legal rights—rights confirmed by two Supreme Court decisions.

The picketers repeated the sardonic verse, clearly enjoying the jab. Riva glanced in their direction and started to edge back toward them, but Michael wanted to talk to her more. "So tell me about the specific goal of this demonstration," he said. "I want to be able to write it in your words."

"It's very simple," she replied. "We want the federal government to stand behind its own laws and court rulings. We want the Kennedys to stand behind their own rhetoric. If local law enforcement won't protect American citizens from violent attacks, the government should send federal marshals. Now, before someone is killed. And make it clear there's no discrimination allowed, on buses, on trains, in terminals, anywhere. The federal government has the power to do that, and it's long overdue."

"Why do you think the administration hasn't acted?"

"You tell me. Maybe they're afraid of the political reaction from southern Democrats. Maybe they don't really give a damn. Maybe they just don't have the balls to do it, and expect us all to be nice little girls and boys and go home. Well, they can forget about that. Those lunch-counter sit-ins last year started something, and it's not going to end because it makes some politicians in Washington unhappy."

Michael, scribbling furiously to capture Riva's staccato quotes, paused, and looked up at her. Her dark brown eyes met his without a hint of wavering. He thought he had never seen a lovelier woman, or a prouder one.

"You've obviously thought a lot about these issues. Have you done this before?"

"When the Greensboro sit-ins started, we picketed at Woolworth stores here in the city, until the company agreed to desegregate. Took months, but they finally did. It shows what people can do, when we stick together and don't take no for an answer."

"Were you scared?"

For the first time since they began talking, Riva's hard shell softened, ever so slightly. "That's a funny question. Yes, at first I was, just a bit. We were picketing a Woolworth's in Times Square, and I had no idea what to expect. I didn't know what the cops would do, what people in the street would do. I'd arranged with my roommate to have some bail money handy, just in case. I didn't tell my parents about it beforehand, because I was sure they would chew me out.

"But it turned out to be fine. The cops just ignored us. We got a few nasty looks and smart-ass comments from people passing by, but some others actually joined our line. When I told my parents afterward, they were upset at first. But after some hemming and hawing, they admitted they were proud of me.

"That was like crossing a threshold. A little while after that, I went down to Nashville to join a sit-in that some Fisk students were organizing at... Aren't you going to take some notes?"

Michael had been staring at her as she was speaking. He coughed and started writing again. "Yes. So tell me about yourself. For my story, that is. How old are you? Where are you from? What do you do? Where do you live?"

The faintest of smiles crossed her face. "I'm 25, I live in the Village, I studied theater and music at NYU. Now I'm auditioning a lot, waiting tables in the meantime. But this isn't about me, and I've got to get back in the line." She rejoined the picketers, just in time to lend her voice to a chorus of "We Shall Overcome."

When she came past him again, Michael drew the deepest of breaths, then took the plunge. "Can I call you?"

Again, that tantalizing hint of a smile. "I'm in the book. R-i-v-a D-a-n-i-e-l-s. You'll need the spelling for your story, I guess. Or I'm taking orders at Cafe Fedora on West Fourth. Tuesdays, Thursdays and Friday nights."

2: Just Coffee

He met Riva for coffee three days later. She was friendly, and he sensed a welcome spark of attraction. She was distracted, however, by the news on the front page of her New York Times. A new group of freedom riders was forming to travel from Tennessee to Alabama, and there was more trouble brewing.

"They're asking for federal marshals to protect them after what happened in Anniston, but nobody in Washington will even talk to them," Riva said, her voice rising in anger. "People are being assaulted simply for traveling together on a bus, and the federal government is just shirking its responsibility."

Michael nodded in agreement. "And those so-called allies who want the freedom riders to stand down are missing the whole point," he said. "This is shining a bright light on what really goes on in the South, and forcing the rest of the country to look. A lot of people won't like what they see."

Riva looked at him curiously, trying to parse his motives. He wasn't the first white person she'd met who'd professed an interest in civil rights, and some had proven to be shallow and insincere. She couldn't discount the possibility that Michael's interest in the issue was intertwined with his self-evident interest in her. Yet she sensed something about him—an underlying honesty, a restless intelligence.

"What got you interested in the movement?" Riva asked.

Michael told her of his respect for the courage of the lunch counter protesters, his eye-opening experiences in the South during his Army days, his years going to an integrated school, and his appreciation for his parents' decision to make that possible.

"But I'm not sure we see eye to eye on this anymore," he said. "My parents have always talked about the importance of equality and treating everyone with respect. But now they've become very invested in the political success of the Kennedy administration, and they tell me I have to see things in context and take the long view. I think what they call taking the long view just amounts to an excuse for being passive, for putting off what needs to be done.

"I got into an argument with them over it the other day. My father tried to tell me that Kennedy is just waiting for the right moment to act on civil rights, and the freedom rides are actually delaying that moment by pushing him into a corner. My mother chimed in with some dusty anecdote from her youth, about her frustration with Roosevelt over something or other, and how life had taught her the virtue of patience.

"It all seemed so weak to me, such a rationalization for doing nothing. There's something you said the other day that really stuck with me: You can't wait around for someone else to change things. And if that makes people uncomfortable, that's a good thing."

Well, he certainly talks a good game, Riva thought, as she listened to Michael's musings. She wondered whether he was prepared to back it up with actions. Something else was more urgent, though, more important than measuring the authenticity of a new acquaintance, however intriguing he might be.

She looked down again at the Times story on the freedom riders. "They're calling for volunteers to join them," she said quietly. "I know some people who're going. I think I have to go, too."

"I'll go with you."

His words had tumbled out in an impulsive rush. In the brief silence that followed, he was buffeted by a torrent of emotions: pride, panic, adrenaline, deep admiration for Riva's courage.

She sat back in surprise.

"Michael, this isn't your fight."

"What if I want it to be? I can't think of a more important issue right now, can you? Besides, I'm a journalist, and this is one hell of a story. My piece on your Foley Square picket is going to get a heavy ride in the next Voice. This is a national story, and if I'm there, I could sell something to a bigger publication."

"Aren't you mixing your motives?"

"Maybe I am. I can live with that."

Riva leaned forward and gave him a hard, searching look. "This isn't going to be like some tame picket line up here in the city. That first group of riders came close to getting killed. Some of them landed in the hospital with cracked skulls. Are you ready for that?"

"Yes, I am," Michael said slowly, doing his best to keep his voice even and still sound confident.

Riva sat back again, still looking straight at him. Michael saw a look of respect spread across her face. He thought he'd be willing to do just about anything for that look.

"Well, okay. We're leaving tomorrow morning, early. Six o'clock sharp. We want to get to Birmingham tomorrow night to meet up with the riders. Travel light, we won't have a lot of room in the car. That is, if you're really up for this."

In fact, Michael wasn't entirely sure he was. But he wasn't about to back out now. He called a Village Voice editor to let him know where he was going. The editor went through the motions of trying to talk him out of putting himself in danger, then readily agreed to run whatever stories Michael could file. He also called an editor at The New Republic magazine, whom he'd met at a journalism conference. That editor made no attempt to talk him out of going and told him he'd be glad to look at a first-hand account of the freedom rides.

Then he called his parents.

His father listened in silence as Michael outlined his plans. There was a long pause when Michael finished speaking. Then Alan's voice exploded out of the phone.

"Son, this is crazy. Crazy on so many levels. First, it's all wrong politically. Of course civil rights is an important issue, but the timing of this is terrible. It's painting Kennedy into a corner just when he's trying to focus on Europe and the Russians, so of course he's going to react badly. I've told you that before, but you won't listen.

"And it's wrong for you. You're not even done with the school year yet. And don't think that being a journalist is going to give you any protection down there. On Sunday. they beat up newsmen and smashed cameras to keep pictures of the Klan busting heads out of the papers. On Mother's Day, no less."

Michael let his father's anger subside, then tried to answer calmly. "Dad, my semester's over. It was all papers and projects and I've done them. If I'm going to make it as a journalist, I can't do it sitting at a desk. And if someone had told you in 1935 not to go to Germany and warn about what was really going on there because the Nazis might get upset and give you a hard time, you'd have laughed in their face.

"As for the politics, we just disagree about that. You keep telling me the same thing—there's always something more important than civil rights, it's never the right time, take the long view. Well, that's all over. People are moving, and I don't think anybody can stop them."

Then it was his mother's turn. Anna tried a more personal tack.

"Michael, I have no problem with people challenging segregation. It's the most hopeful thing that's happened in a long time. But why do you have to join them? Have you read what happened in Alabama? These southerners are just rabid about race, the local authorities aren't doing anything to control them, and the administration up here is just treading water. At least these freedom riders know what they're getting into and have been through a lot of training on how to handle themselves. You'll just be sleepwalking into a combat zone."

"I'm just going down there as a reporter."

"I know you well enough to know that's not completely true," Anna said. "And I also know some of the newsmen who've covered the civil rights story in the South. They say it's practically like being a war correspondent. That's also something that takes training and experience."

"Well, there's only one way to get that experience," Michael retorted. "And I'll make the same argument to you I made to Dad. You ran risks when you were my age to go to Germany to write about life under Hitler. I've always admired you for doing that. And then you went back to Europe to write about the war. Do you think I should be any less willing? Is that the kind of son you raised? Is that the kind of son you want?"

It was tag team for a while, Alan again, then Anna. In the end, none of them had anything left to say.

"I've got to get ready for this trip," Michael said finally. "I'll try to call you when I get to Birmingham, and then I'll check in as often as I can. I love you both very much, and I know you just want me to be okay. But this is something I've got to do."

Alan hung up the phone, poured a couple of generous Scotches, and sat down next to his wife with a sigh. "Well, he's definitely our son," he said wearily. "It's like our past lives are rising up to haunt us."

3: Embattled

The ride to Alabama was a late-model Ford station wagon, loaned by a doctor from Long Island whose sympathy for the movement had overcome a nagging fear that his car would become a casualty of the struggle. It was roomy, but by the time Michael, Riva, five students from NYU and CCNY and a Unitarian minister had piled in, space was at a premium. The group sized up Michael's long legs and awarded him the front seat for the first leg—somewhat to his regret, as Riva was all the way in the back.

His luck improved as they crossed into Maryland. He and Riva wound up together in the middle bench seat, nestled comfortably, if somewhat tentatively, next to each other. She'd ditched her denims in favor of a navy skirt, off-white blouse and gray sweater— "demonstration formal," she called it with a wry smile. Her long hair was pinned up in a conservative bun. She eyed Michael's blazer, Oxford cloth shirt, tie and khakis, and with the same half-smile proclaimed it "Columbia chic."

Riva still wasn't sure what to make of this handsome, slightly awkward young man, an odd blend of pushiness and shyness, who had talked his way into making this trip with her. She was curious about him. Riva understood that he had mixed motives for coming, that activism and journalism were only parts of it; she'd felt the same pulse of attraction. Yet her instincts kept telling her he was sincere about his commitment. Mostly, she hoped he wouldn't become a liability in a crunch. Her instincts were positive about that, too.

Michael might have been reading her mind on that last point. "What can we expect when we get to Alabama?" he asked.

"We should be in Birmingham tonight," she said. "We'll be driving pretty much straight through once we're in the South, because any long stops could invite trouble. Even going to the bathroom is an issue. We'll get more information when we get to Birmingham, but my understanding is that a group of us will board a bus and sit together for a trip to Montgomery. When we get there, there'll be a rally for us at Ralph Abernathy's church. Dr. King is coming in from Atlanta to speak."

"What kind of reception are we expecting? From the locals, I mean—the local whites."

"Your guess is as good as mine. Yesterday, I heard, 10 riders from Nashville got to Birmingham and promptly got tossed in jail. Then Bull Connor drove them back to the Tennessee line and dumped them on the side of the road. I heard he told them, 'I just can't stand your singing anymore.'"

"That's 'cause he's never heard your voice. Even he couldn't resist that."

"You're sweet, Michael. Sappy. But very sweet."

They half-expected trouble as they rolled through Tennessee and crossed into Alabama, but no one paid any attention to them, even though the car had New York plates and interracial passengers. They drove on through the long spring twilight and into the night. At last, they pulled into Birmingham and found their way to the bus station. It was not a comforting sight. Outside, about 50 white people were milling about, some carrying baseball bats and metal pipes. Through a window, they could see about 20 people inside, huddled together in the whites-only section of the terminal. They parked and started walking toward the station door, slowly and deliberately. The whites edged toward them, crowding close, just allowing them to pass.

"Nice to see more o' you folks here from up north," one short, wiry man, who seemed to be the leader, spat out. "We were gettin' worried that we wouldn't have as much fun as the boys in Anniston. The more o' you, the more heads to swing at."

"You tell 'em, Bobby!" another man said. "Let's do it now!"

"Naw, gotta take our time. No hurry. Let 'em sweat for a while."

They pushed through the crowd, single file, the minister in front and Michael at the rear. He realized his knees were shaking, but he kept moving. The last time he'd felt anything like this was three years ago, during his involuntary stint in the Army, when he'd undergone live-fire infantry training, crawling through a Georgia mud field with rifle rounds whizzing overheard. Well, he'd lived through that, he could survive this, too.

There were more taunts from the crowd of whites, muttered and shouted, but nothing more. Inside the station, the minister walked up to a lanky black man in a suit and tie.

"Hello Fred, it's good to see you again. Couldn't you have arranged a more polite reception party?"

"Well, we do our best," replied Fred Shuttlesworth, a local Baptist minister and movement leader. "It's good to see you again, too, Tom."

"What's the situation?"

"We've been here for hours, waiting for a bus to take us to Montgomery. We heard that there was one, but none of the drivers would go with us. After Anniston, they're all afraid. One of 'em told us flat out, 'I have only one life to give, and I'm not giving it to you all.'"

Riva, Michael, and the rest of their carmates greeted the riders and settled down to wait. There was no more room on the benches, so Michael and Riva sat on the floor next to each other, atop their duffle bags. Out of 27 people in the group, seven were white. Although several signs proclaimed the area reserved for whites only, the cops and station personnel made no move to intervene.

"Why do you think they're letting us all sit here?" Michael said.

"I can think of several reasons, some good, some not," Riva replied. "Maybe they're letting us alone so those guys outside can take care of us when we try to leave. Or maybe somebody in

Washington finally got off their butt and put some pressure on the locals to act like they're part of the rest of America."

"I prefer your second explanation," Michael said with a tight smile. He had told no one in the group besides Riva that his parents lived in Washington and had connections there. Before he left New York, he'd briefly considered asking them to intervene with the Kennedys. But it seemed too much like special pleading, and it felt wrong given his parents' views about his participation.

Riva looked away, up at the ceiling, but she edged nearer to him. "I'm worried about those guys outside," she said quietly. "I don't think they're bluffing."

Michael considered the option of striking a pose. He chose honesty. "I am, too. I think I recognized that mouthy little guy outside. He's Bobby Shelton, and he's a grand dragon of the Klan. If there's one Klansman here, there'll be more before it's over."

"Shit. You got any other good news to share?"

"Just that I'm glad I'm here. Here with you."

"I'm glad you're here, too, Michael. You're..." She fell silent, but moved even closer to him.

They stayed together through a long night of waiting and fitful dozing on the hard station floor. The crowd of whites outside dwindled during the night, but at daylight they were back, twice as strong.

The bus arrived mid-morning, with a driver willing to make the trip, if not exactly enthusiastic about it. A reporter for one of the local papers shared the news that Bobby Kennedy had intervened with Greyhound executives and virtually ordered them to find a driver.

They rose, stretched, and walked apprehensively toward the station door, eying the scene outside. The mob had grown to more than 200, but a skirmish line of city police was slowly pushing them away from the front of the terminal. More cops lined the sidewalk from the station to the bus, forming a screen for the riders. Riva and Michael exchanged puzzled looks as they climbed aboard. "I wonder if this is Kennedy's doing, too," Michael said. "Or a Bull Connor setup," Riva replied.

The freedom riders were the only passengers; no one else traveling to Montgomery that day had any desire to join them. The bus pulled out of the station, with two police cruisers in the lead. As it reached the highway, four state Highway Patrol cars joined it. The bus swung onto the road, two police cars in front and two behind, all with sirens wailing. Within minutes, the convoy was hurtling ahead at more than 70 miles per hour. They made the journey to Montgomery, normally a two-hour trip, in little more than an hour.

Any sense of security disappeared when the caravan neared Montgomery. As they slowed at the outskirts of the city, the police cars abruptly peeled off and disappeared. When the bus, now alone and vulnerable, reached the Greyhound station, the riders could see more than a hundred people waiting for them. Michael's hand edged across the armrest and grasped Riva's tightly. The bus pulled onto the station's boarding platform. The driver opened the front door, left the bus, and disappeared. No police were in sight.

They climbed off the bus and sized up their prospects to make it to the station. No chance; the mob blocked the way, and it was moving toward them. Fred Shuttlesworth and John Lewis quickly formed the riders into a circle, just as the mob descended on them.

"Git 'em! Git them bastards!"

Michael locked arms with Riva, just as the mob closed on them.

A bottle flew through the air and hit Riva on the side of the head. She dropped to one knee and clapped a hand to her temple. No blood, but her eyes were dazed. Michael knelt next to her as three men with axe handles reached them. He felt the blows on his shoulders and back. He wrapped one arm tightly around Riva and threw his other across the top of his head, just as a blow landed on it. Pain radiated down his arm. As more blows rained down, he could feel her body shaking. He was trembling himself.

A cacophony of sounds: racist taunts, screams from people being beaten, the dull thud of clubs striking bodies, the crash of breaking

glass as bottles smashed on pavement. The beginnings of a song—
"*Oh, freedom... oh, freedom...*" It died away amid more angry epithets.

The three men grew bored and moved off in search of fresh targets, one offering a parting shot with a kick to Michael's leg. In the brief lull, Michael looked up and saw a flying wooden crate hit John Lewis in the head. He dropped to the pavement and lay there, inert. Another rider, Jim Zwerg, a white student from Wisconsin, was seated near him, blood streaming from his mouth. Michael pulled his Leica out of his jacket. A blow from a baseball bat sent the camera crashing to the ground. The bat wielder smashed at it twice more for good measure.

"No pictures, you son of a bitch! No pictures! You git your sorry ass back up north where you come from! And you do it right quick!"

Riva's head was clearing. Still holding onto Michael, she tried to stand. Michael rose with her. The platform was a tableau of chaos and carnage, with some riders sitting stunned on the pavement, others trying to make it into the terminal, still others fleeing down the street. One young female student was being pursued by a group led by a screaming woman. A car pulled up next to the student, and a man in a business suit got out. Michael recognized him as John Siegenthaler, an aide to Bobby Kennedy. He recalled meeting Siegenthaler at the reception in the Capitol on Inauguration Day, just four months earlier. It now seemed a lifetime ago.

Siegenthaler opened the passenger door and gestured for the student to get in. He took a club to the back of the head and fell unconscious to the pavement. The student bolted, running for her life.

A group of men surrounded Lewis and Zwerg and began kicking and stomping them. The thought struck Michael that he was witnessing a murder; the men seemed determined to finish their victims off. A state trooper appeared, seemingly out of nowhere. "Fun's over, boys. Time to go home." When they ignored him, he pulled his service revolver and repeated the command. This time, they listened.

Just as quickly as the violence had erupted, it was over. More police suddenly materialized and shooed the mob away from the station. The cops paid no attention to the riders, who were scattered across the landscape in various states of distress. Michael helped Riva get fully up on her feet and grasped her by the shoulders. Looking into her eyes, he saw with relief that they were clear and alert. His own shoulders, arm and back ached, but nothing worse than that. He didn't think anything was broken. He put a hand to his head, feeling for blood, but it came away dry.

Jim Zwerg was now upright, but his mouth was still bleeding badly, and he had lost some teeth. John Lewis was stirring, trying to prop himself up on his elbows. Riva and Michael helped Lewis to his knees, then to his feet, and supported him and Zwerg as they headed to the terminal. One by one, the riders walked, limped, and hobbled into the station, like survivors of a disaster. Fred Shuttlesworth was on a pay phone, trying to figure out which hospitals would treat a biracial group of patients and how to transport them.

Michael found some space on a bench, sat Riva down and bent over her for a close look at her head. She winced as he touched her temple, then set her face in a stoic stare. "You've got a big lump forming there, but if I remember my Boy Scout first aid, that's actually a good thing. Better swelling on the outside than on the inside."

"I should have known you were a goddamn Boy Scout."

"You bet. Would've been up for Eagle Scout if I hadn't met you. I think this trip blows that."

Michael sat down beside her. After a moment's hesitation, he wrapped an arm around her, just as she did the same thing. She lay her head on his shoulder and they sat together, silently, breathing slowly, feeling each other, feeling their way into each other, feeling more connected to each other with every passing moment.

4: Dr. King

In late afternoon, some cars came to take them to Ralph Abernathy's First Baptist Church. Some riders were still in the hospital being patched up; most of the others bore signs of the beatings. The lump on Riva's temple had grown to the size of a golf ball, but a nurse at the church who examined her said there was no sign of concussion. Michael's shoulders throbbed, and he found he had difficulty raising his left arm above the shoulder. The church fed them supper in the basement as the building slowly filled up.

By nightfall, more than 1,000 people, a substantial part of Montgomery's black community, were inside. Martin Luther King Jr. was there. So were Jim Farmer of the Congress of Racial Equality, the group that organized the freedom rides, and Fred Shuttlesworth; they had entered the church through a gauntlet of taunting, jeering whites who were gathering outside. Before long, that crowd had swelled to more than twice the size of the group inside, and they were turning nasty. They overturned a car outside the church's front door and set it on fire, then began throwing rocks and bottles through the church windows.

As the smoke from the blazing car wafted inside, and the shouts of the mob rose, parents gathered up their children and hustled them down to the basement. Michael watched in surprise as the children passed, wide-eyed and solemn, but none crying, not even the very small ones. It occurred to him that a black child growing up in Alabama must see a lot of ugliness.

"Paul and Silas bound in jail/Had no money for to go their bail/Keep your eyes on the prize/Hold on, hold on."

Just a few voices at first, then more and more joining, as the tense, frightened people in the church picked up the melody and took heart from it.

"The only thing that we did wrong/Was stayin' in the wilderness a day too long/Keep your eyes on the prize/Hold on, hold on."

Riva's voice soared above the melody line in an effortless harmony. She was joined by a young Fisk student from Nashville, whose alto blended gracefully. The swelling anthem seemed to form a force field that repelled the ugliness outside.

"And the only thing that we did right/Was the day we begun to fight/Keep your eyes on the prize/Hold on, won't you hold on."

Once again, no police were in sight. The only law enforcement on hand was a group of federal marshals, again courtesy of Bobby Kennedy, equipped only with helmets and truncheons. Michael thought they were better than nothing, but he wondered how much use they would be in the face of a determined assault.

He soon found out. Some of the mob forced open the front door and started down the main aisle. About half a dozen marshals inside the church hurled themselves at the intruders, in an old-school football flying wedge, and forced them back outside. It all happened so quickly that no one in the church had time to react. The marshals outside laid down tear gas to drive the mob away from the church. It worked, but some of the gas drifted inside through the church windows.

Michael felt a tap on the shoulder. He turned around and looked into the lean, angular face of Fred Shuttlesworth.

"You're a reporter, aren't you?"

Michael nodded.

"We've got a situation here," Fred said. "There's a group of cab drivers that's formed up not far from here. They want to provide security for us. Problem is, they want to do it with guns. That would be—well, we can't let that happen. You understand why. Reverend King is determined to go see them and talk them down off the ledge, and some of us are going with him.

"We want some journalists to witness what happens. We've got one reporter from the Pittsburgh Courier who's here, and he's willing to go with us, but we could sure use another reporter. To be honest with you, a white reporter, who can report what happens to a different audience. I won't pretend that this is going to be a pleasant little stroll. We're going to have to walk past that crowd out there. It's up to you—but we could sure use your help."

"Give me two minutes," Michael said. "I have to tell a friend I'm going."

Michael found Riva and explained what he was doing. She gasped involuntarily and clutched his jacket. "Michael, you don't have to do this," she said, swallowing hard.

"I think I do," he said. He wrapped his arms around her and hugged her tightly. He pulled back slightly and caressed her cheek. She took his face in both hands, leaned forward and lightly touched her forehead to his. "Come back safe, Boy Scout. Come back safe."

King was at the front of the church, at the head of a dozen men, lined up two by two. Michael joined at the rear and shook hands with his colleague from Pittsburgh, Tom Ackerly. A sudden silence descended as the front door swung open and King led the small group outside. Almost as soon as they were through, the door swung shut behind them.

King led the group down the steps to the sidewalk. The crowd of whites across the street, taken by surprise, stopped their catcalls, unsure of what was happening. Out of the corner of his eye, Michael caught sight of a few marshals on the fringes of the crowd; too few, he calculated, to make much of a difference. King kept the group moving, at a measured pace, almost in march cadence, still two by two, as the whites jeered and heckled. The acrid smells of the burned car and the tear gas lingered in the air. For the second time this day, Michael felt his knees go rubbery. Somehow, he kept walking.

By the time most of the crowd had figured out what was happening, King's group was two blocks from the church and moving steadily away. Most of the whites resumed laying siege to the church; a small group tried to follow King, but soon tired of it and turned back.

After a 10-minute walk through empty streets, the group reached a gas station crowded with cars and a large number of drivers. The men were sober, almost solemn, but they looked very determined, and Michael could see some pistols poking up from trouser waistbands. King walked into the midst of the group and looked around, searching for the leader.

"I think I know why you're here, Reverend," one man said.

"And I think I know why you're here," King replied. "Now, I want to thank you all for wanting to protect us. But this is not the way to go about it."

"We know how you feel," another driver said. "But you have to understand how we feel. We got friends and family inside that church. And you know us, Reverend. We were in the bus boycott in '56. We organized and got people to work and school and church so they didn't have to ride the bus. This is personal for us, and we're just not gonna let those crackers do any harm to our people."

"Now, I'm not asking you to just stand idly by," King replied. "But how we do this is as important as what we do. I've been on the phone three times tonight to Washington, with Attorney General Kennedy. I'm demanding that he fulfill his responsibility to enforce the law and protect innocent people. He's already got some federal marshals out here, and he'll do more before long. He'll get the National Guard down here if he has to.

"Now, he doesn't want to do it. He's very angry with me, and with the freedom riders, because we've put him and his brother on the spot. But he's got no choice. The pictures and stories of peaceful people being pulled off buses and beaten bloody have gone around the country. They've gone around the world. They're embarrassing him. So he'll do what he has to do, what he should do, to keep our people safe. And in the end, the federal government will order an end to segregation on buses—on all forms of travel.

"But we have this leverage only because we've been totally nonviolent. We've created a stark moral contrast. If we yield to the temptation, if we let ourselves be pulled down to the level of those who hate us, we've lost everything. So, I'm asking you, please stand down. Please help us preserve the one great advantage we've got."

The cabbies listened in rapt silence as King spoke. When he finished, they said nothing. King looked at the men, one by one, silently imploring them. Then the driver who had spoken first cleared his throat. "That's a hard thing you're asking of us, Reverend."

"Yes, it is. It's Albert, isn't it? Albert Reynolds? I believe I remember you from the boycott. It *is* a hard thing I'm asking of you, Albert. But it's what we've got to do. Now, please, go home, and let me go back to the church and call Washington again and tell the attorney general that it's time for him to act."

The men looked at each other, not speaking, not moving. Then, as if a silent signal had passed among them, they got in their cars and began to drive away.

The walk back to the church was slower; King was spent, wrung out from the effort of persuasion, and everyone knew the mob would be waiting. It gave Michael time to scribble more notes of what he had witnessed. He realized he had been given a privileged glimpse into why King was such a powerful leader. Not many people could have walked those cab drivers back from the precipice.

The roiling crowd was still outside the church, but once again they were caught off-balance by the reappearance of King and his group. And this time, some marshals pushed forward and helped keep them back. The church door swung open again, and they were back inside.

Riva walked toward Michael, slowly at first, then more quickly. She felt a surge of feelings for this man she hadn't even known a week ago, who had suddenly entered her life and stood beside her during these moments of stress and danger. She flung her arms around him, buried her face in his chest, then lifted her head and kissed him.

He hugged her just as tightly, kissed her on the lips and then on the forehead, and stroked her hair, which had fallen loosely about her shoulders. They stood that way, locked in each other's arms, words superfluous, silent and still amid the storm swirling around them.

Chapter Three
—Grande Dame—

December 1961

1: Anna's Moment

Eleanor Roosevelt was in her 78th year. Her once-tall frame was bent with the weight of her age, and her step was slow as she walked the short distance from head table to podium. Yet one look at her old friend's face told Anna that the fire still burned brightly.

"It is a pleasure for me to address this meeting of the Americans for Democratic Action," Eleanor said in her clipped, high-pitched, precise voice. "It is an even greater pleasure for me to introduce our main speaker, who helped me found our organization almost 15 years ago.

"At that time, the issue of civil rights was not yet high on the nation's agenda. Today, it has moved to near the top of that agenda—and we must work to keep it there. When we formed the ADA, it was unusual for a woman to assume a leadership role in a major political organization. I regret to say, that is still the case today—and we must work to change that.

'But with women like our speaker to offer their leadership, I am sure that we will succeed. Ladies and gentlemen, please welcome our national chairwoman, Anna Arden."

The audience filling the ballroom of Washington's Mayflower Hotel rose and applauded loudly. Anna had no illusions; this standing ovation was more for Franklin Roosevelt's widow, the great doyenne of American liberalism, than for her. Still, she was grateful to Eleanor for lending her enormous cachet to the moment, especially because the message Anna was about to deliver was one that some present would not savor.

After almost a year in office, the Kennedy administration was still struggling to find its political footing. There was great frustration among liberals about this, and sharp differences about how hard to press the president. Amid this debate, the influential organization that Anna led was gathering to set its priorities for the coming year and shape its strategy for swaying the administration. As Anna stepped to the podium, she had no illusions about how difficult the conversation might be.

"We meet today at a time of profound national challenge," Anna said. "That could be said about so many moments in recent years. But this moment is different. And it is different, not because of anything going on here in Washington, but because of what is going on in the hearts and minds—and actions—of everyday Americans. The young people in the civil rights movement are taking matters into their own hands. They have seized the national spotlight, and the nation is profoundly troubled by the ugly bigotry that is being revealed.

"Now, there are some—not inside this ballroom, I am certain—but some who may cling to the illusion that this is a passing thing, that this movement will soon burn itself out and let us return to business as usual," Anna said. "They could not be more wrong. I know the temper of these young people. What we have seen is only the start.

"And like any challenge to the existing order, this one will provoke opposition. Some of it will be direct, virulent, and violent. Some of it will be indirect, employing the tactics of delay and the counsels of patience.

"Our proper role in this pivotal moment could not be clearer. We must give our full support to the civil rights movement. And we must wield whatever influence we have to counterbalance the powerful forces urging the administration to hold back.

"We must do this because it is in our history and our essence as an organization. We must do this because the stain of racial segregation is degrading our country's character and debasing our country's image. And most of all, we must do this because it is right."

Anna paused, and got what she wanted. The audience was back on its feet, applauding. Not everyone, she noticed—but most of them. She hoped it would be enough.

"Now, a little later today, a group of us, including our dear friend Mrs. Roosevelt, will go over to the White House to meet with the president and the attorney general. Of course, we will bring to their attention all the ADA's priorities. But civil rights will be at the top of that list of priorities, as it should be. And I would hope that we will have your full backing when we do so."

In the end, Anna got her resolution of support, with no open dissent. She knew the dissent was out there; even among these committed liberals, there were those who felt that forcing a confrontation on civil rights played into the hands of segregationists in the South and anti-American demagogues abroad. With Mrs. Roosevelt, their great icon, staring down at them, however, no one in the hall was willing to give voice to that thought.

This wasn't the first internal battle Anna had fought, and she suspected it wouldn't be the last. The ADA's core purpose was to advance liberal ideals, but like most organizations in Washington, it was dominated by men—including many men who doubted a woman's capacity to be an effective leader. Anna's ascension to the chair nine months ago had been bumpy. A faction led by a prominent Harvard professor, Ralph Clement Stearns, had done everything possible to block her. The ostensible complaint was that Anna was too far to the left in her views and too assertive in expressing them; she suspected the real objection was that she was too female.

Anna eventually prevailed, helped by Eleanor's firm support, her own formidable advocacy skills, and her opponents' failure to unite behind a single alternative candidate. Even so, the vote had been close, and Anna knew her critics were still out there, perhaps waiting for a moment to challenge her again.

This was an old story; one she had been facing—and overcoming—since her earliest days as an aspiring writer. The first piece she ever sold was a profile of a group of female union workers from the Lawrence textile mills in her home state of Massachusetts. Fresh out of college, she had met them at the huge demonstration on Boston Common in 1927 to protest the execution of the immigrant labor activists Nicola Sacco and Bartolomeo Vanzetti, one of the great left-wing causes of the decade.

The editor of the small magazine who bought the piece told Anna he liked it because it "hit the women's angle." He meant it as praise, but Anna chafed at the patronizing implication. She heard that phrase repeatedly as she pursued her craft. One editor, rejecting a piece she had written on young men made homeless by the Great Depression, told her he had plenty of writers—he meant male writers—to tackle "the big social issues." He told Anna she should stick to—she knew the words by heart now—"the women's angle." He was a prominent editor of a large publication, but Anna was done with diplomacy. She told him to go to hell, and eventually sold the story to a smaller magazine.

In every aspect of her life, Anna made a point of asserting her independence. Her battles with editors to escape being pigeon-holed in a gender enclave mirrored her personal choices. She had decided at a young age that she wanted no part of a life of traditional domesticity. She was clear about this with the men she grew close to. She paid a price, enduring some painful breakups and lonely times, but it was a price she was prepared to pay. And she eventually found in Alan McMaster someone who could accept her decision, who was comfortable with it both intellectually and emotionally.

His acceptance extended to her resolve to keep her own name; she told him she had worked hard to make Anna Arden a well-known byline and was not about to surrender it in any sphere. He also accepted her decision to go to Europe in 1944 to cover World War II for a major American magazine. That required entrusting young Michael to the care of a housekeeper and grandparents; Alan, by then a senior advisor to the Roosevelt administration, was consumed with his own war work and often a part-time parent himself. And it required Anna, like other women journalists, to fight her own war with military authorities who wanted no part of female correspondents.

The excuses ranged from the mundane—no female field latrines—to the absurd: Women would not know how to protect themselves under fire. "I spent a month living in hobo camps to write about migrants," she told one recalcitrant colonel. "I think I can figure out how to dig a foxhole and get into it." Her vivid stories about the soldiers who fought their way into Germany and liberated the Nazi death camps won widespread recognition.

2: Oval Office

The short drive down Connecticut Avenue from the Mayflower to the White House gave Anna a chance for a quick conversation with Mrs. Roosevelt to review their plans for the meeting with the Kennedys. It was well-choreographed; Eleanor would speak first, briefly, thanking the president and his brother for taking the time to meet with them—an ostensible grace note that would serve as a subtle reminder that the Kennedys had been ducking the meeting for weeks. After firing this opening shot, she would turn to Anna to discuss substance.

"How much resistance do you expect?" Anna asked. "Polite skepticism, or all-out rejection? Or will they just listen passively and say nothing?"

"Oh, polite skepticism, I should think," Eleanor said. "They can't say nothing at all, and they won't want to alienate us completely. We have some sway, even if it's not as much as we would wish. I suspect the president will let his bulldog of a brother do most of the talking on civil rights. He'll use Robert to soften us up, just as we're using me for the same purpose."

"A bit like a military campaign, isn't it?" Anna said.

"It always is with them, and with all the high and mighty, in reality," Eleanor replied. "I think their hearts are in the right place on this—at least I choose to believe that, until I'm proven wrong. But we know the Kennedys pride themselves on their pragmatism, on what they call realism. 'Hard' and 'tough' are words they love to use. We need to demonstrate that showing leadership on civil rights is smart in addition to being right."

Eleanor's intuition was on the mark. The president listened impassively, motionless except for an occasional tip forward and back in his oak rocking chair, as Anna outlined the case for action on civil rights—asking that the administration fully enforce the ban on segregation in interstate travel, fulfill a campaign promise to forbid racial discrimination in federal housing, and back legislation to integrate all public accommodations. When she finished, it was Bobby Kennedy who leaned in and spoke. Characteristically, his voice was soft, but his message was anything but that.

"I think we're doing more on this than you may give us credit for. And, frankly, it would help if you would use your influence with Martin Luther King and the rest of his movement to show some restraint and let us work behind the scenes, like I did to protect him and his people in that church in Montgomery last spring. This issue may make for great moral drama, but it's lousy politics for us, I can tell you that. We've got a midterm coming next fall, and if we lose seats, the chances for legislation of any kind go out the window for the next two years."

"There's always a reason not to act," Anna replied, shifting her gaze from brother to brother as she spoke. "There's always an election coming up. What we want to impress on you is that people all over the South, all over the country, aren't willing to wait anymore. They're not going to accept anyone's assurances of working quietly and privately. Don't take my word for it. Talk to them yourselves. We couldn't stop them if we wanted to, and I, for one, wouldn't want to."

Bobby leaned even farther forward across the coffee table that separated the two parallel couches. He started to speak again, but paused as Jack cleared his throat.

"There's a lot at stake here," the president said. "I understand the moral imperative that underlies this issue, and I want to honor it. I certainly understand the power of prejudice. I would remind you that I'm the first Catholic to sit in this office, and it hasn't been an easy journey. It's stirred up some of our bottom-feeders, and they haven't settled down, far from it. They're louder than ever, and they spin their conspiracy theories that I'm turning the country over to the Pope, or the Russians, or both of them at the same time.

"I want this administration to be a success, to serve as a vehicle for all the causes that you and your organization cherish. Right now, to be candid, that's far from certain. So you must understand us and be patient when we choose our moments to act—and to pause."

"Mr. President." Eleanor's voice commanded attention.

"We do understand the considerations you are raising. We also want you and your administration to succeed. If there is one thing we hope to impress upon you, it is our belief that you, and the nation, are fast approaching an inflection point on the issue of civil rights. I am not an oracle, so I cannot tell you exactly when it will arrive, but I believe it is inevitable. Indeed, the paranoid forces of which you spoke are a symptom of this coming crisis, perhaps a harbinger of it.

"What we would urge you to do is to be ready for this moment, to be ready to act, to have a plan in place for acting in accordance with the values that we know you share."

3: Dinner for Four

Anna and Alan sipped Manhattans and glanced at menus as they waited for Michael and Riva. The interlude gave them a chance to chew over the day's events.

"Well done, my dear. You played the Eleanor card quite skillfully this morning," Alan said. His smile was playful, almost sardonic, but he was also sincere. If anyone appreciated a deft maneuver, it was him.

"You might have credited my torrent of eloquence," Anna said with a matching smile. "I can be quite persuasive, you know."

"Oh, I'm well aware of that. But I'm not surprised that even your eloquence, or the Great Eleanor's aura, hasn't won the Kennedys over on civil rights yet. They're catching a lot of hell on it from southern Democrats."

"That's exactly why we went, to balance the scales," she said. "I meant what I said this morning about this movement having staying power, about the mindset of those young people. We of all people should know that, from Michael and Riva. You may not be happy about what they're doing, but it's not going away."

"Now, don't start," Alan replied tartly. "I feel pride in what Michael's doing, although I'll be damned if I'll encourage him by telling him. And I think Riva is wonderful—a wonderful girl, and wonderful for him. I've never seen him so serious with any other girl. They seem completely comfortable with each other, and that makes me happy. But I'm afraid for them, I'll just say it plainly. I'm allowed to be afraid for my son's safety."

"Watching them together makes me happy, too," Anna said. "There's a serenity in him when he's with her, a sense of being grounded, that I haven't seen before. And I have all kinds of fears for them, too, and not just what might happen at a demonstration. The world can be harsh on people who cross a line. They don't seem to know that yet, or don't care, but they're hostage to some dark forces."

"It's only going to get worse if they get their wish and the civil rights issue really heats up," Alan said. "And you know how I feel about the timing. Kennedy's trying to get a legislative program passed, and deal with Khrushchev, and manage crises in Berlin and Cuba and southeast Asia, and along come some hotspurs to demand that he spend political capital that he doesn't have on an issue that he doesn't view as central."

"He's going to have to confront it sooner or later," Anna shot back. "He can temporize until it's a full-blown crisis, as big as any you mentioned, and then try to play catch-up. Or he can get out ahead of it now and lay some groundwork, build some relationships, show some leadership. If I were him, I know which course I'd think was smarter."

This verbal sparring was an old story. She and Alan had been friendly antagonists from the day they had met at the U.S. embassy in Berlin in 1935. Alan was already a rising star in the Foreign Service, and Anna was a young writer battling to make her reputation who had come to Germany to gather material for stories about life in Naziland.

Their paths had crossed at a reception. Anna thought the American diplomats and journalists based in Berlin were pulling their punches about Hitler and playing into the fraudulent Nazi narrative of a benign New Germany, and she told Alan so that day in language that was provocative to the point of being offensive. He might have been angry; instead, almost in spite of himself, he found himself intrigued by this small, birdlike, fearless woman who was flaying him for being soft on a regime that he actually despised.

That was the start of a friendship that bloomed into a love affair, marriage, parenthood, long years together and some apart as their lives arced through demanding careers and intense relationships. They had experienced difficult moments in their marriage, moments that inflicted pain, but that was behind them now as they navigated together through late middle age. The combination of shared experience and undimmed affection bound them together in a way a stranger observing their frequent debates could never have grasped.

Finally, Riva and Michael arrived, somewhat out of breath. A few heads turned as they hurried through the restaurant. Washington was still a southern town in many ways, and interracial couples were far less common here than in New York. Michael noticed the looks, and hoped they were turning to admire Riva's stylish beauty. She also noticed, and was less sanguine.

"I'm really sorry we're so late," Michael said as they sat down. "This was deadline day at the magazine. I've got a piece going on nuclear testing, and my editor got in my ear on a bunch of minor points. I managed to satisfy him, but it took a while. I'm still new, so they're looking at my stuff carefully."

"Well, The New Republic is lucky to have you," Anna said quickly, hoping to head off a debate between Michael and his father about Michael's article, an issue that divided them. "Riva, you look quite lovely. I'm glad you're able to come down for a few days. It's good to see you."

"But not me?" Michael said. "The prodigal returns, but not a word of welcome?"

"You're old news, son," Alan said. "Your mother, different story. She was in the Oval Office today. I'm sure your magazine would love to have that story. But we're off the record here."

"It wasn't anything that would surprise you," Anna said. "We lobbied hard on civil rights. Bobby told us we didn't understand the politics. The president was sympathetic, but mostly noncommittal. And, yes, we're so far off the record that I'm not even here."

"It's all a game of charades," Michael replied. "They won't act until they absolutely have to, until there are more people packing the jail cells and facing down mobs. That's why the demonstrations are so vital. Until that point comes, you're just treading water."

"No, we got some informal understandings," Anna said. "I think he'll sign an executive order on housing discrimination, although probably not until after the midterms. And when the courts order more state universities to desegregate, which could come soon, they'll enforce those orders, even if it means facing down a governor or two. But you're right about one thing—they're politicians, and they respond to pressure."

Anna felt her husband's wingtip Oxford nudge her pump. She knew Alan was not eager to encourage their son's activism, but she thought that ship had long since sailed.

Riva kept her silence during this byplay, as she usually did when the McMasters sparred over politics. She was still finding her footing with this high-powered family, so different from her own. At her parents' dinner table in the Queens neighborhood of Jamaica, the conversation tended to revolve around the state of business at her father's hardware store, her mother's work as a secretary in a real estate office, her younger brother Tommy's performance at school or sports practice. If they discussed politics, it was likely to be local; her parents were on a committee pressing the board of education to end the chronic underfunding of schools in black neighborhoods like Jamaica. They had stopped talking about the civil rights movement when Riva visited. They too wanted to discourage their child's activist instincts out of fear for her safety.

Riva often wondered what a meeting between these families would be like. She sensed some interesting personality convergences. Like Alan, her father Sam had grown a hard shell to cope with the world and could be gruff and abrupt, but in both men she thought it masked an underlying tenderness. Her mother Dorie was the joiner and doer of the family, pulling Sam along to meetings of the school funding committee and serving as treasurer of the neighborhood's Democratic Party committee.

Yet despite these similarities, Riva had difficulty imagining many points of connection. Anna and Alan believed they were in touch with what they called "the Negro community," but Riva noticed that they really knew few black people, and those they did know were atypical high fliers like themselves. Her parents had some experience in dealing with the white world, but it was more of necessity than choice. They found it hard to understand her decision to venture voluntarily into that world and her growing ability to navigate it.

For Riva, that decision had been fraught, but in the end, inevitable. Her ambition in theater and music arose early, kindled by a high school drama teacher who recognized her talent and did everything she could to nurture it. Her singing voice had been honed by years in school glee club and church choir. Her parents had happily encouraged her to attend the local CCNY campus and tolerated, barely, her decision to major in things as impractical as drama and music. When she announced her intention to transfer to NYU, and won a scholarship to pay for it, they tried to talk her out of it.

But Riva realized she was growing out of their world, and she was determined to act on this bittersweet recognition. Even before NYU, she had been drawn to the Village, captivated by its easy interracial informality and its nightlife of jazz, poetry, edgy theater and comedy. James Baldwin's essays and novels kept her company on the long subway rides to lower Manhattan. And she found a powerful role model when Lorraine Hansberry's epochal play about a black family in Chicago, "A Raisin in the Sun," burst onto Broadway.

For all of that, NYU was intimidating at first, and the Village scene had its hidden hierarchy that viewed talented newcomers as unwanted competition. Its sexual openness also was disorienting at the outset. Her first lover was a poet who was charming and charismatic, but relentlessly self-absorbed. On their first full night together, he performed so quickly that she barely had time to realize she was no longer a virgin. He developed no awareness of her needs and feelings, or showed much interest in her talents and ambitions, and her interest in him soon drained away. Better experiences followed, but nothing serious or lasting, until Michael came along.

Michael was different in every respect. He was the first man Riva had known who seemed able to see her as a whole person, with abilities and dreams and widening intellectual horizons. He was genuinely interested in ideas, and for the most part they were the same ideas that fired her mind. He did think a little too well of himself, like most men Riva had met, but he had the intellect and writing talent to back it up. As a lover, he was tender and patient—and handsome.

Riva was not entirely sure why Michael had turned out as he had, but she was grateful for it. She thought that his mother must deserve a lot of the credit. Anna could sometimes be lofty and remote, but Riva sensed an underlying warmth that Michael shared in abundance. She'd tracked down Anna's writings from the '30s and '40s, and found that they were infused with empathy for the orphans of the world's storms—German Jews, dispossessed farmers, gravely wounded soldiers.

At the table, the mood was lightening. Michael, knocking back a beer, was shedding his deadline tension. Alan, mellowing as he finished his third drink, chose to forgo interrogating his son about the intricacies of nuclear policy. Riva was not a big drinker, but she was starting to relax as she sipped her Cinzano. Anna exuded relief at the brightening emotional weather.

"Riva, I understand that you've had some good news?" she said.

"Well, yes, I've landed a role. Small cast, off-Broadway, a hole-in-the-wall theater to be honest, but it's something. The play is kind of free-form and a mélange of genres, but it's interesting. I guess you'd call me the off-lead. I hope you'll come see it when we open next month."

"We would be delighted," Anna said. "Congratulations!" Alan put in a promise to round up some of their New York friends for the opening. Riva was uncertain he would remember this offer later, and also found it a bit patronizing, but decided to leave that thought unspoken. Michael just sat smiling, enjoying Riva's star turn with his family.

They parted at the restaurant door, Riva and Michael walking arm in arm to their hotel, Anna and Alan driving home to northwest Washington. Smelling Alan's breath as they said their goodbyes, Riva was relieved to see Anna get behind the wheel.

Alan's mellow mood lingered as they drove up Wisconsin Avenue. "Michael may not have his head on straight yet politically, but he's really settling into his life. Professionally and personally."

Anna glanced at him for any trace of a sardonic smile, but saw only sincerity. She credited it to Riva's charms, an excellent steak dinner, and, of course, the alcohol. She worried at times about Alan's drinking, but it wasn't a subject he was open to discussing, and he had never embarrassed himself.

"Let's make a long weekend of it when Riva's play opens," she said as they settled in at home. "We could see something on Broadway too, poke around in the galleries, see some friends. We could have dinner with Adlai Stevenson if he's not too busy at the UN, and look in on Mrs. Roosevelt. She seemed frailer physically today than I've ever seen her. I don't know how much longer she'll be with us."

"Ah, our *grande dame* will always be with us," Alan said, prompting a smile from his wife. "She will remain a presence long after she's dead and buried. Any time we are tempted to stray from the straight and narrow path of liberal rectitude, we shall hear that reedy voice scolding us back into line."

Chapter Four
—Crisis—

October 1962

1: Enigma

Experience had taught Alan that a jangling telephone after 10 p.m. rarely brought good news. He exchanged a nervous glance with his wife as he reached for the receiver.

"Mr. McMaster? Please hold for Mr. Bundy."

Oh boy, Alan thought. A call from the White House national security adviser meant that trouble was bubbling up somewhere. His instant guess was Berlin, but the realm of possibilities was disturbingly wide.

"Alan? It's Mac. How are you? Anna well? Good. Sorry to call so late. But we were hoping that you could come by tomorrow. Early tomorrow, if that's possible. Could you be here at 8? I'll explain then. And let's keep this *entre nous*. Excellent. See you in the morning."

Alan knew that McGeorge Bundy was not an effusive man, but even by this standard, his clipped, brusque tone was striking. Mac had sounded stressed and anxious, and did not try to disguise it. And the fact that he was still in the White House at this hour, and lining up a meeting for less than 10 hours from now, also spoke loudly. Whatever was brewing was no small matter.

Anna looked at him curiously as he hung up the phone, but when he fell silent, she knew better than to quiz him. Her husband was a man who compartmentalized rigorously. If it had been a family or personal matter, he would have told her. Plainly, it was business, and he would tell her what he could, when he could. Right now, it was clear, what he could tell her was nothing at all.

"Why don't we finish the Times crossword?" she said. "The clue is 'unsolved mystery.' Six letters, starts with E, ends with A." Alan stared into space for a moment, then turned toward her. "Try 'enigma.'"

Mac Bundy's basement lair in the West Wing was legendary for its cramped austerity, but he liked it that way. Aware of the maxim that proximity to power confers its own authority, he found the tradeoff of space for location well worth it.

Alan had known Mac for years, since Bundy's days as Harvard's dean, and had been in this office for consultations several times during the 21 months of the Kennedy administration. Two topics kept recurring. One was Berlin, the ultimate front line of the Cold War, where the Soviets had erected a wall, a physical barrier bristling with barbed wire and guns, to stem the hemorrhage of East Germans fleeing to the West.

The other was Cuba. Just after taking office, President Kennedy had green-lighted the CIA scheme to overthrow Fidel Castro with a contingent of Cuban exiles, but the operation misfired badly. Since then, Fidel had become ever more provocative in his anti-American rhetoric, and the administration had become ever more aggressive in its search for a covert means of toppling him.

When Alan arrived, he discovered that Mac wasn't alone. Bobby Kennedy, who had become his brother's trusted adviser on matters far beyond his nominal jurisdiction at Justice, had squeezed himself into a corner of the tiny office. As early as it was, Bobby looked like he'd been there a while. His suit jacket was draped carelessly over the back of his chair, his shirtsleeves were rolled up to his elbows and his tie was at half-mast. The thought crossed Alan's mind that he had spent the night at the White House. Bobby's usual air of screw-you cockiness was gone; he looked tired and worried. Mac was more buttoned up, but his angular face was also haggard.

"Here's the situation," Bundy said unceremoniously. "You know, of course, that we've detected an increase in Soviet personnel in Cuba in recent months. You also know that Republican senators like Ken Keating and Homer Capehart have been screaming about it, claiming that Khrushchev is turning Cuba into a forward base right on our doorstep, while we watch passively. And you probably also know that the Soviets have repeatedly assured us that this isn't the case, that any military assets they have in Cuba are defensive, to help Castro repel another invasion."

Alan nodded and waited for the next shoe to fall.

Bundy looked at Kennedy. "Turns out Keating and Capehart were right," Bobby said quietly.

Alan was far too practiced in the arts of power navigation to betray his surprise, but he felt his stomach drop. He waited for Kennedy to continue.

The U.S. had been doing overflights of Cuba with U-2 spy planes for months, Kennedy said, and the most recent aerial photos showed clear evidence that the Soviets were constructing missile bases. The missiles they could house would reach most of the eastern U.S. and half of South America, and could accommodate nuclear warheads.

"This is incredibly reckless," Alan said.

"That may well be, but it's happening," Bundy replied. "Our best estimate is that the first of these missile installations will be operational in a few weeks. And that's not all. There are several Soviet naval vessels en route to Cuba. We've overflown them, too, and the deck cargoes are covered with tarpaulins. We think there are missiles underneath."

"This is a consequence of Khrushchev's perception that he's dealing with a weak and inexperienced leader," Alan said. "He knows Lenin's dictum that a good Bolshevik always probes with a bayonet until he hits something. If it's steel, he stops. If it's soft, he pushes harder."

"Thank you for the lesson in Russian political classics," Bundy bit off. "I'm sure we'll all sign up for your seminar next semester. Right now, we have more immediate concerns. We've got to find a way to forestall what the Soviets are doing—and it would be nice if we could do it without starting a war. We would like your help in pulling off that little trick."

"Of course," Alan said, suppressing a flash of pique over Mac's jab. Playing the role of wise elder to harried government officials sometimes required swallowing slights. "What's the present state of play?"

"We've known about this for five days," Kennedy replied. "The president's convened a group of principals—we're calling it the ExComm—to handle our response. The joint chiefs are unanimous in recommending an immediate series of air strikes on the bases. No warning, no negotiations."

And, Bobby added, the generals argued that there was no certainty air strikes alone would take out all the installations, because some might be underground. So they wanted a follow-on ground invasion to make certain.

"Of course, one byproduct of such an invasion would be the end of the Castro regime," Kennedy said.

"And another byproduct would be a lot of dead Soviets," Alan said. "Do we know how many are in Cuba?"

"Not precisely, but probably dozens, maybe hundreds," Bundy said. "Enough that the Kremlin couldn't ignore it. We'd be in a shooting war with the Soviets, no mistake."

"Where is the rest of the government on this?" Alan asked.

"As I said, the generals are all hot to go in," Bobby replied. "And some civilians, like Lyndon, are with them. McNamara is more cautious, wants to explore other options. Rusk, as usual, is waiting to see which way the wind is blowing. Adlai, to no one's surprise, is dead set against a military strike, and has even proposed a grand bargain with the Soviets to get the missiles out, but he's very isolated."

"And you?"

"I'll repeat what I said at ExComm," Bobby said. "Now I know how the Japanese prime minister felt when he was planning Pearl Harbor. I don't want my brother to be remembered as this generation's Tojo."

"Tell me this, Alan," Bundy said. "The joint chiefs all insist that the Soviets will back down and write Castro off if we go in hard and fast, even if we kill some Russians in the process. What's your assessment?"

"I think that's dangerous, wishful thinking," Alan said. "I have nothing but contempt for the Soviets and their system, as you know, but we have to deal with them as they are, not as we wish them to be. And the very fact that they've taken this gamble means they're deeply invested in it. If they've gone this far, they're not going to go away quietly. They'll find a way to hit back hard, if not in Cuba, then somewhere else, Berlin or Asia. And things like that have a way of escalating."

"That's what the president thinks, too," Bobby said. "And he thinks it could get out of hand very easily. You know Barbara Tuchman's new book about the start of World War I, *The Guns of August*? He keeps referring to it, even quoting lines from it, about how a minor incident in the Balkans snowballed into a war that killed millions because no leader had the intelligence or the imagination to stop it."

"What the president needs is to find a way out, short of war," Bundy said. "It can't be Adlai's way, even if we wanted to go that route. The Pentagon would leak the whole thing in an instant, and the political fallout would be ruinous. What he's tasked us to do is to come up with an alternative to the military option that doesn't back Khrushchev into a corner but applies enough pressure to make him look for an exit. We want your help in finding it.

"And once we figure that out, we want you to help us find a back-channel that will let us explore whether the Soviets are interested. We know you've maintained contacts with Russian diplomats,

Russian journalists, Russian academics. Those contacts could be very useful."

"I'll be glad to help."

"We have two immediate problems," Bobby said. "The first is that we don't have much time. The sites will soon be operational, those Russian ships will arrive in Cuba in a few days, and our generals don't have a lot of patience. Whatever we come up with, we have to do it quickly."

"Right. What's the second problem?"

"The Soviets," Bundy said. "They're lying to our faces about this. The president had the foreign minister in to the Oval Office the other day, and made a point of reminding him of our long-stated policy, that the presence of offensive weapons in Cuba would be totally unacceptable and would carry the gravest consequences. Gromyko just sat there and blandly assured us that his government would never contemplate such a step. That kind of dissembling doesn't inspire great confidence."

"Totally unsurprising," Alan replied. "Sorry to offer another history lesson, but Soviet leaders are well-schooled in another of Lenin's precepts. A lie is perfectly acceptable if it advances the cause of the international proletarian revolution. In fact, such a lie is a service to history. The Russians will continue to deny the existence of those missiles, right up to the day they pull them out."

"You think there's a chance they'll do that?"

"I think there's a chance, yes."

"Any ideas on how we can get to that point?"

"One or two. We could put one of their assets at risk and try for a swap. But that's indirect and could be too slow. Have you thought about a naval blockade of Cuba? I was attached to the Navy Department for a time during the war, and I was very impressed with their operational capabilities."

Mac and Bobby exchanged a long glance. "Tell us more," Bundy said. "How would it work? Why would it work? What's the downside?"

"Well, I'm thinking out loud here," Alan replied. "It has the advantage of using military resources, which might appease the joint chiefs for a time. If the Soviets can't get their missiles into Cuba, the sites themselves aren't an imminent threat, but a more distant one. We might have to interdict Soviet vessels to inspect their cargo, but we could assert our right to do that under the doctrine of self-defense. They might try to resist, but I rather doubt it. We have overwhelming naval and air superiority in the region. The main thing is, it buys everyone some time."

"Downsides?"

"Mostly the converse of the advantages. It's still a military operation, and those involve guns, and men, men who can screw up. The Soviets will keep working on those missile sites, probably speed up the work in fact, and I take it we can't be absolutely certain that they haven't already snuck a missile onto the island. Even one going operational would change the strategic balance. But on the whole, I think the pros outweigh the cons, rather decisively."

"All right. Thank you," Bundy said. "We'll take this back to the president. As you can imagine, we're sounding out a few others for their thoughts, so don't be surprised if you hear some echoes. But I hope you hear nothing, because this is as close-hold as it comes. Don't speak to anyone about this, and I mean anyone, until we get back in touch with you. This thing will have to go public in a few days, but in the meantime, we need to set our strategy and put it in motion. And stay close, Alan."

After Alan left, Kennedy and Bundy sat for a moment and let the meeting sink in. "It's interesting that he came up with the idea of a blockade independently of the others who are pushing it," Bundy said. "And his analysis of the pros and cons was quick and sure, and persuasive. If we sell this to the president, McMaster will be very useful in putting it in play."

"Here's something else," Bobby said. "McMaster's the hardest of hard-liners when it comes to the Soviets. So the fact that he doesn't favor an immediate strike, and offered the naval option himself as an alternative, tells me we'll have some credibility with the hawks when we start to move on it."

2: Quarantine

For the next 48 hours, Alan mostly sat in his study and tried to focus on his overdue article for Foreign Affairs magazine about the implications of the Berlin Wall. Just days ago, it had seemed so timely: an analysis of the central theater of the great global rivalry that would buttress his standing as a fixture of the foreign policy establishment, a sophisticated strategist who advocated toughness while eschewing the excesses of the hard-right anti-Communists.

Yet now the Berlin article felt impossibly remote and irrelevant in the face of this slow-burning subterranean firestorm, hidden from most of the world but capable of erupting into the most devastating inferno. He thought about avoiding Anna and their friends, but decided that would look suspicious. He was skilled in presenting a blank front to the world, although Anna looked at him quizzically a few times. In conversations with friends, he detected a low background buzz about some sort of international crisis in the offing, but no one had any details.

Finally, Bundy called him back. He was alone this time. "We're going with the blockade—except we're calling it a quarantine," he said. "Sounds less bellicose, and more clinical, I guess. The president's going on TV tomorrow night to announce it, and in the meantime we're briefing the Hill and the allies."

"How much time can we give it to work?" Alan asked.

"We don't know. The joint chiefs have bought into it for the moment, very reluctantly, but they'll be quick to turn if it goes wrong. And there's a million things that can go wrong. But for now, at least, that's our strategy. And of course, it can only work if we use whatever time it buys us to feel out the other side."

"So, what can I do to help?"

"Spend some time right now with me and my staff going over everything you know about the cast of characters in Moscow, why they took this gamble, who might be where on it, and what they might take in trade for pulling their missiles out. And once the president has spoken, start working every Russian contact you have to see how they're reacting and who might be useful as a conduit. We'll have a lot of people doing this—even Bobby has a contact in the Soviet embassy—but you know a lot of Russians. Work them."

By the time the president, looking pale and drawn, faced the TV cameras 16 hours later, the chatter in Washington about an impending crisis had reached a crescendo. To Alan's surprise, though, no specifics had leaked.

Kennedy spoke for less than 18 minutes. Sounding tense at first, he soon hit his stride. Alan, who had been rather unimpressed by Kennedy's leadership abilities up to now, thought he was close to pitch perfect tonight. He laid out the Soviet actions, the U.S. response, and didn't sugarcoat the fact that the blockade "may only be the beginning." He left the Soviet leader an out, calling on Khrushchev "to move the world back from the abyss of destruction." Yet the speech's money quote left no doubt about the potential stakes of the crisis:

"It shall be the policy of this nation to regard any nuclear missile launched from Cuba against any nation in the Western Hemisphere as an attack by the Soviet Union on the United States, requiring a full retaliatory response upon the Soviet Union."

If Khrushchev doesn't understand what that means, he's completely delusional, Alan thought as he watched the speech, sitting next to his visibly distraught wife. And if he won't or can't pull back, better to find out now.

• • •

Anna had watched Kennedy with mounting alarm and dismay. By morning, her mood was bleak and raw. She was angry with Alan—

not for concealing the gathering crisis from her, but for backing a course that she considered reckless. She was angry with Khrushchev and Castro for dragging the world to the brink of nuclear war. She was angry with Kennedy for lacking the courage to resist being dragged along with them. She viewed the blockade as a feckless concession to the war hawks that was just as likely to provoke a conflict as to forestall one.

And she was especially angry about her own feeling of powerlessness. At moments like these, Anna realized, she and her cohort of aging New Dealers and youthful liberal activists were largely impotent. While some noisy protests against the blockade were taking place in New York and Washington, most of the country seemed swept up in a fever of support for it. She wondered what Soviet citizens, many old enough to remember what it was like to have a real war fought on their own territory, were thinking.

Alan had tried to convince her that the blockade was the least bad option. She hoped he would be proved right. But she saw this crisis as the inevitable consequence of a policy that had gone awry at the start of the administration, when Kennedy allowed the CIA to sell him on its mad-hatter scheme to invade Cuba with its small, ill-equipped band of exiles. The failure of the Bay of Pigs operation was as predictable as its fallout, which was to bond Castro even more closely to the Soviets.

Ever since then, Anna had been hearing vague, disturbing rumors about the administration's mounting obsession with Castro, and of shadowy ploys to take him down. One side's folly led to the other's, she thought.

She needed to talk to a kindred spirit, someone who would share her fears that the world might be sliding toward a precipice and could offer some wise counsel. She was certain that Adlai Stevenson was appalled by the turn of events, and probably had tried in private to slow the momentum toward war.

Anna had known Stevenson for more than a decade, since the earliest days of his public career. She had campaigned for him, admired his intelligence and wit, despaired at his chronic indecision, enjoyed his friendship, marveled at his uncanny sexual magnetism and tolerated his occasional flirtations.

Now he sounded weary and out of sorts. She knew he was stealing time away from preparations for his presentation to the UN Security Council to return her call, and she thanked him and got straight to the point.

"Is anyone working to put the brakes on this thing? My husband keeps telling me this is the best chance to avoid a war, but it feels incredibly dangerous to me."

"The showdown meeting was Saturday," Stevenson replied. "The military was still arguing for an invasion. If they had prevailed, I suspect we'd be at war with the Soviets now, if we were still alive to know it."

Stevenson recounted how he had argued for postponing any military moves, including a blockade, and exploring a negotiated settlement. He had proposed a formula in which Moscow would remove all missiles and bases from Cuba in return for a public pledge from Washington not to invade the island. In addition, the U.S. would hand its naval base at Guantanamo back to Cuba and withdraw its Jupiter missiles in Turkey that targeted the Soviets. The settlement would be followed by a Kennedy-Khrushchev summit to explore ways of limiting the increasingly dangerous Cold War rivalry.

"It was a waste of time," he said. "I got absolutely nowhere. Bobby pulled me out of the room and told me, in effect, to knock it off and get on the team."

"And will you?"

"I have to. I'm a member of a government in the middle of a dangerous crisis, perhaps the worst since the start of the Korean War. And I'm an American, and what the Soviets have done is irresponsible and can't be justified, no matter what we've done regarding Cuba."

"What have we done?"

"Nothing that comes anywhere close to what Khrushchev has done. We just have to hope that he'll take the opportunity we've given him to reconsider and look for a way out."

Anna had called Stevenson in search of some solace and even some hope, but the conversation only deepened her sense of helplessness. It left her in ill humor as she met Michael for lunch downtown. His mood was equally dark.

"My god, has everyone gone mad?" he said.

"In a way, you could call it a form of psychosis," she answered. "These are powerful, proud men, and they're deeply invested in their power and their position. Some of them are smart enough or humane enough to realize how dangerous and unnecessary this is, but they're trapped by the twisted logic of the situation. They wind up getting carried along by the troglodytes, the ones who just care about dominance and proving they're tougher and stronger than anyone else."

"If we avoid a nuclear war, it'll be a miracle," Michael declared. He told Anna he had spent much of the time since Kennedy's TV appearance on the phone with any sources he could reach, helping his magazine piece together a quick story on the crisis. What he had learned, he said, frightened him even more than the speech.

"Kennedy's contending with some people who are just itching to call Khrushchev's bluff, and I imagine the Soviets have some of the same types," Michael said. "If anyone in government is arguing for stepping back and settling this peacefully, I can't find them."

Anna thought about telling Michael, off the record, about Stevenson's effort, but decided against it. It was Adlai's secret to share, if he chose, and knowing about it without being able to write it would place an unfair burden on her son.

"It may be more complex than that," she said, taking refuge in vagueness. "Your father says the whole point of the blockade is to buy everyone some time so they can explore the contours of a deal."

"I think dad's as crazy as everyone else," he replied. "This isn't even about real-world nuclear strategy anymore. Those missiles in

Cuba won't give the Soviets any nuclear strike capacity they don't already have with their new long-range missiles. This whole thing is about symbolism and saving face—and that's a hell of a thing to take the entire world to the brink for."

Michael's barb touched an inner conflict in Anna. Even as she shared Michael's view of the policy, she bristled at his casual slap at Alan. And so she found herself defending her husband's advocacy of a policy that she herself believed to be misguided.

"He's trying to help the president hold off the cowboys you were just talking about, the ones who want an immediate showdown. He's spent a lot of time building up his credibility with the administration, and he's trying to use it for a good purpose here. It's not fair to condemn him for that, or call him crazy. He's been around Washington for a long time, and he knows how it works, what's possible and what isn't."

"Maybe he's been around too long," Michael shot back. "What's the point of having credibility, as you put it, if you just use it to enable a reckless gamble? You and dad have already had a long run, but people my age, me and Riva and our friends, we'd actually like to have a life, too. We're fed up with living in the shadow of this insane nuclear stalemate. One of these days, somebody's bluff is going to get called, and that'll be the end of us."

Anna winced and shifted uncomfortably in her chair. She tried to move the conversation to safer ground—how Michael's job had been going, the prospects for Riva's role in a new play that was in rehearsal—but neither of them had much appetite for talking about personal matters that seemed suddenly inconsequential. They had little appetite for lunch, either; they picked at it for a while longer, then left.

As they parted on the sidewalk, Anna embraced her son. The thought flashed through her mind that she might never see him again. She hugged him a second time, harder, and told him she loved him. As they parted, she saw a puzzled look on Michael's face. Death isn't truly real to young people, even at a moment like this, she thought. People my age know better.

3: Weak Tea

Two days later, Alan was back in Bundy's office. Bobby was present again, which told Alan that this meeting, unlike the last one, was not purely operational.

"Things are coming to a head, and it's not clear how much longer we can control events," Bundy said without ceremony. "The Soviet ships reached the quarantine line earlier today, but they're in a holding pattern, not advancing or retreating. And one of their subs is lurking about, shadowing one of our destroyers."

"The generals are running out of patience," Bobby said. "Their argument is that the Soviets are playing us, testing our nerve by running their ships right up to the line and then pausing to see if we'll wobble. They keep repeating that time is not on our side because the work on the missile sites is intensifying—and they're not wrong about that. They're pressuring the president to set a hard deadline—72 hours—after which we go in. They keep insisting the Russians will fold if we do."

"Everything I've heard and seen from the Soviets since the president spoke tells me they're just totally wrong about that," Alan replied. "If we listen to them, they'll push us into an actual war. What's our nuclear force status? Have we raised it?"

Once again, Mac and Kennedy exchanged glances. "We went up to Defcon 3 the night the president spoke," Bundy said. "The joint chiefs want us to go to Defcon 2. We've never done that before. They say it would send a signal that we mean business. It might just send a different signal, that we're about to launch a pre-emptive strike." Alan nodded in agreement.

"So we've got to come up with a solution that both sides can live with, and do it fast," Bobby said. "We've gotten some back-channel hints about what might be acceptable to the Soviets. We'd like to hear your thoughts about them. And then we'll want you to help us explore them with the other side. We've got to use every possible channel, given the shortness of time. Have you had any luck reaching out to your Soviet contacts?"

"Yes. One in particular. We've talked on the phone a couple of times, and he's willing to meet me if we have something concrete to discuss."

"Do it. Quickly." Bundy said. "Now, let's talk through some options."

A few hours later, Alan walked into a restaurant on Wisconsin Avenue and took a seat in a corner booth. The Nanking Gate was an unpretentious Chinese eatery sandwiched between a dry cleaner and a drugstore. Its decor was dated and cliched: vinyl-covered banquettes, red paper lanterns and ersatz lacquer screens. The menu was equally unimaginative, but the Nanking had one culinary claim to fame. Its succulent Peking duck, served with no advance order required, made it a McMaster family favorite.

Alan had arrived early. As he waited, he sipped lukewarm tea and glanced at the late edition of the Washington Star. The front page was filled with crisis stories: Stevenson debating the Soviet ambassador at the UN, Castro shouting defiance at the Yankee imperialists, Army reservists mustering in Florida.

A stocky man in a brown business suit entered, looked around for a moment, waved the hostess away, and slipped into the booth, facing Alan. They both glanced around for signs of someone watching, but saw nothing; the restaurant was barely half-filled, and the other diners were preoccupied with their own meals and conversations. Alan guessed that Aleksander Volokshin had been tailed to the restaurant by at least two Soviet minders, and perhaps someone from Alan's side, but if so, they were invisible.

"Would you like some tea, Sasha?"

"Please, spare me. What the Chinese call tea, a Russian would use to water his plants. So weak you can barely taste it."

"Fair enough. I'm not enjoying it much myself."

Alan had known Volokshin for three years. They had met at an embassy reception during the planning for Khrushchev's U.S. visit in 1959. That was in the high summer of U.S.-Soviet detente, before the U-2 spy plane shootdown and the blown Paris summit and Castro's romance with Moscow. They had kept in touch, for both professional and personal reasons; besides being well-connected, Sasha Volokshin was a genuinely engaging man who enjoyed knocking back shots of vodka and became riotously funny after a few glasses. One boozy night at the McMaster home, he had reduced an entire living room to helpless laughter with an off-color impersonation of the Soviet leader that centered on Khrushchev's rural origins and a particularly amorous pig. Officially, he was an accredited correspondent for the Soviet government newspaper Izvestia. Like most Russian journalists in Washington, he was also KGB.

Volokshin lit up—not an American cigarette, which many Soviets in the U.S. gratefully smoked, but a malodorous Russian Belomorkanal. Alan wondered whether Volokshin smoked them as a reminder of home—or a twisted act of homage to his secret institutional masters, who had supplied thousands of prison camp inmates to construct the White Sea Canal for which the cigarettes were named. Volokshin offered one to Alan, who declined it and lit a Winston.

Alan gestured at the newspaper. "This is not heading in a good direction," he said. "There has to be a way to turn it around. We're interested in finding such a way. I can tell you that authoritatively. The question is, are your leaders?"

"I can speak just as confidently, and the answer is yes. But there are pressures back home, just as I'm sure there are on your side. It can't be unilateral. We have to have something."

"Understood. What would it take?"

"To begin, we would need a public pledge at the highest level—from President Kennedy himself—that an invasion of Cuba is off the table. Permanently."

"That may be possible. It won't go down easily with some of our people, but it is possible."

"I'm glad to hear it. I'm glad to hear that the American president will consider declaring his willingness to honor a fundamental provision of international law."

"Please, Sasha. Sarcasm is not helpful."

"Okay. Fair point. So that will help. But because it is such a basic thing, we will need more. Otherwise, our chairman will have a full-scale revolt on his hands in the Politburo."

"I think your chairman is quite capable of handling any Politburo uprisings. But what else did you have in mind?"

"Missiles for missiles."

"You mean Turkey?"

"And Italy."

"Anything else you'd like?" Alan replied. "Want us to throw in the British and French nuclear arsenals, just to make the deal more attractive to your hard-liners?"

"Now who's being sarcastic? Let's stay focused. Your missiles in Turkey had some strategic value several years ago. Today, they're obsolete, because of the ICBMs. You can withdraw them without losing a thing strategically."

"You're forgetting that Turkey is a member of NATO. The Turkish government might not be too happy about being used as a bargaining chip."

"They'll get over it. I'm telling you, that's what it'll take to make this work for us."

"The Turkish missiles could never be public," Alan said. "And it couldn't be simultaneous. After about six months, we could quietly announce that they're being retired from service because of their age, and because of revisions in our overall nuclear force posture. And then we could just never get around to replacing them."

"Could? Or would?"

"Would."

"Okay. Let me take this back and consult. You know, of course, that we're hardly the only people having conversations like this?"

"I would hope that's the case," Alan replied. "Wouldn't want the fate of the world to hang on a single meeting. What if one of us got hit by a bus?"

"Let's just hope that the other conversations are consistent with this one," Sasha said. "Wouldn't want the fate of the world to hang on people who couldn't keep their stories straight, either."

4. After-Action

Once again, Alan found himself in the West Wing basement. Not for long, though; Alan barely had time to shed his raincoat before Bundy led him upstairs to the Oval Office.

The atmosphere in the White House was relaxed, almost celebratory. The great crisis was over, resolved the previous day with the Soviet announcement that they would pull their missiles and installations out of Cuba and the president's no-invasion statement. Nothing was said publicly about missiles in Turkey.

"Alan, I want to thank you for everything you did to help us get this settled," the president said. "Your guidance was essential. Your knowledge of the Soviets and their psychology was invaluable. And your conversations with your friend, the journalist"—Kennedy paused for half a beat and smiled before uttering the word—"were crucial in testing Russian intentions. I don't think we'd be here today, congratulating ourselves, without your help."

Alan was shrewd enough to recognize strategic exaggeration— and to accept it at face value. He knew he had been only one of several role players Kennedy had deployed in the drama.

"Mr. President, I was happy to do what I could. I'm glad it proved useful. And I'll be glad to help again in the future. What is in the works now, if I may ask?"

"The first thing is to keep a close eye on Cuba to make sure the Soviets live up to their word—and a close eye on Moscow for any signs that Khrushchev is in political trouble. You could help us on that second point by letting us know if you pick up any rumblings.

"Then we want to propose setting up a direct telephone link with the Kremlin, so we don't have to communicate through a cranky telex in a crisis. That nearly drove us crazy over the past week. And if Khrushchev is still in the saddle when the dust settles, I want to reopen talks on finally getting a test ban agreement. This was a very near thing, and if we can use that fact to create some momentum toward less nuclear brinksmanship, I want to try."

Anna shoved the new edition of the Saturday Evening Post across the table to her husband. "Look at this. Do you have any idea how this came to be?"

The magazine's cover story was about the missile crisis and Adlai Stevenson's role in it. The writers were personal friends of the president. Their article accused Stevenson of advocating a policy of appeasement, a "Caribbean Munich."

"I have no idea," Alan said, honestly. He could have made a guess, but he was not about to feed this fire.

"It had to come from within the administration," Anna declared. "There's no way Charlie Bartlett and Stew Alsop would have run with this unless they had an inside source. And it's complete BS."

"How can you be so sure?"

"Because, as I told you at the time, I spoke with Adlai the day after Kennedy's speech. And he told me in detail what he'd proposed—which I also told you about, and which you didn't contradict. So I'm quite certain this story is hogwash.

"Yes, Adlai wanted to explore a negotiated settlement—who wouldn't? And in a negotiation, you give something to get something. And, yes, he proposed offering up those wretched missiles in Turkey, which we have no actual use for, anyway. But he never advocated a wholesale abandonment of our bases in the Caribbean, like this article claims. This is a piece of character assassination."

Alan did have an idea where the story might have originated, and why. He understood that its appearance was very useful to the president, helping position him as the tough-minded pragmatist who had rejected the extremes of capitulation and invasion. For all the relief that most Americans felt about the peaceful resolution of the crisis, there were powerful figures in and out of government who believed Kennedy had wasted an opportunity to get rid of Castro.

Alan also knew that the Turkish missiles had been part of the deal, but he was bound to secrecy on that point.

"I'd say that if Adlai Stevenson's *amour propre* is part of the collateral damage from a successful outcome to a crisis of this magnitude, it's a small price to pay," he said.

Anna shook her head angrily. "It's about more than Adlai—although the reputation of a statesman and a personal friend is not nothing. You keep telling me how skillful Kennedy was, how skeptical and questioning, how he outmaneuvered Khrushchev and Castro and his own generals to get what we needed without war. But what kind of groundwork is he laying for the future with a story like this? What happens in the next crisis? Who's going to give honest advice if he fears that advocating restraint will come back to bite him? Who's going to ask tough questions, challenge premises, all the things Kennedy supposedly values? Would you?"

"Ah, I'm in the enviable position of being too old to care about things like that. I just call 'em like I see 'em, and try to make myself useful."

"You can slough it off if you want, but actions have consequences," Anna shot back. "Most people will remember Kennedy as the hero of this drama. Others may take away different lessons."

Chapter Five
–Riva's Roles–

April 1963

1: Good Fortune

Riva awoke first, roused by the bright sunshine streaming through the curtains they had forgotten to close in their ardor last night. She stretched her long body languidly under the blanket, rolled against Michael's back, and gently nuzzled his neck. That was enough to light the spark. Michael stirred and rolled toward her. Soon their kisses were deep and prolonged, their bodies eagerly intertwined, all thought of sleep gone.

As they lay together afterward, nuzzling and fondling each other, Riva's mind danced in a dreamlike state, filled with thoughts of her lover. She reveled in the sweetness of being with him. They had known each other for almost two years, they had lived together for six months, they were deeply intimate in so many ways.

Yet for all their closeness, Michael still seemed elusive to her in many respects, a riddle to be solved. Some nights, after Michael had fallen asleep, she lay awake next to him, her mind filling with questions she could barely articulate. What did he really feel? About her? About his life? About their life together? What would his ultimate priority be, when he had to choose?

She realized something else. Her sense of mystery about Michael mirrored the uncertainties she felt about her own life. She was living an existence she had barely dared dream about only a few years ago, one her parents had told her was an illusion. Yet she had rejected their advice and pressed forward—and here she was, living in the Village, flourishing in its bohemian ecosystem, assembling a network of friends, slowly building a reputation as an actress through real parts in real, professional productions.

Yet she was acutely aware of how tenuous it was. For all its studied liberalism, the world Riva had chosen was still a white world, and black people were admitted on an unspoken probation that could be revoked without notice. And it was a world dominated by men—men who established invisible but powerful limits that acted like a force field, constraining what women could do. Her parents often reminded her of these realities, and she recognized them herself, even as she resented their warnings.

Riva was navigating these waters mostly by instinct, and so far her instincts had guided her well. Greenwich Village was filled with creative, expressive young people with a flair for drama and a taste for edginess. They immersed themselves in political protest and the folk music that formed its soundtrack. They squeezed into small experimental theaters that provided work for aspiring performers like her. They congregated in clubs and coffeehouses that entertained them with jazz, avant-garde poetry, stand-up satire and more folk music. While most of them were white, the Village was as close to an integrated milieu as could be found in New York.

Riva had lived in this world for four years now. Whatever inner doubts she harbored, she exuded self-confidence, and did her best to live the role. She was good as an actress, she was sure of it, and convinced she could get better. The parts she landed varied in size, none of them breakthrough roles, but each offering opportunities to hone her skills. She worked on developing her singing voice and longed for a role in a musical, but that was hard to find, especially off-Broadway, where intense dramas and absurdist comedies predominated. In more honest moments, she wondered whether her voice was strong enough to carry a large role in a musical.

The civil rights movement formed the third pillar of her life. It was another point of tension with her parents, who embraced its goals but could see only danger in it for her. But Riva felt a powerful bond with the movement. She sensed a confluence: as it sought to evoke the country's better angels, she felt it also tapped the best in her, called to her most hopeful and open nature.

Michael stirred, stretched, and kissed Riva lightly. He was content to float in the warm aura created by their passion. His dominant feeling at moments like these was a powerful sense of his good fortune in finding a woman as caring and soulful as Riva. He had many friends who blundered through dates and half-relationships, connecting for a time, and then falling away into alcohol-fueled regrets and recriminations. He had traveled that barren landscape himself before meeting Riva. He was a lucky man, and he knew it.

This sense of being blessed, of not wanting to jeopardize a good thing, made him reluctant to probe his lover's psyche too deeply. He was especially reticent about discussing the most obvious outward difference between them, to a degree Riva found curious. Biracial couples were not rare in New York, especially in their world, but they still evoked an occasional stare or raised eyebrow. Michael refused to acknowledge these reactions, seemed unaware that they even had happened. When she pointed them out to him, he shrugged them off as the fading echoes of a benighted mindset that would soon disappear. Riva wasn't so sure about that.

This was just one part of the Michael puzzle. He was such an odd mixture of self-awareness and reticence. He had no illusions about how privileged his life had been, but he reacted to this realization by refusing to talk about his parents with their friends. When she asked him why, he told her he did not want to be known as the son of Washington power figures, and even confessed to a degree of embarrassment about it. His father's role as a Cold War hawk was especially awkward in their dovish milieu. For the same reason, he was reluctant to talk about his military service. And Riva discovered almost by accident that he spent time volunteering at a church in

Brooklyn that helped tenants who were being cheated or evicted by slumlords; he did not talk much about that, either.

Now the sunlight was flooding their bedroom with light. Michael reluctantly rolled away from Riva, rose, and headed for the shower. Monday was a working day at the magazine for him, but an off-day for Riva, whose play was on a Tuesday-to-Saturday schedule. She was headed for an early lunch with her friend Deana Franklin, then an afternoon working in the local office of the Student Nonviolent Coordinating Committee, or SNCC. one of the movement's most militant groups.

Dressed after his shower, Michael sipped his coffee on the sofa and curled up next to her. He finished his coffee, but showed no sign of finishing his nuzzling. She reciprocated for a time, then gently pushed him away. "Okay, mister, time for you to go out and work so I can be a starving actress without actually starving."

"Yeah, okay, okay, I'm going. I can tell when I've worn out my welcome. See you tonight. We've got that fundraiser for Birmingham."

"Yup. See you there."

They both had vivid memories of Alabama's largest city, from the freedom ride two years ago. Now it was again a battleground, as Dr. King's Southern Christian Leadership Conference and SNCC mounted daily demonstrations to protest racial segregation in the city's stores, restaurants and schools. King and several other leaders had been arrested three days earlier, as the city's belligerent public safety commissioner, the aptly nicknamed Bull Connor, tried to break the back of the budding movement.

Deana was already at the restaurant, sipping tea, when Riva arrived. They had met nearly two years ago, when Riva landed a part in a one-act play that Deana had written. The role was small, the play's run was short, but from it a warm and easy friendship was born.

Deana was slightly older than Riva and had arrived in New York around the same time Riva moved to the Village. She was from

Detroit, the daughter of labor activists; her father had been a leader in organizing his fellow black workers at Ford's massive River Rouge plant to support the strike in 1941 that won union recognition from the last holdout in the auto industry. Both her parents were later accused of being communist sympathizers and called to testify before the House Un-American Activities Committee, but emerged as local heroes for facing down their inquisitors. Deana had studied theater at Wayne State University and acted in productions at the school's innovative Bonstelle Theatre. Then, determined to make it as a playwright, she took the plunge and joined the creative diaspora migrating to New York.

This boldness infused every aspect of Deana's life, and formed a large part of her appeal for Riva. Deana's plays were sharp, uncompromising, sometimes strident; it limited their commercial appeal, and she knew it, but she did not seem to care. Her political opinions were just as unyielding. She was passionate about the civil rights cause, but she viewed it as only one part of a broad global struggle for social justice by the world's nonwhite majority.

And there was something else, something that Deana didn't exactly advertise but didn't conceal, either. She lived more or less openly with her lover, a young white woman from Boston whose vérité-style photographs of city street life had been exhibited in a local gallery. Deana had written for the lesbian magazine The Ladder, and when she got to know Riva well, she shared some of her unpublished poetry, which was personal and unblushing.

It was all a little disorienting, but at the same time bracing and provocative. A conversation with Deana left Riva feeling as if her mental center of gravity had been shifted, her brain stretched and expanded. It was not an unwelcome experience.

Deana greeted Riva with a warm hug and a recommendation. "You should try the omelet. I had it here last month, and I can still taste the onions and Gruyere. You won't be disappointed."

Riva sat down, smiling to herself. Deana could make ordering lunch sound like a sensual experience.

"How's your new play going?" Riva asked as she ordered a coffee.

"I'm stuck. Don't mind admitting it. I wanted this one to be more sweeping than what I've done before, to take in a wider field of vision. But I'm left with the feeling that it just sprawls all over the place with no focus."

"You've never really told me what it's about. I know it's set in the Caribbean and in Harlem, but you haven't shared any more about it."

"And I won't, not just yet," Deana said. "I'm very protective of my children, especially when they're gestating. Tell me about your work. I saw the play when it previewed, and I thought it was very promising, although it had a lot of rough edges. And you know I liked your performance. Has the role developed the way you'd hoped?"

"Yes, and no. It's changed since you saw it, but the main idea is still the conflict between the husband and wife over status and money, kind of an Americanized version of *Look Back in Anger*. My role has evolved, which is actually the biggest change. I started out as a sort of loyal sidekick to the wife, but the director wanted to expand my character, which, of course, is fine with me. But in expanding it, he created a suggestion of some sexual tension between me and the husband. It's an interesting idea, and it gives me a lot to play off of, so I'm happy about that. But I'm not sure it's helped the play as a whole, because it throws off some of the other scenes. I'd be interested in what you think if you saw it again."

Riva's private opinion was that her friend's true calling in the theater would be as a director. Deana could analyze a production's strengths and weaknesses with rare acuity, in a way that she sometimes had difficulty bringing to bear on her own work.

"I'll try to do it. How long do you think it'll run?"

"Hard to say. Audiences have been decent, reviews okay, no outright pans. It's got a little room to run. Frankly, there's a part of me that would welcome an early closing."

"Why in the world would you want that, Riva?"

"Because I want to go to Birmingham, and I don't think I can while *Change of Heart* is running. Even going for the two days we're dark would be risky, because folks like us can get busted for breathing too hard in Birmingham, and that would be a disaster. I'd miss performances. I can't do that."

Deana looked at her searchingly. "You do have an understudy."

"You don't build credentials by missing performances," Riva said. "If I even asked, the director would tell me I have to decide whether I want to be an actress or an activist. He'd also try to guilt me by reminding me what a favor he'd done by expanding my role. And if I went anyway, he'd tell his friends how ungrateful I was, how all performers are just overgrown children, with an aside thrown in about how women are too emotional to be real pros. He'd be too chickenshit to say out loud that black folks have divided loyalties that get in the way of their professional responsibilities, but he'd probably think it, and maybe find some way of hinting at it. By the end, my reputation as a performer would be ruined."

"Of course, you're right. I sometimes forget what complete assholes these men can be. It's a dangerous thing to forget. But, man, Birmingham is going to be a moment. What about Michael? Is he going?"

"He's meeting with his editors today to discuss his next assignment. That's certainly what he wants to write about. And they really liked his piece last fall on James Meredith and Ole Miss. They put it on the cover."

"And how are you two doing? Still got the glow?"

Riva paused for just a moment, asking herself whether she wanted to hedge the answer that had come spontaneously to her lips. No, the time for holding back was past.

"I love him. I love him with all my heart. I know that sounds corny and simplistic, but it's how I feel. There are things that I wish he was more aware of, things about me and things about the world.

But he's young—even younger than I am—and he's got a very big heart. I'm willing to trust that he'll get there."

2: Pure Militance

The SNCC office was in a dingy building on lower Fifth Avenue, halfway between Union Square and Washington Square. It was an open area filled with desks, long tables and folding chairs that occupied most of an upper floor. Some days it was sparsely populated, but today, with the Birmingham campaign heating up and the need for support rising, it was humming with activity.

Riva plopped down on one of the rickety chairs and started stuffing fundraising letters into envelopes. The pitch was straightforward, leading with the campaign's importance as a chance to strike at segregation in the heart of the Deep South, then outlining the need for money to transport volunteers, pay for medical treatment and post bail for jailed demonstrators. Riva stuffed and sealed each envelope and handed it to a college kid from The New School, who addressed it and passed it down the line for stamping.

The well-organized process for getting out the mailing was a bit of an anomaly in a group that viewed structure and hierarchy with suspicion. SNCC was committed to action above all else, and disdained the political alliances that King and other movement figures were nurturing. SNCC's leaders were young, like John Lewis, the group's chairman, whom Riva and Michael had met during the freedom rides, and Diane Nash, a Fisk University student who had organized successful sit-ins in Nashville. They viewed nonviolence as a hallowed principle and militance as a strategic imperative. And, as Riva had learned, they were extraordinarily brave.

She was drawn to their energy, and their willingness to act as the movement's shock troops. She hoped SNCC's political purity could survive in a world that often punished idealists. However, she recalled something that Anna had said in a recent conversation, something that had provoked an argument. Demonstrations were important, they created breakthroughs, she had said. But a breakthrough had to be consolidated, and that meant laws and regulations enacted by sympathetic politicians. Michael had bristled, telling his mother she sounded condescending and dismissive. Riva saw that his comment had stung Anna. She also thought that even if Anna's tone was off-key, she might have a point.

With no performance to call her away, Riva had time to linger for the inevitable political discussion that swirled through the office whenever more than a handful of people were there. Today a young white student from Columbia, wearing a faded sweatshirt and jeans, was perched on a table, sounding a common theme: the perfidy of the Kennedy administration.

"That bill he sent to Congress last month was a joke. Supposed to be a voting rights bill, but no enforcement mechanism of any kind. As if southern whites are ever gonna let Negroes vote just because some federal law says they should. And it didn't even mention public accommodations—nothing."

"We shouldn't expect anything from politicians," a slightly older man, a community activist from Harlem, chipped in. "Their only interest is in keeping a lid on, keeping things stable, and getting re-elected. We have to take the power in our own hands, make them irrelevant."

Once, Riva might have been hesitant to enter this fray, fearful of saying something that would sound naïve or foolish. More than two years of front-line activism and on-stage experience had banished those fears.

"We have to force Kennedy to act," she said. "It's no good ignoring him, because politicians do have power. If we expect nothing from them and demand nothing, that's what we'll get. But you're right that we have to do it for ourselves. We have to make it impossible for Kennedy not to act, to make the cost of not acting so

high that he'll have to propose legislation with some teeth in it—
and actually fight to get it passed. He may not want to, but he'll have
no choice. That's why Birmingham is so important."

The Columbia student snorted in disgust, and the community
activist shook his head sadly, telling Riva that she would eventually
learn the futility of seeking crumbs from the table of the powerful.
Yet she saw other heads around the room nodding in agreement
with her.

The conversation moved on to events on the ground in
Birmingham, and whether the organizers would put out a call for
reinforcements. Riva listened, silent and torn. She knew that many
in this room might soon be exposing themselves to arrest and abuse,
and she hungered to join them. She wondered if she had been too
categorical in dismissing the possibility, if there might be a way
after all.

In this conflicted mood, she headed uptown to meet Michael at
a fundraiser for the Birmingham movement. The subway ride was a
journey between two worlds, from the Village's eclectic funkiness
to the monied elegance of the Upper East Side. In the three-block
walk from the subway, the skies opened in a spring downpour, and
she was soaked by the time she arrived.

The fundraiser was in a spacious brownstone on East 77th Street,
the home of a lawyer who worked for a white-shoe firm and did pro
bono work for liberal causes on the side. Riva dried herself off as
best she could in the foyer, helped by a maid who had a towel at
hand, and headed into the crowded living room.

Michael was already there, sipping a drink and chatting with an
editor of the New York Review of Books, a fledging publication
created to fill the void opened by the city's newspaper strike. When
he spotted Riva, he detached himself and came over to her, his
expression a mixture of concern and involuntary amusement.

"You look like you swam up from downtown. Are you okay?"

"Forgot my damn umbrella. This jacket is wool, too. It'll take forever to dry, and I hate that damp wool smell. How are you, honey? How did your talk with the editors go?"

"Well, I sold them on a reported piece on Birmingham. They're a little skeptical that it'll prove to be as big a deal as I think it will, but it's a good sign that they trust me enough to let me go down, anyway. I'll probably leave toward the end of the week."

That Michael would be there only sharpened Riva's pangs of conflict, but she shunted the feeling aside to share in Michael's evident excitement. "That's wonderful, I'm so glad. I know how much you want to do this."

"How's Deana?"

"Same as ever. Thinks I'm too good for you, but she's willing to give you a chance," Riva said with a smile. "She'll be heading to Birmingham if they want reinforcements. She kind of suggested that I should go, too."

Michael looked at her intently. "Have you changed your mind about going?" he said. "I'm with you either way, you know that. But don't let yourself get guilted into blowing the part. This is going to be a long fight, with plenty of chances to be involved."

"Whatever I do, it won't be out of guilt. I'll have to think about it. But thank you for understanding."

The clink of a fork on glass interrupted them. The host cleared his throat, thanked his guests for coming, and introduced the evening's star attraction, the singer-actor Harry Belafonte.

Belafonte's breakout album of calypso songs in 1956 had launched him into show business stardom, but he did not let his career interfere with his political commitment. He poured his own money into the movement and lent his celebrity to events like this.

"I also want to thank you for being here tonight, and for donating generously, which I know you all have," he said with a wry smile. "And if you haven't yet, we'll be glad to give you the opportunity.

"I think we all understand what's happening in Birmingham, what the stakes are. Bull Connor is trying to break the back of the movement there through mass arrests. And he's jacked up the bail for those arrested. His plan, obviously, is to bleed us dry financially, so we'll have no choice but to call off the campaign. We can't let that happen. If he succeeds, that tactic will be repeated everywhere. We've got to call his bet. We've got to keep on the march in Birmingham and everywhere else—and that's where you good people come in. You can be part of this moment in history just by writing a check. I hope you'll take advantage of this opportunity, and I and Dr. King and everyone in Birmingham are very grateful to you for doing so."

The applause for Belafonte soon devolved into the buzz of resumed conversations. Riva found herself chatting with a well-tailored couple. "I just love his songs," the man said. "Day-O! Day-O! Makes me feel like I'm right there in the banana boat." His wife nodded in agreement. "And he's so—how shall I put it? Well, he's gorgeous. I'm sure you Negro girls must swoon for him. Like we used to go weak in the knees for Frank Sinatra when we were teenagers."

"Yes, and not just Negro girls," her husband said. "We saw him in that movie with that blonde actress. What's her name? Yeah, Inger Stevens. There was real chemistry between them. But in real life, I guess that's a line you cross at your peril."

Riva hoped her folded arms and tight-lipped expression conveyed her discomfort, but body language was lost on them. "Well, it's just a genuine pleasure for us to be able to do some good, and to meet people like you," the woman said. "I told my housekeeper where we were going, and she was so grateful. It made her day."

As Riva walked arm in arm with Michael to the subway, she recounted the conversation, alternately sighing and laughing. "I honestly can't believe what comes out of some folks' mouths when it comes to race," she said. "I guess as long as they cough up a check that'll help bail somebody out of jail, I shouldn't mind listening to them prattle on. But, lord, they sound so foolish."

"Well, speaking of the lord, they say he does move in mysterious ways."

"Tread lightly, mister. You're talking to an old church girl."

"So you keep reminding me. Fortunately, that doesn't seem to get in the way of our love life. Otherwise, you might have to convert me."

"You're about as hopeless a case as I've ever found. But you're in luck. I specialize in redeeming lost souls. My technique is infallible."

Chapter Six
—Family Matters—

May 1963

1: Back to Birmingham

The doors of Birmingham's 16th Street Baptist Church swung open, and the first group of marchers emerged, clapping and singing. Watching from across the street, Michael turned to a colleague, an Associated Press photographer. "It's the kids again," he said.

It was day two of a new tactic for the Birmingham movement in a monthlong campaign dubbed Project C—C for confrontation. The previous day, Michael had watched nearly 1,000 black schoolchildren, ranging from teenagers to some as young as 8, march downtown from the church to support the movement's demands for an end to racial discrimination—and to willingly get arrested. The goal was to fill the city's jails to the bursting point, to provoke a crisis that would force the city's timorous moderate white leaders to step in and negotiate.

The mobilization of the schoolchildren generated intense controversy, not only among whites but within the city's black community. Movement organizers had turned to it in near-desperation, after failing to muster enough adults willing to submit to arrest. It succeeded beyond their expectations. In the city's rigidly segregated black schools, student body leaders and athletes stepped up to organize their classmates. Yesterday's march was peaceful, the atmosphere almost festive, and by the end of the day a jail built to house 900 inmates was packed with more than 1,200.

No one posted bail; the students were committed to win this test of wills.

The first sign that today would be different came from police on bullhorns warning the marchers to turn back "or you'll get wet." As the students reached the far edge of Kelly Ingram Park, across from the church, Michael watched the threat become an ugly reality. At Bull Connor's command, firefighters trained powerful water hoses on the marchers. Students were knocked off their feet, pinned against trees, flattened against buildings. For those who made it past the hoses, Connor's cops had German shepherds waiting. The park and the surrounding streets became a battleground, filled with the sounds of bellowing police officers, snarling dogs and battered schoolchildren.

Connor's tactics were born of his own desperation. White business leaders, facing mounting losses from a black boycott of downtown stores, were wavering. Connor had gambled that the movement wouldn't be able to make good on its threat to fill the jails, but the students had called his bluff. Now he was turning to raw force, hoping to intimidate them off the streets.

And once again, they proved him wrong. Marchers kept streaming out of the church and several other staging sites to converge on downtown. Conner, with no path backward, doubled down on his violent tactics. Michael watched as a high-pressure hose pinned four teenagers against a building. One, completely drenched, tried to shield a classmate, but both were driven to their knees by the powerful spray. Down the street, another teenager was collared by a cop with a leashed dog. At a command, the animal sprang, tearing at the student's shirt. Another dog lunged at a young man and ripped his pant leg open from thigh to ankle.

Michael, in a small knot of journalists, furiously scribbled notes as two photographers snapped away just as frantically. Afterward, he discovered that a good part of what he wrote was indecipherable. It didn't matter; what he saw this day was indelible in his memory.

He caught up with one student, a high school senior named Aaron Sanderson, who had been knocked flat twice by fire hoses. His clothes were soaked and his glasses were cracked, but he was still marching.

"Are you okay?"

"I'm kinda sore. But we gotta keep going. Too many people depending on us. And too many other people are counting on us to just give up if they treat us rough enough. They think we're afraid of them."

"And you're not?"

The student stopped and turned to face Michael. Water was still dripping down his face. His broken glasses were askew. But he held himself erect and looked Michael straight in the eye.

"I don't think we got a choice anymore. If we turn around and go home, it's like we're telling them they can keep treating us like this, keep holding us down like this, for the rest of our lives. I don't want to live like that."

By late afternoon, it was clear how badly Connor had miscalculated. The images of peaceful young black demonstrators willingly enduring violent attacks from dogs and firehoses handed the movement a priceless public relations victory, and the brutality utterly failed to break the marchers' will. More people were arrested than on the previous day, and Connor had nowhere to put them. As the arrests crested above 3,000, he began transporting his prisoners to the state fairgrounds. Short of patrol wagons, he had to press school buses into service to haul away those arrested, which only underscored the demonstrators' youth. On each bus, students lowered the windows and filled the air with the chants and anthems of the movement.

That evening, the graphic footage from Birmingham was the lead story on each television network's national newscast. The next morning, Americans awoke to newspapers displaying a photo of a dog lunging at a student. In Washington, President Kennedy said he was "sickened" by the police tactics, and he dispatched Justice

Department officials to the city as mediators. Bull Connor had made the Birmingham movement a national—an international—news story.

Each day after that brought more marchers, more confrontations, more arrests. The breaking point came four days later, as thousands of marchers evaded police barricades and converged on downtown, filling the streets and staging sit-ins in stores. That day, movement leader Fred Shuttlesworth was targeted by firemen as he left the 16th Street church, and hit with a water spray so strong that it knocked him flat and sent him to the hospital with chest injuries.

Early the following morning, the business leaders, their city all but paralyzed, sued for peace. They met with movement leaders and agreed to most of their demands to desegregate stores, lunch counters and public facilities. Birmingham's political leaders held out for two more days, then capitulated. It was a victory so complete that it sent shock waves throughout the South, spurring activists to mount similar campaigns in many communities. Connor's attempt to kill the movement by showing it could not win had sent exactly the opposite message.

The settlement was almost derailed by a spasm of violence that vividly illustrated the stakes of the struggle—and the alternative that awaited the nation if nonviolent action failed to deliver. Vengeful white racists planted bombs at the motel where Martin Luther King had been staying and at his brother's house. Black residents retaliated with a burst of fury, smashing stores, setting buildings afire and battling police. As Birmingham teetered on the edge of chaos, a makeshift coalition of local black leaders, white business owners and federal mediators managed to calm the city and preserve the agreement—but not before the Kennedy administration had dispatched thousands of federal troops to the area and made it clear they would be deployed in the streets if the mediation effort failed.

As the tension subsided, Michael spent a morning interviewing students as they were released from jail as part of the truce. One girl named Cynthia Parsons, age 17, was looking around anxiously for her parents and her 13-year-old brother, Todd. "I sure hope he got released today," she said, raising herself up to scan the crowd in front of the courthouse. "He acts like a big, tough kid, but he must have been scared in jail."

"How about you?" Michael asked gently.

"You mean, was I scared? Sure, I was. But I didn't care. We can't live like this. I mean, we shouldn't have to. They keep telling us in school, 'This is America, the land of the free,' but it's not. We're not free. Now, maybe we will be."

Just then, she caught sight of her brother. They ran to each other and embraced tightly. That was the end of the interview, but Michael had all he needed.

Riva was in the middle of the milling crowd, helping students find family members or directing them to buses that would take them to the church. She had come on a quick two-day trip, unable to stay longer or risk arrest but determined to play some part in this seminal battle. She and Michael had barely had time to say hello. Now he needed to start writing, and she was leaving in a few hours for the long trip back to New York so she could make her performance the next night.

Michael came up and lightly touched her arm. They were both unsure how an interracial couple would play in this setting. She held his hand briefly, kissed him quickly, then took a nervous step back.

"I'm going to stay for maybe two more days at the most, then fly home," Michael said. "I think this act in the drama is pretty well over."

"Then what?"

"The next scene will be played in Washington. Kennedy is getting dragged, step by step, into greater involvement. The question is, how far will he go after this? The pressure on him is only going to intensify after what happened here. And this is a huge international embarrassment for him."

Riva smiled. "You're turning into quite the political journalist," she said. "The guy I got to know down here two years ago was thinking about the next action. Now you're trying to scope out the geopolitics."

"Do you want that other guy back?"

"I like this guy just fine," Riva replied, still smiling, as a student of about 12 tugged on her sleeve.

As she often did, Riva had touched Michael's innermost thoughts. Throughout his time in Birmingham, Michael had struggled with competing impulses. His heart was entirely with these demonstrators, and a part of him would have wanted to join them. His head told him he had a different role to play, one that required him to stay on the sidelines and observe the battle, write about it, put a human face on it. He was not entirely comfortable with this role. He wondered how long he could assuage his conscience by telling himself that warriors without scribes to tell their story go unheeded by the world.

Riva turned to help the student. "You knock 'em dead with your story and come home, and we'll crack a bottle of wine and talk. I want to chat with you about Memorial Day."

Wondering what she meant, Michael squeezed her hand in farewell and headed to his hotel room and his portable typewriter. His deadline was approaching, and he faced the eternal dilemma of the magazine writer. He had a notebook full of vivid anecdotes and quotes from a week of reporting, but by the time his story appeared in print, much of it would be old news. He needed to use his material to make a larger, more forward-looking point. The question of what the Kennedy administration would do in response to what was now a full-on national crisis over civil rights gave him an angle—and he had an idea for a way to bring the story home.

Opening with the anecdote of the sister and brother finding each other at the courthouse, he pivoted to his nut paragraph, the one that explained the article's larger significance. The success of the Birmingham "children's crusade," he wrote, had elevated southern racism to the top of the national agenda, and created an ever-sharper dilemma for the president. Kennedy had planned to devote most of 1963 to his foreign policy goals, which required drawing a vivid contrast between the Soviet and American systems. "But unless the president acts forcefully and quickly to champion civil rights, he may find that this comparison rings hollow with many of his audiences," Michael wrote.

He landed in Washington just as his magazine's new issue came out. His piece was on the cover, a singular achievement, but he knew this had as much to do with the importance of the Birmingham events as with the quality of his prose. Even more heartening was the reaction of his editors, who were unanimous in their praise. They were especially taken with his linking of civil rights and foreign policy. It was a fresh angle, and it hit exactly the right note. For a left-leaning magazine in a time of Democratic ascendence in Washington, the Holy Grail was to find a way to influence an administration that was nominally on the same side, yet often distrustful of liberals. Michael's piece had delivered the goods.

2: One Step Forward

The subway ride from the Village to Queens took almost an hour, which gave Riva and Michael plenty of time to get nervous all over again. They were headed to her parents' house for a Memorial Day barbecue, with a full contingent of Daniels aunts and uncles and nieces and nephews and cousins on hand. Michael had visited Riva's parents and brother before, but this was to be his first full family gathering.

The night before, they had sat up until two in the morning, sipping wine and talking about their future. Neither could imagine life apart from each other. They felt in tune in every way that mattered. The question that hovered was whether they would take the next step.

"I want to do it. I want to marry you," Michael declared. Riva smiled and cocked her head toward the wine bottle. "No, that has nothing to do with it," he said. "Besides, *in vino veritas.* I'm not saying anything to you now that I won't repeat when I'm cold sober. We love each other. I want to spend my life with you. I think you want to spend your life with me. So why wait?"

"Well, there are implications to think through. For one thing, what about your family?"

"My parents love you. They've told you so many times, and they say the same thing to me when we're alone. They think you're the best thing that's ever happened to me, and they're right. They would be thrilled by the news we're engaged."

"Will they always feel that way?"

"What do you mean? What would make them change their minds?"

This brought them to the cusp of something that Riva thought Michael consistently underestimated. In Michael's mind, racial differences simply did not exist—or if they did, they were to be handled by ignoring them. Riva had noticed many times that when they attracted stares even in oh-so-liberal New York, Michael was either oblivious or chose to offer an alternative explanation.

Riva saw them. Every hard, hostile glance registered, because she was attuned to them. At times she wondered if she was too attuned, if she might be overcompensating, seeing things that weren't there. Deep inside, she doubted it.

And she recalled an awkward conversation with Alan last Christmas in which he tried, in words that were unusually halting for someone so articulate, to discuss the problems that a biracial couple might encounter. He had done it in a friendly, well-intentioned way, but it made Riva wonder whether he and Anna really wanted their son to expose himself to that kind of hostility.

Then there were her parents. They had been fearful when Riva chose to break out of their world. She knew they felt that way out of love for her, but also because, to them, making a place in that world had been a tremendous achievement. They found it hard to understand why their daughter would be dissatisfied with it.

And she had absolutely no idea how they would react if she told them she was marrying Michael. Their initial reaction to him, when she first brought him around, was the puzzled wariness one might exhibit on encountering an exotic animal; they simply had no experience with someone like him. Over time, they had warmed, but Riva sensed that a wariness lingered, unspoken, in the background.

"We live inside a very pleasant, brightly colored bubble," Riva said, edging carefully into the conversation. "We eat in restaurants and drink in bars and listen to music in clubs with all kinds of people, and nobody seems to pay much attention to what we are. I work in a business that prides itself on that kind of ethos. But even here, I can't really forget who I am; the world never lets me for long.

"And your parents' city—it's still a southern town in many ways. The schools were legally segregated until just 10 years ago. You know that because of your own experience, going to a school that only existed because of parents who refused to send their children to segregated schools."

"Of course I understand that," Michael replied. "I understand all of that. That's why the movement is so important. It's going to change the world our children grow up in. We won't have to do what my parents and their friends did, create something out of thin air so our kids can go to an integrated school. And speaking of that, can you imagine the parents who did that objecting to us? Whatever differences I may have with them about tactics or timing, their views on race are a north star for them."

Riva sighed and refilled their wineglasses. It was an unwinnable argument. Michael was a romantic and an idealist, and those were among the qualities that made him so dear to her. Yet those qualities sometimes prevented him from seeing unpleasant realities. He was also accustomed to a world that yielded to his desires rather than resisting them. She could only hope that life wouldn't batter him too fiercely.

"All right, let's take it one step at a time. Tomorrow, after all the relatives go home, let's have a quiet conversation with my parents and take their temperature."

"You want me to ask your father for your hand?" Michael said with a grin. "How quaint."

"Well, he would probably appreciate the gesture," she said, squeezing his hand. "He's a very proper man in his own way. But if you did, he'd probably tell you that I was going to do whatever I wanted regardless of what he said, which happens to be true.

"Look, let's talk to them about how you feel about me, how we feel about each other. Let's get them used to the reality that we're very serious about each other. I think they sort of understand that, but let's make it really clear. Then, if and when the time comes, they'll be more acclimated to it."

"If?"

"You take it one step at a time, too. This lady's no pushover, in case you hadn't noticed."

The rain that had threatened in the morning blew off to the north, allowing the Daniels clan to gather in the backyard of Sam and Dorie's bungalow. By the time Riva and Michael arrived, a dozen people were there, and the grill was going full blast, churning out ribs, chicken, burgers and hot dogs. Sam embraced his daughter and greeted Michael with a cold beer. They fell into conversation about a safe, shared interest: sports. Sam was an old Brooklyn Dodgers fan trying to forget the betrayal of their flight to California by following the expansion Mets, who had not made it easy for him, setting a record for losses last year. Michael had grown up following the equally hapless Senators, who moved to Minnesota just as they showed signs of competence and saddled Washington fans with their own bumbling expansion team. Since they both rooted for tailenders, Michael and Sam had much in common.

Riva had no interest in sports, but a great deal of interest in her younger brother Tommy, who would be a senior at Jamaica High School in the fall. She was enormously proud of him, often telling Michael of her delight in how Tommy maintained top grades in college prep courses while making the varsity in football and basketball. Now, he avidly described how spring football practice left him thinking he had a shot at starting quarterback for his high school team in the fall.

"Coach kept playing me more and more, and I got into a real rhythm with my passing," Tommy said, reaching for a soda. "Both our quarterbacks from last year are graduating, so it's kind of wide open. I think I'm good enough to be the guy."

"Son, you need to hold down that boasting," Sam told him. "Talk with your arm, not your mouth."

"Sure, dad, sure. I hear what you're saying." Some sons would have snapped at an admonishing father or rolled their eyes in silent dismissal. But Tommy was a genuinely unaffected teenager who still wanted his parents' approval. He didn't know quite what to make of his sister and her exotic life, but he and Riva still enjoyed an easy familiarity born of many childhood conspiracies.

"I hope I can get out in the fall to catch one of your games," Michael said.

"You ever play? You look tall enough to be an end."

"My brief, inglorious football career ended at my first practice, when I got blindsided by a linebacker. I thought I was about to catch a pass. He had other ideas. Next thing I knew, a coach was standing over me, asking if I could remember what my name was. He suggested I might make a better contribution to the team by writing about it in the school paper."

Tommy and Sam joined Michael in laughing heartily at the story, and Dorie handed Michael another beer. "This'll take away the sting of that memory," she said, shaking her head one more time at male folly.

Throughout the barbecue, as Riva mixed with her family, she kept one eye on Michael. She was keenly interested in the social dynamics of the afternoon. He was the only white person there, which inevitably made him a subject of quiet curiosity. One by one, family members came by for a close look at the otherworldly creature she had bagged. She could not help but be impressed by Michael's ability to stay afloat in these swirling currents.

Sam and Dorie had been curious why Riva had made a point of asking whether she could bring Michael to the traditional holiday gathering, and were not surprised when the couple outlasted everyone else. The long spring twilight spread slowly across the yard. Tommy excused himself, pleading schoolwork, and went inside.

"We've still got a little time before the bugs come out," Sam said. "And I think we got a few more cold ones left. Here."

Michael popped the cap off the beer and settled into a lawn chair. "This was a great barbecue," he said. "I really enjoyed it. Thank you for inviting me. You have an amazing family."

"Yes, we do. We're very proud of it. Our people have lived around here for a long time, longer than most of the people who think of themselves as native New Yorkers. How about your family? What do they do on a weekend like this?"

"Well, my people were originally from the Midwest. My grandparents came east around the turn of the century. But my family's quite small, compared to yours. We don't do anything big at times like Memorial Day or the Fourth; not enough of us to make it worthwhile. We get together at Thanksgiving and Christmas, of course."

"Sure. Well, family's important," Sam said.

"It certainly is," Michael replied. "I hope to start one someday."

Sam let that thought hang in the air while he cleaned his pipe and refilled it. Dorie, who had been listening attentively, stirred in her chair.

"I want you to know we're not blind," she said quietly. "We see you and Riva together, we see how easy and natural you are with each other. We see how happy Riva is with you. If you love your child, you want her to be happy. So we're happy for her, and happy for you. But I have to tell you, I'm also afraid for her."

"Mom, the world's changing," said Riva, who had sat silently, hardly moving, throughout this conversation.

"Not fast enough, I'm afraid. Your father said our people have lived around here for a long time, and that's right. But there's more to it than that. I'm sort of the family historian, so I looked all this up. Our people came up here before the Civil War, found work as laborers. Lived in a place called Seneca Village, which was in Manhattan, but got chased out when they took the land to build Central Park.

"Then, a few years later, during the Civil War, there were riots. They called them draft riots, but they were really race riots. White riots. Anti-Negro riots. They burned houses, and they lynched people. Eleven people. One of them was named Joseph Stephens. He was my great grandfather's uncle. After that, our people moved to Brooklyn, where they felt safer. Eventually, we came out to here, and we've made a good life.

"So, yes, the world is changing. That doesn't stop me from being afraid for you."

Sam sat silently, puffing on his pipe, while his wife spoke. Riva had teared up. "I never knew that history," she said. "Who was he? Joseph Stephens? What did he do?"

"It's not important what he did," her father said. "What they did to him, that's what's important."

Michael reached out to touch Riva's shoulder. "That's a terrible story," he said. "I have no answer for you, except to say that I believe if we let our fears conquer our hopes, we lose what's best in us. I know those are just words, and that it's easy for me to say them. But I do believe it's true, and I think Riva does, too."

"I don't think it's easy for you to say it," Sam said. "Not for a minute. I know the difference between a blowhard and a serious man. I've met plenty of both. I think I know which one you are. You and Riva have decided to step into something that's very tough, and I think you realize it. I just hope you understand all of it."

"I couldn't possibly. Not like you," Michael said. "But I *can* tell you that whatever happens, I'm in. I'm in all the way. And if anyone ever tries to hurt your daughter, they're gonna have a hell of a fight on their hands."

"I told you this guy was a Boy Scout," Riva said.

Dorie reached over and put her hand on her husband's. "Well, we'll hold you to that promise, and that's for sure. But I don't think we'll have to. I think Sam's got you figured right. So you take care of yourself, and you take care of Riva—as much as she'll let you—and you come back and see us again, and soon, because you're very welcome in our house."

Chapter Seven
—The Paranoid Style—

June 1963

1: Parental Guidance

Michael fiddled with the antenna of the small, battered television until John F. Kennedy's image came into something resembling focus, then plopped down next to Riva on the couch. If the picture was fuzzy, Kennedy's words were anything but that.

"We are confronted primarily with a moral issue," he said. "It is as old as the Scriptures and is as clear as the American Constitution. The heart of the question is whether all Americans are to be afforded equal rights and equal opportunities, whether we are going to treat our fellow Americans as we want to be treated."

As forceful as Kennedy's words were, they were long overdue. For two years, he had been playing for time, acting only when forced by events, trying to avoid a rupture with the segregationists in his own party. Now, finally, he realized that time was up. He was meeting the moment, expressing unequivocal support for the cause of racial equality. And he made it clear that he understood the urgency of the cause, as well as its justice.

"If an American, because his skin is dark, cannot eat lunch in a restaurant open to the public, if he cannot send his children to the best public school available, if he cannot vote for the public officials who will represent him, who among us would be content to have the color of his skin changed and stand in his place? Who among us would then be content with the counsels of patience and delay?"

Kennedy's speech to the nation was the climax of an intense debate within the White House about how to respond to the events that had turned civil rights into a top-tier national issue. Michael, tapping into a network of sources, had captured the crosscurrents in a piece for his magazine.

Kennedy, he wrote, already had an ample domestic agenda before Congress—and it was going nowhere, stymied by the same coalition of Republicans and Southern Democrats who had been throttling progressive legislation for decades. The last thing he wanted was to offer a new measure that would become yet another hostage to this coalition.

But the marches and sit-ins that erupted across the South in the wake of the movement's Birmingham victory left him no choice but to act. And the outbreak of violence in Birmingham raised ominous concerns about whether it would be repeated elsewhere, adding to the pressures on Kennedy. The only questions left to answer were how soon the president would propose a new civil rights bill and how far-reaching it would be. "The likely answers are, soon, and with stringent provisions that require the integration of all public accommodations, from the smallest coffee shop to the largest hotel and department store," Michael wrote.

Michael was sure of his sources, who had described the intense pressures on the president, the counsels of caution from some aides, and Bobby Kennedy's role in tipping the debate toward forceful action. He still breathed a sigh of relief halfway through Kennedy's speech.

"Next week I shall ask the Congress of the United States to act, to make a commitment it has not fully made in this century, to the proposition that race has no place in American life or law," the president said. "I am asking the Congress to enact legislation giving all Americans the right to be served in facilities which are open to the public—hotels, restaurants, theaters, retail stores, and similar establishments.

"This seems to me to be an elementary right. Its denial is an arbitrary indignity that no American in 1963 should have to endure—but many do."

Michael's knowledge of the effort to sway the president was especially authoritative, because some of it had come from his family. His mother had made another visit to the White House with a group of liberals, labor and civil rights leaders. Their message was simple. Birmingham had given Kennedy the one thing he had repeatedly said he was awaiting—a national consensus to act. Now that this moment had arrived, he must seize it.

Michael's father also counseled action, for his own reasons. Throughout the early spring, Alan had been meeting with administration officials to help plan some major foreign policy initiatives, including a European trip by the president that would culminate in a speech at the Berlin Wall calling out the oppressive nature of the Soviet system. As a result, Michael's story after Birmingham on the linkage between civil rights and foreign policy had resonated with Alan very personally.

For two years, he had been telling anyone who would listen that the civil rights militants were pushing too hard, putting too much pressure on a president who was in their corner but needed some breathing room. Now, Alan realized that events were outrunning his old advice—and he knew from experience that advisers who passively allowed this to happen often became ex-advisers.

He began a careful effort to preserve his influence by repositioning himself, adapting his counsel to meet the pressure building on Kennedy. It led to a conversation in the small study just off the Oval Office.

"Mr. President, I have said many times that civil rights leaders were mistaken in trying to force your hand. But now the momentum behind events has become unstoppable. There are going to be demonstrations all over the South this summer, and there is talk about a national march here in Washington."

"I've heard some rumblings about that, and it worries me," Kennedy said. "The potential for it to backfire is tremendous."

"All the more reason to get out in front of this thing now, and buy yourself some leverage with the leaders who will organize the march," Alan replied. "But there's something else, something equally important. Your credibility as the leader of the free world is at stake. Until you commit to act on civil rights, any speech you deliver that draws the contrast between our system and the Soviets will ring hollow."

Both Anna and Alan had given Michael detailed off-the-record accounts of the deliberations that led up to the speech, and Michael had drawn upon them freely to paint his portrait of a president forced into a corner, compelled to shed his reluctance and act. He accepted his parents' privileged intelligence without hesitation, almost casually, in a way that struck Anna as oddly devoid of self-reflection.

"It's almost as if he expected our help as his due," she said to Alan afterward.

"Well, he did thank us. He thanked me, anyway."

"Oh, he thanked me, too, but that's not the point," Anna said. "For years now, he's been in this headlong rush to take distance from us. I suppose that's inevitable, and even necessary. But he seems to have no awareness of how much he's still part of our world, no matter how much he might wish it otherwise. Just as I was with my family, and you with yours."

"I know," Alan said. "He's very willing to tell us in no uncertain terms that we're behind the times, that our entire generation has been in power for too long and needs to move aside. But he's also perfectly willing to make use of us and our inside knowledge when it serves his purposes. And it certainly served his purposes in this case."

2: Only One Answer

The Chicago Chronicle was a sleepy afternoon broadsheet that had been fourth in a four-newspaper town for as long as anyone could remember. Even the industry's postwar consolidation had not improved the Chronicle's position much. It didn't help that the afternoon newspaper market was steadily shrinking as people turned to television for news at the end of the day. When journalists thought of the Chronicle, the adjectives that came to mind were venerable, dull—and doomed.

But three years ago, the paper's longtime owner, Fred Franklin, had retired, passing the leadership to his son Andy. And Andy Franklin had plans for the Chronicle, and for himself.

Andy shared almost nothing with his straitlaced Rotarian father beyond the family name. He had gone east to college at Yale in the '50s and was soon spending weekends, and then many weeknights, in the Village listening to Beat poetry and bebop jazz. Young, handsome and wealthy, he soon attracted a small coterie. He backed a few plays and tried to write one himself. When his father, feeling the weight of years, pulled his credit line and told him to come home and take over as the Chronicle's publisher, Andy was at first resentful. Then he began to see possibilities.

Andy's first move was to seek out an editor in his own image. He found him in Jack Rothstein, an old college buddy who had come back to Chicago after Yale, and quickly made his mark as a city hall reporter and then city editor for the morning Sun-Times. It had taken little to woo him, because Rothstein and Andy Franklin were kindred spirits. They were both brash, distrustful of authority, and full of ambition. They enjoyed a party and the company of attractive women. They admired Jack Kennedy and approved of where he was taking the country. They even had the same eclectic musical tastes: jazz, Motown, Bob Dylan.

In three years of partnership, they had remade the Chronicle into a paper that valued stylish writing and aggressive reporting on local politics, crime, and Chicago's abundant police malfeasance. Although their readership was mostly white, they covered the civil rights movement seriously and had tentatively begun to probe the social dynamics of their rigidly segregated city. The changes had not done much for circulation yet, but Andy had a heavy wallet and nothing better to spend it on.

Now they were ready for their next move, one they hoped would boost the paper into a higher level of the journalistic food chain. The Chronicle's Washington bureau comprised a single reporter, Pete Kelly, who was marking the years until retirement by providing anodyne coverage of the local congressional delegation. The paper's foreign desk was one editor and two wire service teletypes. Andy and Jack—in typical newsroom irreverence they were dubbed "Franknstein"—were determined to change that situation by landing a well-sourced, ambitious D.C. reporter who could range widely and write knowledgeably about both domestic and international issues. And they thought they had found their candidate.

The phone on Michael's desk rang in the middle of a busy afternoon as he scrambled to finish the reporting for a piece on the negotiations for a Soviet-American treaty to ban above-ground nuclear tests. He was expecting a call back from a source in the State Department, and did not hide his disappointment when the voice on the other end was unfamiliar.

"Mr.—Rothstein, is it? Sorry if I was abrupt. Kind of crazy around here today. What can I do for you?"

"Well, you could meet me and my publisher for breakfast tomorrow at the Mayflower. We'd like to talk to you about something."

The next morning, amid eggs Benedict and coffee, Andy and Jack made their pitch. They wanted Michael to come on board as their chief Washington correspondent. He could pick his shots, leaving the routine stories to the wires, jumping in where he saw an opportunity to break news or provide special insight. His primary focus would be Washington, but travel was not out of the question for a good political story or even a foreign assignment. The paper's news hole was by no means huge, but it could accommodate longer stories—if they were worth the space.

"We see this as an opportunity for the paper to take a step up in class," Andy said, "and for you to take a step up with us. I'm sure writing for a high-concept opinion magazine has its rewards, but what we're offering would give you an entrée into mainstream journalism."

"Let me ask you this—why me?"

"We've read your work, and we like it," Jack replied. "You can write, you go after big game, and you obviously have sources. Your pieces from Birmingham were some of the best stuff that was written out of there. And we noticed that you nailed what Kennedy was going to propose on civil rights when a lot of big-name reporters were equivocating.

'You're young, and so are we, and this business is more and more a young man's game. The old generation of hacks who started as copyboys in high school and never went to college or read a book that didn't have pictures is fading away."

"And, to be candid, we're not unaware of who your parents are and who they know," Andy added. "I'm sure you'd be a successful reporter regardless of that, but I also imagine it's an asset for you. We'd like it to be our asset."

Michael was at once offended by Andy's suggestion that he traded on his parents' connections and impressed by his bluntness. It occurred to him that this might be a style, knocking people off balance with selective doses of candor bordering on rudeness.

"My life is in New York. I'm seriously involved with someone, and her career is there. I don't know that I can move to Washington."

"You wouldn't have to," Jack said. "We'd want you here part of the time, of course, but you could keep living in New York and spend a few days each week in D.C. You're probably doing that already. You won't get rich on the salary we'll pay you, but you'll be able to afford renting a room somewhere. Hill staffers and even some congressmen do it all the time, as you know. You might make a new source."

Michael asked about the paper's financial footing. "Chicago is a tough market, and you're not at the head of the class."

"We're keeping our head above water," Andy said. "That's about all you can hope for these days. You can ask around on that if you like."

"I will, of course. Another question: How much resentment will I have to deal with from the veterans if I waltz in and start grabbing plum stories and front-page space?"

"Here in Washington, none at all," Jack said. "Pete Kelly's chief ambition is to make it to retirement three years from now, and you won't threaten that in the slightest. In the newsroom, there are a few mastodons left, but we've brought on a lot of new people, and they're hungry—like you. If you deliver the goods, you'll fit right in."

"One other thing," Michael said. "I'm a journalist, but I've got some strong opinions, especially about civil rights and nuclear weapons. I understand what a reporter for a general-circulation paper has to do, but I'm not going to stop thinking what I think. One pleasure of working for the New Republic is that I don't have to pull my punches."

The two men across the table exchanged glances. Neither said anything for several moments. Then Andy spoke.

"We don't expect you to change who you are. It's because of who you are that we want you. I feel the same way on those issues. Of course, we'll expect your stories to be balanced. But your views about the world are going to shape your judgments about what's news, what's a story, and we're okay with that."

"Do you allow your staff writers to do any freelancing?"

"It would be possible for you to do a magazine piece now and again," Jack said, "as long as it didn't interfere with your work for us or pre-empt something you're doing for us, and was written in a way that didn't compromise your standing as a straight reporter. We'd want to see any such pieces first, of course."

Michael realized that they were going to considerable lengths to accommodate him. They were trying to make it hard to say no, and they were succeeding.

"I need to think this through, and talk it over with a few people—one in particular. Give me two or three days, no more than that, and I'll give you an answer."

Michael's conversation with his parents was quick and simple. They both thought the job offer was a great opportunity. When he sounded out his best friend at the magazine, Barry Edelman, he was equally enthusiastic. His advice was that Michael needed to grow beyond the confines of writing for a small, homogenous audience, and this was a perfect chance to do it. Even if the Chronicle ultimately went under, Michael would emerge with a burnished reputation and a path to a better job.

Riva was another story.

Michael tried to back into the conversation, which was a mistake. Riva had sensed that something was up, and his elliptical way of telling her came across as condescending. She was between roles at the moment and auditioning nonstop, which heightened her sense of being unmoored, and this news made matters worse. Riva moved from the middle of the couch to the end, consciously creating distance between them, crossed her arms, and glared at him fiercely.

"I'm not sure what you want me to say, Michael. Does this mean you'll be moving to Washington? Do you expect me to move there with you? You haven't asked me to, you know. And I'm not sure I can, in any case. I take my professional life every bit as seriously as you take yours, and that life is here in New York."

Michael took a deep breath. He understood that this was a pivotal moment for them, that the next few minutes could reshape their lives together—or apart. He realized that his margin for error had disappeared, and he chose his words with great care.

"I want us to be together. If anything I've said tonight has left you in any doubt about that, then I've failed completely to express how I feel about you, about us, and I apologize for that. I love you, and I want to be with you."

Riva nodded silently, her expression softening ever so slightly, half-mollified but still tense.

"I don't want you to give up your work. I want you to succeed at it. I know that means New York."

Another nod, a little less tension in her posture.

"I've worked it out with them that I wouldn't have to move to D.C. I could still live here, with you. I'd have to spend some time in Washington, maybe three days a week on average, sometimes more, depending on what's going on. I'd have to travel some, too, make some White House trips, cover big demonstrations like Birmingham, make reporting trips for political stories, things like that. But my home base would be here. Here with you."

What Michael said next was totally unplanned, but suddenly seemed right to him.

"I think we could handle all of that—especially if you take me up on what we talked about over Memorial Day."

"Your timing might not be ideal on that one, mister."

"Why? Why isn't it? What better time to talk about it than when we're at a crossroads like this? You want me to get down on one knee? I'll do it. You want me to give you a ring? I don't have one handy, but I can fix that up quickly enough tomorrow."

Now it was Riva who paused, fully sensing the weight of the moment. Michael leaned forward and took her hand—the one that would wear the ring—and it was impossible to read anything but love in his eyes. She realized that the time for hesitation was over.

As those thoughts went through her mind, he spoke again.

"I love you. I want to spend my life with you. I can't imagine my life without you. Please marry me, Riva."

Only one answer was possible.

3: Fever Swamp

They set a date for early December, midway between Thanksgiving and Christmas. They both wanted a small, simple wedding, just family and some close friends. They told their parents, together and in person, and found their reactions interesting. Riva expected Dorie and Sam to be welcoming but reserved. Instead, they exploded with warmth. They hugged their daughter, Sam clapped Michael on the back so hard it stung, and Dorie, seeing him wince, gently put her arms around him and welcomed him to their family. There were tears in everyone's eyes.

Anna and Alan took the news in stride at first, showing less emotion than Michael expected. He had a sense that they had been expecting it, perhaps wondering what was taking them so long. He began to worry that their lack of reaction would make Riva feel unwelcomed, but just then his mother rose and embraced her. "I'm very happy for you, for you both," she said.

Alan, the model host, found a bottle of champagne at the back of the refrigerator and filled four flutes. "To our newest family member, and to your long life together," he said as he lifted his glass. "And to our son's good judgment, and his good fortune," Anna added, smiling at Riva. Michael and Riva fell asleep that night feeling loved and blessed.

July and August went by in a blur. Riva auditioned for an ambitious musical, *Tambourines to Glory*, adapted from a Langston Hughes novel, and was called back for a second and then a third look. As she waited anxiously to hear about the role, Michael was in the midst of his job transition. He spent some time in Chicago getting to know the people at the Chronicle and the rhythms of a daily newspaper, so different from those of a weekly magazine. Then he plunged in, covering the civil rights march that brought a quarter of a million people to Washington in late August. Two weeks later, he was back in Birmingham to cover a horrible story: the Ku Klux Klan bombing of the 16th Street Baptist Church that killed four choirgirls. It was the same church where Michael had watched the schoolchildren march out in May. The killings left Michael shaken and angry, but they hit Riva especially close to home. The thought that there were people so consumed with hate that they could murder young black children in a church cast a long shadow over what should have been a hopeful, optimistic moment.

For as summer ended, Riva was making her own transition—to her first Broadway role. After several callbacks, she had won a part in *Tambourines to Glory* and was working nonstop to prepare for the opening in early November. Amid these passages, the couple found little time to spend together. "I say I'll marry you, and then I never see you again," Riva joked one sleepy morning. "Good preparation for married life," Michael kidded back.

Through the fall, Michael gave careful thought to the subject of his first big political feature for the Chronicle. It would be a kind of coming-out for him, and he wanted to be sure it did not misfire. When the White House announced that the president would travel to Texas just before Thanksgiving, he decided he had found the story.

The trip would be a mission to forge a truce between the warring conservative and liberal wings of the Texas Democratic Party, a conflict that threatened Kennedy's prospects for winning a crucial state in his re-election campaign next year. The story seemed made to order for a major piece. In addition to high political stakes, the personalities were vivid: Ralph Yarborough, a flamboyant senator who led the liberal faction; Governor John Connally, the flinty head of the conservatives; and Vice President Lyndon Johnson, once the powerful Senate majority leader, now a marginalized figure and the butt of rumors that he would be dumped from the ticket.

The story would also give Michael a way into another theme he wanted to develop: Kennedy's growing stature and confidence. The successful resolution of the Cuban crisis, the negotiation of a test ban treaty, and the decision to lead rather than follow on civil rights had put to rest many of the doubts Americans harbored about their young president. His liberal critics were appeased, but it was broader than that. His Gallup poll approval rating was nearing 60 percent, and the polls showed him leading every likely Republican challenger. It was not universal; he remained in many ways a polarizing figure, and his legislative program still faced significant opposition in Congress. Yet there was a growing sense, in Washington and in the country, that Kennedy had found his stride and was positioned to realize the great promise of his presidency. The Texas trip would be a test of his new political clout.

The paper's national editor, Bob Patterson, another Franknstein hire, loved the idea of a Texas story; he was a refugee from the Dallas Morning News, an ultra-conservative paper that took delight in mocking the Kennedys. Michael made plans to fly out to Texas before Kennedy arrived, spend some time reporting on the state's Byzantine politics, and join the White House entourage when it arrived in San Antonio on Nov. 21.

What he saw and heard on the ground led him to conclude that Kennedy had a difficult and perhaps impossible task before him. Texas Democrats were so riven that they could barely speak to each other in civil terms. Yarborough believed that the conservatives in his own party would try to sabotage him when he ran for re-election the following year, and they did nothing to allay his fears. Both sides talked about Johnson as yesterday's man, bereft of influence and headed for the political graveyard.

Even more ominous, in Michael's view, was the state's overall political climate, which struck him as a virulent fever swamp.

Billboards demanding the impeachment of Supreme Court Chief Justice Earl Warren, author of the 1954 ruling that segregated schools were unconstitutional, dotted Texas highways. Houston and Dallas were centers of activity by anti-Castro Cuban exiles, who openly reviled Kennedy for what they regarded as his betrayal of the men lost in the Bay of Pigs operation. In Dallas, just a month earlier, Adlai Stevenson had been spat upon and physically assaulted by right-wing demonstrators when he spoke at an event to promote the United Nations. A former general, Edwin Walker, who had been forced out of the Army after trying to indoctrinate his troops with far-right propaganda, was a major political figure in the city.

Bob Patterson's old paper, run by rabid conservative Ted Dealey, took every opportunity to inflame the situation. Two years earlier, at a White House lunch, Dealey had insulted the president to his face, calling him and his administration "weak sisters" and telling him, "We need a man on horseback to lead this nation, and many people in Texas and the Southwest think that you are riding Caroline's tricycle." Morning News editorials repeatedly excoriated the president, and Michael had picked up chatter that the paper would greet Kennedy by running an ad from a right-wing group accusing his administration of being "soft on Communists."

Michael had taken Richard Hofstadter's class on American political history at Columbia and read his new book, "Anti-Intellectualism in American Life." What he was seeing in Texas brought to fresh life Hofstadter's thesis that a deep and toxic strain of irrational nativist populism ran through the country's history. The strain lay dormant for long periods, but burst forth in moments of crisis and rapid change.

The book was a work of history, but Michael saw in these ultra-conservative Texans a living embodiment of Hofstadter's theme. Kennedy was challenging the American postwar consensus in both domestic and foreign policy by aligning the federal government with the civil rights cause and taking steps to ease tensions with the

Soviets. While most Americans supported him, he was awakening the malign subterranean forces Hofstadter had described.

Yet when Kennedy arrived in San Antonio, Michael wondered if he'd been chasing a mirage. More than 100,000 people lined the motorcade route from Bergstrom Air Force Base through downtown to Brooks Medical Center, where the president spoke. The crowd was enthusiastic to the point of frenzy; many were part of the city's substantial Hispanic community and waved hand-lettered signs reading "Bienvenido Mr. President." It was another side of Texas; the city's Democratic Party and its labor organizations were using the visit to show that, as one young Mexican-American nurse at the medical center told Michael, "the Kennedy-haters don't speak for us."

4: Dallas

The welcome for the president in Houston later that day was almost as exuberant as in San Antonio. And it was more than matched in Dallas on Friday. The rumors about the Morning News' anti-Kennedy ad proved true: under a sarcastic headline "welcoming" the president to Dallas, it read like a bill of particulars in an indictment. Downtown, however, a huge crowd was waiting, shouting their support for the president and his beautiful wife, who sat next to him in an open limousine. As the street narrowed, Kennedy fans standing eight deep on the sidewalks surged against police lines, slowing the motorcade's progress. The cheers and cries echoed off the tall office buildings, creating a cauldron of noise, heat, and emotion.

Michael, riding in the press bus near the rear of the long motorcade, at first experienced the city's response to Kennedy as a delayed-reaction wave, a wall of sound washing back at him. Soon, the entire cortege was in the midst of the crowd, and the din was deafening. Michael, in a window seat, scribbled notes furiously, noting the occasional hostile signs and Confederate flags and the much more prevalent friendly ones. Office workers were leaning out windows to wave. Out the front window of the bus, he could see the convertibles carrying the photographers, but the pressing crowd and the police officers obscured the rest of the motorcade. As it snaked through the mini-Manhattan cavern of downtown Dallas, he could glimpse open sky far ahead.

At the end of the cavern, the bus turned right. The front of the procession, now barely visible ahead, had already made that turn and another to the left, past a nondescript brick building with a Hertz car rental sign and a flock of pigeons on its roof. The streets were clearing now, but the motorcade still proceeded at a crawl. Michael wondered why, then decided it was to give onlookers ahead a good glimpse of the first family. The crowd din was behind them now, fading with each passing moment. That made the sound ahead of them, the sound of what Michael thought might be a firecracker, plainly audible.

The pigeons, startled by the noise, lifted off the roof in a flutter of wings. In quick succession, two more explosions. During his Army service, Michael had trained for a time as an infantry rifleman. This did not sound like fireworks after all. It sounded like gunfire.

The bus sped up, then slowed to negotiate a hairpin left turn in front of the brick building. As it passed into the plaza beyond, Michael stood up for a better view out the front window. The head of the motorcade was no longer visible. Vehicles in front of the bus were slowing almost to a stop, uncertain where to go. Out the side window, Michael, in disbelief, took in a scene of chaos.

Some police officers were pointing urgently to the brick building behind them, others in a different direction. Spectators who had come to see the president had dropped to the ground, one man covering a young child as if to protect him. Protect him from what? Could that really have been gunfire? Where the hell was the president?

The bus, and the rest of the motorcade in the plaza, seemed to hang suspended in time. Then all the vehicles accelerated, and Michael was thrown back into his seat. The bus swung right, onto a freeway ramp, barreled up the road and arrived in a few minutes at the Dallas Trade Mart, where the president was scheduled to speak at a luncheon.

In the Trade Mart parking lot, more confusion: police cruisers parked at odd angles, but no sign of the presidential limousine or any other vehicle at the head of the motorcade. Cops and late-arriving lunch guests milled about, looking bewildered. Michael walked up to one officer, showed his press credentials, and asked what was going on.

"Kennedy's been shot."

"That's a poor joke."

"I'm not joking. We heard it on the police radio. They've taken him to Parkland."

"What's that? Where's that?"

"The nearest hospital. About a mile from here. That way, straight down Harry Hines Boulevard."

Michael looked at his watch. Christ. Quarter to one. Fifteen minutes to the paper's last deadline. He raced up to the building's press entrance, flashed his credentials again, and found a pay phone in the lobby.

"Bob, it's Michael from Dallas. Something's happened. We're at the next stop, but no Kennedy, and a cop just told me he's been shot."

"We got a bulletin from UPI about 10 minutes ago. The goddamn wire machine rang five alert bells. Five. Twenty years in the business, I've never heard five bells. I thought we must be at war with the Russians."

"What did the story say? Any details?"

"Just shots fired at Kennedy's motorcade. Nothing more than that."

"Well, I can give you a little more. My cop said Kennedy's been hit, and that they've taken him to the hospital. Parkland Hospital. He said he heard it on his police radio. I got his name. Officer Ray Burley, Dallas Police."

"Okay, thanks," Patterson said. "We're remaking page one and we're blowing deadline. If Kennedy's been seriously wounded, we may have to do an extra. You get over to that hospital—and keep filing."

Michael went back outside and looked around desperately for a lift. He saw a colleague from Newsweek, with whom he'd swapped beers and stories in the hotel bar the previous evening, cadging a ride from a Texas Ranger. The Ranger was motioning him into the back seat as Michael walked up. The Newsweek man and the Ranger nodded, and Michael squeezed in gratefully. He silently blessed his generosity in picking up the bar tab last night.

The hospital was afflicted with the same air of chaos he had left behind at the plaza and Trade Mart. Cars were parked haphazardly, some in the middle of driveways, some on lawns, some abandoned with doors open and engines running. An image formed in Michael's mind of an entire city suddenly stricken by a raging, malevolent force that tossed people and machines about like playthings.

The Ranger pulled around to the emergency entrance. The presidential limousine sat at the ambulance bay, abandoned. As Michael and the Newsweek reporter walked past it to the ER doorway, they looked in. The leather rear seat was stained with blood; more blood was pooled on the carpeted floor. Several red roses lay in the pool. Michael recalled that Jackie Kennedy had been handed a bouquet of roses on the airport tarmac. He had noticed how the flowers contrasted and yet harmonized with her bright pink suit.

Inside, a melee of medical personnel, cops, Secret Service agents and forgotten passengers from the front cars of the motorcade. They saw Ralph Yarborough leaning against a wall, looking at the floor, dazed. Michael asked him if he'd seen what happened.

Yarborough barely looked up. "Gentlemen, this has been a deed of horror," he said.

That was poetic, but it didn't exactly help Michael understand what condition the president of the United States was in. At that moment, a hospital official came up and chased them away, saying all press were to gather in rooms 101-102, which proved to be a double classroom for nursing students. They would be briefed there, the official said.

But they weren't. As precious time ticked away, and the classroom slowly filled with reporters, nothing happened. Michael made one foray upstairs to find a pay phone, and learned from his desk that the two wire services were reporting wildly conflicting things: Mrs. Kennedy had been hit, Mrs. Kennedy had not been hit; the vice president had been wounded, the vice president was unscathed. The one thing they agreed on was that the president had been shot, but his condition was unknown. He also learned that his paper was holding open its last scheduled edition of the day and preparing to publish an extra that evening if events warranted it. That gave him some welcome breathing room on deadlines.

It was nearing 1:30, a full hour after the motorcade had passed through the plaza. Hugh Sidey, the veteran Time magazine correspondent, entered the classroom and generously shared a conversation he'd just had with a priest outside the hospital. Sidey, sensing that the clergyman had been called to administer last rites, asked if the president was dead. "He's dead, all right," Sidey quoted the priest as saying, and spelled the name for his colleagues: Father Oscar Huber.

Some reporters made a break for the pay phones, and Michael considered joining them. Then he spotted Mac Kilduff, the White House press spokesman for the trip, entering the room. Kilduff's ashen face telegraphed what he was about to announce. As he walked toward the small podium at the head of the classroom, reporters flung questions at him. Others shouted for quiet. Kilduff started to speak, then halted, unable to continue. Michael looked down at his watch and noted the time: 1:33.

"President John F. Kennedy died at approximately one o'clock Central Standard Time today here in Dallas," Kilduff said at last. "He died of a gunshot wound in the brain. I have no other details regarding the assassination of the president. Mrs. Kennedy was not hit. Governor Connally was hit. The vice president was not hit."

Other journalists peppered the shaken spokesman with questions about Johnson's swearing-in, with demands for a medical briefing from Kennedy's doctors, but Michael did not wait around to hear the answers. The competition for a pay phone was stiffer this time, but he finally found one and reached Bob Patterson.

"Okay, good work," Patterson said. "We're right on top of deadline, but we've just got time to retop our wire story with your lead. You can dictate it to me. Lemme get some copy paper in my typewriter. Okay. You ready?"

Well, that's the question, Michael thought, taking a deep breath. Am I ready? I guess we'll find out.

"Dateline Dallas. President John F. Kennedy was assassinated today as he and his wife rode through the streets of this city. The president was shot in the head, and died about half an hour later, according to White House spokesman Malcolm Kilduff. Spelling is K-i-l-d-u-f-f. New paragraph.

"Kilduff announced the president's death at Parkland Hospital, where Kennedy was taken after being shot. P-a-r-k-l-a-n-d. Kilduff said Mrs. Kennedy and Vice President Lyndon Johnson were not hit. However, he said, Texas Governor John Connally, who was also riding in the presidential limousine, was wounded. His condition is unknown. New graf.

"Just before the shooting, Kennedy had basked in the cheers of thousands of supporters who thronged downtown Dallas on a warm, cloudless day. The gunfire sent spectators sprawling for cover in the plaza where the shooting occurred. That give you enough to retop with?"

Michael heard Patterson rip the sheet from his typewriter and shout for a copyboy. Then he came back on the line. "That's great work. You really came through. We'll have a lead story with a staff writer's byline on the streets this afternoon, just as people are getting out of work.

"Now, Jack has already ordered up an extra. Deadline is five o'clock. We can't bend that one. So report the hell out of it for the next two hours, and I'll get our best rewrite guy to take your dictate and put it together with what the wires have."

Michael had been functioning on instinct and adrenaline, narrowly focused on the task at hand. As he hung up the phone and made way for the next impatient reporter, the knowledge of what had happened hit him full force. John Kennedy was dead. Lyndon Johnson was president. It seemed a tragedy of unimaginable dimensions, for the country, for all the causes and people Michael cared about. Like Ralph Yarborough at the hospital entrance, Michael sagged against a wall, disoriented to the point of dizziness.

As he slowly recovered his balance, the questions that formed in his mind were, who? And why? The most obvious answers pointed directly to the hard-right conservatives who dominated Dallas' political life. Some of Michael's colleagues were voicing suspicions that the assassination could be part of a right-wing coup.

However, the man that Dallas police arrested that afternoon, and paraded before Michael and a gaggle of sweaty, shoving reporters that evening, hardly fit this profile. Lee Harvey Oswald was a left-wing loner, a pro-Castro campaigner, a onetime defector to the Soviet Union who had returned with a Russian wife. It seemed to make no sense.

In his brief perp walk, Oswald denied killing the president. "I don't know what this is all about," he said, adding cryptically, "I'm just a patsy." Yet police insisted that they had their man, telling reporters Oswald had shot Kennedy from a sixth-floor window of the brick building, a school textbook warehouse where he worked, and shortly afterward had gunned down a police officer who tried to question him. They displayed, like a trophy, the high-powered Mannlicher-Carcano rifle that they said Oswald had used to kill the president.

Michael's sense of disorientation was accentuated by the scene at police headquarters, which was utterly disorganized, with people randomly coming and going and little effort made to provide security. It fit the tenor of this terrible day perfectly.

5: Adrift

The next morning, Michael and his editors considered his next move. The choice was to stay in Dallas and report on the investigation into the assassination, or fly to Washington to cover the transition. They agreed that the Dallas press and the wires were best positioned to handle what was in the end a police story. Michael headed for the airport.

It was a sorrowful flight, and a somber Saturday homecoming under rainy, overcast skies. The streets of the capital were all but deserted, the few people out huddled in raincoats and private thoughts. On his way up the White House driveway to the press room, Michael walked by a clutter of items that were being removed from the Oval Office to make way for its next occupant. Kennedy's padded oak rocker was unmistakable.

That evening, as the deadline-induced adrenaline rush subsided again, Michael ached for the comfort of people he loved. Riva was in New York, but she promised to join him on Sunday. He spent the night with his parents, glad for the solace of their company. Michael poured out his fears that Kennedy's death meant the end of his initiatives. Interestingly, his parents, who now often disagreed about politics, had the same view on this.

"I wouldn't be so quick to dismiss Johnson," Anna said. "I was appalled at first when Kennedy picked him. But he's tried to show an understanding of why we need to move ahead on civil rights. The speech he gave in Gettysburg on Memorial Day didn't get the attention it deserved, but it was all you could have hoped for in a national leader."

Alan went further. "Johnson is an operator. To some people, that's an insult, but not to me. He knows the Hill far better than Kennedy did, or anyone Kennedy had around him, and he can get the wheels turning again up there. He'll understand what he needs to do to become president in his own right, and that's embracing Kennedy's program and convincing people that he's not a Southern politician anymore. My primary concern about him, you won't be surprised to hear, is over foreign policy. He's completely untested there. I hope he has the good sense to keep Kennedy's national security team intact and listen to them."

Michael smiled, despite his grim mood. "What you're really saying is that you hope he'll listen to you and your friends," he said. Alan raised his eyebrows and pursed his lips, but offered no disagreement.

Riva came the next evening, arriving just as Michael was getting off deadline after another grueling day. The entire nation was now in deep mourning, millions of people transfixed and bound together by the endless television images as all three networks dumped commercial programming and covered the events in Washington and Texas nonstop.

The sense of surreality was deepened by another burst of violence. As the clueless Dallas cops paraded Oswald before another media mob, a man pushed forward and shot the prisoner to death. He turned out to be a strip club owner named Jack Ruby, who had connections to both the cops and the Mafia. His story was that he shot Oswald because he deeply loved and admired John F. Kennedy and was determined to visit revenge on his killer and spare his widow the ordeal of a trial. Michael wasn't alone in thinking Ruby a curious candidate for avenging angel.

Riva was dealing with her own discontinuity, coming down off the high of her first Broadway role as *Tambourines to Glory* closed its run. Her part had not been a major one, but it was a first for her and had dominated her life for many weeks. With the wedding coming up, and the holidays after that, she was reluctant to plunge into a round of auditions. She and Michael had seen little of each other lately, and simply being together helped lift the gloom.

They briefly considered, then dismissed, postponing the wedding. If the idea of celebrating a joyful personal milestone at such a time seemed discordant, the thought of surrendering to the darkness of the moment was even less palatable. The matter was settled when Anna told them an affirmation of love and commitment was the most powerful antidote to sadness and tragedy she could imagine.

Riva's parents had hoped for a church wedding, but she and Michael had to disappoint them. They were determined to do this in their own way, true to their own spirit. So the families gathered in a bright, wood-paneled room on the NYU campus to watch Riva and Michael stand hand in hand before a municipal judge and share the vows they had written for each other. Riva wore a long, flowing white dress that perfectly accentuated her natural beauty. Michael wore a dark blue business suit.

"I have loved your independent spirit since the day I met you, not far from here," he told her. "I will honor that spirit every day of our lives together, because in doing so I honor the best part of myself. My love for you lifts me up, it makes me a better man, because I want always to be worthy of your love."

"My love for you will never falter, because to abandon our love would be to betray myself," she said in reply. "I know you are strong, and kind, and wise, and gentle. I knew your heart before I knew your mind, and your heart called to me. It still does, it always will. And I will always answer, with my heart, and with my love."

After the ceremony, Michael's small family and Riva's much larger one mingled—tentatively at first, but with growing brio as the wine and warm feelings flowed. Michael worried a bit about his father's tendency to overindulge, but Anna was vigilant.

They held the wedding dinner at the Minetta Tavern, a touch of irony, as it was one of many spots where Riva had waited on tables during college and between roles. The maître d' professed to remember her and dubbed her an honored alumna for the night. He chipped in with a bottle of champagne on the house, so she offered no complaint.

When the time for toasts arrived, Alan stepped up to the plate first. Michael again had a moment of worry, but his father was restrained and gracious. "We came to know Riva soon after she and Michael met, and we quickly came to love her, and to understand why our son so loved her. A parent sometimes doubts a son's choices and judgment. On this vital matter, this affair of the heart, we know our son chose well."

Sam more than matched him. "A father thinks no man could ever be good enough for his little girl," he said. "When we met Michael, and we saw the joy he gave to our daughter, the pleasure she took in just being with him, our minds were set at ease. Now, I think it's time for me to stop talking, and for all of us to drink to the happy couple, and to a long life together."

A few days later, Riva and Michael sat on a Caribbean beach, trying to make sense of the hurricane that had blown through their lives. They had chosen their honeymoon spot carefully, thinking Jamaica was a place where a biracial couple would be at ease. They were mostly right, but they attracted a couple of chilly glances from the tourists, all of them white, and a few curious looks from the hotel staffers, who were almost exclusively black. And the gulf that separated affluent visitors and struggling islanders was inescapable. It made them uncomfortable and clouded the pleasure of the trip.

Still, they were married, and they were happy to be married. The sun was warm; the water was pleasant to swim in and pleasant to look at from their balcony, green in the shallows and blue in the deeps. The world of gunfire and grief seemed far away.

It was a moment to draw a long breath and take stock. They talked of their lives and their love for each other, and all of that made sense. They were doing what they wanted to do. They were good at it and getting better. Riva was steadily building a reputation in the theater world. It was a fickle world, and she was still searching for the big breakthrough part, but she was getting noticed. Her last role had allowed her to show her musical talent on a big stage. Michael was a star at his paper and was establishing a presence in Washington's insular tribe of journalists. Most of all, they loved each other deeply.

But how to make sense of the world around them? How to account for its caprice, its casual cruelty and calculated violence, its sudden descents into darkness? There had been moments this past year when they felt in sync with the rhythms of history, when it seemed that life was bending low to embrace their most cherished hopes. Then it was blown apart, in the roar of the Birmingham church bomb and the crack of Oswald's rifle. What could be relied on in the face of such arbitrary insanity?

They talked of these things, and they clung to each other, like survivors of a shipwreck, cast adrift and lost.

BOOK TWO

Chapter Eight
–Texas Two-Step–

December 1963

1: The Johnson Treatment

Anna had visited the West Wing of the White House several times over the past three years. Now she was back, and outwardly nothing was different; it was the same crowded, cluttered, frenetic beehive. Yet she knew that beneath this familiar surface, everything had changed, because the man at the top had changed.

Anna had been through a transition as well. Shortly before Dallas, she had faced down a challenge to her leadership of the ADA. With the passing of her patron Eleanor Roosevelt, the men who had opposed her initial selection as chair tried to block her re-election. Their pretext was Anna's advocacy of a provision in the civil rights bill to outlaw job discrimination by gender as well as race; they argued this would make a difficult selling job for the bill even harder. Anna and her allies retorted that it would actually increase support by spreading the benefits—and was the right thing to do.

As before, Anna outmaneuvered her opponents by exploiting their internal divisions and their habit of underestimating her. She won the showdown vote, emerged with her authority enhanced, excised her adversaries from the ADA board—and now had landed on the new administration's list of people worth meeting.

Horace Busby met Anna in the West Wing lobby and led her to a cramped conference room. He was a small, precise, buttoned-down man who had worked for Lyndon Johnson since his Senate days in a variety of capacities: speechwriter, idea generator, and emissary. As they entered the room, Bill Moyers, another old Johnson hand, rose to greet her. I'm getting double-teamed, Anna thought. This must be important to them.

"Thank you for coming in so close to the holidays," Busby said as they sat down around a narrow table. "I know you must be very busy with family things. But this is a tricky moment, and we hope you can help."

Johnson had been president for all of two weeks. He had navigated the initial, emotion-wracked days of his sudden ascension and given a well-received speech to a joint session of Congress, pledging fealty to John Kennedy's program and ideals. For most of the nation, however, he was a puzzle, and his grip on power was still uncertain.

"I'll be happy to do whatever I can to advance the goals that the president laid out," Anna said, choosing her words carefully. "How do you think I can help?"

"You can help persuade people that the president means what he says," Moyers said. "I mean people who think as you do, people who loved Jack Kennedy—as I did—and want to see his legacy enshrined in concrete acts of law. Starting with civil rights. You noticed, I'm sure, that the civil rights bill was the first priority he mentioned in his speech."

Moyers was a shrewd choice for this meeting, Anna thought. He was a Johnson man, but with strong Kennedy ties. He had been the liaison between the Johnson and Kennedy camps during the 1960 campaign, and it appeared he was going to play a similar role for the new president. Kennedy had trusted him sufficiently to name him deputy director of the Peace Corps, one of Kennedy's pet projects. Moyers' liberal credentials were unassailable.

"I thought the speech was excellent," Anna said. "His pledge to pursue the Kennedy agenda, and perhaps even go beyond it, was music to my ears—as I'm sure it was intended to be. The question I have for you is the obvious one: How can we be sure he means what he says?"

"You can ask him yourself," Busby said, as he and Moyers rose to their feet.

Anna turned and found Lyndon Johnson standing in the doorway. She rose as well, and found her right hand swallowed up in both of Johnson's large mitts. He towered over her and his aides; the room seemed barely big enough to contain his outsized physical presence. Anna recalled how one senator who had received the "Johnson treatment" had described the experience: "He seems to grow two inches taller for every minute he talks to you."

"I can't stay long, but I just wanted to drop by and thank you for coming in to chat with Buzz and Bill," the president said. "I know you're very busy this time of year with family. Speaking of which, congratulations on your son's wedding. I'm sure you and Alan must be thrilled about Michael. He's doing you proud."

A deft grace note, Anna thought, as she thanked the president. The wedding had not been a high-profile social event, but Johnson's staff had taken the trouble to learn of it, even amid the maelstrom of the transition.

"I know you've probably got a million questions about what I plan to do and where I intend to take this country," Johnson continued. "My boys here can fill you in on the details, but I just want to tell you this: I meant every word I said up on the Hill. The best way we can honor Jack Kennedy's memory is to pass his program, starting with a strong civil rights bill that outlaws segregation in public facilities, and then the tax cut, the health care bill, and so on.

"One of my top men advised me not to emphasize the civil rights bill in the speech because its chances are so uncertain. I had a very simple answer: What's the point of being president if you're going to duck the tough fights?"

This too was sweet music for Anna. "Well, of course, I couldn't agree more, Mr. President," she said. "I thought your speech hit every note perfectly. And I'm also in full agreement with you about using your presidency for big purposes. This country is still reeling right now, but people are hungry for leadership. They appreciate John Kennedy more now that he's gone than they did when he was alive. This creates a great opportunity for you. You can seize that momentum and lead this country to a place that was unimaginable a short time ago."

Johnson exchanged swift glances with his aides. "Did you have anything specific in mind?"

Anna was uncertain if Johnson was sincerely soliciting her policy advice—or subtly mocking her temerity in offering it. She chose to take his question as an opening.

"Attack the roots of inequality, not just the symptoms," she said. "Use the power and the purse of the federal government to make an all-out assault on poverty and economic injustice. In the cities, of course, but also in the rural areas, where poverty afflicts people of all races. This is a national problem, and it demands a national solution."

"Anything else?"

Again, she asked herself, was Johnson's question genuine, or tinged with sarcasm? Only one way to find out.

"Oh, many things, but let me just mention one: I believe the provisions of the civil rights bill must extend to job discrimination by sex, as well as race. Women are entering the workforce in numbers again, and the labor laws don't afford as much protection against bias as they should. Besides being good policy, it will also be good politics; the more people who benefit from the bill, the more support there'll be for it."

"You've got a lot of ideas, and they're very interesting," Johnson said. "You think your liberal friends would be inclined to support me if I did all these things?"

Anna chuckled, again wondering if she was being played. "Yes, I think we would, Mr. President," she deadpanned.

"Well, I appreciate your sharing your views. I want to hear more from you as I go forward, so I hope you'll come by and see us again, and soon. But what I really need from you right now is to go out and talk to your friends and get them fired up. I mean people like Joe Rauh and Walter Reuther and Ken Galbraith. And the Kennedy people, too, like Arthur Schlesinger. Some of them are hopeless. Bobby hates me and always will. I don't know why, but he does. I'm sure he's already plotting to shove me aside. But some of them can be reasoned with.

"I've already talked to them myself, of course, but hearing it from you will count for a lot. Tell them about this conversation. Tell them I'm serious about moving forward, and I need their support to make it happen."

As Anna emerged from the presence, two thoughts struck her most forcefully. The first was a realization of how much the balance of power had shifted in favor of her and her fellow liberals. John Kennedy had tolerated them, and at times embraced their ideas and programs, but he had never fully trusted them. They needed him more than he needed them, and he knew it.

Yet many Americans still viewed Lyndon Johnson as a sectional figure, not a national one, and he needed to change that perception in a hurry. He also needed to unite the clans and factions of his party around him. As the meeting made clear, that meant he needed the support of liberals much more than Kennedy ever had, and that need was likely to grow, not diminish, as the 1964 election season beckoned.

The second realization was the depth of Johnson's distrust of Robert Kennedy. That offhand remark — "Bobby hates me and always will" — spoke volumes to her, and saddened her. It carried a strong whiff of paranoia—but she recalled the aphorism that even paranoids had enemies, and she had no doubt that Bobby reciprocated the venomous sentiment. She recalled the scene on the night of the assassination, when Air Force One landed at Andrews Air Force Base on its return from Dallas. Lyndon Johnson was now the president of the United States, and Robert Kennedy was a serving member of his cabinet, yet Bobby pushed past him as if he hadn't existed. This was a blood feud that would never be resolved, and she felt it held nothing but trouble for both sides.

Still, the upshot of her conversation was clear. Anna was prepared to take the new president's pledges at face value, in large part because they aligned with his current political interests. Only time would tell about whether his invitation to sound off about policy ideas had been genuine, but his request for her help spoke to a genuine need for support.

And she could not help but be impressed by the force of Johnson's personality. He's already growing into the role, she thought. She hoped he could use that aura of command to sway the lawmakers who had bottled up Kennedy's program.

Over dinner that evening, Alan peppered her with questions. He felt mildly envious. He had talked with McGeorge Bundy, who was staying on as national security adviser, and received assurances that Johnson wanted his counsel on foreign policy. He had yet to meet with the man himself.

"So you're going to be Lyndon's water carrier?"

"I'm going to seize a golden opportunity that comes along maybe once in a generation," she said. "Johnson needs us, and he's prepared to pay in kind. We'd be idiots if we didn't take him up on it."

"You know, he's probably had the same conversation with half a dozen other people, maybe more," Alan said.

"Of course. So what? If I can serve his purposes, I can keep his ear. You've played that game with more than one president, and it's worked. You'll play it with this one, too, for the issues you care about. Once you get the chance, that is."

That last comment triggered an involuntary wince from her husband, and Anna half-regretted it. But Alan was a big boy, and there was a power dynamic in their marriage, just as there was in the wider world of Washington. If it was flowing in her direction for the moment, why not enjoy that moment?

Alan had his turn soon enough, in a conversation with Johnson and Mac Bundy in the president's small study just off the Oval Office. While LBJ's mind was mostly on domestic issues, he was thinking ahead to the Christmas holidays, when he planned to invite several important guests to the Johnson ranch in Texas. One was Ludwig Erhard, the new chancellor of West Germany. Alan knew him well and had worked with him for years, going back to the days right after the war when Erhard crafted the program that revived the German economy. Johnson had many questions about how Erhard could be enlisted to serve as a counterweight to French President Charles De Gaulle in the NATO alliance.

There was also the nagging question of what to do about Southeast Asia. The civil war in Laos between communists and royalists had been quelled, for now, by an uneasy truce. But neighboring South Vietnam had devolved into political chaos, and even the commitment of more than 15,000 American troops— Kennedy had coyly called them "advisers"—had not improved the military balance between the wobbly government army and communist Viet Cong insurgents. The communists had been fighting to win control of Vietnam for more than 20 years, and they showed no signs of buckling. One of Kennedy's last acts was an executive order contemplating the withdrawal of some U.S. forces immediately and all of them within 13 months. Johnson wanted to know what Alan thought of that step toward disengagement.

"Mr. President, I don't think we can afford to show any sign of weakness or hesitation, there or anywhere else in the world. I know the Viet Cong and their North Vietnamese backers are tough customers, and I know what some of those reporters have been writing about all the problems the South Vietnamese army is having. But Vietnam is a proxy war more than anything else, and if we pull out and let the communists win, it'll only embolden the

Soviets and Chinese. It will have ramifications throughout the region. Indonesia would be their next target, and then the Philippines."

"Well, that's what I think, too," Johnson replied. "And McNamara and Bundy and the military men tell me those know-it-all reporters have it wrong, as usual. Our people say the South Vietnamese are learning how to handle the Viet Cong, and that our forces are critical to that effort. I've never been to that part of the world myself. Have you?"

"No, but I'd say if you've seen one communist insurgency, you've seen 'em all," Alan said. "They're all cut from the same cloth, and the pattern was made in Moscow. The local details don't matter much."

It was a typical conversation between two powerful men in a powerful nation about a small faraway country that was annoying them by refusing to bend to their will or fulfill their preconceived expectations. It was the kind of conversation that could have occurred in London two centuries earlier, as a king and his ministers discussed how to stamp out a pesky insurgency in the American colonies, or in Rome nearly 2,000 years ago as an emperor gave orders to bring stubborn Teutonic tribes to heel. For those living at what they regarded as the center of the world, the local details on the periphery never seemed important. Sometimes, they were right.

The talk moved on to Khrushchev, and NATO, and the prospects for a fresh round of tariff reductions, and then to Latin America and Africa. By the end, they had traveled around the globe, and Alan's views had been solicited on every major foreign policy issue facing the new president. As he drove home, Alan realized that this conversation had lasted far longer than any he had ever had with Jack Kennedy. Like his wife, Alan sensed opportunity. This new president was a naif on foreign policy, Alan thought, and he needed wise men to provide expert advice. Alan was only too happy to oblige.

2: Vapor Trails

Anna, for her part, happily dove into the task that Johnson had set for her. His early conduct in the White House eased her path. He had focused his considerable powers of persuasion on the Hill, and the results were encouraging. The Kennedy tax bill would be freed from the purgatory of the Senate Finance Committee. Even more important, the House would vote on the civil rights bill in January. That left ample time on the legislative calendar to marshal support to defeat the inevitable filibuster in the Senate.

The fact that the new president was backing up his words with action gave Anna crucial talking points, and she used them.

She also discovered that Johnson had blazed the trail she was traveling. One of her first calls was to Adlai Stevenson. She found that LBJ had already met with him and promised that his counsel would count for more in a Johnson administration than it had with his predecessor. Stevenson believed him, and Anna made no attempt to dissuade him; Adlai's credulity made it that much easier to line him up in her campaign, and his enduring reputation in liberal circles made him an asset.

She spoke with another influential liberal, Senator Hubert Humphrey, and found him equally receptive. Humphrey had launched his political career on the civil rights issue, and the prospect of a president willing to go all-in on it made him forget the doubts he once harbored about Johnson. Humphrey had known Anna and Alan since the days of the Truman administration, and Anna's willingness to accept Johnson's sincerity counted with him.

Anna also had a conversation with one of the civil rights leaders she had come to know well during the White House meetings after Birmingham. Roger Jefferson had started his work in the movement as a community organizer in Los Angeles and risen to a position of national leadership in the Voter Education Project, a joint effort by the major civil rights groups and the Kennedy administration to register black voters in the South.

Anna knew that Johnson had his own lines of communication into the country's black leadership. Her goal in talking with Jefferson was not to convey information, but to receive it. She was very curious about how the new president's pledge of fealty to civil rights was being received by those with the most direct stake in the effort.

What she learned from Roger was that Johnson had begun reaching out to civil rights leaders almost immediately after Dallas, seeking to convince them of his sincerity and win their loyalty. Jefferson said he'd been in one of those meetings and described a mood that began in skepticism but ended in a belief that the president was genuinely committed to the effort. What he described was a parallel to the experiences of white liberals like herself.

"With Kennedy, I never had the feeling that he was fully committed," Roger said. "He had to be pushed by events, and even then, he was more dutiful than passionate. There was always the sense that, in his mind, we were the suitors, we needed him more than he needed us.

"With Lyndon, it's different. He comes across as all-in on this, emotionally as well as politically. That could be theatrics, and only time and events will really tell. But he presented himself almost as an equal partner, not a reluctant overlord."

A few days later, Anna flew to Detroit to meet with Walter Reuther, the president of the United Auto Workers union. With him, there was some history to overcome. Reuther had played a central part in the effort to block Johnson's nomination as Kennedy's running mate at the 1960 convention. However, he had swung his powerful union strongly behind the civil rights movement, and the new president's commitment to push the legislation across the finish line resonated with Reuther.

That night, Anna spoke at a meeting of Democratic Party members in the nearby college town of Ann Arbor. The Michigan state party was one of the most liberal in the country, and those present reflected its diverse strands: union officials, civil rights activists, professors and students from the University of Michigan. Like Reuther and Humphrey, they regarded civil rights as their litmus test, and they listened to Anna's assurances of the new president's commitment to it with undisguised relief.

Arthur Schlesinger was a tougher sell. The bookish, bow-tied historian had bonded closely with Jack Kennedy during his years as a White House adviser, and his first instinct after the assassination was to join the exodus of Kennedy loyalists who could not imagine working for Lyndon Johnson—or any other leader, really. The new president had convinced Arthur to stay on temporarily, but he made it clear that he would soon leave and start work on a history of the Kennedy presidency.

Anna did not particularly care whether Schlesinger stayed or left, but she cared very much about his attitude toward the new president. He had great cachet in liberal circles and among the Ivy League academics who had admired and advised Kennedy, but regarded LBJ as a creature from another planet.

Anna had known Schlesinger for years, since their days as co-founders of the ADA, and cherished hopes that she could leverage their long relationship to line him up in helping bridge the gulf between Johnson and the Kennedy clan. She hadn't yet approached Bobby, knowing how raw the wound still was, but it could not be avoided much longer. He was now the political paterfamilias, and she heard he was meeting with loyalists to plot out his next moves. One option was to try to muscle his way onto the 1964 ticket as LBJ's running mate. Another was a bid to be on the ticket—at the top.

Anna regarded the former as impossible, because Johnson would never agree to it, and the latter as suicidal. She hoped that Schlesinger could help her deflect Bobby onto a more sensible path, one that would not split the party just as it seemed poised to accomplish so many long-cherished goals.

What she found in Arthur was a conflicted man who fulfilled the caricature of the indecisive intellectual that had dogged him throughout his White House tenure. At one moment, Schlesinger talked of Johnson as a usurper, a man unfit to carry his predecessor's briefcase, a placeholder to be pushed aside for the rightful heir. The next moment, he was speaking with enthusiasm about the great promise of the moment for achieving liberal aims, and how Johnson could prove useful in realizing this potential.

In the end, Anna settled for half a loaf. Arthur agreed to help persuade their fellow liberals to get behind Lyndon so long as he fought for their programs, and he also promised to steer clear of any anti-Johnson cabals. But he refused to talk to Bobby about stepping back from a challenge to LBJ in 1964, saying he could not do it with a clear conscience. Anna would have to fly that mission solo.

Just getting Bobby to agree to meet proved arduous, even though they had known each other for several years. Kennedy was still deep in his own private mourning and seeing very few people. He spent most of his time holed up at Hickory Hill, his rambling house in the Virginia countryside, or at Hyannis Port with his parents, his brother's widow and her suddenly fatherless young children. Finally, after several tries, she wangled a reluctant invitation to come out to Hickory Hill.

It wasn't a particularly good place for him to escape his ghosts, she thought. It was here on November 22 that he had received word of the shooting, followed by an almost gleeful phone call from FBI Director J. Edgar Hoover telling him that his brother was dead. Today, the countryside was brown and bare, the skies leaden and lowering, the big house hushed and empty. When he greeted Anna, she barely suppressed a gasp, even though she had been forewarned. Bobby, always a slight man, now seemed gaunt and shrunken, his face the color of the clouds, dark circles under his intense blue eyes.

"It was good of you to see me. I don't know how to begin to express my and Alan's sorrow for your loss. We loved your brother, both as a leader and as a human being, and we will feel his absence for the rest of our lives."

"I'm haunted by the fact that I may have unwittingly been responsible," Bobby said, in a voice so low Anna had to lean forward to catch his words. "I know the prevailing theory is that Oswald acted alone, but I can't help but wonder. We went after Castro very hard. I was the point man, and Oswald had those strange Cuban connections. And then there's the mob. I made the Mafia a personal project at Justice. Jack Ruby had all those underworld links. Very convenient that he silenced Oswald. I just don't know."

"I'm not sure it's productive to chase those vapor trails," she said gently.

"No, probably not," Bobby said. "Jack was always very fatalistic about life. He'd been through so much, survived so much, always came out on top, he just refused to worry about it. I should adopt his attitude. I've been reading a lot lately, classical tragedy, and I found this quote from Aeschylus: 'He who learns must suffer. And even in our sleep, pain that cannot forget falls drop by drop upon the heart, and in our own despair, against our will, comes wisdom to us by the awful grace of God.'"

Anna felt her heart rise in her throat, and her eyes dampen. At the same time, she thought that Greek tragedy might not be the best reading material for this man in his present state of mind.

"I had a reason for wishing to see you today, besides personally expressing my grief. Like Aeschylus, I too am concerned about wisdom. And like you, I'm concerned about the fate of your brother's programs, and the party that he led so well."

"I wish nothing but success for his programs, especially his civil rights bill—*his* civil rights bill—and for the Democratic Party next year," Bobby said.

"I know you do," Anna said. "The question, as always, is the best way to achieve that success."

"Things seem to be taking care of themselves, if what I read in the papers is right."

Anna shook her head slightly. "We both know that things like important legislation never just take care of themselves, not while so many conservatives have their hands on the levers of power in Congress. It takes strong leadership to loosen their grip. My belief is that Lyndon Johnson can provide that leadership, and that he's prepared to provide it."

At the mention of the name, Bobby sat back abruptly, as if he'd been slapped. His face, soft with melancholy a moment ago, hardened and set.

"Did he ask you to come see me?"

"He did not ask that. He did ask me to tell anyone who would listen that he's completely sincere about pushing your brother's program through to enactment, and absolutely determined to make a success of that effort, no matter how long it takes or how tough the opposition. And I've been doing that, because I believe him, and because I can't think of a better memorial to John F. Kennedy than passage of the civil rights bill and the other measures."

"I know you've been making the rounds," Bobby said. "People still talk to me, you know. And I believe your motives are sincere, that you're not angling for anything from him and carrying his water to get it. We've known each other for some time now, and I've always respected your commitment to your principles."

Anna nodded, even as she noticed that Bobby had used the same phrase as her husband—"carrying his water." What is it about these men that makes them view politics in such feudal, liege-and-vassal terms?

"So what would you have me do?" Bobby said after a long silence.

"First, take him at his word about supporting your brother's program, at least until he proves otherwise. Don't do anything that will impede what will have to be an all-out effort next year, in Congress and in the country. And, if you're able to, ask your friends and your allies to be part of that effort."

Bobby answered with a slight nod. "What else?"

Anna sat back and took a deep breath. This part was going to be difficult.

"You're going to be president one day. We both know it. The only question is when. But if you try for it next year, I fear it will bring only the worst, for you and for what we want to achieve. You'll force the entire party to choose sides, and the only beneficiaries will be the Republicans. It's probably the only way they could win. And you'll convince a lot of people that the old 'ruthless Bobby' canard has merit.

"You say you've been reading Greek tragedy. Perhaps you've come across this line, often attributed to Euripides: 'Those whom the gods would destroy, they first make mad.'"

Bobby sat back again, this time slowly, a faint smile playing across his face. It was gone a moment later. When he spoke, his tone was measured, but his face had hardened again.

"Lyndon Johnson is an ill-mannered boor. He enjoys humiliating people when he has power over them. He grovels to people who have power over him. I've seen him do both, up close, and it's not pretty. He's also a crook, a corrupt Texas pol who's had his greasy hand out for years with the special interests who could enrich him in exchange for favors. And he's given those favors freely.

"The fact that he's in my brother's place makes me sick, physically ill. I did everything I could to stop Jack from picking him at the convention, but I couldn't. Now we're stuck with him, for the moment."

Bobby paused to let those sentiments sink in.

"I won't do anything to interfere with getting the president's legislative agenda passed," he continued. "In fact, if I'm asked to, I'll be very active in supporting the civil rights bill, and so will my people at Justice.

"But I don't think for a minute that Lyndon sincerely believes in civil rights, or racial equality, or fighting injustice. He sincerely believes in his own political interests, and right now those interests are best served by aligning himself with the president's program. The minute he decides otherwise, he'll disappear on us like a magician's rabbit. I don't intend to go around broadcasting those views; anybody who knows me already knows what I think. But if anyone asks me, privately, that's what I'll tell them.

"As for next year, who knows? It's eight months till our convention. A lot could happen in that time. I haven't made any commitments about anything to anyone—and believe me, people have asked. I appreciate what you say about not splitting the party. I hope you'll appreciate that I have responsibilities to a lot of people and a lot of causes, and I have to keep my options open."

It was the best Anna could hope for under the circumstances, and she accepted it with good grace. As she said her goodbyes, she had a sudden impulse. She turned and hugged Bobby, just briefly. It surprised them both. They were reserved people, not inclined to such displays outside their families. Yet it felt to Anna like the right thing to do. Bobby seemed so vulnerable, so unprotected, so emotionally exposed. He was consumed by grief and loss, and his slow passage through this tortured landscape was awakening qualities that Anna had not seen in him before, an emerging capacity for introspection and emotional depth, even empathy. She certainly had never heard the pre-Dallas Bobby quote Aeschylus.

She noticed something else. When he used the words "the president," he applied them exclusively to his brother. When he spoke of the man who actually sat in the Oval Office now, it was always the name, never the title.

3: War Footing

As Anna reflected on the sum of her efforts, she thought the returns were promising. Most of those she had spoken with were encouraged by LBJ's early actions and willing to grant him time and maneuvering room. If he were able to deliver real legislative victories, Anna felt those sentiments would crystallize into full support, and Johnson would have a clear path to the nomination and then to election in November. And if he used the moment to go beyond Kennedy's agenda and propose more far-reaching economic and social programs, he would no longer be Kennedy's accidental successor. He would be president in his own right.

As Anna pondered the best approach for reaching out to the White House to share these findings, a phone call from Horace Busby resolved the problem. The call was about the president's working vacation at his Texas ranch over the holidays. It would be a hectic time, with people important to Johnson shuttling in and out for meetings as well as socializing. He wanted Alan and Anna, both of them, to come.

It was flattering, even though they understood the motives behind the invitation. Lyndon Johnson was still finding his footing as president and as party leader. He needed advice and support from people who could help him walk with confidence in both roles. That he regarded Alan and Anna as among those people was not displeasing.

It was a long journey, first by plane to Austin and then by helicopter to the ranch, another 50 miles west, in the Texas hill country. Their first glimpse of the region in the rapidly fading twilight revealed a stark setting: undulating hills, winter-barren and windswept, and then the Johnson ranch complex, popping into view astride the thin brown ribbon of the Pedernales River.

They arrived the day before Erhard; Johnson wanted Alan there as a friendly face when the West German leader showed up. Alan played the role to the hilt, exchanging hearty backslaps and fat cigars and reminiscences of conferences in Bonn and Brussels with the portly, florid chancellor. Erhard was also new to the world stage, and also suffered from the disadvantage of a high-profile predecessor: Konrad Adenauer, the legendary "Der Alte," creator of the postwar West German state.

The invitation to the ranch was the best Christmas present Erhard could have imagined, and he lapped up the attention and the Texas version of *gemütlichkeit*, complete with barbecued ribs, square dancing and Christmas carols sung in German. Johnson kept the substantive discussions with Erhard short and general, knowing they both were still finding their legs on foreign affairs. He could be reasonably certain, however, that when the inevitable trouble with De Gaulle over NATO policy arose, Erhard would lend Johnson a sympathetic ear.

Erhard wasn't the only visitor to get the LBJ treatment. Johnson cycled Washington reporters, including Michael, in and out for brief stays that featured small-group interviews and ranch tours. He used the journalists to demonstrate that he had his own style, earthy and informal, entirely different from Kennedy's. And he used them to stage a crude, cruel display of alpha-male dominance that not coincidentally cast a Kennedy acolyte as the butt of the joke.

Pierre Salinger had served John Kennedy since his Senate days and had become a close confidant. He put aside his grief over the assassination and agreed to stay on as White House press secretary to help Johnson navigate the transition. He was a skilled spokesman, popular with the press, but also an easy mark for teasing because of his short, rotund physique. He had always looked out of place among the athletic, stylish Kennedys, and he stood out even more on a Texas ranch.

For Johnson, Salinger's physical awkwardness was an asset to be exploited. After holding an impromptu press conference on the lawn outside the ranch house, the president delighted the photographers by jumping atop a tall black horse. He pleased them even more by calling Salinger over and beckoning him toward a smaller mount. As the press secretary perched precariously on the horse, Johnson paraded for the cameras, then took off at a brisk pace. Salinger bounced along behind him, a panicked look on his face, desperately trying to stay in the saddle.

With the photo ops finished, Johnson returned to his substantive agenda, and the next item was Vietnam, the problem that wouldn't go away. The security situation had deteriorated since Alan's last conversation with the president, despite the generals' assurances that the much-maligned South Vietnamese army was making progress. Mike Mansfield, the Senate majority leader and a legitimate expert on Asia, responded to the new troubles with a detailed memo arguing for military disengagement and a political solution. A worried Johnson asked his senior security officials to weigh in with memos of their own.

In a long evening conversation with Alan over bourbon in the ranch's living room, the president summarized the memos' recommendations. They added up to escalation, not disengagement: scrapping Kennedy's plan for troop withdrawals, sending more U.S. forces to the critical Mekong Delta region where the Viet Cong insurgency was strongest, and initiating covert military actions against communist North Vietnam, which nurtured the insurgents. Those operations included secretly deploying U.S. warships to shell North Vietnamese coastal installations in the Gulf of Tonkin.

"I think these recommendations all make sense, if—and it's a big if—they're carried out within a clear strategic context," Alan said. "And our long-term strategy has got to be one of exacting a steadily greater toll on the North Vietnamese, making them pay an ever-steeper price for their support of this insurgency. The Viet Cong can't succeed without that support; in fact, it couldn't exist for long without it."

Engaging the insurgents in the Mekong Delta was fine as a first step, Alan said, but it was only coping with a symptom. Taking the war directly to the North would deal with the cause. The president should be prepared to do that. If not, he should take the Mansfield path and start putting out feelers for a political settlement.

"I'm not gonna go the Mansfield route," Johnson responded. "I'm not about to be the president who loses us Vietnam. And I'm sure as hell not gonna do it in an election year. I remember what happened when the Reds took China in '49. The Republicans killed us with it. They screamed 'Who lost China?' for the next four elections. And they won three of those elections."

Johnson fell silent for a moment, sipping his drink. "When you say make the North pay a greater price, what specifically are we talking about?"

"I think we have to be prepared to use our air power, Mr. President," Alan replied. "Shelling coastal installations is a start, but those installations aren't that important to the North. The Ho Chi Minh Trail is important. It's the Viet Cong's lifeline, and it's vulnerable to strategic bombing."

"Okay. What else?"

"If necessary, we have to contemplate bombing North Vietnam itself," Alan said. "That would certainly get their attention and make them understand we're serious."

"And if that doesn't work?"

"We may have to drop the advisor fiction and send regular Army and Marine units," Alan said. "That would instantly change the military balance in the South. And it would buck up that wobbly government in Saigon."

Johnson shot Alan a skeptical look. "And what will the Russians and Chinese be doing while all this is going on?" he asked.

"Not much, Mr. President. They're too busy trying to get at each other's throats to pay much attention. And southeast Asia is a peripheral concern to them, even the Chinese. They're both delighted that we're struggling a bit in Vietnam, and they'd be happy to profit from the fallout if we fail, but they're not going to invest any substantial amount of assets there."

Johnson paused for several moments to process Alan's comments.

"Well, thank you for your counsel," he said at last. "You've provided me with more forward-looking strategic clarity than the people who are actually on my payroll. They're mostly concerned with the short term and with keeping my favor, not the big picture.

"I can tell you this much. I'm not about to cut and run, but I don't want to turn myself into a wartime president, not just yet, not in an election year. The moves you're talking about may have to be made at some point, but for now I'm going to limit it to okaying what McNamara and Rusk and Bundy are recommending, and do it as quietly as possible, and hope that it's enough to hold things together.

"And if any smartass reporters or congressmen or Republican candidates ask me what my Vietnam policy is, I'll tell 'em I'm not gonna send American boys to do a job that Asian boys should be doing for themselves. That's a pretty good line, don't you think?"

Alan came away from this conversation with some revealing insights into Johnson's thinking on Vietnam. One was that it was shaped primarily by domestic politics, and the raw fear of being blamed for a failure there. Another was that he had no intention of leveling with the American public, or their congressional representatives, for that matter, about the steps he was about to take.

The first point didn't bother Alan very much. If Johnson chose to adopt a sound policy for a base reason, he wouldn't be the first, and what mattered was the policy. The second point did worry him. He had no objection in principle to secrecy, but Johnson would need political support in Congress and the country for the steps down the road that Alan thought might be needed to stabilize Vietnam. Escalating in the shadows was no way to build that support.

The next day, it was Anna's turn to be closeted with Johnson. He would deliver the State of the Union speech shortly after he returned to Washington, and he had made it clear that he wanted to use the moment to put his own stamp on the presidency. Anna had caught glimpses of speechwriter Ted Sorensen huddled over a typewriter in a small office at one end of the ranch house, working on a draft of the address.

Anna's conversation with the president took place not in the living room but in a smaller private room in another part of the rambling house. The thought crossed her mind that LBJ might want to conceal the fact that he was consulting her. She searched for reasons that might be so, and one came to mind: of all the people who were at the ranch to advise Johnson, she was the only woman.

Well, even under wraps, a one-on-one with the president was still an opportunity, and she was eager to hear what Johnson wanted to talk about.

"I was intrigued by your thought, the last time we spoke, about thinking big, thinking beyond President Kennedy's legislative agenda," he said. "I'd like to explore your thinking on that."

"My thinking is that it's time to commit the federal government to an all-out assault on economic inequality," Anna replied. "We're the richest country in the world, in the history of the world, and yet 20 percent of our citizens are trapped in poverty with little hope of escape. We both know that's not right. It also doesn't square with most Americans' image of their country, and that creates an opening."

Anna mentioned a recent book by the social critic Michael Harrington, *The Other America*. It had caught the attention of Jack Kennedy—but Anna deftly omitted bringing up that detail. "He trained a spotlight on the poverty that persists in the inner cities and the rural parts of the country. You can turn up the intensity of that spotlight, make the problem plain to the whole country, and propose a program for dealing with it."

"And what would that program look like?"

Anna was ready for that one. She ticked off several items, making it clear that she was not freelancing, that she was talking about programs that would enjoy strong support among many liberal groups and activists: Expand Kennedy's proposal for federal health insurance for the elderly to include low-income adults of all ages and their children. Set up a federally funded preschool program for poor children that would bring them to kindergarten on an equal footing with others. Create a modern version of FDR's Civilian Conservative Corps that would get young people off the streets and train them for work. Make Washington a partner with local governments and community groups to clear slums and promote economic development.

"And, most important, tie these programs together under a common theme, make them part of a common effort to attack and defeat poverty and inequality once and for all," Anna said. "Make this a national goal, with the federal government as the tip of the spear. The country's mood right now is receptive to a challenge, a big challenge, and there's none bigger than this. Americans will respond to it, and you'll have the public support you need to push these programs through Congress."

Johnson, who had been hunched forward during Anna's monologue, leaned back and expelled a long breath. "Well, you certainly have thought about this, I can see that," he said.

"I have, and I'm not alone. You'll be able to tap the thinking of a lot of smart people in academia and the think tanks like Brookings, people who have been talking and writing about these ideas for years. You'll certainly have the support of liberal groups and the unions and the civil rights organizations, and a lot of mayors.

"What's needed is strong leadership at the top to galvanize all that brainpower and enthusiasm. Mr. President, that's where you come in. Only you can provide that leadership."

It didn't surprise Anna that LBJ was coyly noncommittal at the end of their conversation. She knew that many people were advising Johnson on the speech. Yet her instincts told her she had connected. She had taken care to work in two points that would appeal to Johnson: the notion of going beyond Kennedy's proposals even while embracing them, and the allusion to his youthful political hero, FDR.

Yet her biggest selling point, she thought, was more primal. Lyndon Johnson had a very large ego.

So it also did not surprise her, when they were back in Washington, that an invitation arrived for her and Alan to watch the State of the Union address from the House gallery in seats reserved for White House guests.

The spacious chamber, bathed in brilliant light for the television cameras, was filled and brimming with anticipation long before Johnson's arrival. The State of the Union was a Washington ritual, with a well-established hierarchy and set of protocols. In the front of the chamber, special sections were reserved for special groups: the Cabinet, the Supreme Court, the military's Joint Chiefs of Staff, the diplomatic corps. Behind them, in tiers, sat the combined membership of the House and Senate, 535 lawmakers if all attended—and tonight, all were there to take the measure of a still-new president. The culminating ritual came when the chamber's rear doors swung open, House Doorkeeper William "Fishbait" Miller's stentorian voice cut through the chatter— "Mr. Speaker, the president of the United States" —and Johnson strode down the center aisle to the rostrum.

He began with a plea for the civil rights and tax cut bills, a pledge to cut unneeded federal spending, a ritual bow to his predecessor and his programs. And then, for Anna, came the money quote:

"Unfortunately, many Americans live on the outskirts of hope— some because of their poverty, and some because of their color, and all too many because of both. Our task is to help replace their despair with opportunity."

Johnson's voice rose in pitch and timbre to punctuate his next words.

"This administration today, here and now, declares unconditional war on poverty in America," he said. "We shall not rest until that war is won."

As Johnson paused to acknowledge the applause rolling across the chamber, Alan turned to his wife. "Well done," he said. "You've got your war. I wonder if I'll get mine."

Chapter Nine
–Freedom Summer–

August 1964

1: Plantation Politics

Fannie Lou Hamer had grown up on a Mississippi cotton plantation, the daughter of sharecroppers, the youngest of their 20 children. She started working in the fields at age 6 and had to leave school altogether at 12 to help her family earn enough to survive the brutal strictures of the sharecropping system. But she had a natural gift for words and storytelling, gifts that were recognized and honed during Bible study classes at her church. And she possessed an instinctive dignity, an unshakeable belief in her self-worth and that of people like her, and a deep reservoir of personal courage. All these qualities made her a natural leader.

Hamer first attempted to register to vote in Sunflower County in 1962. She was rejected by the county's white registrars, who said she had flunked a literacy test, and she was kicked off the plantation where she lived with her husband for simply making the attempt. She survived a drive-by shooting by some local racists. And she kept returning to the registrar's office. Four months after her first try, she succeeded in registering—only to be told that she still couldn't vote because she hadn't paid Mississippi's onerous poll tax.

Michael first met Hamer and heard her story in June, when she was helping to lead the civil rights movement's Freedom Summer project to register black voters in her home state. The drive brought hundreds of volunteers, black and white, into Mississippi from around the country. As the campaign intensified, white rage and violence grew as well. These simmering tensions boiled over on a June night, when three Freedom Summer workers went missing while investigating a church burning in Neshoba County. Their disappearance became a national drama that led the federal government to dispatch hundreds of FBI agents and Navy personnel to Mississippi to search for them. Their bodies were found buried under an earthen dam, more than a month after they disappeared.

Now, just a few weeks after that terrible discovery, Michael was squeezed into the rear of a hot, overcrowded meeting room in Atlantic City, New Jersey. He was listening to Fannie Lou Hamer tell the credentials committee of the Democratic National Convention why it should refuse to seat the all-white delegation that the all-white Mississippi Democratic Party had sent to the convention, and should instead recognize the mostly black Freedom Democratic Party as the rightful representative of the state.

Speaking in a clear, unwavering voice, Hamer narrated the long history of her attempts to register to vote, and the similar efforts of other black people in Mississippi. She described how they had been harassed and threatened with violence, how they had been arrested for trying to use a restaurant bathroom on a trip back home from a voting rights conference. She described how she and the other arrested activists had been systematically beaten for the sin of refusing to address their jailers as "sir."

The credentials hearing was being carried by the television networks, and the back of the room was filled with reporters. What Hamer said next resonated widely, and for a long time.

"All of this is on account of we want to register, to become first-class citizens," she told the committee. "And if the Freedom Democratic Party is not seated now, I question America. Is this America, the land of the free and the home of the brave? Where we have to sleep with our telephones off the hooks because our lives be threatened daily, because we want to live as decent human beings, in America?"

A short time later, with Hamer's words still resounding in his mind, Michael emerged into the bright August sunlight flooding the Atlantic City boardwalk. The Mississippi challenge was quickly becoming a high-profile issue at the convention, a symbolic test of where the party stood on civil rights. And after this hearing, he felt reasonably certain how the delegates would vote on it—if they got the chance. The challengers enjoyed widespread sympathy among the Democrats who had gathered in this faded seaside resort to nominate Lyndon Johnson for president. And there was little affection for the official state delegation, whose members were openly supporting Johnson's Republican opponent, Barry Goldwater, and had just passed a defiant resolution declaring their belief in racial segregation.

He also knew that the full convention might never get the chance to vote on the Mississippi challenge, because Lyndon Johnson had other ideas.

By all indications, Johnson was on top of the world. He was far ahead of Goldwater in all the polls. He was running on a genuine record of achievement. He had seized the reins after John Kennedy's assassination nine months ago and united his often-fractious party around him. He had allayed the suspicions of its liberal wing by winning passage of a sweeping civil rights bill and proposing a wide-ranging series of initiatives to eradicate poverty, just as Anna and other liberals had urged him to do.

These successes now made him risk-adverse. He obsessively pored over his favorable poll numbers. He was determined to prevent anything that might jeopardize his victory in November or diminish its size. He wanted this convention to be a celebration of his leadership, a week-long paean to his primacy. He made his wishes clear to all around him and made it equally clear that anyone who thwarted this desire in the smallest way would incur his formidable wrath.

As for the Freedom Democrats, Johnson was not about to risk the party's veneer of harmony by backing a bid by some upstarts to expel the Mississippi regulars, a move that might trigger a walkout by other southern delegations. And he certainly wanted no noisy floor fights over the issue.

And Michael had learned that Johnson possessed some important leverage to get his way, because he had Hubert Humphrey in his pocket.

No one in the Democratic Party leadership was more associated with the civil rights cause than Humphrey; no one was closer to the movement's leaders. Humphrey had begun his national political career with a passionate speech championing civil rights at the Democratic convention in 1948, long before the issue was fashionable. But now Humphrey wanted something, wanted it badly, and only the president had the power to confer it. Humphrey wanted to be Johnson's running mate, as a step toward sitting in the White House himself when LBJ's presidency was over.

Walking down the boardwalk to his hotel, Michael paused briefly to talk with some of the Freedom Democrats as they boarded a bus back to their motel on the edge of town. Bob Moses, a veteran SNCC activist who was one of the key organizers of the Freedom Summer campaign, told Michael he was optimistic about the challenge. Hamer's powerful testimony, he said, would make a difference.

"It's important that reporters like you were here to hear it," Moses said. "And forgive me for saying this, Michael, but it's even more important that the TV cameras were here."

"No need to apologize. But you heard what LBJ did? He called an impromptu press conference, to announce nothing of any importance, right in the middle of her testimony. Pretty obvious ploy to distract attention."

Moses' face fell momentarily. Then he shrugged. "Shabby little tricks like that won't matter in the end. A lot of people will still see the testimony. I'm sure we'll make the TV newscasts. And folks like you'll write about it, right?"

"Oh, you can be sure of that. This is a slow news day, and you're the best thing going for us. In fact, I've got to get moving if I'm going to make deadline."

Two hours later, Michael walked into the Shelburne Hotel dining room to meet his parents, who were ensconced at a corner table.

"So, what's the big story today?" Alan asked as Michael sat down.

"Mississippi. The Freedom Democrats. As if you had to ask."

"Well, I suppose it's good they're getting their moment in the sun," Anna said. "I hear it was great theater, but they're not going to get what they want. Personally, I wish it were otherwise. But this is the president's convention, and he's made his wishes very clear. They're not going to be seated."

"Why not?" Michael shot back, irritated by her certitude. "Because Johnson would rather seat a lily-white delegation full of people who don't support him and, in fact, call him a traitor to the South? I'd say a floor fight over it could be very interesting.

"And, in any case, you're going along with this? How can you? If anyone has earned the right to represent the people of Mississippi— I mean *all* the people of Mississippi—it's the Freedom Democrats. They've paid the price, many times over. And part of that price has been paid in blood."

Alan gave him a withering glare. "You have a flair for the dramatic, son. You also have an unfortunate tendency to turn practical political questions into stark moral issues. That's a bad habit, as I, and your mother, and anyone else who's had any experience in politics can tell you. I learned that the hard way many years ago, when I tried to convince President Roosevelt that we were obligated to get involved in Spain—"

"Oh, my god, that again?" Michael had been hearing for years about Alan's quixotic support for the Spanish loyalists, and he did not think the story improved with age. "You were right on the merits back then, even if it would have been politically difficult for Roosevelt to do the right thing. I'm right on the merits now—and this time, it isn't even that politically difficult to do the right thing. Who's Johnson afraid of pissing off? A bunch of white supremacists who aren't going to vote for him anyway?"

"Okay, let me get this straight," Alan said. "Lyndon Johnson has just signed the toughest, most far-reaching civil rights law this country has ever seen. He rejected every attempt to dilute it, and he went all-in for it, even when a lot of people close to him were telling him it wasn't smart to do it—"

"Were you one of those people, dad?"

"Never mind that. The point is, he did it. He took a big political risk for civil rights, and he won. And now he's basing his campaign on the most ambitious social and economic reform program any president has dared to propose since FDR. So what are the people who should be the most grateful for it doing? Praising him? Giving him a little leeway in an election year? No. They're putting him on the spot, forcing him into a no-win situation."

The conversation had an edge to it, born of another recent disagreement, one that had nothing to do with Mississippi. A few weeks ago, just as the search for the three murdered civil rights workers reached its tragic end, the president had told the nation that two U.S. warships cruising in international waters in the Gulf of Tonkin had been attacked by North Vietnamese torpedo boats. In retaliation, Johnson ordered a series of air strikes against North Vietnamese shore installations. And he demanded and got from Congress a broad, vaguely worded resolution that authorized him to take any further military action he deemed necessary to "prevent further aggression."

Alan was openly delighted by this turn of events; he had been advocating deeper U.S. involvement in Vietnam for many months, and saw the naval engagement as a glittering opportunity to move the administration further down the path to full intervention. Michael was just as openly suspicious of Johnson's claims about the incident, and deeply uneasy about a greater U.S. role in a messy conflict that was best steered clear of. They quarreled noisily over the matter, and neither was completely over it.

Anna had stayed out of that dispute. She had no hesitance about weighing in on Mississippi. "Seating the Freedom Democrats would make for great symbolic drama, and there's a part of me that would love to see it," she said. "It would also cause a walkout by most of the other southern delegations, and would amount to handing the South to Goldwater on a platter. You can't blame the president for wanting to avoid that outcome.

"So there's going to be a compromise worked out, one that recognizes the legitimacy of the issues the Freedom Democrats are raising, but without causing a complete blowup. That's the way this thing is destined to end—and it would help a great deal if your friends in the movement would show some flexibility to help us get to a successful resolution. You might even help out by telling them so."

"My friends? I'm a reporter, not a political operative. I don't presume to tell Bob Moses or Fannie Lou Hamer or anyone else in the movement what to do. And if I were advising them, you wouldn't like it, because what I'd tell them is to drop your compromise in the nearest wastebasket and force a floor fight. Because they just might win it. And then the Democratic Party would be aligning itself with the South's future, not its past."

2: Selling the Deal

If Johnson held most of the high cards, the Freedom Democrats had one ace in their hand. Their challenge was the only note of real tension at this convention, and the army of journalists who were flooding into Atlantic City jumped on it gratefully. Most of them, including Michael, had been in San Francisco the previous month for a Republican convention that had been filled with drama, as the party of Lincoln was hijacked by a candidate and his supporters who reviled the civil rights act and shouted down moderate Republicans when they tried to speak. It was a scary moment for the nation, but it made for great stories.

Here, though, it was Johnson's show from start to finish, and he was doing everything in his power to make it drama-free. The only news to be broken was LBJ's choice for his running mate—and that story was just as likely to come out of Washington as here. So the bored, frustrated press contingent embraced the Freedom Democrats and their fight to oust the white Mississippi regulars as a gift from the gods.

The credentials committee hearing gave them plenty to work with. As Bob Moses had predicted, Hamer's testimony was prominently replayed on the Saturday evening TV newscasts. The story made the front page of the Sunday New York Times and most other newspapers, including Michael's. The committee was due to vote tomorrow on the Mississippi challenge, and Johnson controlled enough votes on it to ensure that the challenge would be rejected. Yet if just 10 percent of its members voted the other way, they would have the right to present a minority report to the full convention, and demand a vote on their report. And the outcome of *that* vote was far from certain.

This meant that for the next 24 hours, a bright, unblinking spotlight would be trained on the committee and its members. It meant that those members, most of them relatively obscure politicians unaccustomed to national attention, would be subject to intense pressure.

Michael came across one of them, a congressman from Chicago whom he knew fairly well, as he walked through the lobby of the Haddon Hall Hotel on Sunday morning. He did not look eager to be interviewed, but Michael managed to corner the wary pol before he could duck into the elevator.

"I'm getting it from both sides, and I'm screwed no matter which way I go," he told Michael, after specifying that they were off the record. "If I vote to seat the regulars, half my district will think I'm a racist. If I vote the other way, I'll never get another bill onto the House calendar, even if it's just to rename a post office. I wish my phone had been out of order the day they called to offer me a seat on this goddamn committee."

Michael knew for a fact that the congressman had actually lobbied quite hard to get himself on the committee back in June, when it looked like a risk-free way to raise his profile. Still, Michael expressed his sympathy for the pol's conundrum, negotiated the wording on a couple of usable quotes, and moved on.

The Freedom Democrats had a few big guns in their ranks. Martin Luther King was in town, and had testified in support of their bid on Saturday. Roy Wilkins, head of the NAACP, and James Foreman of the Congress of Racial Equality were also supportive. A senior Democratic House member from Oregon, Edith Green, agreed to work on their behalf.

Their most effective weapon, however, was the raw emotional power of their challenge, the moral authority derived from the sacrifices and suffering of black life in Mississippi, the stark contrast they created simply by walking into a room. That created great sympathy for them among rank-and-file Democrats, and created a significant problem for Johnson and his allies. It made outright rejection of the Mississippi challenge impossible. As Anna had predicted, some sort of face-saving compromise had to be found. And someone had to be found to sell that compromise—someone who had credibility with the civil rights leadership.

Michael learned the terms of the deal from a thoroughly conflicted aide to Pierre Salinger, now a California senator, on Sunday afternoon.

"The regulars will be seated, but they'll have to pledge to support the ticket," the aide said. "And starting in 1968, any delegation from a state that doesn't allow full voting rights regardless of race won't be recognized."

"What about the Freedom Democrats?"

"We're going to give them two seats. They'll be at-large seats, but they'll be allowed to vote."

"You're serious? This is the great compromise?"

The aide sighed heavily. "I'm not crazy about it, and neither is my boss. But, yes, that's the deal."

"Two seats," Michael said. "And at-large seats at that, not even representing Mississippi. You really expect them to buy this, after everything that's happened down there this year?"

"I don't know. I hope they do, because if they don't, they'll come away empty-handed. That's as far as the president and his people are prepared to go. In fact, he's pretty pissed off things have gone this far. He told my guy that he thinks they're deliberately trying to embarrass him."

"Embarrass him. He's the president of the United States, he's the most powerful man in the world, and he's upset because some people from a state that really is an embarrassment, who've been denied their rights and then jailed and beaten when they protested over it, aren't rolling over and licking his boots, like everyone else at this convention. Poor baby."

That was more than the aide and his uneasy conscience could abide. "Look, Michael, you wanted me to tell you what the state of play was, and I told you. If you don't like it, I'm sorry, but save your sarcasm and your moral posturing for someone else."

"You're right, Phil. *I'm* sorry. This issue hits home to me, for several reasons. One is that I was down in Mississippi this summer, and I saw what life is like there, and what happens when you try to challenge it. But I shouldn't have gone off on you. And I appreciate your help, so thank you."

"You're welcome. And don't worry about it. Conventions always make everyone a little crazy. Even when there's no doubt about the outcome."

Remembering to bite his tongue, Michael was able to confirm the terms of the deal with two other sources. The next piece of the reporting puzzle was to figure out whether it could be sold—and who would do the selling.

From his contacts in the Michigan delegation, Michael learned that Walter Reuther had been recruited for the effort. The leader of the auto workers' union was a powerful figure in the national party. Through his support for the civil rights movement, he had forged personal relationships with most of its leaders. And he owed a political debt to the president, because of his vocal role in the liberals' effort to block Johnson's nomination as Kennedy's running mate four years ago. Some might regard that as ancient history— but not Lyndon Johnson. And Reuther, an eminently pragmatic operator himself, certainly was aware of Johnson's long memory for such slights. All that made him an ideal choice as emissary.

Yet Reuther might not be enough. The Mississippi activists and their SNCC allies didn't care much about political alliances, and they certainly didn't care about Lyndon Johnson's wounded ego. And support for their cause was building. On Sunday afternoon, delegates going to and from their hotels had to walk past a crowd of several hundred movement supporters who were parading on the boardwalk in support of the Mississippi challengers. Democrats in Atlantic City were getting an earful from Democrats back home, people who had heard the testimony at the platform committee hearing and were moved by it. A groundswell was building. It needed to be headed off—and fast.

Enter Hubert Humphrey.

A member of the Minnesota delegation filled Michael in on the strategy for putting the deal across, and Humphrey's role in. Humphrey was leveraging his connections to sell the compromise to movement leaders like King, Foreman and Wilkins—and to SNCC Chairman John Lewis, if possible. And they, in turn, would exert pressure on the Freedom Democrats to accept their two at-large seats, or at least to not force a floor showdown. Humphrey's argument to the movement leaders was that the arrangement was a big step forward, that most of the white Mississippi regulars would refuse to support the ticket and be forced to leave—and that the movement would acquire a powerful and time-tested ally at the heart of the Johnson administration. Putting this compromise over, Humphrey intimated, was LBJ's price for making him vice president.

Michael was quite confident that Humphrey would have no luck with Lewis, who had spent most of the spring and summer in Mississippi. When he hadn't been in the state, he had traveled around the country recruiting volunteers to work on Freedom Summer. That left him feeling a personal responsibility for the murdered activists. When Michael caught up with him on Sunday evening, Lewis confirmed he had refused to endorse the compromise.

"This is ultimately up to the Mississippi people, and I'm not going to pressure them one way or the other," Lewis told him. "But if they ask me for my opinion, I'll tell them I think it's an insulting piece of tokenism."

"Where are the other movement leaders?"

"Roy Wilkins says to take the deal. No surprise there. Jim Foreman hasn't said anything yet. Martin has said quite a bit, but on both sides of the issue. Everybody's getting a lot of pressure to back down. But we have a counterstrategy."

Michael looked up at John, pen poised over his notebook.

"I don't think you'll need to take any notes on this, because it's pretty obvious. We'll hold firm, we'll let the support for us build from the bottom up, and we'll try to force a floor fight on Tuesday. If we can get the full convention to vote, I think we'll win."

That put the onus squarely on the credentials committee. On Monday, Michael's checking showed that enough members would vote with the Freedom Democrats to cross the threshold needed to allow a minority report and bring the issue to the full convention.

Whatever pressure was being exerted had not succeeded—yet. The platform committee chairman, an old party wheelhorse named David Lawrence, was getting nervous. He kicked the issue to a special subcommittee and played for time by postponing the decision until Tuesday.

By Tuesday afternoon, the pressure from above had reduced support for the Freedom Democrats to below the threshold needed for a minority report. The two-seat compromise was rammed through on a voice vote. All but three of the white Mississippi regulars refused to pledge their loyalty to the ticket and went home. That left a sea of empty chairs in the Mississippi delegation when the Tuesday night convention session opened—and created one last opportunity for the Freedom Democrats.

They spent the afternoon collecting floor passes for the session from sympathetic delegates. Once on the floor, they headed straight for the empty Mississippi seats and filled them. When security people arrived to evict them, they locked arms and started to sing.

"We shall not, we shall not be moved. We shall not, we shall not be moved. Just like a tree that's planted by the water, we shall not be moved!"

The civil rights movement was staging a sit-in on national TV in the middle of Lyndon Johnson's coronation. Outside, on the boardwalk, the crowd of demonstrators marching to support the Freedom Democrats had swelled to more than 2,000. Michael filled his notebook with quotes from those inside and outside the hall. Fannie Lou Hamer summed up the group's decision to reject the compromise: "We didn't come all this way for no two seats." John Lewis drew a larger lesson: He told Michael that whatever flickering faith he had in the strategy of building alliances with liberal politicians had been extinguished for good. "They kept telling us the system could be made to work. Well, here we are, at the very center of the system. We played by the rules, we did everything we were supposed to do, and we arrived at the doorstep. And we found the door slammed in our face."

3: All or Nothing

Michael had been too busy during the frantic days and nights of the convention to spend any time with his parents. On Friday morning, he caught up with them over breakfast. Anna and Alan were in a mellow mood, with Johnson duly nominated, Humphrey anointed as his running mate, and the convention gaveled to a close with no further drama. The path looked broad and smooth to a sweeping victory in November that would expand the Democratic majorities in Congress and open up possibilities for new initiatives in both domestic and foreign policy.

Michael was leaving Atlantic City with a sour taste in his mouth. He had witnessed a betrayal, for in his mind there was no other word for what had been done to the Freedom Democrats. It had been done at the behest of a president who was supposed to be an ally of the civil rights cause, but had shown himself willing to sacrifice that cause when doing so was politically expedient. And the betrayal had been carried out, not by conservative southern Democrats, but by some of the party's most prominent liberals. Like John Lewis, Michael saw the moment as one that demanded a rethinking of some fundamental assumptions.

Anna tried to talk him out of his bleak mood. "This may seem hugely important right now, but it'll be overtaken by five more big things before you know it. That's the way the world is today. It moves so fast that it frightens me sometimes. But three months from now, few people will even remember what the fight over the Mississippi delegation was all about."

"I'm willing to bet that the people from Mississippi who came here looking for a little justice will remember," Michael said. "They won't have a choice. They'll remember because they'll still be living in a feudal backwater that denies them their most fundamental rights and then jails and beats them, or worse, when they try to change things. And they'll remember that Lyndon Johnson and his party had a chance to do something about it, and decided it wasn't that important to them."

"Listen, for the last time, your friends were offered a perfectly reasonable compromise," Alan shot back. "It moves the ball forward in ways that will affect how this party and its conventions operate for years to come. And they decided that preserving their precious purity was more important to them. They're the ones who had a chance to do something meaningful and turned it down. They could have made a lot of friends here this week, and instead they made a lot of enemies."

Anna jumped in. "As for your larger point, about this being such a seminal moment that requires rethinking your whole approach to politics—well, rethink all you want, but understand that at some point you have to decide whether you want to stay in the wilderness and remain unsullied but impotent, or come inside and actually get something done. I spent a long time on one side of that line, and I've never regretted crossing over to the other side."

Michael looked across the table at his parents with growing frustration.

"You just don't understand, do you? People in Mississippi don't care about what rules the national party will operate under four years from now. That's like the far side of the moon to them. What they do care about is whether they're ever going to get the right to vote, which would begin to give them some power over their lives, and over the local officials who ignore or mistreat them now. They care about building a real movement, one that isn't dependent on the whims of some power broker because it's put down real roots among people in local communities and can deliver some real victories for those people. Don't take my word for it. Talk to them yourself.

"And for Lyndon, it turns out that it's all about power, too— about demonstrating his power to dictate to other people, to make them dance to his tune, and to show everyone that he could make them do it.

"Maybe you're right that he's on his way to a landslide that will usher in the second coming of the New Deal. Maybe you're right that people in Washington will soon forget all about the Freedom Democrats and the way they were run over this week. But I think forgetting about that would be a serious mistake, because Lyndon Johnson has just shown us something about himself, and about the way he operates, and it's rather ugly. And a lot of other people have shown us something about themselves, too."

Anna fell silent, suddenly filled with a deep sadness. She thought about how this conversation would have played with her younger self—the young woman who had told a nominally liberal congressman to his face that he was unfit for office because he lacked the courage to stand up to the isolationists and anti-Semites in his own district. Like Michael now, Anna in her youth had felt nothing but disdain for the trimmers, the timid people who split the difference, who settled for what was offered and maybe a few morsels more. That way of operating did not lend itself to dramatic narratives or heroic codas. But it might just be the only way to—what was Alan's phrase? To move the ball forward, to move it at all, in a country where most people want heroism confined to movie screens and real life to be reassuringly dull. Take your shot when you see an opening, push as hard as you can—but be prepared to take the deal in the end.

She knew better than to expect Michael to accept that perspective, or even understand it. Deep inside, she wouldn't have wanted him to. She would have been disappointed in him if he had. What did that make her? Two-faced? Schizophrenic? No, just older and wiser—as boring and pedestrian as that phrase might be.

Well, older, certainly. Was she kidding herself about the wiser part? That wasn't out of the question. Yet she had lived by this creed for a long time now. Whether it was wisdom or folly, riches or fool's gold, she was bound to it. Just as she was bound to face her son's scorn.

Chapter Ten
– Business As Usual –
March 1965

1: Selma

The reasons Michael might find himself in a house of worship could be counted on the fingers of one hand. A wedding. A funeral. His volunteer work for an activist church in Brooklyn. And finally— most likely these days—the movement.

So he was not surprised when a journey that started with a phone call from John Lewis led him to a church in Selma, a middling Alabama city 50 miles west of the state capital of Montgomery. Brown's Chapel was a local center of the movement, and today it was the jumping-off point for what Lewis and his fellow activists hoped would be the next big thing.

"We're going to march from Selma to Montgomery to protest the fact that we still can't vote in Alabama, or almost anywhere in the South," Lewis told Michael. "At least, that's what we're going to try to do. They got a county sheriff here name of Jim Clark who reminds me of Bull Connor, and he seems to be calling the shots. If you can get down here on Sunday, it could be quite a story, one way or the other."

Michael had known John since their paths first crossed during the freedom rides four years ago, and the SNCC chairman had never misled him by hyping an action. Michael had great respect for Lewis' personal integrity, as well as his dedication and courage. And he was fully aware that, with racial segregation in public facilities now illegal as a result of the civil rights law enacted last year, the denial of black voting rights was the last legal bastion for southern white supremacy.

So Michael found himself at Brown's Chapel on a cloudy morning, part of a sizable knot of journalists. John Lewis had made quite a few phone calls, it seemed. Whatever was about to happen, it was going to be well covered.

Michael's preliminary reporting about the situation had turned up more than enough to convince him and his editors that the story would not be a dud, because Selma was seething. The campaign here had been launched two months ago by Martin Luther King's organization, the Southern Christian Leadership Conference, along with SNCC, in an effort to follow up on last year's Mississippi campaign and make voting rights a top-tier national issue. They organized large-scale attempts by black residents to register to vote at the county courthouse, backed up by marches and rallies. The would-be voters were rejected with the calculated humiliations that southern racists reserved for black people who didn't "know their place": so-called literacy tests filled with trick questions that were impossible to answer correctly. The marches and rallies were met with beatings and arrests by Sheriff Clark's deputies and Governor George Wallace's state troopers.

The official violence reached a peak when a young demonstrator, Jimmie Lee Jackson, was shot to death by an officer. With emotions running high in the wake of this killing, SCLC conceived the idea of a march to Montgomery to channel the community's anger into a productive—and peaceful—effort.

The church door opened, and Lewis and Hosea Williams of the SCLC led the marchers out, clapping and singing.

"We shall overcome, we shall overcome, we shall overcome someday. Oh, deep in my heart, I do believe, that we shall overcome someday."

Michael's first impression was that the turnout was disappointingly small. The authorities' threats had worked, he thought. Wallace had ordered his state troopers out in force to back up his threat to shut down the march. In case they needed help, Clark had put out a call for every white adult man in the county to show up at the courthouse and be deputized into a posse.

That meant the 500 or so marchers were nearly outnumbered when they reached the troopers and deputies waiting at the far end of the Edmund Pettis Bridge, which took Highway 80 across the Alabama River on its way to Montgomery. To Michael's eye, this had the look of an ambush, and the nervous expressions on the faces of the marchers reinforced his impression.

Michael moved ahead and joined a clutch of reporters, photographers, and TV cameramen on the other side of the bridge. Cameras rolled and shutters clicked as the marchers crested the bridge and descended toward the troopers.

"Ain't gonna let nobody turn me round, turn me round, turn me round. I gotta keep on a-walkin', keep on a-talkin', marching on to freedom land."

The marchers paused and fell silent as they neared the skirmish line of troopers, and for a few moments there was a tense, hushed standoff. As Michael watched the wordless test of wills, he found himself holding his breath.

The silence was broken by a trooper with a bullhorn. "It would be detrimental to your safety to continue this march," he said. "I'm telling you that this is an unlawful assembly. You are ordered to disperse. This march will not continue."

As he was speaking, the other troopers began donning gas masks. At a command, they advanced on the motionless marchers, slowly at first, then at a dead run. They barreled into Lewis and Williams and shoved them hard with their truncheons. The two men toppled, knocking over the marchers crowded in behind them, creating a domino effect. Tear gas canisters arced through the air, landing on the bridge and spewing their noxious contents.

In moments, the scene dissolved into chaos. The troopers clubbed and trampled marchers as they forced them back up the bridge, administering systematic beatings to those who lost their footing, men and women alike. In the troopers' wake came Clark's posse, mounted on horseback, riding through the marchers like Cossacks straight out of Tsarist Russia. Lewis was struck down by a blow to the head and then clubbed repeatedly. A local activist who had helped organize the march, 53-year-old Amelia Boynton, was knocked to the ground by a mounted officer and beaten into unconsciousness.

Cries of pain and panic filled the air. A dense cloud of tear gas shrouded the foot of the bridge. Through the choking haze, Michael could see marchers carrying the injured as they fell back, struggling to support the dazed and bloodied people up the steep slope of the span.

The one-sided confrontation was over in less than half an hour, but its reverberations lasted for many days. Sunday tends to be the lightest day of the week for news, and an ancient journalistic adage warns about the perils of screwing up on a slow news day. The sheriff and the governor had done exactly that.

Michael's story about the rout of the marchers claimed most of his paper's front page the next day, alongside an AP photo of Lewis on his knees with a trooper standing over him, poised for another swing. A photo of Boynton lying helpless on the bridge ran on an inside page. Newspapers across the country played Selma as front-page news. The graphic film footage led the evening TV newscasts. One network interrupted its prime-time movie-of-the-week presentation to show the clip. The film was "Judgment at Nuremberg," a drama about a Nazi war crimes trial.

Like Bull Connor in Birmingham two years earlier, Clark and Wallace had unwittingly done the movement an enormous favor. The violence against the marchers on what quickly became known as Bloody Sunday became a huge international news story, and the reaction was immediate and widespread. Activists and sympathetic clergy began pouring into Selma from across the country. Movement leaders announced plans for another march to Montgomery, this one far larger. Support demonstrations erupted throughout the nation, demanding that the federal government intervene to protect the marchers and that the Johnson administration submit legislation to ensure voting rights.

Before Bloody Sunday, the president had not been happy about the movement's decision to force a confrontation over voting rights. He wanted to use the political capital he had gained from his landslide victory over Goldwater to enact his ambitious legislative agenda of economic and social programs. He believed the political marketplace's appetite for civil rights reforms had been sated by last year's law, and that the issue of voting rights was best left for later.

He was not alone. Anna expressed the same view in a phone conversation with Michael just before he left for Selma. "This isn't a matter of principle, it's a matter of timing," she told him. It was a moment for passing big, sweeping programs, and voting rights activists would have to wait their turn. "Just like the Freedom Democrats," he replied. "I believe they're still waiting."

Yet Johnson also possessed finely tuned political instincts, and a keen sense for recognizing a moment of opportunity. Now, in the growing public furor over what happened in Selma, he saw just such a moment, and he decided to seize it.

Eight days after the confrontation on the bridge, Michael climbed into the press gallery of the House chamber in Washington and watched the president throw the full weight of the federal government behind the civil rights movement. He announced the introduction of legislation that would take the authority for voter registration away from southern officials and give it to special federal examiners, who would be instructed to register every qualified voter regardless of race. He did it in a prime-time speech delivered to a joint session of Congress and a national television audience. And he did it with words that civil rights activists never imagined would ever be spoken by a president.

"At times, history and fate meet at a single time in a single place to shape a turning point in man's unending search for freedom,"

Johnson said. "So it was at Lexington and Concord. So it was a century ago at Appomattox. So it was last week in Selma, Alabama.

"What happened in Selma is part of a far larger movement which reaches into every section and state of America. It is the effort of American Negroes to secure for themselves the full blessings of American life. Their cause must be our cause, too. Because it is not just Negroes, but really it is all of us, who must overcome the crippling legacy of bigotry and injustice.

"And we *shall* overcome."

When Michael got off deadline and came home, long after midnight, Riva, who had come down from New York to be with him, was still awake. She poured him a glass of wine and leaned against his shoulder.

"I'm still a little dazed. I half-expected Joan Baez to pop out from behind the dais and start humming freedom songs while he was speaking," she said.

"She would have been redundant. He stole the movement's favorite anthem for his biggest applause line. And he knew exactly what he was doing and how it would come off."

"The question is, can we believe the words?"

"I think the answer is yes," Michael said. "He's got nowhere else to go now. He's lost white southerners, at least the ones who can't or won't evolve on race, no matter what he does. And most of the rest of the country is with him, and us, on this. The bigots like Wallace have made sure of that."

"That's all political tactics, and that's all fine," Riva said. "But we both know we're running out of the big symbolic issues like segregation and voting rights, issues that are focused on the South, issues that allow most northern whites to hold on to the illusion that racism is just a southern problem. The deeper issues affect the entire country, and they're economic and social."

"I think Johnson already recognizes that," Michael said. "That's what his war-on-poverty programs are designed to address."

"Yes. So here's two more questions," Riva said. "Will he still have most of the country behind him if he really tackles those problems? And will he have the stomach for the fight if the going gets tough? White people, North and South, benefit from racism in ways that most have never thought about. It's just part of the natural order of things to them. When someone comes along and tells them different, they may not be quite so willing to sing *We Shall Overcome*."

2: Driving While Black

Shortly after Johnson's speech, the Justice Department got a court injunction ordering Alabama officials to allow the reprise of the Selma-to-Montgomery march. Johnson put the state's National Guard under federal command and ordered it to protect the marchers. When they stepped off again from Brown's Chapel, the core group of 500 that marched on Bloody Sunday had swelled to 8,000. Martin Luther King was in the vanguard. Lewis, shaking off the effects of his beating, joined him in the front row. Hollywood celebrities rubbed elbows with local activists and clergy from around the country. The marchers made their way onto Highway 80 and across the now-memorable bridge, walking behind American and United Nations flags under a protective canopy of military helicopters.

Four days later, they paraded into the square in front of the state Capitol, past the Dexter Avenue Baptist Church where King first made his mark a decade earlier as leader of the Montgomery bus boycott. Wallace fled the Capitol to avoid meeting the march leaders. More than 25,000 people, black and white, filled the square to hear King hit new heights of oratorical power.

"How long will justice be crucified? How long? Not long. Because no lie can live forever. How long? Not long. Because you shall reap what you sow. How long? Not long. Because the arc of the moral universe is long, but it bends toward justice."

The press contingent on hand for the march was big enough to cover a national political convention. Michael was among them, and Riva had planned to travel with him to join the march. But the night before they were to leave, the phone in their apartment rang.

Riva answered, and mostly listened during the call, rubbing her temple as if her head suddenly ached. When she put down the receiver, her jaw was clenched and her cheeks were tear-stained.

"That was my mother. Tommy's in the hospital. He got into some kind of trouble with the police. A cop beat him up. Beat him so badly that he's got a fractured skull, a concussion and a broken cheekbone."

"My god, that's terrible. What happened?"

"She didn't have a lot of details. It sounds like Tommy and some of his friends were driving out to Jones Beach to meet some other friends, and got pulled over on the parkway. His friends are in jail. He's in Long Island Jewish. He was in the intensive care unit at first, because he was unconscious when they brought him in, but they've moved him to a ward. I guess that's good news, right?"

Riva slept very little that night. Michael heard her pacing in the living room, alternately crying quietly and swearing softly to herself. Tommy was 20, over 6 feet tall and a muscular 180 pounds, but to Riva he was her little brother and she was fiercely protective of him.

They changed to a later flight and headed to the hospital in the morning. Sam and Dorie were there, sitting next to Tommy's bed. He was asleep, his skull swathed in bandages and more gauze wrapped diagonally across the left side of his face. Sam was holding his hand.

"He's been awake a little this morning," Dorie said. "The doctor said that was good. But he's going to be here for several days, they say, and he may need physical therapy after that."

"Do you know any more about what happened?" Riva asked.

"I talked to one of the kids in the car," Sam said. "Tommy wasn't even driving. The kid swears they weren't speeding, weren't doing anything wrong. These cops pulled them over for no reason. When the cops walked up to their car, Tommy rolled down the window and asked why they pulled them over. Not angry, the kid said, not sassy, just asking.

"The cop told him to get out of the car. When he did, the cop told him he was a smart-mouthed punk and he should keep his black mouth shut. Tommy told him he had no cause to talk to him that way. The cop hit him in the face with his club and then cracked him on the head."

"The other three boys in the car all got hauled in for, get this, resisting arrest," Dorie said. "Once Michael's out of the hospital, he'll have to appear on the same charge. For nothing. For absolutely nothing. For driving out to the beach, because it was a warm day."

"For being black and driving out to the beach," Riva said.

There was a controlled rage in their voices that Michael had never heard in them before. He understood its source completely; one glance at the battered young man in the bed was enough to make it clear. At the same time, it rocked him, and it frightened him a little. In Michael's life, injustice was something that he cared about, wrote about, fought against, but it was something that happened to other people, something he experienced at a distance. For Riva and her family, it was very personal. And he realized, as he should have known already, that this was not a new experience for them.

Riva said little on the trip back to the city. When they got home, she told Michael to go to Alabama without her. "My family's going to need me," she said. "And I have to tell you, the way I feel right now, I have no interest in taking part in some great festival of interracial harmony."

Michael nodded, but his face must have betrayed his inner unease.

"I'm glad the march is going to happen," Riva said, trying to explain. "I'm glad the government finally got off its ass and sent troops to protect the marchers. I'm glad there's going to be a voting rights bill. But when it's over, America—I mean white America—is going to pat itself on the back for all the wonderful progress it's making and then go back to business as usual. And we've just had a little taste of what business as usual really is."

3: On the Fence

Even before Selma intervened to draw his attention, Lyndon Johnson was wrestling with the deteriorating situation in Vietnam. He had defused it as a campaign issue last year by manufacturing the naval incident in the Gulf of Tonkin and using it as a pretext to bomb North Vietnamese military installations. That one-off action had been enough to silence the Republicans for the moment. It also gave him an excuse to ask Congress for the open-ended resolution allowing military force in the future. Johnson coupled this request with a repetition of his standard line that he would not send Americans to do a job that Asians needed to do, and that was enough to quiet the skeptics. The resolution passed in the Senate with only two dissenting votes. In November, Vietnam was a non-issue.

Yet if the airstrikes pacified the political battlefield, they had the opposite effect on the real one. North Vietnam's leaders responded by beefing up their forces. They began engaging South Vietnamese units in set-piece battles for the first time and won most of them.

To most Americans, Vietnam was still an obscure country that couldn't be located on a map. To anyone paying attention, however, it was a mess and getting worse, in both military and political terms. As the South Vietnamese army's battlefield performance worsened, the infighting in Saigon intensified; the generals seemed far more interested in jousting with each other for political advantage than in taking on the enemy in the field. Johnson had postponed the hard decisions until after the election, but now the time for evasion and improvisation was over.

The president began reaching out with growing urgency to people he trusted, to give him advice and to serve as sounding boards for his own tortured musings. His fundamental dilemma had not changed since Alan first counseled him at the dawn of his presidency. He feared that turning Vietnam into an American war would undermine his great domestic reforms, but he feared even more the prospect of becoming the president who lost Vietnam to the communists.

On a gray and chilly winter morning, just days after the pomp and pageantry of Johnson's inauguration, Alan was closeted in the Oval Office with the president, Walt Rostow and Mac Bundy. Rostow, a senior State Department official, was known to be an unrelenting hawk on Vietnam who was urging a massive escalation of U.S. involvement. Bundy, still serving as national security adviser for Johnson as he had for Kennedy, had yet to weigh in, Alan's sources told him.

That made Bundy a key figure in the administration's deliberations. And it meant that Alan was speaking to him, as much as to the president, although he had to mask that reality carefully to avoid offending Johnson's capacious vanity.

"Mr. President, I believe it all boils down to three options. I know that's the classic ploy of the buck-passing bureaucrat, but in this case, it has the virtue of being true."

"Okay, Alan, let me hear them."

The first option, Alan said, would be to announce a withdrawal of U.S. forces, let the South Vietnamese army fight on alone, and call for talks on the country's political future. It was a poor option, he said, because the North Vietnamese believed they were winning and thus had no incentive to engage in meaningful negotiations. And given the current military balance, even if there were to be a political settlement now, it would eventually result in a North Vietnamese takeover of the South.

"You make option one sound so attractive," Rostow said with a tight smile.

Alan ignored the comment and plowed ahead. The second option, he said, was to Americanize the war immediately. That held the promise of transforming the military situation, and might shock the communists in the North into agreeing to peace talks—perhaps quite quickly.

"That's the first problem with this option: a premature peace deal, before our intervention has really changed things on the ground," Alan said. "But the larger problem is that we haven't prepared the American public for a war effort, and that would be fatal."

"Why do I sense that we're about to hear your preferred solution?" Rostow said.

Again, Alan resisted taking the bait, and outlined his third option: a gradual move toward increased U.S. involvement, making it clear to the communists that they would pay an ever-greater price for their actions, but also making it clear at every step that they had an alternative. Begin with a sustained bombing campaign against targets in the North as well as the South, Alan said, and follow it with a buildup of American ground forces. Be prepared to send more troops if needed—and make the case to the country that keeping South Vietnam out of communist hands was worth the sacrifices it would entail.

"As my friend Walt has so cleverly divined, it's the third option that I would urge you to adopt," Alan said. "We need to squeeze the North Vietnamese, slowly but ever more firmly, until they realize they can't win. Then we can get them to the table to discuss a real peace deal, one that preserves South Vietnam's independence.

"But I can't stress enough to you the importance of talking straight to the American people and getting them behind this policy, because without that we can't possibly succeed. I was in government when Harry Truman tried to wage a war in Asia without sufficient domestic political support. It undermined the war effort, and it destroyed his presidency."

Despite his sarcastic interjections, Rostow had nodded several times during Alan's presentation of his third option. Alan suspected his assent was tactical, that he found Alan's recommendations insufficiently aggressive but felt they would inevitably lead to stronger measures. Johnson listened intently, fidgeting a little but keeping his intense brown eyes focused on Alan. Mac was inscrutable, silent and motionless.

When Alan finished, it was Bundy who spoke first. "I'm going to be going out there in a few days for a first-hand look," he said. "Perhaps I'll gain some insights as to why there's such a gap between the optimism of our people in Saigon and the course of events in the field. That will help me advise the president on the decisions that, I think we all agree, can't be postponed any longer."

Johnson shifted in his chair, leaned back and looked off into space for a moment.

"I can't believe I'm sitting here between the flags, the leader of the free world, wracking my brains about how to handle a raggedy-ass fourth-rate country," he said at last. "But here I am. And we've got to get this right. Because one thing I do believe: If we lose there, those Republicans will ram Vietnam up *my* ass and keep it there, and I'll never be able to accomplish another thing. I remember Harry Truman, too. He was one hell of a president, had plenty of balls, achieved a lot of things. But once China went to the Reds, they hung it around his neck and never let him forget it."

Nothing's changed, Alan thought. With him, it's still about fear, the raw fear of the domestic political fallout. Well, that's not the worst thing in the world if it steers him in the right direction.

And he was struck by something else, by a dog that didn't bark. Alan had anticipated that Johnson and his aides would fire questions at him about his recommendations: how practical they were, how the enemy might respond, how that might shape future American decisions. This was a standard part of such policy discussions—but not this one. Not one question. He realized he was talking to people who had already made a decision, and were coming to him not for advice but for validation. After a flash of irritation, he decided he could live with that, too. The important thing was to get Johnson headed down the right road, regardless of how he got there.

4: Off the Fence

A few days later, Mac Bundy left for Vietnam. He was barely in-country when the Viet Cong offered their welcome: an attack on a U.S. air installation in Pleiku, in the central highlands, that killed eight Americans and wounded 60 others. The U.S. launched a retaliatory air strike on the North; the insurgents responded to that move with an attack on another American installation; Washington ordered a second air strike. The ride up the escalator had begun.

A week after the Pleiku attack, with Mac back in Washington and recommending military action, Johnson jumped off the fence. He approved a sustained bombing campaign against targets in the southern part of North Vietnam, a plan that carried the evocative name of Rolling Thunder. It was supposed to be temporary, and it was supposed to be an alternative to committing ground forces. Yet the president also agreed to send a contingent of Marines, ostensibly to provide security for the airfields involved in the bombing campaign.

This took place while most of the country was preoccupied with the drama playing out in Alabama and its reverberations in Washington. But Anna was paying attention, fully aware that her husband was in the middle of these events, and they filled her with unease. She was not about to criticize a president who was delivering on so many long-sought domestic priorities. Yet when she thought about the course he had adopted on Vietnam, she foresaw mostly trouble ahead.

"How can you be so certain that this will work?" she asked Alan one night as they watched Johnson on the evening news. "These people have been fighting one foreign power after another since the early days of World War II. Why will they fold at the first sign of American firepower?"

"Because they're not fools," Alan replied. "They may not give in immediately. We may have to apply greater degrees of pressure. But sooner or later, the reality will sink in that they can't do to us what they did to the French."

"Sooner or later. Those words don't comfort me. It sounds like what you're talking about is a recipe for ever-increasing commitment, with no clear end in sight. With every step, it'll be harder to turn back. And, speaking of sooner or later, this will cost money, and political capital, and eventually it's got to undermine his domestic programs."

"You know what the president calls people who talk like that?" Alan retorted. "Nervous Nellies. Like a bunch of old women who sit around wringing their hands and worrying instead of acting decisively."

"I think that's an insulting term, one that reeks of misogyny. I'm rather appalled that my husband would quote it approvingly. If you ask me, the president and the men around him could do a lot worse than listen to what us Nervous Nellies have to say."

When Anna canvassed her liberal friends, however, she found that most were either unconcerned, or unwilling to pay much attention to Vietnam. And even the few who shared her apprehensions were feeling pressure to stay silent. They, like her, were reluctant to cross a president who was championing their agenda. In addition, their political antennae were up, and they found the experience of their old friend Hubert Humphrey highly instructive. The vice president had spoken forcefully in a White House strategy meeting right after the Pleiku attack against a retaliatory strike. It was the last meeting about Vietnam he was invited to attend.

If Anna was conflicted, Michael was incredulous. He was well-sourced at the White House and on the Hill, and those sources told him that Rolling Thunder and the Marines were just the start. No formal decisions had been made, but if Hanoi did not buckle quickly, Johnson was prepared to keep bombing and send more troops, this time heavily equipped Army units. The Pentagon had already drawn up detailed plans for these moves, and a few select, reliable lawmakers were being briefed by White House aides. This planning directly contradicted one of the stated strategic premises of Rolling Thunder, which was ostensibly to *avoid* the need to send more U.S. forces.

"I can't believe he's willing to stake so much on such a flimsy reed," Michael said one night as he ate dinner with his parents. "It's not only that the Saigon government and its army are so undependable. He's putting his entire domestic program at risk for something that's just not that important. Even if you're a dedicated Cold Warrior, like you, dad, you must realize that this isn't where it's going to be won or lost."

Alan dismissed that argument as short-sighted. No battlegrounds were unimportant, he said. The nuclear stalemate with the Soviets had spawned a series of proxy wars: Berlin, Cuba, now Vietnam. A loss anywhere was unacceptable, because the first defeat would be the last.

"Berlin is at the heart of Europe," Michael countered. "Cuba is on our doorstep. Vietnam is 10,000 miles away, and it isn't even central in Asian terms, it's on the periphery even there. The only people who really care about Vietnam are the people who live there—which is another reason this is so misbegotten. The North Vietnamese care about it a lot more than we do, and that will give them staying power."

"That cuts both ways, son. It means the South Vietnamese care, too."

"Well, I haven't seen any great evidence of that," Michael said. "And while we're on the subject of the Vietnamese, what do you think happens to the people on the business end of all the ordnance we're dropping? I mean the civilians, the people who live in those villages and towns. We both know that you can't bomb from 30,000 feet and expect precision. We're probably killing and wounding a lot of ordinary people, and their livestock, and destroying their crops in the bargain. You expect them to love us for it?"

"Now you're turning a geopolitical argument into a moral one," Alan said. "You have a habit of doing that. Get your story straight. Pick your ground and stay on it."

"They're one and the same," Michael shot back. "If we bomb, we kill Vietnamese, and that's ugly and unnecessary and wrong. And when we kill Vietnamese, we alienate the very people we're supposed to be fighting for."

"It won't matter in the end," Alan retorted. "We have the firepower, and we'll use it. If it costs some lives to turn back the communists, it's worth it. We killed a lot of German civilians with our bombing, but it was a price worth paying to destroy the Nazis."

"Oh my god, dad, think about what you're saying for just a moment. The German people voted for Hitler and cheered him on as long as he was winning. And Germany was a major power, a big industrial nation that conquered most of Europe and wanted more. The Vietnamese just want to be left alone to farm their crops and run their own affairs, without any more Western powers dictating to them."

"Well, they're going to be disappointed. Whether they like it or not, their country is a front in a global conflict. We stopped the communists in Europe, we stopped them in Korea, and we're going to do it in Vietnam. If you don't or can't understand why that's important, you're what Lenin called a useful idiot."

"Here we go again, this manic, unthinking anti-communism of yours! This isn't Europe, and it isn't 1948. Surely you've noticed that the communist world isn't monolithic anymore. The Soviets and the Chinese distrust each other as much as they distrust us. And Ho Chi Minh and his people are nationalists first and foremost. This whole thing is twisted and immoral. And if you're part of it, so are you."

Anna listened to this increasingly heated argument between two people she deeply loved with profound disquiet. Her husband and her son were leaning across the dining room table, voices raised and faces reddened, and she felt powerless to ease their anger. She had lived her whole life by the power of words, but she had no idea what words of hers could calm the passions that this embryonic war had unleashed in her family.

As angry as he was, Michael was glad that Riva wasn't there for this argument, because her presence would have made it even more acrimonious. She shared Michael's views about Vietnam, but she saw something else, something worse. She saw Vietnam as a white man's war against a non-white nation, a neocolonial power trying to subjugate a small country that had only recently severed the leash of Western rule. She had read Frantz Fanon, the theorist of anticolonial revolt, and saw in Vietnam's peasants and insurgents a clear Asian analogue to Fanon's North African wretched of the earth.

Besides Fanon, Riva was reading Malcolm X, the onetime Nation of Islam leader who had split from that group and then was assassinated while giving a speech in Harlem. Before he died, Malcolm had renounced the Nation of Islam precept that all whites were inevitably "devils." But he remained absolutely clear on one point: black people had to take command of their own lives and their own organizations, and stop relying on the benevolence of white people, even those with the best of intentions. In Riva's current mood, these arguments resonated with great power.

5: Cry of Pain

Riva was spending time with her brother, and was increasingly worried about him. He recovered from most of his physical injuries more rapidly than predicted. However, he complained of frequent, intense headaches, which his doctors ascribed to the aftereffects of his concussion. And the changes in his personality were unmistakable. Tommy had been naturally upbeat, energetic, and outgoing, but now he was often lethargic and moody. He had been nearing the end of his first year at Hofstra. His grades were solid, and he thought he stood a decent chance of being the starting quarterback in the fall. Now, he showed no interest in either school or football, and one day in June, he abruptly announced that he was dropping out. He spent many days in his room alone.

Riva's anger over what had happened to Tommy burned like a slow-acting fuse. It was only increased by the aftermath. The Nassau County authorities were embarrassed by the affair, especially after a reporter for Newsday, an old Columbia classmate of Michael's, had taken an interest—but not so embarrassed as to discipline the cops involved in any way. They quietly dropped the charges against Tommy and his friends and hoped the whole incident would be forgotten. Riva wanted to contact a lawyer about a civil suit. Tommy showed no more interest in that than in anything else.

Sam and Dorie counseled patience, expressing hope that their son would gradually regain his bearings. Riva had her eye on another looming problem.

The U.S. bombing campaign failed to bring the North Vietnamese to heel, and South Vietnam's fighting performance showed no improvement. An ever-wider stream of U.S. Army units flowed into Vietnam through the spring and summer, and in July, Johnson announced a major jump, another 50,000 troops. As Michael reported this story, he picked up indications at the Pentagon that the buildup would require a significant increase in the monthly draft calls.

For the Daniels family, this was no abstract matter. Tommy had gotten a student draft deferment when he entered Hofstra. If he followed through on his intention to drop out, he would lose the deferment and risk being swept up in the rising demand for more draftees.

"He stands a good chance of flunking the physical," Michael told Riva as they discussed the problem. "He's still recovering from a skull fracture and a concussion, and we can get a doctor to certify the personality changes they've caused. I think the Army might not want him."

"And I think that's wishful thinking," Riva said. "Maybe that would work for a middle-class white kid who'd lost his deferment. But you can bet that the draft quotas are going to be a lot higher in black neighborhoods, and they're going to be a lot less picky about finding ways to fill them."

Michael started to object, then thought better of it. He thought the relentless pressure for more manpower would make the Army an equal-opportunity conscripter, taking anyone it could get regardless of race. Yet he realized it would not matter much either way for Tommy. If he left school, he would be vulnerable.

Riva and Michael had been a couple for almost four years. They still cared deeply about each other, enjoyed spending time together, both alone and with their friends, and shared a vibrant sexual relationship. Still, the inevitable strains of marriage were there, and they were aware of them, even if they avoided confronting them. The blossoming of Michael's professional career meant he spent a great deal of time away, either in Washington or on the road, and often when he was home his evenings were consumed by work. When Riva was working, she also was often preoccupied. But her acting career seemed to have stalled, and she began to think that a black performer, especially a black woman, faced invisible but unbreachable limitations. It added another layer of anxiety as she tried to gain some perspective on her life.

One big question growing in her mind was whether the civil rights movement's model of integration achieved through biracial action was still valid. She realized that this held deep implications for her own life, a life constructed on the premise that she could successfully navigate an interracial world—and that there would be an interracial world to navigate.

She still had several contacts in SNCC, and she knew that some of its leaders, like Stokely Carmichael, were arguing that it was time for white activists to take a subordinate role in the movement—or leave altogether and work separately to combat whites' racism. As Riva had foreseen, the attainment of the movement's immediate goals was creating stress fractures, within it and in society at large, that would only widen over time. Even language became a point of division. A growing number of activists were rejecting the term Negro, adopting Malcolm's argument that it was a slave label, and insisting on black as the appropriate description.

These debates became far less abstract in August, when Watts, a black neighborhood in south-central Los Angeles, exploded in six days of violence. The match that lit the fuse was a scuffle between a black motorist and some cops arresting him for a traffic violation. Crowds gathered and pelted police with rocks and bottles. The community's simmering resentments over police brutality and price-gouging merchants boiled over in an epic eruption. White-owned businesses were looted and burned in an ever-widening arc. More than 4,000 National Guard soldiers and 16,000 police officers were deployed against the thousands of people in the streets, many of them chanting an impromptu slogan: "Burn, baby, burn." The final tally: 34 dead, more than 3,000 arrested, $40 million in property damage.

Almost as soon as the flames died down, the debate over the causes and meaning of the violence began. Once again, language became contentious; was Watts a "riot" or a "rebellion"? One term connoted a mindless, criminal mob, the other a purposeful, legitimate response to oppression. Martin Luther King tried to bridge the gap, coupling a rejection of violence with a plea for understanding the real and deep grievances that sparked it.

Many whites were not listening. The state's governor, Pat Brown—a Democrat who had been elected with the help of black voters—said the violence had been perpetrated by "guerrillas" and "gangsters." L.A. police chief William Parker, long resented by black residents, went Brown one better, comparing the rioters to Viet Cong insurgents. He intended the comment as an insult, but quite a few black people, both leaders and everyday citizens, thought

Parker had unintentionally gotten it right for once. Watts truly was an insurgency, and more were coming.

Watts became the next flash point for Michael's family, and this time, Riva was on hand for the fireworks. The family had gathered at its summer home on the Delaware shore for Labor Day, but the events of the day pressed in relentlessly, blocking out the ocean breezes and lapping waves.

"How's Lyndon Johnson supposed to get his legislative agenda passed when the people he's trying to help are tearing up their own neighborhoods and screaming 'get whitey' on national TV?" Alan said. "He's the best friend the civil rights movement has ever had, and he's battling some very tough opposition in Congress to get the anti-poverty programs funded properly."

"You mean when he's not sending more soldiers to Southeast Asia to bomb and bully the Vietnamese into line?" Michael retorted.

"These things are not mutually exclusive," Anna said. "To use one of the president's more colorful metaphors—a cleaned-up version of it, anyway—we can walk and chew gum at the same time."

"We can't, ultimately," Michael shot back. "We won't have the money, and he won't have the political capital. He's going to have to choose between a war on poverty or a war in Vietnam, and I think it's clear what his choice will be. My sources say he's already signaling to the Hill that he'll trim domestic spending if he has to, in order to accommodate the military buildup."

"Your sources are all wet," Alan said. "You need to find some new ones, people who actually know what's going on."

Michael's face flushed bright red. A political argument was one thing. Denigrating his reporting was quite another. Before he could return fire, his wife spoke.

"The programs you're so concerned about are Band-Aids, nothing more," she said, her voice quiet at first but soon rising in frustration. "Those people in Watts—and a lot of other black neighborhoods—don't care about Johnson's exalted war on poverty, because they know it won't change anything. They care about bad housing and storekeepers who cheat them. They care about cops who crack them over the head for looking at them crossways. I can tell you something about that. And they care about being stuck in dead-end jobs that don't pay enough to live on, even when they can find them.

"What happened in Watts was a cry of pain from people who've been ignored and abused for a long time, and then on top of it are told that things are changing for the better when they know different. And you're going to be hearing a lot more cries of pain like that, because a lot of black people in a lot of places are feeling that same pain."

As Riva spoke, Michael turned and looked at her in surprise. It was the first time he could recall that she had really taken on his parents in a political argument. "Well, now you're truly a member of the family," he said. "We don't think it's a successful gathering unless we're tearing into each other about politics."

Riva's expression softened ever so slightly, and she reached out to touch Michael's hand. She understood why he would want to defuse the situation, because it was so obviously awkward. Anna's body language radiated regret and chagrin. Alan's face was tight with anger, but he held his tongue, unwilling to tell her out loud that she did not know what was best for her own people, even though he so obviously thought that was the case.

The question is, Riva thought, does my husband think so, too? She thought the answer was no. She would find out for certain when they were alone. But the fact that she even had to ask herself the question, that she didn't instinctively know the answer, bothered her. It bothered her a great deal.

Chapter Eleven
–In–Country–
September 1966

1: Outbound

When the Daniels and McMaster families gathered, it was usually a happy moment, a celebration of a holiday or anniversary. Today, there was no joy in the occasion. They were together at the Daniels house in Queens for a double farewell, to see their sons off on long, perilous voyages. Both Michael and Tommy were about to leave for Vietnam.

Their moods could not have been more different. Michael was on his way voluntarily, even enthusiastically. He had lobbied his editors for weeks to land the assignment. His paper had been relying on wire services and the occasional stringer to cover the steadily escalating conflict. Now, with hundreds of thousands of American forces in-country and no end in sight, Jack Rothstein agreed to send Michael for up to three months, and with a wide remit. It included linking up with American military units for a ground-level look at the war, as well as reporting on the political situation in Saigon and the official U.S. view of the conflict.

Tommy Daniels was not going voluntarily, and he was sullen and silent. He had been drafted in the winter, passing the Army physical despite his history of concussion, skull fracture and subsequent headaches. The war's unrelenting manpower demands had ensnared him, and after 10 weeks of basic training at Fort Dix and three months of infantry school at Fort Benning, he was ticketed for Vietnam.

For Dorie and Sam, Anna and Alan, this was a stressful, worrying day. They talked to each other in low tones, offering rote reassurances that everything would be well, then spent time with their sons. There wasn't much to say; they mostly sat next to them and hoped their presence would convey their feelings.

For Riva, this was a double nightmare. She had done everything in her power to persuade her brother to stay in college and keep his student draft deferment, but nothing worked. His beating by a police officer had changed him in ways that no one could completely understand, least of all him, and he steadily retreated from his old life and friends. He mostly stayed in his room, brooding, and when he went out, it was with new companions who reinforced his alienation and apathy. Riva strongly suspected they were smoking a lot of pot, and maybe using other drugs, but her efforts to broach the subject got her nowhere.

To have her brother bound for Vietnam was awful news, but not surprising; she had known it was coming ever since Tommy was drafted. To have her husband going as well was a thunderclap. When Michael first raised the subject, she reacted with shock, then anger. When he persisted, trying to explain that this was an opportunity he had to grasp, it triggered the worst fight of their marriage. Riva was so furious that she spent two nights away from Michael, sleeping on her friend Deana Franklin's living room couch. She came home after that, her anger giving way to sadness and apprehension, but it hurt her deeply that her husband knew how distraught she was about his plans and still plowed ahead with them.

Now, Riva sat apart from everyone, wordless and withdrawn. She was afraid that if she spoke to anyone, she would begin to cry, and she wanted at all costs to avoid that. She was haunted by a premonition that she would never see either Tommy or Michael again. This terrifying thought had been growing in her mind for days, but she felt unable to talk about it with anyone in her family, out of fear that she would make the parting harder for them. And it wasn't a burden she felt comfortable sharing with a friend. So she swallowed her fears, and was consumed by them.

Tommy was leaving first, being picked up by two other members of his unit. They had gone in together to rent a car for a last stateside road trip before shipping out, a leisurely three-day drive to Austin, Texas. There, at Bergstrom Air Force Base, they would board a military transport for the long trip to Vietnam.

When they heard the horn honk outside, Tommy's parents embraced him, told him they loved him and would miss him, urged him to stay safe and write often. He nodded, saying little, embarrassed and uncomfortable.

Riva hung back, then rose, walked up to Tommy and hugged him tightly. "You take care, bro, and you come back to us. Not gonna be the same around here with you gone." Then she squeezed his hand, turned and sat down again, staring straight ahead as the rest of the two families said their final goodbyes and Tommy went out the door.

Michael sat down next to her and tentatively put his hand in hers. She did not withdraw it, but didn't look at him. They sat wordlessly for several moments, the silence enveloping them, weighing on them, becoming too painful to endure. "I'm sure Tommy will be okay," he said. "I'll make a point of seeing him when I'm over there." Riva nodded, still silent, still looking straight ahead.

A little later, it was time for Michael to leave. His parents were driving him to Kennedy Airport for a flight to San Francisco, where he would catch another plane bound for Asia. Dorie and Sam had offered to come as well, but Michael sensed that they needed time to process Tommy's departure, and politely declined. Riva made no such offer.

Michael embraced Sam and Dorie, repeated his assurances about Tommy, and turned to his wife. She was back in her solitary seat, again staring straight ahead, not looking at anyone.

Once more, Michael sat down next to her. "I hope you can understand," he began. "This is something I have to do. If I passed it up, I would spend my life regretting it, wondering what it would have been like, wondering how I would have done."

Riva said nothing, first nodding slightly, then shaking her head, looking away, the tears very close now. Goddamn it, I don't want to cry. Lord, let me not cry. Anything but that.

His parents hovered nearby, unwilling to intrude, but he caught them in his peripheral vision. Their body language conveyed that it was time to leave. He slowly got to his feet, and then turned back to Riva. She still could not speak yet, but she rose and put her arms around his neck.

"I love you, Riva. I always will. I hate that this is hurting you. The timing couldn't be worse. But it'll go by fast. I'll be back soon. So will Tommy."

"I know. I know. I love you, too. Please...please take care of yourself. And say a little prayer for Tommy."

They spent a long time holding each other. Then, suddenly, with one last hug and a long look back, Michael was gone.

2: The Hard Line

Lyndon Johnson was not a stupid man. He was unpolished; at times he was crude, corny, even cruel; and he had pronounced weak spots in his knowledge and experience, two of which were foreign and military affairs. But his long climb to the pinnacle of power was fueled by formidable assets: great energy, innate shrewdness, and an instinct for reading people and their needs and weaknesses.

His gamble on war in Vietnam was well into its second year, and showed no signs of paying off anytime soon. He had bought into a strategy of steadily increasing military pressure on the North Vietnamese and Viet Cong, based on the premise that at some point they would realize the futility of their struggle and agree to a political settlement. At every step up the ladder of escalation, his advisors told him, he would have options.

The pressure had been applied, the set-piece battles fought and mostly won, yet Hanoi showed not the slightest sign of weakening. Johnson simply could not grasp that kind of thinking; it was irrational, it defied conventional understanding. When he tried to comprehend it, he fell back on the lazy Cold War trope of the communist fanatic, too blinded by Marxist dogma to recognize reality. It did not occur to him that there was a much simpler and quite logical explanation for the other side's stubbornness: the animating force of nationalism, combined with the confidence born of fighting foreign invaders for more than 25 years and not being beaten yet.

As for options, he discovered they did not really exist. Each new escalation closed off choices, made it harder to backtrack, because the investment in men and money and blood was that much greater. The original commitment of 16,000 U.S. troops that Johnson inherited from Kennedy had swelled to more than 400,000, the initial bombing campaign had steadily expanded in scope, and Johnson had no doubt that he would soon be asked for more of both.

His generals told him all was going well, increasing numbers of the enemy were being killed, ever larger amounts of territory were being cleansed and pacified. His civilian advisors agreed, and added that the Saigon government was showing greater signs of stability, and that its army, known as the ARVN, was steadying itself and could soon fight on its own.

He wanted to believe it. Unlike his predecessor, he was somewhat in awe of the generals, and he was still dazzled by the erudition and Ivy League sheen of the Kennedy team of civilian advisors he had also inherited. Deep down, though, he began to harbor doubts about whether the rosy assessments were really accurate. He shared these doubts with a very select number of confidants, people like Dick Russell, the Georgia senator who had been his mentor long ago when he first arrived in the Senate, raw and damaged by a tainted election. Russell agreed with his darkening outlook, but he also agreed with Johnson that the problem was insoluble for political reasons. LBJ was still unwilling to bear the onus of being the president who lost Vietnam, and that placed him in a trap from which there was no escape.

Perversely, even as his doubts grew, Johnson became more reliant on the hard-liners around him. He grew impatient with Bob McNamara because he sensed—or thought he sensed—that the defense secretary, once so convincing in his predictions of victory, was beginning to waver. McNamara stayed on, but Mac Bundy was gone, and LBJ did not seem to mind much; he replaced him as national security advisor with Walt Rostow, a true believer if ever there was one. He excoriated Bill Fulbright, an old Senate ally but now increasingly critical of the war, telling aides that the Foreign Relations Committee chairman was being disloyal to the country.

As the president shut out the skeptics and turned to the hawks for affirmation, Alan McMaster became something of a favorite. Alan had a fully integrated view of Vietnam, and it had not changed in any way over the many months that he had been counseling Johnson. American military power was ultimately irresistible, so long as it was applied with increasing pressure. And Vietnam was important in the broader Cold War struggle; the critics who called it peripheral and a distraction failed to understand that losing any territory to the communists was a fatal first step down a very slippery slope.

When McNamara persuaded the president to order a pause in the bombing campaign at the end of 1965 as a peace overture, Alan advised against it and warned that Hanoi would see it only as a sign of weakening American resolve. When the North Vietnamese showed no inclination to reciprocate, Alan's stock in the Oval Office rose considerably. When Fulbright held public hearings on the war and gave a national platform to eminent critics like George Kennan and James Gavin, Alan was at hand to tell LBJ it was mere political theater that would have no lasting effect on public opinion. At every turn, his advice was consistent: stay the course, tough it out, and sooner or later, the bet will pay off handsomely.

"Mr. President, this is a defining moment, for your presidency and for the course of the Cold War struggle," Alan told him during one White House visit. "Advisors like me will come and go, and some will trim their advice to fit the prevailing political winds. But you will remain here, at your post, and years from now, men will remember with gratitude the decisions you made and the resolution you displayed in the face of doubt and division."

Johnson looked at him intently across the big Oval Office desk, saying nothing at first. When he did speak, he leaned back and looked away, and he seemed to be speaking more to his own inner conflicts than to Alan.

"I keep remembering a story I heard about Woodrow Wilson," he said. "He was elected to be a reform president, to pursue an agenda of domestic renewal. When he got to Washington, he supposedly told a friend, 'Wouldn't it be ironic if I wound up preoccupied instead with foreign affairs?' And of course that's what happened, and ultimately it destroyed him—destroyed his presidency, destroyed his health."

"My father knew Woodrow Wilson," Alan replied. "He regarded him as a great man, and his failure to bring America into the League of Nations after World War I as a great tragedy. The people who are criticizing you on Vietnam are the heirs of those wretched isolationists who brought Wilson low. If they prevail again, it will repeat that tragedy. But you have assets that Wilson lacked, and you will succeed where he failed."

Johnson sat up and looked at Alan again, returning from his inner reverie. It never hurt, Alan found, to stroke LBJ's outsized ego.

"I hear your son is over there now, writing about it," the president said. "I hope he gets at the truth of what we're trying to do. When he's back, tell him to call Bill Moyers, and we'll try to arrange an interview. I'd like to hear about what he saw."

Alan knew that journalists just returned from Vietnam were unlikely candidates for a sit-down with the president, because they rarely brought him good news. Most were easily co-opted by the culture of negativity that prevailed in the Saigon press corps. Yet Alan also marveled at the politician's knack for knowing personal details. He started to mention that Tommy was also there, then thought better of it. Reminding Lyndon Johnson that he was sending draftees to Vietnam was not a way to win favor.

Michael prepped for his Vietnam assignment by covering the Fulbright hearings gavel to gavel. They became a moment, not only in Washington but in the country at large thanks to television coverage. Fulbright gave ample time to administration witnesses, including General Maxwell Taylor and Secretary of State Dean Rusk. But the most memorable testimony came from critics like Kennan, the legendary diplomat who formulated the Cold War strategy of containing the Soviets, and Gavin, a World War II hero who had gone on to become a three-star general. These were not student protesters from Ann Arbor or Berkeley who could be dismissed as naïve or unpatriotic; they were senior figures in the national security establishment, and their views were stated in the sophisticated language of strategic thinking and careful calculation of the national interest. Their testimony legitimized dissent and fueled a growing debate over the war.

For Michael, the hearings merely confirmed long-held views. For Anna, they crystallized doubts that had been growing for many months—but also the political dilemma created by those doubts. For her, Johnson was still the president who had brought to fruition so many important priorities, who had banished the frustration and impotence that had plagued liberals for years, who had capped it by proclaiming "we shall overcome" from the House dais. And there was more that needed to be accomplished, for which a committed president was crucial. She understood the argument of dissenters like Senator George McGovern—and, increasingly, Bobby Kennedy, now a senator from New York—that the war would inevitably undermine the administration's domestic programs. But breaking with Johnson, even criticizing him openly, was a place she could not go.

Alan dismissed the hearings as a kabuki, staged by hypocritical men whose principal motive was to strike back at a president who had insulted their egos by spurning their advice. "George Kennan is an arrogant elitist who got sidelined at State years ago because he couldn't follow the logic of his own theories," he told Anna. "Jim Gavin is a showboat who still sees himself as parachuting into hostile territory like he did on D-Day.

"And Bill Fulbright—well, screw Bill Fulbright. He didn't make a peep when the Tonkin Gulf resolution passed, in fact he helped shepherd it through the Senate. Now he's discovered all these principled differences with the president. It's bullshit. And I'll tell you something else: He's voted against every civil rights bill that's ever been proposed. If this were a war to save white people from falling under communist domination, he'd have a different view of it."

Anna thought this last remark was gratuitous and grossly unfair, and she said so. It did not improve the mood in the house. She was glad that Michael was not there, because of the explosion it would have caused. She had urged him, in fact, to keep a low profile with his father during the hearings, in hopes of maintaining some measure of family peace.

The hearings kicked off a national debate that was long overdue. Yet, if Fulbright hoped they would provoke a process of rethinking within the administration, he was deeply disappointed. Johnson hunkered down with his most hawkish advisors and shut out the critics. The war ground on, the casualties mounted, the troop deployments increased, the draft calls rose with them. By the time Michael arrived in Vietnam in late summer, U.S. forces there outnumbered the entire South Vietnamese Army.

3: Five O'Clock Follies

The first thing that hit Michael was the heat. Stepping off the plane onto the tarmac in Saigon felt like walking into an oven. He had never been in Asia before, and even Washington's notoriously muggy summers were no preparation for this tropical steam bath.

His second impression was of noise and confusion. The war had swollen Saigon's population to almost three times its original size, and the city was ill-equipped to handle it. Beneath the facades of French colonial architecture, the streets teemed with cars, trucks, bicycles, motorbikes, military vehicles, and an astonishing number of pedestrians who somehow managed to weave through the chaotic traffic without being flattened.

The larger news organizations had offices in Saigon, but for now, Michael would work out of a hotel and file his stories through the Associated Press. He snagged a small room at the Continental Palace, a four-story hotel that looked like it had been lifted from a Parisian boulevard and plopped down on Tu Do Street. It had an illustrious history—Graham Greene wrote much of "The Quiet American," his novel set in the French Indochina war, in room 214— and was now a favored hangout for many American journalists.

Michael found some of them clustered in the hotel bar, even though it was only midafternoon. He ordered a beer and nodded a greeting at the fellow on the next stool, a large, sandy-haired man who was working on something that looked a lot stronger than Budweiser.

"You new? Come out to join our little frolic? Welcome to the Continental Shelf—that's what we call this dive. I'm Jim Allerson, Newsweek. Nice to meet you."

"Pleasure, Jim. Michael McMaster, Chicago Chronicle. Yes, just arrived yesterday, as a matter of fact. You been out here long?"

"Six months and counting. Second tour. First time, I was with UPI, cleaning up Neil Sheehan's leftovers. Filing once a week now seems positively luxurious. That's about the only thing that's luxurious about this place, though. You coming to today's Five O'Clock Follies? Give you a good introduction to surrealism, Saigon-style."

Michael had been told—warned might be a better word—about the daily American press briefing, and the sardonic nickname attached to it by reporters who found it increasingly unreliable but had to attend in case any actual news was announced. Its venue was the Rex Hotel, another colonial-era establishment with a rooftop bar that was a melting pot of journalists, government officials, hookers, and the odd spy.

The briefing room was barely half-filled today, and the mood was languid. It had been relatively quiet lately, no big American operations or major North Vietnamese attacks underway, just another week in a war that ground onward, with no clear end in sight. Neither victory nor defeat seemed close at hand, and most correspondents would have had difficulty defining what either of those outcomes might look like.

Shortly after five, the chief briefer, Barry Zorthian, strode into the room. He was a plump, round-faced man with the nonchalant but wary manner of a circus lion tamer who senses the beast is drowsy, but knows it can awaken with a snarl at any moment. He began by pointing to the lapel of his cream-colored tropical suit. "Like my new pin?"

Those in the first row leaned forward and squinted. The lapel pin read, "Ambushed at credibility gap."

"Not bad, Barry," said the AP bureau chief, Ed White. "The issue is, are you the ambushee, or the ambusher?"

"Is that your opening question?" Zorthian shot back. "In that case, I'll move on to UPI."

"What, no announcements today?"

"Actually, a few. A brigade from the First Infantry Division, working with the ARVN's 51st Infantry Regiment, engaged and defeated an NV unit trying to infiltrate in the Central Highlands early this morning. A total of 55 enemy soldiers were confirmed killed. The ARVN regiment suffered two dead and seven wounded. One American was wounded, no U.S. killed.

"In the Pleiku region, there was an engagement between a 4th Infantry brigade and a VC unit. We count 20 VC dead, no U.S. casualties.

"And in the Delta, the 12th Infantry Regiment along with an ARVN unit—sorry, I don't have the name of the ARVN unit, I'll get it for you—encountered an enemy unit preparing for a raid on a strategic hamlet and successfully engaged it. Two Americans, five ARVN and 37 VC killed.

"So that brings us to a total of 112 enemy killed in the last 24 hours, as against two Americans and seven ARVN, if I've done my arithmetic right. I have? You've checked me, Phil? Great, thanks. Not a bad day's work, I'd say. Now I'll take your questions, which I'm confident will be penetrating and elegantly phrased."

The disconnect in the process was obvious to Michael as he listened to the reporters trying to probe Zorthian's assertions. None of them had been with the troops who fought these engagements. If any journalists had been there, they were still in the field with their units, and might not be back in Saigon for days. By then, the battles Zorthian had just narrated would be old news, displaced in everyone's mind by a dozen fresh developments. The reality was that American spokesmen could claim whatever they wanted with little fear that they would ever be called on it. They could offer up body counts that created an image of progress and forward momentum, and no one listening would know if they bore any relation to reality.

The people who did know—the mid-level military officers, State Department officials and development aid specialists, among others—were wary, and not exactly fond of spilling their guts to a journalist they barely knew. So Michael spent a frustrating first few weeks in Saigon, trying to orient himself and build up some sources, feeding his paper's maw with feature stories about life and death in a war zone. The closest he got to anything resembling action was the cafe that a guerrilla blew up with a planted bomb shortly after Michael walked by. He was close enough to feel the blast wave as well as to hear the explosion, and he doubled back—quickly at first, then more slowly as he recalled that the Viet Cong sometimes set a second bomb, timed to go off as rescue workers arrived. This time there was no follow-on explosion, just a jumble of shattered glass, smashed tables and bloodied bodies, alive and dead, on the street in front of the cafe.

He talked to one survivor, a Vietnamese student who had stopped off for a drink on his way home from class. He sat on the pavement, covered in plaster dust, blood from a cut scalp drying on his forehead. His mind slowly clearing, he told Michael he recalled seeing a young man get up from the bar and walk out, leaving behind a duffle bag. He said he started to follow the man out, to tell him he had forgotten his bag. "I think that's the only reason I'm alive," he said. As he reached the door, the bomb exploded, propelling him out into the street.

An American military policeman, overhearing this conversation, shared it with a South Vietnamese soldier, who lifted the student up roughly and shoved him toward a jeep. Michael followed, trying to ask the soldier why he was manhandling an injured victim. The soldier ignored Michael and threw the student into the back of the jeep.

As Michael tried to persist, the MP clapped his hand on Michael's shoulder. "Take it easy, fella," he said. "If that guy saw something, they'll want to know about it, get a description. You can understand that."

"How about getting him some medical attention first? He's probably got a concussion, and that cut on his head could easily get infected. He needs to go to the hospital."

The MP stiffened. "His first duty is to tell what he knows. And they'll want to make sure he's really just a bystander, not VC himself. They have ways of doing that. Then he can get treatment."

"So you're fucking telling me that being the victim of a bombing automatically makes you a suspect in the bombing?"

"I'm fucking telling you to mind your own fucking business. You're in a war zone, not back home in Washington or New York or wherever the hell you came from. Next time, it could be you lying in the street covered in blood."

4: Phin Quoi

The choppers lifted off from Bien Hoi Air Base in mid-morning, to give the company plenty of time to get into position for the operation, which was planned to start and finish in daylight. Michael, strapped into a canvas bench seat facing the rear of the helicopter, swiveled his head to take in the view out the side windows. There wasn't much to see; from more than 1,000 feet above, the green canopy of vegetation looked remarkably uniform. He pulled out his Leica and snapped a couple of shots, more to pass the time than for any other reason. In the facing seat, a photographer from Reuters puckishly produced his Nikon and captured Michael, capturing not much of anything. An hour later, the Huey copters were landing at a fire support base in the Mekong Delta.

After a hasty meal, Michael's company and two others swung out on the day's mission. A village about two kilometers away—two "clicks" in soldier slang—had been reported by the South Vietnamese army as Viet Cong-infiltrated. Air strikes had been called in to rout the guerrillas. For good measure, artillery from the firebase opened up after the air strikes ended, pounding the village with howitzer fire. The companies' assignment was to reach the village, engage any remaining Viet Cong, render whatever was left of the place unusable to the enemy—and, of vital importance, conduct the body count.

If any civilians remained, a South Vietnamese unit would be called in to herd them to the nearest strategic hamlet. These were closely guarded compounds set up by the Saigon government, ostensibly to care for displaced villagers, but in reality to separate the civilian population from the Viet Cong. The existence of the strategic hamlets was a tacit admission by the government that the insurgents and the peasants were natural allies who had to be kept apart at all costs. Michael had visited one shortly after his arrival. It was presumably a model hamlet, since the public affairs office was conducting tours for journalists, but it struck him as a tidied-up concentration camp. The entire site was surrounded by barbed wire, the perimeter was patrolled by soldiers, and residents could leave to visit relatives only with timed passes.

Michael had been told to stay in the middle of his company and not wander or lag behind, and he took care to follow those instructions. He had wondered if he would be fit enough to keep up with trained combat troops, but these soldiers, made wary by weeks in the field, were in no hurry to reach their destination. They fanned out and kept moving at a steady, deliberate pace, heads swiveling constantly, keeping especially alert on the unit's exposed left flank. To his right, Michael could hear, but not see, the other two companies making their way through the thick terrain at the same steady pace. He wondered who else might be out there, observing them. He wondered what this would feel like if it were a night patrol, with visual contact nonexistent, but every noise magnified.

If anyone was watching, they stayed well hidden and did nothing to impede the soldiers' progress. The companies reached the village shortly after midday, as the tropical sun emerged from behind a cloud bank and bathed the scene in brilliant light and withering heat.

Very little was left of the place. A few small peasant huts— "hooches," in U.S. military argot—were still standing, but a great mass of charred wood, ashes and blackened earth told the story of a village that had been largely destroyed by the air and artillery fire.

There was no sign of any living creature, human or animal. What was there, in abundance, were bodies. The corpses were scattered across the scorched ground in various poses of death. Some face down, with an arm thrown across the back of the head in vain hope of protection. Some on their back or side, so that their faces, twisted in a last grimace, were visible. Some so badly burned that they were just charred remains of what had once been human beings. The village's animals, herded into what had been a pen, lay dead a short distance off.

After the soldiers secured the perimeter and confirmed the absence of any insurgents, the other two companies fanned out from the site to see if they could pick up the trail of the Viet Cong who had been reported in the vicinity. They returned an hour later, reporting no sign of any hostile forces. In the meantime, Michael's company occupied itself with the tasks of searching for any hidden Vietnamese, military or civilian, counting the bodies, and then finishing the job of making the village of no value to any Viet Cong who returned—or anyone else.

They were almost at the point of giving up the search for survivors when a corporal shouted out, "Lieutenant, come over here and look at this." The officer led a small party in that direction, weapons at the ready, accompanied by Michael and the Reuters photog. The corporal pointed with his M16 rifle at a tunnel dug into the base of a small hill. Deep inside were three women and four children, cowering in fear.

The company's South Vietnamese army interpreter shouted at them, presumably telling them to come out and that they would not be harmed, and they slowly emerged. Looking at the women's faces, Michael guessed an extended family; mother, adult daughter, grandmother. The children seemed to range from five to nine, but that was pure surmise.

"Ask them where their men are," the lieutenant told the interpreter. The women shrugged and muttered a few short sentences. "They say when the bombs started, the men told them to hide in the tunnel and then ran off. They don't know where the men are now."

"How many men?"

"They say three. A father, a grandfather, and one son."

"Were they VC? Any of them?"

This produced the most animated response the women had shown, vigorous shouts of denial accompanied by much shaking of their heads.

"Did they see any VC here? Not their men, but others?" The women looked at each other, not answering immediately. "Did they? Goddamn it, were there VC here? Ask them."

Finally, hesitantly, the mother answered. "She says they came three nights ago. She says the villagers asked them to leave, but they just laughed. When the bombs came, they left. Quickly."

"Does she know where they went? Which way they went?" That question produced a shrug and another head shake.

The officer turned away in frustration. The interpreter told the women they and the children would be taken to a strategic hamlet soon. The grandmother asked if she could look among the bodies for other family members. Michael's last glimpse of her was as she bent over a corpse—he couldn't tell if it was male or female—weeping and murmuring.

Then the body count began. When it reached 75, the lieutenant told his men to knock off and get some food.

Michael walked over to the officer. "Can I ask you something, lieutenant? Why stop counting? There are some more bodies over there."

"Seventy-five is plenty. HQ will be more than happy with that number. No need to run up the score."

"Will you report them as dead civilians, or dead VC?"

"I'll report them as dead Vietnamese. That's what I can see, and that's what they are. I'll let other people decide whether they were civilians or VC."

"It seems obvious they weren't Viet Cong. There isn't a single weapon of any kind here."

"It's not obvious at all. Weapons are a precious commodity for the VC. They take pains to retrieve them from their dead before they disappear."

"Some of these corpses seem to be female."

"Some VC are female. And a lot of these bodies are so badly burned or blown apart, you can't tell what they are. What they were, that is. They ain't nothin' now, that's for sure."

All three companies joined in the task of setting fire to the hooches that were still standing. With the rising smoke and flames as an infernal backdrop, the men formed up for the return march to the fire support base.

When Michael got back to Saigon, he made a point of tracking down the public affairs office's reporting of the strikes on the village. It was not easy. The name of the place, Phin Quoi, was hard for Americans to spell and appeared differently in various reports. And individual actions sometimes were lumped together, making them difficult to isolate. Finally, with the help of a sympathetic public affairs officer, he tracked it down. Phin Quoi went into the books as 75 VC killed.

5. Bar Talk

Michael managed to link up with Tommy once while he was in-country. Tommy snagged a two-day leave, and they met at the Continental Shelf. Michael ordered some food, figuring Tommy would appreciate a break from Army rations, but Tommy mostly wanted to drink. He was quiet at first, but he became a bit more talkative after a few beers.

Tommy's unit was based in the highlands. He hadn't seen much yet in the way of action, just some patrols that produced no VC contact. But another platoon in his company had been badly mauled in an ambush and suffered half a dozen casualties; he heard that one soldier wounded in the action had died in a base hospital. Tommy narrated this with the understated fatalism that Michael had become accustomed to hearing from soldiers in Vietnam.

"It's just a job, man. Just something to get through. I'm here for a year, that's the standard tour. So I'll get it over with, and get the hell out of this fucked-up place, and spend the rest of my Army days stateside, probably training new kids at infantry school. In the meantime, I try to have a little fun."

"You keep in touch with your parents and Riva?"

"They write me, a lot. I write them back, a little. It's hard to find time for letters. But I let them know I'm okay."

"And are you okay?"

Tommy shrugged and downed a big swallow of beer. "I'm alive. That's something in this goddamn place."

After several rounds, Tommy proposed a move to a more adventurous setting: a nightclub that several guys in his unit had recommended. As they descended the stairs to the basement bar, Michael was hit by the smell; a blend of stale beer, cigarette smoke, human sweat, and a faint whiff of urine. The place was dim, most of the light coming from red paper lanterns strung from the low ceiling or propped on the tables. It was, literally and figuratively, a dive.

As Michael's eyes adjusted to the light, he saw that the place was about half-filled. Lots of soldiers on leave, dressed in goofy civilian outfits. A few especially beefy guys, probably construction workers. And several young Vietnamese women in low-cut dresses, dancing with Americans to the beat of a Roy Orbison tune blasting from a large jukebox.

"Pretty woman, yeah yeah yeah. Pretty woman, look my way. Pretty woman, say you'll stay—with me-ee."

Tommy disappeared for a few minutes, then returned with a couple of joints. He lit one, dragged deeply, and passed it to Michael.

"Second one's for later," he said. "Be careful with this shit if you're not used to it. Weed here's a lot stronger than back home."

That proved to be an understatement. After two tokes, Michael was floating on the ceiling. He ordered a couple of drinks, more to quench his sudden thirst than for the alcohol. They sat and drank, not saying much, conversation inhibited by the powerful pot and the blaring jukebox. Orbison had given way to Mitch Ryder.

"Devil with a blue dress, blue dress, blue dress, devil with a blue dress on—yeah-a!"

Tommy left again and returned with two girls in tow. Peering at them through the haze, Michael guessed they were 16, 17 at most. They might have been sisters, but such fine familial distinctions were beyond Michael's mental capacity for the moment. "They wanna dance with us," Tommy shouted over the music.

"You do recall that I'm married to your sister?"

"We're talkin' about dancing, Michael. That's all."

"Okay, okay. Sorry. Sure, let's do it."

They danced with the girls through a couple of numbers. The place was filling up now, and there was little room to do much more than sway in place. Michael made a couple of attempts at conversation with his partner, but between the din and the language barrier, he didn't get far. Finally, the girls drifted off, promising they'd be back later, and Tommy and Michael drifted back to their table.

They talked for a while, but before long the conversation lagged. The place was getting on Michael's nerves. "I think I'll head back to my hotel. You got a place to bunk for the night?"

"I think I'll make out okay."

"Well, be careful, man. Out there, and here, too. I'll give your love to Riva and your parents. Good luck, and keep your head down."

Michael's last glimpse of him, as he unsteadily mounted the stairs, was of Tommy sitting alone, pulling on a beer, looking out at the dance floor, looking a bit lost.

6: Clash By Night

Once again, Michael was strapped into the seat of a Huey, this time on the move with a battalion of the First Air Cavalry. They were bound for an area of the Central Highlands northwest of Pleiku, near the Cambodian border. The mission was to interdict traffic coming off the Ho Chi Minh Trail, the legendary North Vietnamese supply route that ran the length of the long, curving border that separated Laos and Cambodia from Vietnam. Well-disguised branches of the main trail cut into the narrow neck of the highlands to feed men and materiel to Viet Cong units operating in the region. The battalion's assignment was to find these tributaries and sever them.

The terrain was all in favor of the insurgents: thick jungle, broken by rugged, heavily forested hills. The trail had been established more than six years ago, some of it overlaid on trade routes that had existed for centuries. As parts of it were choked off by U.S. air strikes or ground operations, the North Vietnamese adapted by opening new branches and bypasses. It was a shell game, with the Americans cast in the role of the marks.

The choppers dropped the battalion at the landing zone, and the men formed up. The battalion's executive officer, a major who hailed from Oregon, conducted a quick briefing, and then they headed out. This was to be a multi-day operation, and the chances of engaging the Viet Cong were high. The four companies involved were divided into two teams, each with about 300 soldiers. The count should have been higher, but few units were operating at full strength these days.

The first two days of the mission passed with no contact. Yet there were signs of recent VC activity—beaten-down vegetation, a few discarded items not of U.S. origin—so there was no doubt this was an active area for infiltration. It increased everyone's wariness.

Late in the afternoon of the third day, they were traversing a small hill, heading west into the setting sun. The captain leading the company ordered his men to tack at 45-degree angles to the sun to minimize the glare. Michael was once again in the middle of the unit, paired with a television crew from CBS. There was a muffled explosion up ahead and to the right. Then all hell broke loose.

One soldier walking point had tripped a small mine, hastily laid by a Viet Cong unit to protect one of its flanks. The unit had heard the Americans coming and hunkered down in the dense foliage, hoping to remain unnoticed until the Americans had passed and then attack from the rear. When the mine exploded, they opened up with rifle fire and grenades.

The men quickly broke formation and fanned out. The CBS crew followed a pair of corporals and disappeared. A private, Michael's assigned buddy for the day, grabbed his arm and shouted "Stay with me" over the rising din of the firefight. Michael did not need to be told twice. The vegetation was so thick that it was difficult to see beyond a few feet in any direction. The limited visual sense was more than balanced by an overload of sound: bursts of gunfire, explosions, shouted commands, cries of pain.

Michael crouched low next to the private, trying to keep his bearings. The soldier moved forward warily, trying to keep in visual contact with men on his left and right. Something he heard or saw in front of him caused him to lay down a burst of rifle fire. A return volley passed over Michael's head as he hugged the ground. He heard a man to his left groan and curse. The private rose to a half-crouch and fired three more bursts, then lobbed a grenade in the direction of the volley. This time there was no responding fire.

They moved forward and found the bodies of two Viet Cong. One had taken a round in the neck, the other's chest was blown open by the grenade explosion. They saw a trail of beaten-down underbrush leading away, suggesting that some VC had survived the encounter and were retreating. They followed the trail for a short distance, then turned back.

The man who had groaned was being patched up by a medical corpsman. He had been nicked in the shoulder, a superficial wound that still required careful treatment because it could easily become infected in the heat and humidity. He sat on the ground, smoking a Marlboro and muttering to the corpsman about his luck.

It had seemed to Michael that the firefight lasted an eternity, but in reality, it was over in 10 minutes. The VC unit had silently melted away, and tracking it down was impractical, given the fading light and thick foliage. They found 11 VC corpses. Seven Americans had suffered gunshot wounds. The soldier who tripped the mine was dead.

They had no real sense of the size of the unit they had engaged, whether it was part of a larger force or a reconnaissance team operating far afield. They suspected the Viet Cong unit was equally in the dark about them. It seemed an apt microcosm of the larger conflict. As his breathing and heart rate returned to normal, Michael's mind turned to some lines from Matthew Arnold's poem, "Dover Beach":

And we are here as on a darkling plain
Swept with confused alarms of struggle and flight,
Where ignorant armies clash by night.

As the company bivouacked that evening, Michael shared a smoke with the captain and talked about the encounter. Ray Machado's Boston origins were apparent in his heavy New England accent. He had gotten through UMass with the help of a ROTC scholarship and had gone almost directly from commencement to the Army's Officer Candidate School. He had arrived in Vietnam 11 months ago as a second lieutenant and been promoted twice—the first time because the first lieutenant leading his platoon had been killed.

He and Michael had talked a fair amount in the past three days, but Ray had been rather guarded. Tonight was different. Perhaps it was the lingering adrenaline rush from the engagement, perhaps he felt Michael had passed some sort of unspoken test out there. For whatever reason, he opened up.

"What you've seen sums up the whole goddamn thing," he said. "During the day, we can move pretty much at will. We can get ambushed, and if it's a well-laid trap, we take casualties, but we still win all the firefights. The VC bloodies us up and then backs off, and tracking them in this terrain is almost impossible. Fighting them is like trying to nail jello to a tree. And then at night—well, at night, who knows what the fuck goes on, or where the VC is, or what they're up to. We've got equipment that's supposed to give us night visibility, but it's heavy and hard to use and not very reliable."

Michael listened for a moment as the nighttime sounds swept over them. The wind rustling the trees mixed with the noises of nocturnal animals and insects. Trying to discern any human movement, especially if the human was stealthy and skilled at moving through the terrain, would be very difficult.

"What about air power? Does that level the field, or tilt it in our favor?"

"Sure, we can call in nighttime air strikes to where we think they are, but the truth is, we're usually guessing. Sometimes we get lucky, but it's hit or miss. And we kill civilians that way, a lot of civilians sometimes, which doesn't exactly improve our popularity with the locals. One battalion commander told me once, 'No such thing as a civilian out here. As far as I'm concerned, they're all VC.' That pissed me off at first, but when I thought about it, I decided he was unintentionally right. The more civilians we kill, the more recruits we make for the VC.

"And then sometimes we guess really wrong and hit our own units. Happened to me early in my tour. I tell you, I've never been half as scared of the VC as I was of our own ordnance that night. Damn near a quarter of my platoon wound up with some sort of wound, some serious. I was lucky. All I got was some superficial shrapnel cuts and an ear that was partially deaf for a week. It was one fucked-up mess. This whole thing is one fucked-up mess, if you ask me."

"This is really interesting. Thanks for talking to me about it. You mind if I quote you? By name, I mean? Or you want some cover?"

"Go ahead. I'm short. I should be stateside in less than a month. Then another few weeks and I'll be separated. I don't intend to make the Army a career."

Chapter Twelve
–Fathers and Sons–

November 1966

1: Fools Like Us

Michael had written several spot news stories and features during his stay in Vietnam, but he did not want to write his big wrap-up piece while he was still in-country. He doubted that anyone from the embassy or the military would give him any trouble, but he decided to play it safe. He holed up in a Tokyo hotel room and spent three days going through his notes and putting the piece together.

His take on the war was that it was unwinnable on any terms that Americans would find acceptable. The gap between official optimism in Saigon and the nasty realities on the ground was wide and growing greater. The South Vietnamese government had no real political support outside the small elites that were living off it. The South Vietnamese army, after five years of American hand-holding, still couldn't function independently and there was no reason to think that would change. U.S. battle tactics inevitably created resentment in a civilian population that was already alienated from the government.

The North Vietnamese and Viet Cong were hardly saints; Michael quoted villagers who had been abused by the insurgents or had seen relatives brutally murdered for real or imagined cooperation with South Vietnamese or U.S. forces. He had talked with refugees from the North who spoke of a society that was spartan and regimented, where anyone who dissented in the smallest way was harshly punished. He found no reason to doubt these stories. Yet he also had spoken with many South Vietnamese intellectuals and professional people who told him—always off the record, because they feared government retaliation—that the irreducible element in the equation was nationalism, and that the other side owned that franchise and always would.

He wrote it that way, describing a stalemate in both the military and political situations, one from which there was no real escape because the other side had shown it was willing and able to match any American escalation.

If the U.S. upped the ante again by increasing its forces and level of violence, that would only sharpen the political dilemma, Michael wrote. More bombing and search-and-destroy operations would create more civilian casualties, and thus more enemies, among the population. More U.S. forces would increase, not lessen, Saigon's dependence on the Americans. And in the end, he concluded, "there is no reason to think it will deter Hanoi from calling the U.S.'s bet, and probably raising."

Michael filed his piece from Tokyo and booked a flight to the States for the following day. He soon found himself in a running battle with his paper's foreign editor, Derek Iverson, that started in Tokyo, continued during his stopover in Los Angeles, and resumed when he landed in New York.

"I don't think we can run such a downbeat piece," Iverson told him. "It's so totally at odds with what's coming out of the White House and the Pentagon, and out of Saigon. We'll look like we've signed up with the anti-war movement."

"Look, Derek, the paper sent me out there to see what's going on. This is what's going on. If you have a specific problem with a specific piece of reporting, let's talk that through. I've got very detailed notes to back everything up."

What followed was an extended negotiation that dragged on over three days, as Iverson pulled the story apart and questioned Michael about every aspect of it. In the end, Michael won most of the battles, but not before he called on Jack Rothstein to referee the final rounds. Michael hated doing that, because he genuinely liked Iverson and thought he was a strong editor. He also knew that Derek was an ex-Marine who was very proud of his service in the Pacific. He suspected that might be coloring Derek's judgment, perhaps in ways he was not aware of consciously.

When the story finally ran, it led the Sunday paper, stripped across the top of the front page with a photo Michael had taken of the burning hooches in Phin Quoi. The wire syndicate that the Chronicle was part of also carried it. The next day, he went down to Washington, to talk his story up among sources and colleagues, and to be there in person for any official blowback.

He was pleased to discover that his piece was getting some attention. The Chronicle was not on any Washington must-read list, but it was a heartland paper that had endorsed Johnson in '64 and editorialized in favor of his Vietnam policy. When such a newspaper ran a deeply reported story questioning that policy, it got noticed.

In the afternoon, his mother phoned and asked him over for dinner.

"You sure it wouldn't be better to do this at a restaurant? Dad might be more restrained in a public setting."

"He's going to tell you what he thinks, whether it's in our dining room or The Palm. You know him well enough to understand that."

What Alan McMaster thought, and had no hesitance in expressing, was that Michael's piece amounted to propaganda for the enemy, and that his son had enlisted in a movement that was serving the interests of the communists, whether those involved knew it or not.

"Were you there, dad? Do you think I just fantasized those engagements in the delta and the highlands? Sure would've been a lot easier to do it that way, and a lot safer, too." He saw his mother wince and regretted that last comment.

"I think you saw what you wanted to see, what you expected to see before you ever set foot in Vietnam," Alan said. "It's a case of confirmation bias, not conscious deception. It amounts to the same thing, because you're helping to undermine public support for an absolutely vital military effort. You could've witnessed an unequivocal U.S. victory, and you'd figure out some way to cast it as a defeat."

"If anyone is guilty of confirmation bias, it's you," Michael shot back. "The evidence keeps piling up that this isn't working—not just my stories, almost all the reporting—and you just keep ignoring it. You always find some element, some justification, some reason for telling us that black is white. I don't know what you're telling Johnson when you talk with him, but someone needs to tell him the truth about what's happening there."

"It's *President* Johnson, goddamn it, and what I tell him is that he needs to ignore fools like you and keep on a steady course, because the slightest hint of wavering signals to the enemy that they can wait us out."

"Fools like me. Nice one, dad. Well, there's just one problem. They *can* wait us out. They happen to live in Vietnam, in case you hadn't noticed. That's why they call them Vietnamese. They were there before we came, and they'll be there after we go, whenever that is. And you'd understand that if you weren't so blinded by your Cold War dogma, your inability to see the world in any other terms other than the great monolithic Red Menace."

They went on in that vein, their voices rising in anger, their remarks growing more cutting and personal. Anna sat in pained silence, a role she found herself playing with ever greater frequency when Alan was present and the subject of Vietnam arose. She had invited Michael over in the belief that it would be better for Alan to vent now, rather than allow the anger to fester. Now she wasn't so sure. Perhaps it would have been better to let some time elapse; he might have been distracted by other problems and forgotten about Michael's story. No, it wouldn't have mattered; her husband had a long memory for things like this.

Finally, the argument burned itself out, as much from emotional exhaustion as anything else. Alan disappeared into his study; Michael left, saying he preferred not to repeat the confrontation over breakfast. She offered to call him a cab, but he said he wanted to walk over to Connecticut Avenue and hail a taxi there. The exercise would help him clear his mind, he said.

After he left, Anna sat alone for a long time, with a glass of wine and her thoughts for company. A father-son rivalry was natural and inevitable, and the fact that Michael was an only child meant there was no sibling, no second son, to deflect the tension. But this was growing worse, not better, and that seemed unnatural. Michael was in his late 20s, he was married, he was successful professionally. The need to diminish and compete with his father should be abating, not growing. As for Alan, aren't people supposed to mellow with age, become more tolerant and understanding, especially of their children? Not happening, either. There was an ugly dynamic building up between them, and she was at a loss about how to alter it.

Finally, feeling weary and defeated, she rose and headed to bed. As she walked past the study, she looked in. Her husband was sitting in an armchair, drinking a Scotch and leafing through a book. His back was to the door, and he was too absorbed or too drained to sense her presence. She craned her head to see what he was reading. She could just make out the title. It was Turgenev's novel of angry generational conflict, *Fathers and Sons*.

2: Regrets

Michael and Riva had not talked much while he was away. The 11-hour time difference inhibited telephoning, and Riva said she didn't need reminders that two people she loved were in Vietnam.

Michael feared that Riva's anger over his going would linger and chill the homecoming. He found to his relief that Riva was past that and simply glad to see him, alive and unhurt. She had never shared her premonition that he wouldn't return, out of fear that it would skew his mental state in a situation that was stressful enough. Now, she just allowed herself to feel her delight in having Michael back, and to express that delight in many ways. For long hours, they just sat together, enjoying their intimacy. They made love frequently those first few days, and their passion had an emotional resonance that was deep and sublime.

Riva listened to Michael's experiences in Vietnam and read his stories appreciatively, but she found little in them to surprise her. Before Tommy was drafted, she had been reflexively opposed to the war; once he was in the Army, her knowledge about Vietnam deepened and her opposition hardened. She went to anti-war demonstrations, but found them tame and futile. The old SNCC activist in her believed in direct action, and the draft resistance movement appealed to her. She took a training course on counseling young men on how to avoid being drafted and men already in the military on how to escape its clutches. For two months, she had been helping to staff draft counseling centers at NYU and Columbia, and two weeks ago she and five others set up a center in Harlem. This brought her into contact with some black militants who had just established a New York branch of a group that was attracting a lot of attention in California over its confrontational tactics against the police. It was called the Black Panthers.

As they talked about politics, Michael noticed an unmistakably harder edge to Riva's views. One reason she found the mainstream anti-war movement disappointing was that, in an effort to reach the broadest potential audience, it downplayed an aspect of the war that Riva found especially objectionable. In her view, it was impossible to separate Vietnam from American racism. This war was at its heart a white nation bringing its immense destructive power to bear on a non-white population. The fact that the United

States was forcing black soldiers, like her brother, to serve as instruments of this wholesale killing only made the crime worse.

Riva was still deeply invested in fighting America's racism. But she increasingly saw the civil rights movement's approach as irrelevant. She found confirmation during the summer as Dr. King tried to take the model of interracial activism north to challenge housing segregation in Chicago. King and his marchers were pelted with rocks, bottles, and a selection of racial epithets worthy of the worst southern bigot, and the rest of the country barely reacted. After a few months, King retreated with only a vaguely worded truce to show for his bruises.

Riva no longer had much contact with SNCC, as it refocused its energies on organizing black voters in Alabama, but she heartily agreed with the group's new leaders when they bluntly told its white members it was time to leave and find some other vehicle for their activism. Black people had to run their own organizations and make their own decisions, the SNCC leaders said. They adopted a succinct slogan to crystallize the thought: Black Power.

Riva's activism did not leave a great deal of time for her professional career. Her last stage role had ended six months ago, and she had auditioned only sporadically since then. She did some work on skits and street theater performed at anti-war actions, and she lent her ever-lovely voice to benefit concerts that raised money for draft resisters. She told herself she could pick up her career again when the moment was right, but a part of her wondered if that was really true.

Michael shared almost all of Riva's views about the war. He saw the political system as increasingly dysfunctional. The Fulbright hearings had made a splash, but the administration neutralized the dissenting senators with embarrassing ease. The Democratic Party was Lyndon Johnson's party, and most of its leaders and members were not about to cross him, no matter how uneasy they might feel about his war. Michael felt a rustle of hope when Bobby Kennedy called for a bombing halt and a renewed effort to start negotiations with Hanoi, but the administration simply ignored him and Kennedy failed to follow up aggressively. Michael had more hope for the anti-war movement than Riva, even as he acknowledged the limitations she pointed out. He sensed something stirring on college campuses that might form the nucleus of a force that could compel the politicians to take note.

Increasingly, Michael found himself at odds politically not only with his father but his mother as well. The tensions came to a head during a phone call shortly after the blowup over Michael's Vietnam story. Anna had called as a conciliatory gesture, to express her regret over Alan's hostile tone, but the conversation soon headed into troubled waters.

"Look, I appreciate your calling, but I have to say that it's really dad's place to offer regrets—if he has any," Michael said. "And I have to say this as well: It's time to stop enabling this terrible policy by keeping silent about it. You've shared your private doubts with me, but you've also kept them private. We're way past the point where that does any good."

That comment plainly hit a nerve.

"Well, son, I don't think I need any lectures about how to conduct myself politically," Anna snapped back. "I've been at this a long time, a lot longer than you have, and I think I understand something about how to handle a good leader who makes a bad decision. And that's exactly what Lyndon Johnson is. I agree with you that he's leading us down a dangerous path on Vietnam, and we need to find a way to turn him around on it. But we've got to do it in a way that doesn't destroy his administration. There are so many domestic priorities—"

"Seriously? You're seriously going to keep telling me that he's still the great liberal sugar daddy, and we've got to forgive him this little peccadillo of a war, even though it's killing thousands and thousands of people, so we can get some watered-down housing appropriations bill passed?"

"That housing bill you're dismissing so sarcastically can improve the lives of a lot of poor people—people that you say you care about," Anna retorted. "And if dissent over the war winds up letting the Republicans get back in power, we'll get the worst of both worlds—more war and less domestic progress."

"That's always what it comes down to for you—winning the next election, keeping your crowd in, keeping the other crowd out. That only matters to me if they stand for different policies, and right now I don't see any differences that matter. And if you're really worried that the war will sink the Democrats, deal with the cause and not the symptom. Find a way to put some real pressure on Johnson to change course. You tell me you've been playing this game for a long time. Maybe you've been playing it too long."

Michael came away from this conversation with regrets of his own, for the confrontational tone he had taken. If he had second thoughts about his attitude, however, he had none about the substance of his argument. In his view, Anna's generation had only one model, one strategy for bringing about change: working within the Democratic Party and leveraging the support of its officeholders, to whatever degree was possible. That playbook placed strict limits on what they could advocate and how they could advocate it, and it forced them into complicity when their putative allies adopted disastrous and immoral policies abroad.

The alternative was neither simple nor easy, he acknowledged, but it did exist: organizing independent movements to pressure the system from outside, supporting the pols when they delivered on their promises but having no hesitance about opposing them—publicly and vocally—when circumstances required it.

Anna was stung by the dispute and did not try to hide it. In her mind, Michael was committing a classic piece of youthful folly, acting as if this were Year Zero and there was no prior history worth learning. She felt he was willfully ignorant of the hard-earned lessons of her generation of activists, who had spent years in the wilderness shouting impotently into the wind, with government at all levels dominated by uncaring men who ignored them because they could, because they paid no political price for doing so. When that changed, starting in the 1930s, it was because a new set of politicians was elected through the votes of people who were fed up with the status quo and demanded change. And those politicians understood the votes could keep flowing—or be cut off. But both sides also understood that this was a two-way street, and that achieving some progress often required accepting limitations and compromises and, at times, outright betrayals.

Anna had been furious with Franklin Roosevelt for refusing to offer the smallest token of support to the Spanish loyalists who were fighting to stave off fascism. A few years later, in the period between the fall of France and Pearl Harbor, she thought he was too slow in moving the country toward a war footing against Nazi Germany. She had vented her feelings in private conversations with Mrs. Roosevelt. The first lady told her she agreed wholeheartedly, but that political realities prevented her husband from moving any faster. The only thing to do, she said, was to swallow hard and trust that a well-intentioned leader would come through in the end. And in the end, she was proven right.

Michael shared Riva's views about another important matter: the pervasiveness of racism. She had been on the mark right after Selma when she predicted northern whites would be far less generous about ceding their own privileges than in overturning southern segregation. Racial attitudes were hardening across the country. Black leaders warned that the Watts violence of the previous year was not an anomaly and could be repeated in any number of cities, because the grievances that provoked it were so widespread. White mayors responded by beefing up their police forces, and congressional support for what was left of Johnson's Great Society agenda ebbed. When a black neighborhood in Cleveland exploded during the summer, both sides claimed vindication.

Michael and Riva could not ignore the personal dimensions of this problem. They were an interracial couple in a time of deepening racial polarization and stiffening battle lines. They were in danger of being trapped in a racial no-man's-land, caught in a crossfire of rising resentment.

Michael detested racism, loathed it to his core. His deepest fear was that this was not enough, that Riva would come to see him as just one more ineffectual white liberal who only talked a good game. He decided to open up to Riva about this fear, and was relieved when she responded warmly and sympathetically.

"We know each other, Michael. We know our deepest thoughts and longings. We've been through a lot together. We can wall ourselves and our love for each other off from the ugliness outside. I really believe we can."

Michael hugged her happily and hoped with all his heart she was right.

They settled in for the holidays, accepting Sam and Dorie's invitation to spend Thanksgiving with them in Queens. Michael hoped that the passage of a little time might lessen the tensions with his own parents, at least enough to allow a friction-free visit during Christmas.

A couple of weeks after Thanksgiving, Michael was in the AP's New York bureau, where he often worked when he was in the city. As he looked over the latest wire stories from Saigon, the ringing telephone pulled him back to his desk.

"It's me," Riva said in a low, affectless voice that filled him with more worry than if it had been brimming with emotion. "Please come home right now."

When he arrived, Riva was sitting with her parents. She handed him a telegram.

"The Secretary of the Army has asked me to inform you that your son, Private Thomas Daniels, was wounded on December 6. He received injuries to his shoulder and back. He was treated at a field hospital and transferred to the 2nd Surgical Hospital in Qui Nhon. His condition is reported as serious. Your anxiety is realized and you are assured that he is receiving the best of care. As more information is available, it will be shared with you."

Chapter Thirteen
–Set The Night On Fire–

June 1967

1: Homecoming

The Daniels family waited as a long stream of passengers on the TWA flight from San Francisco trickled through the gate. They had been told that wheelchair passengers were sometimes the first to be taken off the plane, sometimes the last. On this flight, apparently, they were at the end of the line.

An elderly couple was wheeled off by two flight attendants. Then a middle-aged woman with one leg in a cast. Finally, Tommy.

He had spent more than five months in hospitals and rehab facilities in Vietnam and Japan, recovering from his wounds and two surgeries to repair some of the damage. His internal injuries had mostly healed, and he could sit erect. But one bullet had severed his spinal cord, and he was paralyzed from the waist down. Permanently paralyzed, the doctors said.

Last year, when Tommy left for Vietnam, Riva had fought fiercely to hold back her tears. Today, she didn't care. She wept as she held her brother, carefully at first, unsure of how fragile he might be, then more tightly as she choked out how much she loved him. She wasn't alone. Dorie sobbed softly as she embraced her son. Sam was crying as he shook Tommy's hand and then held it in both of his own. A few feet away, Michael teared up as he watched.

As passengers swirled around them, several paused to look at the homecoming. One man, in a Marine uniform, started to walk over, then thought better of intruding. He caught Michael's eye, mouthed "good luck" and walked on.

Another young man, a civilian wearing a backpack, headed in Tommy's direction, and Michael did not think he was coming to offer best wishes.

"Something I can do for you?" Michael said, planting himself in his path.

The kid—Michael could see now that he was no more than 20—looked up at him with a mixture of fear and defiance. "Yeah, you can tell your baby-killer friend I think he got what he deserved."

Michael stared at him in disbelief, frozen by the cruelty of his words. Then he came alive, as if awakening from a dream, took one step forward and shoved him in the chest, hard. "And you can turn around and get lost, or you'll get what you deserve."

With a muttered curse, the kid took off. The Daniels family, fortunately, had missed the exchange.

Michael had heard about the rough greeting returning servicemen were receiving from anti-war civilians, but this was his first direct encounter with it. For all his opposition to the war, he could not fathom the insensitivity of casting blame on an individual soldier—especially when the soldier was likely to be a draftee, and the accuser was probably safe because of the good fortune of a draft deferment. More than once, he had wondered what he would have done if he were just a few years younger, and hadn't done his military service before Vietnam.

Sam wheeled Tommy out to the curb while Dorie retrieved the family car, and they carefully lifted him out of the wheelchair and into the back seat. His upper body had regained some of its strength, but he was still generally weak. The Daniels had traded in their sedan for a station wagon to provide more space, and outfitted their house with a ramp up to the front door and a first-floor bedroom. Tommy talked hardly at all during the short ride home, and not much more when they arrived. He quietly thanked his family for being so accommodating, told them he was glad to see them, assured them he would be comfortable in the house, and that was about it.

Neither Tommy nor the Army had told the family much about the circumstances of how he was wounded. When Michael made some inquiries and learned the details, he understood why the Army wanted to bury the incident. That was not about to happen, though, because there were dozens of casualties that day, and one was the son of a congressman. It wasn't a pretty story, and it hardly helped the Daniels' peace of mind.

Tommy's company had engaged a North Vietnamese unit just south of the demilitarized zone that bisected North and South Vietnam, and after a hard fight was chasing the retreating enemy as night was falling. On its flank, another American company had also tangled with an enemy unit and was trying to cut it off before it could reach the DMZ. Both engagements developed quickly, and the two American companies were not aware of each other's positions. All four units collided in the dark, and a wild scrum ensued, in which much of the fire was American on American. By the time the chaos was brought under control, 15 Americans were dead, another 36 were wounded, and what was left of the North Vietnamese units had slipped away in the confusion and darkness.

When the congressman learned these sorry details, he made sure there was a full internal investigation into the incident, and in the end, the battalion commander was reprimanded and forced to retire. Yet it was never determined whether the fire that hit Tommy, or many of the other casualties, was friendly or hostile.

So Tommy was home from the wars—but his family soon discovered that his presence was more ghostly than real. He was still in considerable pain, which meant taking large doses of painkillers that left him groggy and uncommunicative. Mostly, he stayed in his room and listened to music on headphones; his old love of Motown had morphed into a taste for heavy-metal bands like Iron Butterfly and Black Widow. Sam, Dorie and Riva all tried to draw him out, collectively and individually, with little result. Gradually, his plundered soul came to dominate the Daniels home, and it drained the house of joy and spirit.

2: Language of the Unheard

The music coming out of the radio in Riva and Michael's apartment wasn't heavy metal; it was the Doors, blasting out the refrain of their chart-topping hit: "Try to set the night on fire!"

The song was a paean to sexual desire, not violence, but it had taken on an unintended meaning. A week ago, on a hot July evening, two white cops in Newark had needlessly pulled over and then brutalized a black cab driver in front of a crowd of angry witnesses. Now, the papers related the toll of the resulting explosion: 26 people dead, 1,000 under arrest and $10 million worth of property up in smoke.

The events were a bloody fulfillment of the predictions of black leaders that the country was in for a "long, hot summer." Michael recalled a speech by Dr. King three months ago, in which he warned that American cities had become powder kegs. "A riot is the language of the unheard," he said. Many whites heard those words as a threat, not a forecast.

Riva soon discovered just how frightened some whites felt. Newark was right across the Hudson River from Manhattan. New York had experienced its own disorders in Harlem in 1964, and the Newark violence sparked a current of fear that a repetition was looming. Riva found that some white neighbors, even white friends, were looking at her differently, with suspicion or hostility. She felt isolated in a way that she had never experienced in all her years in the city. She thought she might be imagining things until she talked with some black friends. They were getting the same reactions.

Michael, usually sensitive to her moods, didn't pick up on her discomfort. She wanted to talk to him about it, but hesitated, for fear he would think her paranoid.

On a Sunday morning a few days after the Newark violence burned itself out, Michael answered the phone in their apartment. The paper's weekend editor, John Sturgis, was on the other end. "I don't know if you've heard, but Detroit blew last night," he said. "It's not dying down today, it's actually getting worse. We've got a reporter and a photog on the way, but the reporter is Al Dannis, and he's never covered anything like this. We'd like you to go, too. If this is anything like Newark, it's going to be like covering a war zone, and you're our most experienced guy for that."

"Sure, I understand. I'll try to get a flight this afternoon. But let me ask you, do we have any black reporters we could send, too? That would really help our coverage. They'd see and hear things we'd miss."

There was a long pause. "Michael, we've got two black reporters on staff. Two. One is Andy Samson, and he's on vacation. I think he's off camping somewhere. The other one is Vanessa Brentley, and there's no way we're sending a woman into a riot zone."

Michael had worked with Vanessa on some stories, and was certain she would know how to handle herself. He let John know that, but he also realized this ultimately wasn't John's call, so he didn't push the point.

Riva listened to Michael's end of this conversation with growing apprehension. She was not happy about him going away at such a moment. She felt exposed and vulnerable, caught on the wrong side of a line that had barely been visible to her until now. Yet she didn't know how to tell him what she was feeling. She worried that he would see her as surrendering to exaggerated fears. A part of her felt that way herself; she didn't like to imagine herself as weak or fearful. And so another brick in a wall of miscommunication was laid.

Getting to Detroit proved difficult, because most of the flights to the city had been cancelled. Michael managed to get a flight to Toledo and drove the rest of the way in a rental car. As he rolled north on I-75, he saw a long stream of traffic going in the other direction. He had the inbound lanes to himself. He spun the radio dial in search of news, but found only normal programming. The strange silence about the trouble, along with the abnormal traffic flow and the beautiful midsummer weather, cast a surreal spell on the day.

Hungry for information, Michael stopped at a gas station and phoned his paper. He learned that the disorder was indeed metastasizing, with stores looted and set ablaze and crowds confronting police. The lack of information on the radio, John Sturgis told him, resulted from a local news blackout, requested by city officials in the vain hope that ignoring the violence would make it go away.

The wire services were not observing the blackout, and John read him the latest AP dispatch. The triggering incident, it reported, was a police raid early that morning on an after-hours bar, a "blind pig" in local parlance. Michael learned more details later. The bar had been crowded with a welcome-home party for two Vietnam vets. The cops insisted on arresting everyone, but they were under-manned, and it took a long time to bring everyone out to the patrol wagons. It was a hot, airless night, and a crowd soon gathered, taunting the officers. A bottle flew through the air and smashed into a police cruiser. A roar of approval went up. The cops retreated with their prisoners under a hail of missiles. The fuse had been lit, and the explosion soon followed.

Michael found the suburban hotel where Al Dannis and their photographer, Dave Flanigan, had put up. Together, they drove into the city on a broad, six-lane thoroughfare. As on the interstate, almost all the traffic was heading out of Detroit.

The city was low and flat, creating a long horizon. To the northeast, the cloudless sky was marred by a gray-black smudge. As they drew closer, the smudge grew into a dense pall of smoke hanging over the epicenter of the disorder. Michael was immediately reminded of the burning peasant huts in Phin Quoi. John Sturgis was right. He was back in a combat zone.

When they headed toward the column of smoke, they were redirected to a side street by a cop who told them the main roads were being kept clear for law enforcement and fire vehicles. The detour led them into a neighborhood of wood frame houses and small apartment buildings. People were milling about in the narrow street, talking and pointing to the billowing smoke just to the north. It was slow going, and they were getting some hostile stares. No cops were in sight.

"I'm not sure this is such a great idea," Al said. Michael, behind the wheel, began considering escape maneuvers.

The insistent ring of a burglar alarm erupted from a convenience store. Several people had broken in and were carrying out cases of beer. Some in the watching crowd shouted their approval. A few moved forward to join in.

Then came sirens, and two police cruisers barreled down the street, scattering the crowd. The cars screeched to a halt in front of the store, and four officers emerged, service weapons drawn. "Freeze, goddamn it!" one shouted at the scattering looters. The looters kept running, some dropping their booty, others hauling it with them. The cops started to pursue them, then retreated to the store, awaiting reinforcements. Dave snapped several frames of the cops and the shattered storefront through the car window.

With the street momentarily clear, Michael wheeled around and headed back to the boulevard. He would take his chances on the main roads, he decided, rather than risk being trapped on a side street again. At another police barricade, they were told flatly that no cars were being allowed through. They parked and stood behind the barricade, mingling with the cops. All were wearing helmets and several carried shotguns. Michael noted that all but one were white.

Up the street, about three blocks away, they could see crowds of people smashing store windows. An officer told Michael that the outnumbered police had given up trying to stop the looting and burning. "They ordered us to pull back and try to seal off the area," he said. "Maybe that's a good idea, but it means the fires are just gonna keep burning. We got no way to protect firemen."

"Did you see this coming?" Michael asked.

The cop shrugged. Then he lowered his voice, eying the lone black officer at the barricade and making sure he wasn't overheard. "We stopped showing 'em who's boss," he said. "This is what happens."

Al, Dave, and Michael decided to move forward on foot. The cops looked at them as if they were crazy, but did not stop them. They walked cautiously up the street, Dave clicking away, Michael constantly swiveling his head to make sure they had a clear route of retreat. He'd seen soldiers doing that in Vietnam, and recalled being taught to do it during his Army training. He'd never had to use that training during his military service, but it was suddenly useful.

As they neared the crowd, they met a reporter and photographer from the city's morning daily, the Detroit Free Press. They'd been in the area for hours and were making a last foray before their deadline. They said the mood in the street was totally unpredictable; some people were friendly, or at least willing to talk, while others had taunted and cursed them.

They encountered a little of both on this street. Mostly, the crowd was occupied with the task at hand, which was breaking into businesses and emptying their contents: a pharmacy and a record store on one side of the street, a grocery directly across. Two blocks ahead, smoke rose from a pawnshop. One man on the edge of the crowd explained that the looters were trying to focus on white-owned stores, which he said were widely resented for offering inferior goods at inflated prices. But, he said, not everyone was so disciplined, and black businesses were also being hit.

"Are you surprised this is happening?" Michael asked him.

The man reacted with a harsh laugh. "You kidding? This's been coming for a long time. Just a question of when, and what would set it off. Cops ride around here like they own the goddamn place. Look you up and down like you're nothing, you're garbage, just a piece of shit. Well, the cops don't own the place today, do they?"

The man appeared to be in his 30s. He was dressed in a short-sleeve shirt and dark slacks. He had a muscular build, and his hands were rough and worn. "Where do you work?" Michael asked.

"Ford's. River Rouge. Assembly plant. Eight years now. Trying to get in the skilled trades, but that's tough."

"Can I get your name?"

"Ah, no way, man. You're the fourth reporter to ask. I'm okay to talk to you guys, but I don't want the cops to come looking for me when this is over. Got enough trouble in my life as is. You just tell people we're tired. Tired of the cops fuckin' with us all the time. Tired of getting ripped off by these store owners. Just tired of the whole goddamn scene. This is the result, and maybe it'll get somebody's attention. Nothing else has, that's for damn sure."

As they talked, the crowd had surged back and forth, and the center of it was now moving in their direction. Michael and his four colleagues were beginning to get hostile looks and even more hostile taunts. "Hey, white boys, what the fuck you come round here for?" one man shouted at them. "You motherfuckers come looking for trouble, you gonna find it," another told them.

"I think it may be time to pack it in," the Free Press reporter said. At that moment, a whiskey bottle arced through the air and conked him on the head. He stumbled but kept his feet. He reached up to touch his head, and his hand came away bloody. Another bottle slammed into Michael's back, between his shoulder blades. "You best be going," the auto worker said.

They headed back the way they had come, resisting the temptation to run. Several people followed them for a while, taunting them, but they grew bored and turned back to rejoin the looters. The Free Press reporter was able to walk on his own, although blood was flowing down the side of his face and onto his shirt.

At the police barricade, a cop with some EMT training cleaned up the reporter's cut and bandaged it. The wound turned out to be superficial. "Just about any head cut is gonna bleed a lot, even if it's pretty light," the cop said. The reporter wisecracked that his bloody shirt would become a battle trophy in his newsroom. His photographer recorded it for posterity.

Michael, Al, and Dave debated their next move. They decided to head downtown to the Associated Press bureau. There, Dave could process and transmit his photos, and Al and Michael could stay abreast of developments and send their story.

The drive was an excursion in the surreal. The streets were mostly empty of traffic. What little there was ignored red lights and kept moving. To the north, the cloud of smoke was spreading as more buildings were set afire. The immediate area was eerily quiet, but they could hear in the distance a dull roar, a mixture of sirens, crashing glass, and indistinct shouting.

At the AP bureau, they learned that the scene they had witnessed was one small blaze in a rapidly spreading conflagration. The police effort to pull back and contain the situation had not worked; the rioters easily leapfrogged the perimeters established by the cops and spread the disorders to new neighborhoods, forcing the outflanked police to pull back further in an ever-widening arc. And with almost all available police concentrated on the west side, where the disorder had started, there was none to deploy on the east side when rioting broke out there.

As the looting and burning spread, the politicians circled each other, issuing dueling statements and selective leaks seeking to deflect blame. Detroit's mayor was a politically ambitious Democrat, Jerry Cavanagh. Michigan's governor was an even more ambitious Republican, George Romney, who was preparing to run for president. Cavanagh, insisting at first that his cops could handle things, resisted asking Romney for state police and National Guard help until the situation was out of control. When he finally made the request, Romney announced he would refuse to grant it without a formal declaration from the mayor that state help was required. Amid the gamesmanship, precious time was lost.

Now, with the disorder spreading rapidly, it occurred to Romney that his own National Guard might be inadequate. He sounded out federal authorities and got a dose of his own medicine. No informal requests would be honored, he was told. If Romney wanted the U.S. Army in Detroit, he would have to make an official declaration that an insurrection was underway—and make it to President Johnson, the man he was planning to run against next year. Michael understood exactly what was going on: Like Romney with Cavanagh, Johnson wanted to be sure that a potential adversary was on the record, admitting that he couldn't handle the situation.

3. On Guard

As Michael was sending his story, he overheard that an AP reporter and photographer were about to go out with a National Guard contingent on a patrol. They said they had room for one more. Michael and the AP staffers hopped onto the back of the truck and introduced themselves to the 12 Guardsmen.

Every one was white. Some were Vietnam vets, but at least half had done their overseas Army duty in Korea or Germany and had never seen combat. They were suburban or small-town guys who worked at civilian jobs during the week and gathered on weekends to fulfill their Guard obligation. When Detroit erupted, they were taking part in an annual drill in rural Camp Grayling, hundreds of miles from inner-city Detroit in physical distance and light years away in social experience.

Between Michael's Army service and his time in Vietnam, he had an idea of what military professionalism looked like—and these guys looked nothing like it. They were scared part-time soldiers entering what they regarded as hostile territory, nervously fingering their assault rifles. It was a scene that did not inspire confidence.

Their orders were to escort a couple of fire wagons into the west side riot zone and provide cover while the firefighters tried to quell some of the blazes. Fire crews had been showered with rocks and bottles earlier in the day, and then gunfire in the evening. They rolled up to a burning shoe store, and the Guardsmen jumped down to form a perimeter around the firefighters as they hooked up their hoses. "You guys stay put," one soldier told them. Michael crouched down and watched as the AP photog started snapping away.

A small crowd approached, and some bottles flew. The Guardsmen lowered their rifles, with bayonets fixed, and the crowd retreated. The firefighters began dousing the blaze. A crack of sound—Michael recognized it instantly as a gunshot. Two more. A firefighter standing next to his truck grabbed his shoulder and cursed. Two Guardsmen pointed at a second-floor window in a building across the street. A volley of rifle fire peppered the building, then several more. Michael never heard an order to open fire.

Two police cars pulled up, along with an EMT crew to treat the wounded firefighter. Michael, still crouching in the back of the truck, watched six cops, all carrying shotguns, cautiously approach the building and disappear inside. They emerged 15 minutes later. Michael overheard one officer telling a soldier what they had found.

"Sniper's long gone," the cop said. "But we found a family living in the next apartment. They were flat on the floor, probably still are, scared out of their goddamn minds. Two young kids. The mother's trying to calm 'em down. Not having much luck."

Michael jumped down to talk with the cop. He said the walls of the family's apartment were pockmarked with bullet holes. "A miracle no one was hit," the cop told Michael. Then in a low voice, turning away from the Guardsmen and cocking his head toward them: "These motherfuckers are fuckin' crazy. They're scared shitless, and they'll fire on anything. Been happening all night. Not gonna help calm things down."

With the violence spreading, Romney bowed to reality and formally requested federal troops. Some of those sent were from the Army's 101st Airborne Division, a storied unit that had fought heroically in World War II and served in Vietnam. Michael had crossed paths with them in the Central Highlands.

Once the 101st was in the city, Michael drove over to where they were deployed, and looked around for familiar faces. He soon found one, a corporal—he had been a PFC the year before—and renewed acquaintances. As in Vietnam, Ray Johnson was happy to swap a cigarette for some conversation, very candid but not for attribution. He was a slender black youth from Chicago's South Side who had been drafted right out of high school and was nearing the end of his Army service. He hadn't been happy about being in 'Nam, and he wasn't much happier to be in Detroit.

"The guys in my unit are mostly okay, a lot of us are brothers. We're just here to try to cool things out without looking to waste anybody," he said. "Wish I could say the same for the cops."

"Some people I've talked with say they're a big part of the problem."

"They're just like the cops I knew back home—guys with big chips on their shoulders. They're taking this whole thing very personally, like they're a gang and their turf is being violated. They may wear badges, but they're not much different from the Blackstone Rangers in my old neighborhood."

Michael asked about the National Guardsmen, whom the paratroopers had replaced on the streets of the east side. Ray lit up another Marlboro and rolled his eyes. "Bunch of scared white dudes with itchy fingers," he said. "They were glad to get out of here, and I was glad to see 'em go. Not safe to be around."

Michael found this pattern repeating itself. Near where he had witnessed the sniper and the soldiers' reaction, a report of a gunman sparked a fusillade from Guardsmen, including fire from a

50-caliber machine gun mounted on a truck. One round killed a four-year-old girl, Tonia Blanding. The sniper report turned out to be wrong; one of the girl's relatives had lit a cigarette, and the flame from his lighter was mistaken for a muzzle flash by twitchy Guardsmen. On the edge of the riot zone, a visiting businesswoman went to her hotel room window to see what was going on outside. She died from a stray National Guard bullet.

As the week wore on, the deaths piled up. A store owner trying to protect his business from looters. A firefighter electrocuted by a high-voltage security fence. Another firefighter shot—possibly by a sniper, possibly by friendly fire, no one could say for sure—as he battled a blaze. A young mother sitting in the passenger seat of her husband's car. Looters, and others mistaken for looters. In the end, 43 people died.

The most egregious incident did not come to light until days after the disorder died down, when the Free Press and a local black congressman uncovered it. In a motel close to where the businesswoman was killed, police responding to a report of gunfire found several young black men together with two white women. When the officers left the Algiers Motel two hours later, three of the black men were dead. The police report attributed the deaths to sniper fire. Eyewitnesses' accounts and a pathologist's report told a different story: The men had been shot at close range by cops after being beaten.

4: The Price

Michael's paper could not get enough of his coverage, and he wound up staying the entire week. His national editor, Bob Patterson, told him readers seemed to have a weirdly morbid fascination for the story.

"It's like they're watching a slow-motion train wreck, and they can't turn away, no matter how grisly it is," Patterson told him.

"And you know, it's not like this is happening on the far side of the moon."

"What do you mean, Bob?"

"I mean that everybody in Chicago understands it could happen here. Jack pulled together an editors' meeting this morning, just to plan out how we'd cover a blowup. We may need your expertise, and Al and Dave's. You're our riot pros."

"Lucky us," Michael said.

As in his war coverage, Michael wanted to get beyond the "bang-bang," the easy stories chronicling the carnage, and try to make sense of what he had seen. What he saw in the week-long spasm was a marker signaling the end of many lazy, comforting illusions about the nature of race and racism in America, and he centered a story around that theme:

"Detroit's bitter irony is that it has, until now, prided itself on being a model of racial progress. Its humming auto plants provided well-paid work to thousands of black migrants from the rural South. The auto workers' union has a cadre of senior black leaders, and its president, Walter Reuther, marched beside Martin Luther King. Both Detroit's mayor and Michigan's governor forged their political reputations as civil rights supporters and won office with support from black voters."

Yet in the end, he wrote, Detroit's assumptions about itself were wrong. A liberal mayor and a reform-minded police chief did not lessen the resentment that many black Detroiters felt toward the police. Steady auto paychecks didn't make dilapidated housing or dishonest merchants palatable. And once the conflagration was ignited, the liberal delusions of Detroit's leaders prevented them from understanding what was happening until it was beyond anyone's control.

"In the wake of what happened here," Michael concluded, "the question that every city and every city leader should be asking is a simple one: If Detroit can descend into this abyss, is any place immune?"

For Lyndon Johnson, Michael wrote, Detroit was also a pivotal political moment. A president who had gone all in for civil rights now faced the prospect that panicked white voters would turn against all measures to help black people—and turn on him in next year's election. So he made Romney practically grovel for federal troops and made sure in his televised remarks announcing the commitment of the soldiers to note that the governor had lost control of the situation.

In those remarks, Johnson also tried to inoculate himself with frightened whites. "Pillage, looting, murder, and arson have nothing to do with civil rights," Johnson said. "We will not tolerate lawlessness. We will not endure violence. ... This nation will do whatever it is necessary to do to suppress and punish those who engage in it."

Michael returned from Detroit to a chilly reception. His father, who made a point of following his stories, told him in a testy phone call that he had been far too easy on the rioters. His mother, still a Johnson supporter despite her growing qualms about Vietnam, thought his analysis of the president's actions and motives was overly harsh. Neither seemed able to grasp his main point, which was that the urban conflagrations had created an inflection point that signaled the need to rethink all the old assumptions.

If his parents failed to see that, Riva had no difficulty—and drew lessons that brought Michael up short. She saw in Detroit, she told him, the living embodiment of the promise of a black revolution that she had been reading about in the works of Malcolm X, LeRoi Jones and Eldridge Cleaver.

Her attitude was hardened by the continued deterioration of her brother. Tommy increasingly depended on drugs of various kinds and was withdrawing more and more, his spirit wounded even more severely than his body. "It all goes back to that racist cop," she said. "He ruined Tommy's life, and he walked away like nothing happened."

The result was a powerful attraction to the Black Panther Party, a Bay Area group that centered its program on confronting the police— "pigs," they called them—with guns if necessary. The nascent New York Black Panthers held a special meeting in Harlem to commemorate "the revolutionary brothers of Detroit," and Riva returned from it afire with the spirit of the moment. Michael tried, tentatively, to offer a cautionary note, but he did not get far.

"The grievances that led to this are completely legitimate, but I have to wonder what was accomplished in the end," he said. "Most of the people killed were black. All the houses and a lot of the businesses that went up in smoke were owned by blacks. And the political fallout is going to be devastating. How do we create support for solutions to all these problems in a poisonous, polarized atmosphere like this?"

Riva started to snap back at him, then stopped herself. He was still Michael, and she still cared about him, even if she thought he was increasingly clueless about what was happening in America. So she softened her voice, if not her words.

"Michael, you have to understand. That's all over. Trying to slap Band-Aids on the kinds of gaping wounds that black people have suffered wasn't much of a strategy to begin with, and it gets more useless every day. More and more of us understand that, and that's why these rebellions are happening, and are going to keep happening. We're done playing nice or settling for half a loaf."

"What about the human cost? There were 43 people who died in Detroit, and 33 of them were black. That's a 3-to-1 ratio. Not great odds, I'd say."

"That's the cost of a revolution. It's been that way in every revolution. Algeria, Kenya, Cuba, Vietnam, you name it. The people at the bottom always take the highest casualties. But we always win in the end. It's a price worth paying."

Michael had gone into this conversation intending to measure his words carefully. But Riva's last remark, with its tone of ideological certitude, led him to say something he regretted for a long time afterward.

"Isn't that easy for you to say, sitting here in New York, watching other people do the dying?"

"It's not at all easy for me to say, because it's my brothers and sisters who are doing the dying. *My* people. Not yours."

Michael had no answer for that. What he did have was a heavy heart, and a growing fear about where Riva was headed in her thinking—and where they were headed as a couple. The city steamed and shimmered in midsummer heat, but he felt a sudden chill, a foretaste of an early frost.

Chapter Fourteen
—Exorcising Demons—

September 1967

1: 'Dump Johnson'

Allard Lowenstein was an odd duck. Everybody who knew him agreed on that, if little else. And many people knew him, because he was a dynamo of energy who never seemed to pause for food or sleep once he got an idea in his head.

He had been seized by a lot of ideas during his 39 years. He worked at various times as a lawyer, college professor, congressional staffer and speechwriter. In 1964, he was a volunteer in the Mississippi Freedom Summer campaign, and then attended the GOP convention that nominated Barry Goldwater because one of his best friends was a conservative Republican. Michael had met him several times, at civil rights demonstrations and in Washington, and now Lowenstein was reaching out to him again.

The idea that had seized Allard at this moment seemed quixotic in the extreme. He summed it up in a two-word slogan: "Dump Johnson." Lowenstein was convinced that LBJ was vulnerable to a challenge by an anti-war Democrat, and could be denied renomination. He wasn't fazed in the slightest by the fact that no president who had actively sought his party's nomination had been rejected in almost a century. Undeterred, Allard and a couple of young cohorts plotted out an elaborate strategic plan for how the latent discontent over Vietnam could be mobilized and harnessed by the right candidate, using the growing alienation of young people over the war as the starting point. Then they set out to find that candidate.

Their first choice was an obvious one. Allard knew Bobby Kennedy, having helped him write the memorable speech Bobby delivered in Cape Town the previous year challenging South Africa's apartheid regime on its home turf. He reached out to Kennedy, and with typical brashness told Bobby he should run and that he, Allard Lowenstein, would manage his campaign and take him straight to the White House.

Allard was also an inveterate press schmoozer, and for this effort he saw publicity as all upside. He knew Kennedy would be a difficult sell, and the more buzz he could create, the better his chances. So he called several reporters he knew, including Michael, outlined what he was trying to organize, and made it very clear it was all on the record.

Michael also knew Bobby fairly well, going back to Kennedy's difficult New York Senate campaign in 1964, when he had been burdened with the double accusation of being a ruthless opportunist and a carpetbagger to boot. Bobby had won, but he ran more than a million votes behind LBJ—a fact the president never failed to recall during their increasingly infrequent meetings.

Michael made a point of maintaining the relationship over the years, and had moved from skepticism to an appreciation of Bobby's growth as both a public and private person. Anna, who had known Kennedy longer, told him that Jack's death had changed Bobby in a way few people are altered once they reach adulthood. The single-minded operative who lived solely to serve his brother had evolved into a thoughtful, self-reflective, rather fatalistic man who was groping toward some unknown epiphany.

Where most journalists viewed Kennedy's turn toward opposition on Vietnam as a purely tactical move to exploit a Johnson weakness, Michael saw something else: a genuine effort to think through the proper uses and limits of American power, and an understanding of how the war was dividing the country and making it so much harder to deal with its many problems.

Michael heard that Allard and Bobby had met, and Lowenstein confirmed it, but was uncharacteristically coy about the outcome. "It's still a work in progress," he said. "You should talk to Bobby yourself." Michael was not entirely sure what that meant, but he followed through and arranged to meet Kennedy in his big corner office in the Old Senate Office Building.

Bobby agreed to talk about his meeting with Allard, but only if the conversation was totally off the record. "This is political dynamite for me," he said. "I can't stop other people from talking, but I won't do anything to feed the rumor mill."

Michael agreed to the terms, and quickly got to the point. Bobby was just as direct in his answer. "I can't do it," he said. "Even if I thought Allard had a sound plan—and I'm far from certain about that—I can't be the man who executes it."

"Why not? What's holding you back?"

"Three things, mainly. First, there's the old 'ruthless' trope. I've been trying to shed that image for three years, and I think I've made some progress. If I run against Lyndon, it will all come back, three times as strong. Second, there's the fact that a lot of Democrats aren't ready to desert Johnson yet, even though they suspect that he's blundered badly on the war."

"Are you sure about that?"

"Try asking your mother. I'm sorry to put it in such personal terms, but you have a one-woman focus group right in your own family. I know Anna very well, we talk often. Do you think she's ready to dump Lyndon and back me in a showdown?"

Michael knew the answer to that question. "And the third reason?"

"Lyndon and I can't stand the sight of each other, as you know quite well. The people around us have internalized that hatred. Maybe it was a mistake to let that happen, but it has. And that means if I challenge him, it will get very personal, very fast, and the entire party will get pulled into it. How we come out of that and still win in November is beyond me."

Michael thought for several moments about what Bobby had said, and how to reply. When he did, it was as much a statement as a question.

"Isn't there an overarching issue here, of what's happening to this country? I was in Detroit. It was like I was back in Vietnam. It was like that New Left slogan, 'bring the war home,' had come to life. I don't think it was an aberration. It's only going to get worse, because Johnson is completely out of touch—that speech he made railing against 'lawlessness' was an embarrassment—and the Republicans would be worse. And now we've got George Wallace in the race, running around the country stoking racial fears."

"I'm well aware of all these things," Kennedy replied. "I've been trying to sound the alarm about them for two years."

"In that case, aren't you obligated to run? You're the only politician who has any chance of bringing people together behind a program of ending this wretched war and attacking the social problems that are tearing us apart. I'm not talking about Washington pols, who'll fall in line behind anyone with power. I'm talking about everyday people, who know their country is spiraling out of control and know they're paying the price."

Kennedy leaned back and smiled. "Sounds like you're practicing politics without a license."

"Maybe. Tell me where I'm wrong."

Kennedy expelled a long breath. "I'm not used to reporters talking to me like activists," he said at last. "Mostly, you guys just want to know when I'm planning to stick a knife in Lyndon's back. So this is a little disconcerting.

"I don't disagree at all with your fears about where we're heading. I just don't think I'm the man, right now, to play the role that Allard and a lot of other people want me to play. I told Allard that, and suggested he talk to George McGovern. I don't know if George is interested, but he'd be a good candidate. And having someone run against Lyndon might put some pressure on him to change course.

"And I've noticed that Gene McCarthy has become really vocal about the war, in a way that I've never heard him talk before. You know Gene, he tends to sound like a seminarian, not exactly a rabble-rouser. But his latest speeches on Vietnam have been anything but academic. When you put your reporter hat back on, you might want to talk to him."

Michael thanked Bobby for the time and the tip, but he came away from the conversation profoundly depressed. His concern for the country's shredding social fabric had become personal for him. Riva's turn toward black radical politics, and the growing gap between them that resulted, weighed heavily on him. He had no illusions about a magical cure, but he saw in Bobby Kennedy a politician who might—might—be able to pull disaffected people like Riva back from the edge. He was at war with himself about it; one part of him dismissed those hopes as naïve illusions. Yet he could not help nurturing them, because of his deep love for her.

He followed up and talked to McGovern and then McCarthy. McGovern ruled himself out. But McCarthy, while typically speaking elliptically, left Michael with the strong impression that he would go against LBJ if no one else came forward.

Those interviews gave Michael enough to write a story outlining the dump-Johnson strategy and suggesting that Lowenstein may have found a halfway credible candidate to execute it. The story looked prescient when McCarthy began dropping hints about his availability.

In October, Michael made a reporting trip to New Hampshire, where the first presidential primary would be held in five months. What he found suggested that Lowenstein was not tilting at windmills. It was a conservative state, overwhelmingly white, largely rural and instinctively Republican, but his interviews with local Democrats and everyday people alike revealed deep disquiet about the war and a sense that Johnson was out of touch.

"I served in Korea, and I'm proud of that service," one middle-aged man told him at an American Legion fish fry. "But my son got drafted in the spring, and he'll probably be in Vietnam before too long. What's the point? What are we fighting for? I can't tell you, and I don't know anyone who can."

Another Army veteran told him that he had no objection to the overall goal of the war, but had serious problems with the way Johnson was executing it. "If we're going to do it, just do it," he said. "No half-measures, no 'bomb here but not there.' Get it over with and get the hell out."

Michael also noticed that New Hampshire's laws contained a quirk that could benefit an insurgent candidate. This notoriously cantankerous state contained a sizable pool of voters who were not registered in any party. These voters were free to cast a ballot in either major party's primary. It meant that independents who wanted to send a message that they disliked the war, or simply wanted to weaken Johnson, could vote for a Democratic challenger.

His story from New Hampshire concluded that there was fertile ground to be plowed there by a serious anti-war candidate. Michael had achieved some standing as a Washington journalist, and his piece helped establish the credibility of the dump-Johnson effort with other political reporters.

2. Trial Balloon

Johnson was not entirely oblivious to the discontent building up over the war. He regarded people like McCarthy and Lowenstein as minor irritants. His dread of Bobby Kennedy had only deepened, however, and he viewed Kennedy's criticisms of the war as a potential prelude to a challenge from the one Democrat who could give him serious trouble. He and his inner circle began considering maneuvers that might pre-empt the problem. Their thoughts quickly centered on a classic Washington ploy: finding a scapegoat who could be sacrificed to appease the dissenters.

After running through a list of possibilities, they soon came to rest on General William Westmoreland, the commander of U.S. forces in Vietnam. In many ways, Westmoreland was perfect for the role. He was important enough to matter, he was resented by many war critics because of his imperious public manner, and there was a ready-made replacement in his well-regarded deputy, Creighton Abrams. Yet there also was the potential for substantial blowback, because "Westy" was an intensely political general who had taken care to develop strong ties with hawkish members of Congress.

So Johnson and his advisors made use of another tried-and-true maneuver: the trial balloon.

Anna Maria's Italian Restaurant, on Connecticut Avenue just north of Dupont Circle, was not known for the authenticity or quality of its cuisine. It had two virtues. In a town notorious for early closings, it was open until 1 a.m. for those wanting a late supper. And it was just the right distance from downtown D.C. to be convenient for discreet lunch meetings.

Michael walked in, waited for his eyes to adjust to the dark interior, and looked around until he spotted Horace Busby at a corner table. Busby had officially left the White House two years ago, but those familiar with the inner workings of the Johnson administration knew that Buzz still made himself available to LBJ for surreptitious undertakings.

Michael picked at a rather wilted Caesar's salad and waited for Busby to get around to the reason he had asked Michael to lunch.

"Have you written anything about General Westmoreland?"

"I wrote a profile last year, when I was in-country. Nothing much since then."

"You might want to revisit the subject."

"Oh? Why is that? Something up with him?"

"There might be."

"That's a little cryptic, Buzz."

"Let me put it this way, Michael. If you were to write a story saying the president had become uncertain about the general's leadership of U.S. forces and was starting to look at possible alternatives, you could look very smart."

"Would I, now? Or I could look very stupid. What are you telling me? That LBJ has decided to replace him?"

Busby's only response to that question was to swallow another mouthful of lasagna. Michael tried a different tack.

"What's the motivation for this? Why has the president suddenly lost confidence in Westmoreland?"

"You know the situation on the ground better than I do. You were there. Do you think things are going well for us?"

Busby's habit of answering a question with another question was beginning to irritate Michael, but he couldn't ignore what he was being told.

"Okay, and if he does decide to ditch Westy, who would he replace him with?"

"Isn't that pretty obvious? He does have a deputy, doesn't he?"

The rest of the meal produced nothing else that was useful, but Michael already had plenty to digest. He ignored the passing taxis and made his way back to his office on foot, hoping the half-hour walk would help clear his mind. The conversation with Busby had been maddeningly enigmatic. Buzz had never said definitively that Johnson was thinking of replacing his top general. He had only hinted at it, albeit broadly. And Busby had insisted that the conversation be on background, with only the vaguest of attributions: someone familiar with the president's thinking. Those were arguments for extreme wariness. On the other hand, Busby's close connection to the White House was undeniable. And, as always, there was the competitive aspect. If Buzz was talking to Michael about this, he—or someone else in Johnson's orbit—might well be talking to other reporters.

When Michael got back to his office, he got the deputy White House press secretary on the phone. After a lot of verbal fencing, the flack said he could confirm—completely off the record—that the gist of what Busby had said was accurate. That did not really settle the matter, because if the White House wanted Michael to write the story, its press office certainly wouldn't be refuting it. A round of calls to congressional sources, both pro-war and anti-war, produced nothing of any value. Either the White House wasn't talking about this on the Hill, which seemed unlikely if it were true, or lawmakers on both sides were holding their fire, waiting to see what would happen next.

Michael reached out to a widening circle of potential sources who might know something. The results were inconclusive. Nobody knocked the story down, but nobody really confirmed it, either. Yet it seemed clear that people were aware of the chatter about Westmoreland. That left Michael with the worst of both worlds: a story that had just enough uncertainty to hold a risk of making him look foolish, but just enough substance to hold a risk of being beaten by a rival.

The story that Michael wound up writing was carefully hedged, reporting only that the president was beginning to consider the possibility of a change in commanders. The hedging didn't matter in the slightest. In the increasingly volatile atmosphere prevailing in Washington, the story triggered a powerful reaction, as some journalists tried to match it, others tried to knock it down, and the congressional sources who had been of no help to Michael before the story ran began issuing loud reactions. The loudest came from Westmoreland's fans on the Hill; the chairman of the House Armed Services Committee, a right-wing South Carolina Democrat named Mendel Rivers, issued a statement calling Westmoreland a "fine American patriot" who had guided American forces to the brink of victory and should be allowed to finish the job. "Replacing this superb commander at this moment would undermine our entire war effort," Rivers said.

Two days after Michael's story ran, the White House press secretary, George Christian, held a briefing for reporters. "The president regards General Westmoreland as a superb commander," he said. "He is convinced that we are winning the fight in Vietnam, and that General Westmoreland is the right leader to carry that fight through to a victorious conclusion. Any reports to the contrary—any reports about replacing him—are categorically false."

Michael was in the back of the room during this briefing. As he filed out with the rest of the press corps when it ended, he noticed his colleagues were averting their gaze and giving him a wide berth. He felt as if he were suddenly radioactive.

Michael's first call was to Jack Rothstein. Jack listened in silence as Michael offered his apologies, and then his explanation of how it had come about. "If you feel like I need to resign to protect the paper, I will," Michael said. "I feel terrible about this."

"Don't be ridiculous. If I got rid of every reporter who made a mistake, I wouldn't have anyone left, because we all do it. Even editors. You're still a damn good reporter, and you're still our guy in D.C. So shake it off, and learn what you can from it, and get ready for the next story."

"Okay, Jack. Thank you. But I still feel like shit about it."

He called Horace Busby several times. Buzz never returned his call. He had more luck connecting with the deputy press secretary, who offered no apologies, just a terse explanation.

"The reaction on the Hill was volcanic. Simple as that. You may have noticed that George used the exact words that Chairman Rivers used to describe Westmoreland—'superb commander.' That wasn't a coincidence."

"So you used me to float a trial balloon, and when it got shot down, you all bailed out as fast as you could," Michael replied. "Thanks a lot."

"Oh, grow up, will you? You came to me, as I recall, not the other way around. You asked me a question, and I gave you an answer—an answer that was accurate as of that moment."

"Well, I may have come to you, but only because Horace Busby came to me."

"Who? Does Horace Busby work at the White House? I seem to have a distinct memory of attending his goodbye party a couple of years ago. It was a pretty good party, too."

"You used me. And you misled me."

"You misled yourself. You wanted that story, you wanted the scoop. If it had turned out differently, you'd be calling me today to thank me. Or, more likely, you wouldn't have called at all, because you'd have forgotten all about how I'd helped you."

That evening, Michael nursed his wounds over dinner at his parents' house. He got little sympathy there, either.

"If you'd bothered to call me before you wrote that dead fish, I could've warned you off the story," Alan told him. "I know the state of play, and there's no way in hell the president would change commanders right now, just when things are falling into place so nicely."

Michael thought the situation in Vietnam was hardly falling into place, but he didn't have the emotional energy to get into a debate about it. "I thought about calling you, but I didn't think it would be right to use you as a source on this, given how much we disagree about the war."

For the second time that day, Michael found himself being told to grow up.

"Really, son? You're not willing to call me when I could help you, in this case help you avoid stepping in it? But you're more than willing to sit around here and soak up the intelligence that your mother and I provide you, simply by talking about the state of the world? And you've been doing that for years, and we've been happy to do it for you. So, tell me—what the hell is the difference?"

3: Color Blind

While Michael was away in New Hampshire, Riva had dinner with Deana Franklin. They wound up going back to Deana's apartment for drinks, and talked long into the night. They were old friends, and they spoke candidly about their lives and sorrows. Deana had recently split up with her longtime partner and was in a melancholy mood. It had been a long time in coming, she said, so it wasn't a shock, but she still felt as if a part of her had been wrenched from its roots.

Riva found the failure of another biracial relationship unsettling, and asked if race had played a role in the breakup. Deana was a long time in answering.

"I never really thought about race that much when we were together," she said at last. "Alicia seemed so totally color-blind, and our gender was so much in the foreground, and figuring out how to navigate in a world that often wasn't friendly to our kind of relationship. But when I think about it now, yes, it probably had something to do with it. No matter how much we cared about each other, and no matter how much we had in common, we came from such different worlds."

That led to a discussion about the larger context of race. Riva was surprised by Deana's mixed reaction to the rebellions of the summer. Deana saw Detroit and Newark as a natural response to years of grinding oppression, symptoms of a society that was nearing a fundamental crisis. The fact that people at the bottom were breaking free of all the old constraints was a source of hope to her. But she also cautioned Riva that the anger in the streets needed to find a political direction, that it had to become the motor force of a genuine revolutionary movement. When Riva mentioned the Panthers as a model for that movement, Deana said she liked their boldness, their capacity to inspire, their willingness to draw stark lines of separation—but she also questioned whether a program based mostly on confrontations with the cops and macho swagger was enough to meet the moment.

As was often the case when she talked with Deana, Riva felt an almost palpable sense of her mind being stretched as she took in her friend's distinctive slant on the world, large and small. The experience was at once stimulating and unsettling.

They fell silent for a moment. Deana looked at her intently. "You haven't said much about Michael, and your own relationship. Haven't said anything, actually."

"I'm not sure where to begin. What you said earlier about you and Alicia, coming from such different worlds—I didn't think it would matter, but now it seems to matter more and more. He's the best man I've ever known, and the best white person, man or woman. He's as close to color-blind as you can be. He just doesn't seem to see race."

"And you used to think that was a blessing, but now you're not so sure?"

Riva looked at her friend, and realized that this was familiar territory to her.

"Yes, that's right, Deana. I'm finding that race matters to me— my race matters. There's no escaping it. I'm starting to wonder if I've been kidding myself, thinking that I was somehow special, unique, and the laws of racial gravity didn't apply to me. Starting to wonder if I can live the way I've been living, a black woman in a mostly white world. No, not starting to wonder; I've been wondering about it for a long time now. And if I can't live in that world, I don't know how I can live with Michael. And I don't know how to talk to him about it."

"Wow. You've got quite a problem, my dear. Or several problems."

"Don't I know it. And I think he does, too, somewhere deep inside, even though we don't talk about it. He's certainly not stupid, and he knows me well enough to read my moods. Lately we've been tiptoeing around each other, almost afraid to engage in anything beyond superficial conversations."

"Do you still—are you still attracted to each other?"

"We don't make it as often as we used to, but when we do—yeah, we really make it. He's still a wonderful lover. Attentive, tender, passionate. That's part of what makes this so hard. If we had cooled off, it would be a lot easier to walk away."

"Is that what you want to do? Walk away?"

"No. Yes. God, Deana, I don't fucking know what I want to do."

They sat silently, side by side, on Deana's ratty sofa. They edged closer. Riva leaned into her friend's shoulder and began to cry softly. Deana's arms were around her, and her tears were flowing freely. Deana held her for a long time, until her weeping gradually ceased.

Afterward, Riva thought long and hard, trying to understand the emotions that had poured out of her so unexpectedly. She realized there was no single source for her tears, that she was weeping for many things. Her marriage and its descent into a pallid limbo, of course. But also her sense of herself, or at least her old sense, the one she had erected so carefully over so many years, the one that was now falling apart, piece by piece, no matter how hard she tried to buttress it. That made her especially sad—and also made her angry.

She was not accustomed to feeling helpless, unmoored, swept out to sea by an irresistible tide. She was used to feeling in control; used to feeling an easiness, a sureness, a sense that her life was in sync with the world. A feeling that she'd cracked the code, mastered the rhythm. She felt anything but that now.

She had to regain some degree of command over her life. She was determined to do that. How? She wasn't at all sure. That lack of certainty truly was cause for sorrow, and rage, and something else— a touch of panic.

Then another thought formed in her mind: a powerful sense that she needed above all to embrace her own feelings, to stop denying or questioning them, to stop compromising with them. She remembered something James Baldwin had written: "You have to decide who you are and force the world to deal with you, not with its idea of you."

If race really did matter to her, she needed to follow the logic of that insight. She had to be willing to organize her life around it, around being black. If that meant giving up on living in a biracial world—really, a mostly white world—well, she would do it. If that had implications for her marriage and for her husband—if Michael's color-blindness wasn't the unalloyed virtue she once thought it was, but a form of self-delusion, a willful denial of reality—she needed to take that on, as well. And so did he. She had to make him see it and act on it. If he could. And if he couldn't, she needed to find that out, and soon.

The panicky feeling hadn't disappeared. It still lurked there, just beneath the surface. But she felt as if she'd forced it to retreat, drained some of its toxic power. She felt back in control of her life, at least a bit. Not as much as she wanted to be. Certainly not as much as she needed to be. Well, it was a start.

4: Belly of the Beast

Michael had first encountered the anti-Vietnam war movement on a frigid January day in 1965, watching a few hundred people parade through Times Square thrusting leaflets into the hands of bemused bystanders. It left him doubly disappointed: as a journalist, because it hadn't made for much of a story, and as an old, instinctive activist, because the whole affair seemed so futile and so inadequate to the stakes at hand.

Since then, he had watched as opposition to the war swelled into a major force. As draft calls mounted and images of violence flooded American television screens, demonstrations large and small spread across the country. Some were polite and orderly, others provocative and disruptive. Students burned draft cards and chanted that Johnson was a murderer and a war criminal. In the spring of 1967, Martin Luther King spoke out against the war, and more than 300,000 marched from Central Park to the United Nations. Polls showed a majority of Americans disapproved of the protests and still favored the war, but the margin of support was slipping.

Now, Michael was preparing to cover the anti-war movement's most ambitious effort yet: a rally at the Lincoln Memorial in Washington, followed by a march to the Pentagon to "confront the warmakers" at the source. The day was planned to bridge a divide in the anti-war camp between moderates who wanted to appeal to middle-class Americans and uneasy lawmakers, and radicals who believed disruption and confrontation were essential elements of any successful action. The rally would be massive in size, mainstream in tone and decorous in manner. Once it was over, those with an appetite for something more adventurous would take the field.

Michael came home to New York for a few days before the Washington march. He discovered, somewhat to his surprise, that Riva was planning to go. She had no use for rallies, she said, but the prospect of a confrontation at the Pentagon was very much to her taste. She planned to march with a black anti-war group that included draft resisters and military deserters. She showed Michael one of the group's banners for the march. It was emblazoned with a large black clenched fist.

Michael suggested they travel to D.C. together, but Riva told him, half embarrassed and half defiant, that she was going with her group on a bus. She agreed to link up with him at the end of the day.

The rally fulfilled all of its goals. It was large, with more than 100,000 attending. Its roster of speakers embraced all factions in the movement. And as a result, it was long and increasingly boring, especially to the hotbloods girding for action.

Michael listened to the speeches with half an ear and scribbled a few quotes. His assignment was to concentrate on an overarching story that captured the sweep and meaning of the day, and the oratory was only a small part of it.

Riva and her cohort skipped the rally altogether. They wanted to be in the vanguard of whatever was to happen at the Pentagon, so they positioned themselves to be in the forefront of the marchers once they moved out.

Finally, the orators ran out of steam, and marchers began streaming out onto Memorial Bridge. They walked at a measured pace, past twin bronze statues of warriors that guarded the eastern end of the bridge, and out onto the span. Under a brilliant blue sky, the Custis-Lee mansion above Arlington Cemetery on the far side of the Potomac gleamed in the sunlight. At the end of the bridge, a left turn took them into the Pentagon's north parking lot, where yet another rally with more speeches was planned.

Some stopped to listen, but most kept moving through the parking lot toward the massive stone structure that loomed ahead. Michael, tired of oratory, kept moving too, looking for a higher vantage point to observe what would unfold.

Riva was near the front of the marchers as they crossed the parking lot and a highway and headed toward an area in front of the Pentagon called the mall. At the top of a grassy slope, a temporary fence barred the way. Only briefly, though; several people grabbed the flimsy wire mesh, pulled and twisted, and a four-foot-wide section was torn away. As marchers streamed through the opening, a burst of laughter erupted. "Did they really think that was going to stop us?" a young man next to Riva said with a chuckle.

Michael, circling and climbing, watched the crowd squeeze through the gap and fan out again as they headed for the long, pillared entrance. No one was here to impede the marchers, but at the end of the mall, where it rose to meet the level of the building, Michael could see a line of helmeted, uniformed men.

Riva and the crowd around her surged forward, energized by their easy penetration of the fence, then slowed as they approached a ramp and a short flight of steps. At the top of the steps a rope was strung, and behind it stood a line of helmeted military police and federal marshals carrying clubs.

Michael watched the head of the marchers, numbering in the hundreds by now, fill up the steps and pause before the rope. Turning, Michael saw a long column stretching back across the mall and onto the bridge, with more waiting at the far end of the span to cross. He estimated that 10,000 people were taking part.

Riva was in the second row behind the rope line, just below the top step. The line of MPs and marshals took several steps forward and positioned themselves barely a foot from the barrier. Everyone seemed to freeze in place. Protesters began calling out, some pleading with those on the other side to join them, others shouting profane insults.

Someone in the front row grabbed the rope and began to lift it. At a barked command, the entire line of marshals and MPs advanced, swinging clubs. A man directly in front of Riva took a blow and tumbled backward into her, nearly knocking her down the steps. As she steadied herself, a truncheon landed heavily on her shoulder, another on her temple. For the second time in her life, she fell to one knee and felt her head spin.

The marshals pushed the crowd down to the bottom of the steps and formed a new skirmish line in front of them. Another group of MPs came up to form a second line. Nobody was shouting "Join us!" anymore; insults were flying furiously now, along with some bottles and stones. The approaching crowd of marchers packed in behind them until there was no room to move. Riva, still shaky from the blows, had the unsettling feeling of being trapped.

Michael took in the confrontation at the rope line, then watched as an uneasy equilibrium set in. With that front appearing stable for the moment, he circled around to catch what promised to be one of the day's weirder events. On a makeshift stage, a gaggle of pranksters had gathered at the behest of Abbie Hoffman, a veteran activist who had come to believe that ridicule and surreal street theater were the movement's most powerful weapons. His idea for today was a ceremony to exorcise the war demons haunting the Pentagon, ending in a finale that he promised would levitate the building 300 feet.

Amid the pungent smell of pot, Ed Sanders, a founder of the rock band The Fugs, chanted "Out demons out!" over and over. He announced what he called a first for the Pentagon: "a grope-in" to serve as a "seminal culmination in the spirit of peace and brotherhood, a real grope for peace." Hoffman rounded up couples willing to fulfill the mission. Beat poet Allen Ginsberg punctuated Sanders' rap with Hindu mantras. A line of MPs guarding the building watched impassively.

Michael tried to get his mind around the dissonance: a scene straight out of a Marx Brothers comedy taking place a short distance away from a violent confrontation that left people bruised and bloodied. Like so much of what was happening in America, the images refused to mesh into any kind of coherent pattern. They were shards of reality that spun around each other, collided, and then flew apart, like subatomic particles in an especially unstable isotope.

The Pentagon remained earthbound, and Riva and her friends grew tired of hunkering down in an inert crowd at the bottom of the steps. They worked their way free and tried to circle back and to the left to reach the river entrance to the building, where they heard another confrontation was brewing. They pushed through a patch of low trees and shrubbery, climbed a small rise, and walked head-on into a unit of soldiers wearing gas masks. As more protesters piled up behind Riva, the soldiers lowered their bayoneted rifles. She never saw the tear gas, but suddenly she was coughing and choking. She stumbled back down the hill, gasping for breath.

The sun was setting behind the Pentagon, casting a long shadow across the pavement, as Michael made his way back to the parking lot and looked for Riva's bus. He found it, and her as well, sitting on the ground with the group she had traveled with, waiting for the driver. She couldn't talk much, her throat still inflamed from the gas. She had a small bruise on her temple, and her jeans jacket was ripped in a couple of places. When Michael embraced her and asked how she was doing, she shrugged and looked away. "I'm okay," she rasped.

Michael didn't think she looked so okay, but her face was set in an expression of stubborn defiance that did not invite solicitude. He knew that look well and respected its boundaries.

Michael knew the leader of the group, Curtis Marbury, from his SNCC days in Alabama, and asked if he could interview him. Marbury was reluctant at first. He finally agreed to make a few comments about his group, which had plans to launch a national campaign to encourage young black men to resist the draft. "This war is another form of genocide against us," he said. "We're being drafted at twice the rate of whites, and we're taking twice as many casualties. So saying 'hell no' isn't a choice for us, like it is for white folks. It's a matter of survival."

While Michael was talking to Marbury, members of the group were eying him, some curiously, many others warily. Riva looked conflicted and embarrassed. She's too decent to tell me straight up that I'm not welcome here, Michael thought, but that's the reality. He finished his interview and walked over to her.

"I hope your sore throat clears up. Take it easy. I'll see you home tomorrow. I love you."

Riva nodded, nothing more. As he walked away, Michael took one look back. The expression on his wife's face was unmistakable. It was one of relief.

Chapter Fifteen
—Breaking Point—

January 1968

1: Tet

Michael had no use for the background briefing. It was an antiquated piece of Washington arcana that brought together a politician and a group of reporters under ground rules that stipulated everything was off the record unless the pol retroactively agreed to be quoted on something specific. The underlying rationale was that protective anonymity encouraged candor. Michael's experience was that most politicians stuck to their habitual caution anyway and then used the rules to shape self-serving quotes.

Today's backgrounder was different. The guest was Bobby Kennedy, and the moment could not have been more fraught.

The New Hampshire primary, the opening act of the 1968 presidential campaign, was just six weeks away. Gene McCarthy had been waging a desultory campaign against LBJ and the war for two months, trying to execute Allard Lowenstein's dump-Johnson strategy. Yet Washington still buzzed with chatter that McCarthy was a stalking horse, a placeholder for the president's real opponent, who would step in when the moment was right: Robert Kennedy. Both Johnson and McCarthy, in their own ways and for their own purposes, fed these rumors, and Bobby's disavowals were increasingly unconvincing.

So Michael was seated at a breakfast table in a private room at the National Press Club in Washington, toying with a plate of watery scrambled eggs, as Kennedy faced a group of political reporters and columnists. It did not take long for the money question to land on Kennedy's plate: "Are there any circumstances under which you would challenge the president for the Democratic nomination this year?"

"No, I can't conceive of any circumstances."

"No circumstances whatsoever?" The questioner threw out some possibilities. "What if the president decides not to run?"

"Now you're talking about an act of God," Kennedy replied.

It sounded about as definitive as any modern-day politician could be. And yet, as the session continued and Bobby talked about the situation in the country and the Johnson administration's failures, he sounded to Michael much more like a potential candidate than a committed noncombatant.

The war in Vietnam, Bobby told the group, was plainly tearing the country apart. Yet America was a society already riven by deep problems of racial and economic inequality, despite a veneer of prosperity. The result was profound alienation and discontent—not just among the usual suspects, black people and young people, but among many other groups as well. The war was exacerbating this division and alienation, but it was as much a symptom as a cause.

"The cause hasn't been analyzed and dealt with," Kennedy said. "There's affluence, yet a feeling of unhappiness in the country. If someone touched the heart of that, and how to bring the country back together—if he could bind the wounds, appeal to the generous nature of Americans. If I thought there was anything I could do about it, I would do it."

But there was, obviously, something he could do about it, and he wasn't. As Bobby went on, it seemed to Michael that he was being given a window into Kennedy's inner turmoil. He named his reasons for not running, which had not changed since Michael's conversation with him in the fall: It would tear the party apart, it would deliver the White House and perhaps Congress as well to the

Republicans, it would damage his credibility as an advocate for the causes he embraced.

In almost the same breath, he acknowledged that this reasoning made him sound weak and timid. "I know that isn't very satisfactory, but I don't see that there is anything I can do about it."

As the backgrounder neared its end, it devolved into the usual haggling about what would be put on the record and how the quotes would be worded. Amid this dickering, a journalist handed Kennedy a wire service dispatch from Saigon. The Viet Cong, it reported, had launched a coordinated series of high-intensity attacks across Vietnam. Bobby read the dispatch and handed it back to the reporter with a sardonic smile. "Yeah, we're winning," he said.

Winning was what Lyndon Johnson had promised, and the fall and winter had been full of predictions from the president and his top aides and generals that victory was drawing near. Worried about slippage in the polls, they launched a "success offensive" designed to convince skeptics that the enemy was on its last legs. It culminated with a speech by General Westmoreland, still firmly in command of U.S forces, in which he asserted that "we have reached an important point when the end begins to come into view." The enemy, Westmoreland said, simply could not mount a major offensive. In an interview with Time magazine, he upped the ante: "I hope they try something, because we are looking for a fight."

Now Westmoreland was getting what he had asked for, and a lot more. As Bobby and the journalists were sparring in Washington, it was already nighttime halfway around the world in Vietnam, and under the cover of that darkness, 80,000 North Vietnamese and Viet Cong troops were swinging into action in a well-prepared general offensive.

Over the next several hours, they launched attacks on more than 100 towns and cities, including two-thirds of South Vietnam's provincial capitals. In Saigon, insurgent teams that had infiltrated the city attacked the main U.S. air base, the South Vietnamese military's general staff and naval headquarters, the national radio station and the presidential palace. Smaller units struck scores of police stations, military posts and army billets, killing officers from a carefully prepared list. As the attacks spread, a sense of panic enveloped the capital.

The greatest blow to U.S. prestige came when a 19-member Viet Cong team blew a hole in the wall surrounding the new U.S. embassy and charged through it. Unable to shoot their way into the main building, the commandos hunkered down in the courtyard and fought a running battle with Marines and MPs that lasted for six hours. It ended only when troops were dropped onto the embassy roof by helicopter and managed to kill the remaining insurgents. By that time, film footage of the embassy fight was airing on American TV screens, providing vivid visual evidence of the Viet Cong's capacity to penetrate the heart of U.S. power in the country.

These assaults were the start of what came to be called the Tet Offensive, named for the lunar New Year that began the same night as the attacks. It took days of bitter, bloody fighting for U.S. and South Vietnamese troops to roll back the enemy's gains and recapture the territory it had seized. In Hue, a large provincial capital, the insurgents occupied the entire city, killed thousands of government sympathizers, and held on for almost a month before being dislodged.

The intensity of Tet's violence was crystallized in a single photograph, by AP photographer Eddie Adams, that ran on the front pages of scores of American newspapers. It captured a South Vietnamese general holding a pistol to the temple of a young Viet Cong insurgent an instant before he pulled the trigger.

One week into the offensive, insurgents overran a town called Ben Tre deep in the Mekong Delta. U.S. forces responded with an intense barrage of bombs, rockets and napalm. The firepower drove the Viet Cong out. It also left the town in ruins and killed hundreds of villagers. When AP reporter Peter Arnett asked a U.S. officer why the action had been taken, his answer became an iconic, Orwellian epitaph for Ben Tre and the entire war: "It became necessary to destroy the town to save it."

The price of Tet to the communist side was high; tens of thousands of its soldiers were casualties, and the goal of touching off a general uprising against the South Vietnamese government went unfulfilled. Yet the cost to the U.S. was higher. The reality that a supposedly beaten enemy could carry out such a campaign exposed the hollowness of the government's predictions of imminent victory. When Johnson held a press conference and proclaimed the offensive a "complete failure," the reaction was widespread disbelief and even derision.

In private, officials knew better, Michael learned from his sources. Defense Secretary McNamara, on his way out because he had lost LBJ's confidence, told the president Tet showed two things: the U.S. had underestimated the enemy's capabilities, and that enemy would remain a formidable force despite its losses. When Alan McMaster—still a true believer despite Tet's carnage—attended a meeting of advisors called to pull together recommendations for Johnson, he was stunned by the prevailing pessimism. When Alan advocated telling the president to stay the course, he found himself almost alone.

The breaking point came a few days later, when Westmoreland delivered his recommendations for how to respond to Tet. The general coupled his bland assertion that the offensive had been a great military defeat for the enemy with a request for a commitment of more than 200,000 additional U.S. troops, on top of the 550,000 that were already in-country.

The incoming defense secretary, Clark Clifford, was a wily Washington operative who had no institutional or personal investment in the war and could look at the situation with fresh eyes. The more he learned, the clearer it became to him that Vietnam was a bottomless pit, that neither the generals nor the civilian officials had any real strategy beyond more men, more bombing, more public proclamations of imminent victory. When he discovered that Johnson, shell-shocked and sleepwalking through the aftermath of Tet, was about to rubber-stamp Westmoreland's request, he called a time-out and began a stealthy, skillful, concerted effort to turn the policy around.

Michael was torn between covering the maneuvering in Washington or the political impact of Tet. His instincts told him the campaign trail in New Hampshire was the better story, and he was not disappointed. On Michael's last foray to the state, in early January, McCarthy had seemed perfunctory, almost bored, in his campaigning. Now, as he sensed with a politician's instinct a turn in public opinion, he was energized and on the attack. He still spoke in an elliptical, almost professorial style, but he had found a message and kept hammering it: Tet exposed the bankruptcy of Johnson's war policies, and New Hampshire voters had an opportunity to send the president an unmistakable message that it was time to change course.

Equally important, Michael found that the small state was slowly being inundated by Al Lowenstein's student army. Academia was still the heart of the anti-war movement, and in Boston, just across the state line, were 40 colleges, with more in western Massachusetts and Connecticut. From a storefront office in the state capital of Concord, scores of student volunteers fanned out across New Hampshire, knocking on doors, chatting up shoppers and leafleting factory gates. Admonished to get "clean for Gene," they dressed neatly and modestly, tied back long hair in ponytails and shaved beards. Michael, who had sported a beard since grad school, felt absolutely bohemian in their midst.

The polls still showed McCarthy at just 20 percent, despite Tet, but some of the local pols were not so sure. The Johnson campaign in the state was almost nonexistent, they told Michael; the president was passively relying on the cachet of incumbency and the local Democratic organization to smother the McCarthy insurgency under its weight. It might have worked before Tet, but things had changed. The potential for independents to vote in the

Democratic primary increased Johnson's vulnerability; there were plenty of voters in this fundamentally conservative state who felt that LBJ's mistake was not that he had gone into Vietnam, but that he had gone in with insufficient ruthlessness.

Michael summed it up in the nut paragraph—the "so-what?"—of his story from the trail. Johnson's peril, he wrote, was not so much that he might lose the primary, but that no one was sure any longer what victory might look like. Incumbent presidents were supposed to be invulnerable, and the expectations for McCarthy had been set so low that anything less than a Johnson landslide could easily look like a setback for the beleaguered president. "And in the wake of the profound questions about the war that the Tet offensive has raised," he wrote, "very few people here anticipate an LBJ landslide."

2: All in the Family

Michael flew to Washington from New Hampshire and walked into the middle of another family battle. He and Alan were barely speaking to each other, their differences over the war so deep that any conversation quickly escalated into a shouting match.

Anna also avoided discussing the war with Alan. She was even angrier at the dissident Democrats, who in her view were undermining the only politician who stood between the country and her worst nightmare: Richard Nixon. Anna had despised Nixon since his red-baiting days in the 1940s, and his resurrection from the political graveyard filled her with dread. On that point, she and her husband agreed.

"You want a good story, and McCarthy and his children's crusade fill the bill, but for god's sake, think about the consequences," she told Michael. "If he really damages the president, there will be only one beneficiary, and we both know who that'll be. In case you haven't noticed, Tricky Dick is now the Republican frontrunner."

Johnson's vulnerability was entirely his own doing, Michael replied. McCarthy was the symptom, not the cause. The problem was the war, not the voters who had turned against it and its architect.

"It doesn't matter if Nixon—or just about any other Republican, for that matter—winds up in the White House," Anna said. "You think they'll be any more disposed to getting out of Vietnam?"

"I think it matters less with each passing day whether Lyndon or Nixon is president," Michael replied. "They both stand for the same things in the end. They're both part of a political system that's become broken and bankrupt, and more and more people understand it. Especially young people, who aren't invested in the system.

"And besides that, you're overlooking another possibility. We both know Bobby has been holding quiet strategy sessions with a small circle, gaming out what a Kennedy campaign would look like. He's the one politician who could really transform things. What would your attitude toward LBJ be if Bobby got in?"

Anna didn't bite. "We used to have a saying in my family when I was growing up: We'll jump off that bridge when we come to it."

"We may come to it sooner than you think."

"I'll believe it when I see it," she said. "Robert Kennedy is a dear friend and someone I admire greatly. I know what he thinks about the war, and about where the country is heading, and I don't disagree with him. But he also has a good political head on his shoulders, and he knows how divisive his candidacy would be. He doesn't want to deliver the presidency to Nixon any more than I do."

There the argument stood for the moment. Michael spent a couple of days interviewing congressmen about the latest developments on the war and the campaign, and then headed home to New York. It was Valentine's Day, but he knew Riva wouldn't be there. She was at her parents' house, huddling with them in an increasingly desperate search for some way to brake Tommy's downward spiral.

He was routinely skipping physical therapy sessions, which meant his physical condition was stagnating at a low point. He was no better about attending counseling sessions at the VA center. He was in pain, and taking a variety of painkillers, including a powerful opioid drug called Percodan, which his VA doctors prescribed freely.

He talked very little to his family and saw few friends. And the people he did hang out with made Riva deeply suspicious. They seemed like dopers who were interested in Tommy because of the pain medications he had in plentiful supply, and she strongly suspected they were bringing other drugs to the party. The whole situation made her deeply fearful for Tommy, but he turned aside her efforts to talk to him about it with an apathetic shrug.

Michael offered to come out to Queens and try to talk to Tommy. Riva at first turned him down, then agreed, more in desperation than hope. Michael rolled Tommy down the icy sidewalk to the corner tavern, ordered a couple of Budweisers and then a couple more.

"So, that night at the club in Saigon? I always wondered, whatever happened to those two girls we danced with? Did you ever catch up with them later?"

Tommy looked up from his beer, trying to focus on what he realized should be a pleasurable memory. "Two girls? Trying to remember. Yeah, I think I do. We did, actually. Kind of shy at first, but we had a few laughs. Helped take the edge off."

"I thought they might be twins, or at least sisters."

"Nah, I don't think so. Just a couple of village girls trying to score some money for their families, actually. Saigon was full of girls like that. Well, that kind of thing's all over for me now."

"Look, this isn't entirely my business, Tommy, but maybe physical therapy and counseling would help. Certainly couldn't hurt, right?"

Tommy's expression changed from guarded reserve to wary suspicion. "My sister put you up to this?"

"I put myself up to it. I care a lot about her, and the way you are, it's hurting her, hurting her deeply. As well as hurting your parents. And hurting yourself. I can't see any winners in this."

"Well, yeah. Seems like I stopped winning a long time ago. A little late now to turn things around."

"It's never too late, Tommy."

"Easy for you to say, man. You're not sitting in a wheelchair."

"Well, think about it, okay?"

"Yeah. Sure. I'll do that. I got plenty of time these days to think. No distractions, you know? Makes it easy. It's just what I think about that's hard."

3: Lame Duck

Tet had done nothing to change Alan McMaster's view of the war. The offensive was a huge gamble by the North Vietnamese, and he believed they had lost the bet. Some 40,000 of their best troops were dead, their cherished uprising against the Saigon government hadn't happened, and the South Vietnamese army hadn't buckled. The generals were right to call Tet a massive military defeat for the enemy, and the president was right to argue that we must deny them even the cold comfort of a psychological victory. The only thing to do was to hit back hard with more bombing, more ground operations, and more troops in the field. If only we could shake off the shock of the offensive, avoid a sense of panic, stop drowning in two feet of water, the situation would soon improve.

Yet Alan also had a sensitive political barometer, and he soon detected subtle shifts in the weather. He was delighted at first when Clifford was named to replace the wavering McNamara, because Clifford was said to be a hawk. Yet soon after the new secretary was in place at the Pentagon, Alan noticed that the level of meetings to which he was invited had shifted downward. And the meetings he did attend contained few allies. He was being edged, slowly but unmistakably, toward the periphery of power. When he inquired about having an opportunity to brief the president directly, as he had often done in the past, he was told that Johnson was seeing fewer people these days.

Alan still had sources, and he learned that Clifford had concluded that any U.S. increase in troop strength or operational tempo would inevitably be matched by the other side, just creating a new stalemate at a higher level of violence. Acting on this conclusion, Clifford was carefully assembling a team of advisors and allies to urge a new course: capping rather than increasing U.S. troop strength, starting to turn over combat responsibility to the South Vietnamese, and seeking negotiations with Hanoi for a political settlement, even if that meant a pause in bombing the North as a token of good faith.

To Alan, it was a terrible mistake, a classic case of snatching defeat from the jaws of victory, but he felt powerless to prevent it. His remaining allies in the administration were also being marginalized. They were demoralized, and they reported that the president shared their mood. LBJ's eyes were turning, belatedly, to the political thunderheads gathering on the northern horizon.

When that storm broke, it was with a force no one fully expected. McCarthy won 42 percent of the Democratic vote in New Hampshire to Johnson's 49 percent; when McCarthy write-ins on Republican ballots were tallied, he was within 230 votes of a sitting president. The delegate count was even more amazing; 20 of the state's 24 elected delegates would be pledged to McCarthy at the Democratic convention in Chicago.

As the stunning returns rolled in, Michael wedged himself into the packed ballroom of the Sheraton-Wayfarer Hotel in Manchester and filled his notebook with jubilant quotes from young Clean-for-Gene acolytes as they waited for the senator. He emerged shortly after midnight, setting off explosive chants of "Chi-ca-go! Chi-ca-go!" McCarthy could read the room, and he also knew who had fueled his campaign, so he made sure to pay tribute to his young fans. "People have remarked that this campaign has brought young people back into the system," he said. "But it's the other way around. The young people have brought the country back into the system." Anyone who still considered McCarthy politically inept, Michael thought, was deluding themselves.

Michael also recalled his remark to Anna shortly before the primary about a broken political system. Were McCarthy and his young supporters showing that he was wrong? Was the system still functional? Could it accommodate and channel the growing discontent over the war, in a way that made a real difference?

Events now began to move at a speed that threatened to outpace the human ability to absorb them. The day after the primary, as Michael was flying home, Bobby Kennedy announced he was reassessing his attitude toward the presidential contest. There was little suspense about what that really meant, and three days later Kennedy made it official: He was running.

If Bobby expected he would easily inherit the forces unleashed by the McCarthy campaign, he was mistaken. The candidate who once could have had the support of anti-war Democrats for the asking found himself in a nasty internecine battle. McCarthy, having gotten a taste of success, had no intention of yielding, and many of his supporters now regarded Bobby as a crass opportunist. All the old Kennedy caricatures of the ruthless, cold-blooded operator leaped back to life. The next primary was in Wisconsin in a few weeks, and it was too late for Kennedy to get on the ballot there. With Johnson's support ebbing by the day, McCarthy was headed toward a resounding victory and a fresh burst of momentum for future contests.

The next thunderclap came two days before the Wisconsin vote. The president went on national television to announce the results of his Vietnam policy review. It was a total victory for Clark Clifford. Johnson announced that he was unilaterally halting the bombing in most of North Vietnam and called on Hanoi to begin peace negotiations. No massive troop increase would happen, and combat responsibilities would be shifted to South Vietnamese forces wherever possible. After three years of escalation and more than 30,000 American combat deaths, the administration was taking the first tentative steps toward disengagement from Vietnam and its torments.

Michael had learned most of this before the speech, so his story was largely written before LBJ began speaking. As he listened to the president and followed the prepared text released just before the start of the speech, he filled in some details in his story, added a few quotes, and waited for LBJ to conclude before filing. At one point in the evening, he had considered sending his story early and cleaning up any glitches later on the phone, to give his editors in Chicago a head start on a late night. Johnson's closer made him glad he had waited.

"I have concluded that I should not permit the presidency to become involved in the partisan divisions that are developing in this political year," LBJ said. "I do not believe that I should devote an hour or a day of my time to any personal partisan causes or to any duties other than the awesome duties of this office, the presidency of your country.

"Accordingly, I shall not seek, and I will not accept, the nomination of my party for another term as your president."

Two frantic hours later, Michael rewrote his lead paragraph one last time, patched in a final quote from a reeling Democratic politician, and filed his story. Feeling the familiar big-story buzz of adrenaline overload combined with exhaustion, he headed upstairs to the press club bar. Normally deserted on a Sunday night, it was crowded with reporters, political staffers, and lobbyists. All were in the same fragile state of jangled nerves, fraying tempers and near-complete cognitive dissonance.

"What the fuck just happened?" one press aide to a Democratic senator said to no one in particular as he downed a shot. "Presidents just don't do that. Especially not presidents like Lyndon, who'd break your balls to get a yes vote on a motion to proceed. The idea of him just renouncing power like this—it's crazy."

"I think he's a patriot," a columnist for a St. Louis paper put in. "He's going to devote his time to seeking peace, and he wants to take Vietnam out of the political realm."

"I think he's a goddamn hypocrite," snapped a correspondent for a Philadelphia daily, whom Michael knew fairly well. "He's making a virtue out of necessity. He's going to get his clock cleaned in Wisconsin on Tuesday, and after that, Bobby and the whole Kennedy apparatus is lying in wait. Anybody who credits him with any noble motives for this should go back and take third grade over again."

The columnist deflated like a popped balloon and moved off in search of fairer weather. Michael squeezed in at the bar next to the Philly guy and clapped him on the shoulder. "Go easy on old Chalmers," he said. "He's had a rough few weeks, with all his predictions about the war and the campaign blowing up like a bunch of cheap firecrackers, and tonight was the capper."

"Yeah, I know. I shouldn't have barked at him like that. I'll go over and apologize in a minute. I just find that son of a bitch so insufferable. LBJ, I mean, not Chalmers Winston the third, or the fourth, or whatever the hell he is. He's taken this country on a ride through hell, and killed a lot of people along the way. And now that it's all exploded in his face, and he can't deny the reality of the failure anymore, it's, 'Oops, guess we'll stop bombing and start negotiating after all, and by the way, I'm riding off into the sunset. See ya, suckers.'"

Michael ordered a beer, changed his mind and switched to Jack Daniel's, and turned to look at the source of a commotion across the room. A reporter from one of the newsweeklies was standing on a chair, giving a bibulous, scatological rendition of Johnson's withdrawal speech, complete with poorly faked Texas twang:

"Ah've been screwin' y'all fuh foh yeahs now, but tonight ah'm tellin' y'all that ah've dee-cided to pull out."

Michael had no love for Lyndon Johnson or his war. Yet just a few hours ago, he reflected, that same reporter probably had been pleading with a White House aide for an off-the-record fill on what the president was going to announce. Now, Johnson, suddenly a lame duck, was the butt of the reporter's boozy humor.

Lovely place, Washington. Harry Truman's old wisecrack came to mind: Want a friend in this town? Get a dog.

Two nights later, the Wisconsin tide rolled in, carrying McCarthy to a clear win with 56 percent of the vote. Now there was no chance he would yield to Kennedy. The two anti-war candidates were headed for a fratricidal collision next month in Indiana. As they circled each other, Hubert Humphrey began preparations for his own candidacy as the administration's new standard-bearer.

The night after the Wisconsin primary, Michael sat in his parents' living room, chewing over the vastly altered political landscape with them. He and his father were speaking again, sort of, on the condition that they not discuss the war directly. If Vietnam was out of bounds, however, presidential politics wasn't.

Alan said he was prepared to support Humphrey. He didn't really trust him on the war, remembering all too well how the vice president had argued against the initial decision to escalate in 1965. But Alan observed that Humphrey had learned his lesson from that indiscretion. In retaliation, LBJ excluded him from any further high-level meetings and stopped speaking to him for several weeks. Hubert soon became a dutiful cheerleader for the war, so slavish in his loyalty that he became regular fodder for political satirists. He would stay on that side of the argument now, Alan said, if for no other reason than that it was his only path to the nomination.

Alan was convinced that his own isolation was temporary, that the policy pendulum would swing back in his direction. The North Vietnamese had no interest in a real peace settlement, he said, and once that became clear, the only option would be the full-bore escalation that Johnson had just rejected. The fever swamps of the McCarthy and Kennedy camps would be drained, the young peaceniks would move on to new distractions, Humphrey would be nominated, and the country would get on with the business of finishing off the enemy.

Michael leaned forward, poised to dismantle this fantasy, but was stayed by a withering look from Anna. She had no use for the war, but her principal concern remained keeping the White House out of Republican hands, especially Nixon's hands. The Democrats were a mess, but a salvageable mess—barely. McCarthy was a dreamy Don Quixote, liable to charge off in the direction of some new windmill at any moment. Humphrey was an old ally, but he had turned himself into a joke, a bargain-basement hawk who parroted his patron's lines with less credibility each day. Under Nixon's menacing scorn, he would wilt like a flower in a sandstorm.

That left Bobby. And that was the square on which Anna would land, still fearful that her party would be split beyond repair, but believing that Kennedy was the only Democrat who stood any chance of holding it together long enough to win in November.

Michael regarded the Kennedy-McCarthy conflict as a tragedy, and could not shake the feeling that it would end in frustration and disappointment. The old gibe about liberals organizing a firing squad by forming a circle seemed to be coming true before his eyes. The only hope either candidate had of winning the nomination was to show such overwhelming popular strength that the party wouldn't dare deny them. Now, they would careen through the primaries, dividing the anti-war vote even as it was expanding. Humphrey would not have to win a single contest; he could bide his time and let McCarthy and Kennedy kill each other off.

A part of Michael was repelled by Bobby's icy calculation of letting McCarthy take all the risks and then curtly cutting in once McCarthy had exposed LBJ's weakness. Another part understood that, for all his opportunism, Kennedy commanded a breadth of appeal and a largeness of spirit that made him a unique candidate.

At one time, Michael had nurtured the hope that a Kennedy campaign might pull Riva away from the black radical milieu she found so attractive. When he got back to New York, he discovered the foolishness of that hope. Yet it was not the Black Panthers who were dominating her life, for Riva had little interest in politics of any flavor at the moment. She was in increasing despair over her brother. While Michael had been in Washington, she had found Tommy in his room, slumped in his chair, unconscious. It took the ambulance tech more than 10 minutes to revive him. At the hospital, Tommy's blood work came back showing the presence of so many drugs that the doctor could not say which one, or ones, had caused him to black out. They kept him overnight and sent him home with a warning to stick to one painkiller and follow the dosage closely. Tommy responded to that admonition with a blank stare.

"I'm trying to save his life," Riva said. "I just don't know how. He's dying slowly before our eyes, and trying to stop him is like holding water in your hand and trying to keep it from running through your fingers."

"I'll do anything to help. Is there anything I can do?"

Riva shook her head, slowly and sadly. "It means a lot to me that you tried to talk to him back in February. But he's not listening to anybody, except maybe his druggie friends, who I would like to run off with a shotgun. Not that it would do any good. He'd just find some new doper pals. They know he's got easy access to all kinds of shit through the VA.

"And I hate those damn VA doctors even more. They hand out drugs like chewing gum. Lately they've been giving him something new called oxycodone, which they claim is less addictive, but it just blanks him out, takes him further away from us. And he never sees the same doctor twice, so it's easy for him to bullshit his way to another prescription. When I tried to talk to one of them about it, he just looked at me like I was a witch, and asked me why I wanted my brother to be in pain. I wanted to clock the sanctimonious son of a bitch."

"I could try to talk to someone at the VA about the situation."

"You'd be wasting your time. They probably wouldn't even see you because you're not immediate family. And they don't care, that's the truth. They've got so many wounded men coming at them, they don't have the time or the inclination to do anything more than basic maintenance. For someone like Tommy, that means what they call keeping him comfortable."

As she talked, Michael sensed a sadness in Riva that he had never seen before. He loved her, more than he ever had, and her fierce devotion to her broken brother filled him with fresh admiration. But he feared she was slipping away from him, much like Tommy was slipping away from life. And he felt just as powerless to stop it.

"Okay. If anything occurs to you, let me know. I'm supposed to fly out to Indiana with Kennedy tomorrow and spend a few days with him on the trail. You want me to cancel? I will if you want me to."

"No. You need to do your work, and there isn't anything you can do to help here. I'm not sure what anyone can do."

Chapter Sixteen
—Goodbye to All That—
April 1968

1: Our Own Despair

The Kennedy campaign plane was on the tarmac with its engines revving, ready to take off for the quick hop from Muncie to Indianapolis. Michael ducked into the small terminal building for a quick check-in with his office. The national desk phone, which usually was answered immediately, rang several times before a clerk picked up. In the background, Michael could hear a loud buzz of conversation and a few shouted orders.

"Have you heard?" the clerk asked.

"Heard what?"

"Martin Luther King's been shot. In Memphis. He's in the hospital, or heading there. We don't know anything about his condition."

No one aboard the plane had heard the news, either. Michael shared it with a Kennedy aide, Fred Dutton. When Dutton relayed it to the candidate, Bobby's face drained of color. On the short flight, Kennedy huddled with a few aides at the front of the plane. The schedule called for him to go directly from the Indianapolis airport to an open-air rally in a largely black neighborhood. Michael guessed that the candidate and his staffers were debating what to do about the event. It depended in part, he thought, on King's condition. As soon as the plane was on the ground, Dutton hurried across the tarmac to the airport's police office. He returned a few minutes later with the news that King was dead.

The debate at the front of the plane resumed. Michael and a couple of colleagues hovered nearby, openly eavesdropping. Campaign staffers were too disoriented to chase them away. Michael overheard someone saying that the city's police chief had advised against going, and would provide no officers for security. Abruptly, the debate ended. "We're doing it. Let's go," Bobby announced.

The small motorcade arrived at the rally site and pulled up as close to the platform as possible. It was clear to Michael that they were preparing for a fast getaway if things turned ugly. The crowd was large, more than 1,000 people, most of them black, and most had not heard the news; the mood was still festive and rally-boisterous. Bobby climbed onto the platform, hunched within himself in a black raincoat against the gathering evening chill. He looked shaken, almost haunted. He has to be reliving Dallas, Michael thought.

"I have some very sad news for all of you," Kennedy began, "and sad news for all of our fellow citizens, and people who love peace all over the world, and that is that Martin Luther King was shot and killed tonight."

There were gasps and shouts of "No!" from people near the podium. The sound system was iffy, however, and much of the crowd didn't immediately grasp what Kennedy was telling them. As he went on, his grim demeanor and somber tone communicated the message almost as much as his words. Michael noticed he was speaking without notes, winging it on what might be the most important speech of his life.

"In this difficult day, in this difficult time for the United States, it is perhaps well to ask what kind of nation we are and what direction we want to move in. For those of you who are black ... you can be filled with bitterness, and with hatred, and a desire for revenge. We can move in that direction as a country, in greater polarization, black people amongst blacks, and white amongst whites, filled with hatred toward one another.

"Or we can make the effort, as Martin Luther King did, to understand, and to comprehend, and to replace that violence, that stain of bloodshed that has spread across our land, with an effort to understand, compassion, and love."

The crowd was entirely quiet now, almost hushed. Michael could hear some weeping softly as the news of King's death sank in.

"For those of you who are black and are tempted to be filled with hatred and mistrust of the injustice of such an act, against all white people, I would only say that I can also feel in my own heart the same kind of feeling. I had a member of my family killed. But he was killed by a white man. But we have to make an effort ... to understand, to go beyond these rather difficult times."

Michael had never before heard Bobby mention his brother's death, and aides had told him Kennedy once vowed never to talk about it in public.

He went on to quote the lines from Aeschylus that he had embraced and drawn comfort from in the days following Jack's death: "Even in our sleep, pain which cannot forget falls drop by drop upon the heart until, in our own despair, against our will, comes wisdom, through the awful grace of God."

Michael paused in his note-taking and took in the scene. A presidential candidate was quoting an ancient Greek writer to a rally crowd that could turn hostile at any moment, he thought. And they're hanging on every word. Like a congregation in church.

Bobby's words were tumbling out now, propelled by an intensity of feeling that pulled the crowd in and bonded it with the speaker.

"What we need in the United States is not division. What we need in the United States is not hatred. What we need in the United States is not violence and lawlessness—but is love, and wisdom, and compassion toward one another, a feeling of justice toward those who still suffer within our country, whether they be white or they be black.

"So I shall ask you tonight to return home, to say a prayer for the family of Martin Luther King, but more importantly to say a prayer for our own country, which all of us love—a prayer for understanding, and that compassion of which I spoke.

"Let us dedicate ourselves to what the Greeks wrote so many years ago: to tame the savageness of man and make gentle the life of this world. Let us dedicate ourselves to that, and say a prayer for our country and for our people."

They reboarded the vehicles—the security precautions were unnecessary, the crowd was quiet, almost solemn, as it slowly dispersed—and rode downtown in almost total silence. Looking over his notes, Michael found that after the Aeschylus quote he had written: "This is a leader. This is a president."

In his hotel room, Michael called his office to let them know what he had, then phoned Riva. No answer. He called her parents' home and reached Dorie, who said Riva was there, in Tommy's room, talking with her brother. "No need to interrupt her," he said. "Tell her I called, and I love her, and—god. What an awful night."

"Yes. I'll tell her. I wish I could say I was surprised. It's what happens to people who—to people who try to do right by the world. Hold on, Michael, she just walked in the room. Here she is."

"Riva, I—I can't believe the news."

"I can," she said. "With no difficulty. I'm just surprised it hasn't happened before now."

"God, we're killing off our best, the only people who could chart a path out of this insanity. I don't understand why that's happening."

"It's happening because America—white America—doesn't really want a way out. Nobody wants to say that out loud, but that's the reality. This country is violent and racist, and too many people like it that way. When you try to change that, it's just a matter of time before you become the next sacrifice."

Michael wanted to say something to assuage the hurt and anger that came across so plainly in Riva's voice. He couldn't think of a single thing. He recognized the relentless logic in what she said, even as fear welled up inside him about where that logic was taking Riva—and taking them.

With those thoughts reverberating in his mind, he began putting together his story, with the television on in the background. The networks had canceled their regular schedules to cover the news. And the news was growing more dire by the minute. Violence was erupting in one city after another as people learned of King's death. By midnight, it was spreading across Chicago, Pittsburgh, Cincinnati, Washington, and many other places.

Only a few large cities were spared. One was Indianapolis.

By the next day, as Michael flew back to Washington, he learned that the paroxysm of anger was coursing across the country. It was Detroit all over again, but on a national scale, the raw rage as contagious as the flames that leaped from building to building. In city after city, police and firefighters retreated in the face of sustained attacks ranging from rocks and bottles to sniper fire.

Michael's editors barely had time to talk with him. They had their hands full as disorders spread across Chicago's west side. From a fellow passenger's transistor radio, he learned about Mayor Richard Daley's response: a public order to his police to shoot to kill arsonists on sight and "maim or cripple" looters. It was pure Daley, Michael thought, full of bluster and intimidation, but it was far too late to scare people back into passivity.

As Michael's flight approached National Airport, the plane flew down the Potomac from the northwest, the iconic city visible on the left. A thick plume of smoke hung over it, another gray-black cloud shrouding another war zone in Michael's growing collection.

The violence in Washington had started at the center of the city's black commercial and cultural district at 14th and U Streets. It then spread up and down 14th, coming within a few blocks of the White House and the National Press Building, where Michael's office was located. From a high window, he could see soldiers patrolling on 14th Street. The White House, a short walk away, was surrounded by Army infantrymen. At the Capitol, he saw Marines manning machine guns on the steps. The nation's capital looked like a city under siege.

As the embers still smoldered, Michael headed to Atlanta to cover King's funeral. It was a stark contrast to the anguish of the cities. At the service in King's own church, Ebenezer Baptist, he eulogized himself, through a recording of a speech he had delivered two months earlier. He had decried what he'd called the "drum major" syndrome of self-importance and egotism, then said: "If you want to say that I was a drum major, say that I was a drum major for justice. Say that I was a drum major for peace. I was a drum major for righteousness. And all of the other shallow things will not matter."

King's casket was loaded onto a wooden farm wagon and pulled by two mules along the three-mile route to Morehouse College. More than 100,000 people lined the streets to watch it pass, in almost total silence, broken occasionally by movement anthems. At the head of the procession, Michael spotted John Lewis, King aides Jesse Jackson and Andrew Young, and King's widow, Coretta, veiled in black. Politicians and show business celebrities followed them.

The colliding images of violence and mourning, Michael wrote, suggested the passing of an era. King's movement, and his whole approach, were being challenged by younger black leaders who had little interest in patient interracial coalition-building. And recent events showed that people in the streets had even less interest in nonviolent activism.

"The freedom songs that were sung at King's funeral procession once lifted the hearts of civil rights demonstrators as they marched against southern racism," Michael wrote. "Today they were dirges, not only for a man, but quite possibly for a movement."

One man who hoped otherwise, Michael reported, was Robert Kennedy. King's murder and its aftermath had frozen presidential politics in place. But the campaign would soon resume, and when it did, Michael wrote that Bobby planned to center his on the need to address racism and inequality. A Kennedy aide pointed him toward a speech Bobby had delivered the day after King's death, as violence was spreading across the country, as a window into where he would take his message.

"Too often we honor swagger and bluster and the wielders of force; too often we excuse those who are willing to build their own lives on the shattered dreams of others," Kennedy had said. "Some look for scapegoats, others look for conspiracies, but this much is clear: Violence breeds violence, repression brings retaliation, and only a cleaning of our whole society can remove this sickness from our soul."

There was more than one kind of violence, Bobby said. There was the slow, pernicious violence done to people by institutions that were indifferent and uncaring.

"This is the violence that afflicts the poor. This is a slow destruction of a child by hunger, and schools without books, and homes without heat in the winter. This is the breaking of a man's spirit by denying him the chance to stand as a father and as a man among other men."

In Atlanta, Bobby spent the night before the funeral in a series of meetings in his hotel suite with black leaders from a wide variety of fields. They were supposed to be private meetings, but Michael picked up some hints about them, tapped his civil rights sources, and pieced together a story.

He learned that Bobby had positioned himself in a corner of the room, not at the center, and sat mostly silently as one speaker after another talked about the racial crisis stalking the nation and what might be done about it. Some comments were angry and personal, some demanded explicit commitments to certain programs, but he refused to be drawn. He was there to listen, learn and pay tribute to King, he said.

The meetings lasted nearly six hours, until almost 3 in the morning. Michael reported that, besides giving Bobby a window into the thinking of black leaders at a moment of national crisis, they served a second purpose: to allow Bobby to signal to those leaders the strategic turn that his campaign was about to take.

2. Gone

When Michael returned to New York the day after King's funeral, Riva wasn't in their apartment. He phoned her parents, but got a busy signal. Several retries yielded the same result. He was looking up the number of Riva's uncle when the door opened and she walked in.

One look told him something was terribly wrong. He started to form the question, but it died on his lips. He waited as she sat down, across the room from him, and gathered herself.

"We found Tommy this morning. Found him—an overdose. They tried to revive him, like the last time, but this time they couldn't. This time, he was gone. Just gone." Her voice broke at those last words.

Michael started to speak, then rose and walked over to embrace her. She froze him with an upraised hand.

"I'm not here to be consoled. I'm here to get a few things together."

"You're leaving?" He heard his words, but couldn't believe he was speaking them.

"Yes."

He went back to his chair and sat down. They both sat silently for several moments.

"I can try to explain," she said finally. "I don't know if you'll understand—you always did, but this is so different. I still love you, Michael. I always will love you. But I can't be with you anymore. I can't be in this world anymore. It's over."

"I don't know what to say. I know I've been gone a lot—"

"That has nothing to do with it," she said. "This is not about you. It's about me. I've changed. The world has changed, and it's changed me. For better or worse, I have no idea, but I know it has."

The silence descended again. Once again, she broke it.

"You remember when we first met? How we first met?"

He nodded in wordless misery.

"We met on a civil rights picket line. We fell in love on a freedom ride. It was such a hopeful time—god, was it hopeful. Our love was born in that hope, that sense that we could change the world by the force of our good intentions.

"We were wrong. That's all done now. You can't deny it. The signs are all around us. My brother"—her voice broke again, but only for an instant—"my brother was a sacrifice to that reality. And our love is a casualty too, dying on the same altar."

Michael recalled the story he had written just a day ago, a virtual obituary for the civil rights era. He had not realized he was writing an epitaph for his marriage as well.

His mind reeling, his heart pounding, he tried to summon some argument that would persuade her to stay. Even as he did, he recognized how futile it was. He knew Riva well, knew how determined she was when she made up her mind. And a part of him realized that this had been coming for a long time, that the signs had been there, if he had only acted on them.

Finally, there was nothing more that he could say.

"Where will you go? What will you do?"

"I don't know. Stay with my parents for now. Help them bury Tommy. Then crash with a friend, find a roommate. I'll get by."

Riva rose, walked into the bedroom, and emerged a few minutes later with a small bag. Michael got up and took a tentative step toward her. She hesitated for a moment, then came to him and flung her arms around him. He could feel her wet cheek on his shoulder. Through his own tears, he watched her push away, turn and walk through the door.

She was gone.

BOOK THREE

Chapter Seventeen
–Campaign–
April 1968

1: Alma Mater

Michael remembered Columbia University from his student days a decade ago as a stately, brick-lined refuge from the bustle of Upper Manhattan, populated by serious, slightly manic students whose primary concerns were grades and getting into grad school.

It was a refuge no longer. Students protesting racism and the war were occupying five campus buildings and refusing to leave unless the university complied with a long and growing list of demands. The New Left had barged into the polite precincts of the Ivy League like an unruly intruder, leaving a trail of muddy footprints and broken crockery.

It had been two weeks since Riva left. The first few days for Michael were a gray fog of regret and recrimination, mostly aimed at himself. He barely left the apartment, which was unhealthy, as it was filled with memories of her and their life together. He was not ready to talk to his friends or family about the breakup, so he stayed home and brooded. Finally, boredom overcame his lethargy. When Columbia blew up and his editor suggested he cover it, he pushed aside his melancholy and headed uptown.

As Michael walked through the university's wrought-iron main gate at 116th Street and Broadway, he saw knots of students milling about on College Walk, the campus's east-west axis, in a heated debate over the takeovers. Outside the occupied buildings, students and faculty opposed to the protesters shouted at them to give it up. Supporters retorted with chants of encouragement.

The Columbia revolt was a national story, because almost anything unusual that happened in New York became a national story. But it was only the latest outbreak in a long series of student protests. They had spread beyond the traditional incubators of campus radicalism—Berkeley, Ann Arbor, Madison—to places once thought immune from the contagion, including the nation's most elite private institutions. And they were not confined to America. Youthful anger over Vietnam and the inequities of western society was fueling protests in Paris, West Berlin, Rome and London. The spirit of revolt even leaped the East-West divide; in Czechoslovakia, a liberal communist regime struck a chord with young people hungry for a break with their country's ossified Soviet-style system.

Michael walked up to Low Library, one of the occupied buildings, and started scribbling notes as he listened to a debate taking place on its steps. A young woman was exhorting the crowd to support the protesters and their demands, deftly deflecting several hecklers. As he got closer, Michael smiled in recognition. It was Marta Hauser.

Michael had known Marta since journalism school. They had dated a few times back then, although nothing serious came of it. In those days, Marta was an aspiring journalist with an activist bent; over the years, Michael had seen her pieces in the Village Voice, the East Village Other and Ramparts magazine. She was talented, if a bit strident, he thought.

Now, it seemed, Marta was reinventing herself as a campus radical leader. She had not changed much: small and wiry; long wavy hair, pulled back from her round face; dark, intense eyes. Marta was a few years older than most of the protesters, but she had always looked a bit younger than her age.

"This university likes to portray itself as a lordly refuge of learning, but we know better," she shouted through a bullhorn. "We know that behind the facade of academic neutrality, Columbia has been cozying up to the warlords, secretly doing research for the Pentagon but too ashamed to admit it publicly. And we know that it's been a bad neighbor to Harlem, steadily encroaching to build lofty edifices that are reserved for the white elite that attends Columbia but off-limits to the black community."

"Why don't you go back to whatever cave you crawled out of?" one listener shouted.

"Why don't you take off your blinders and take a hard look at what the university is doing?" she retorted. "It's not a pretty sight. We're trying to do something about it."

"Go fuck yourself, you commie bitch!"

"Are you always this articulate, or is today one of your good days?"

The rippling laughter deflated the heckler, and she resumed her flaying of the university and its gray, bureaucratic administrators, who clearly had no idea how to respond to the revolt. As she concluded with a pitch to take part in the protest, several groups of occupiers, as if on cue, leaned out from second-floor windows and chanted, "Join us!"

A part of the crowd did just that, climbing the steps and filtering through the one open doorway. As Marta started to follow them, Michael called to her.

"Well, hello, stranger," she said. "What brings you back to dear old alma mater? The administration trying to recruit alumni to calm things down?"

"Not exactly. I'm here to cover your little camp-out. And, personally, I've got no problem with it. If any place needed shaking up, it's Columbia. Can I talk to you about it, for the story? To quote you? How'd you get involved?"

"I've been working with an SDS collective here for about a year," Marta said. "Most of them are pretty young, and new at this, and it seems I've compiled a bit of a resume between writing about actions and taking part in them. So I guess I've become one of the leaders, although we absolutely hate that term. Call us facilitators, if you don't mind."

They both smiled at the preciousness of the euphemism. One thing about Marta that Michael had always liked was her rich sense of the absurd, her ability to poke fun at herself and her own side, despite—or perhaps because of—her underlying seriousness.

"Well, you seem to be good at it. You shut down that heckler like a pro, and you got quite a few people to join. So, how are you? This wild radical career seems to agree with you. You're looking well."

"You're not. You look rather ... shopworn. Everything okay with you?"

Ah, yes, Michael thought, another one of Marta's qualities—bluntness. She always prided herself on being a truth-teller. Is the truth about me that obvious?

He glossed over his situation in a few sentences, then steered the conversation back to interviewing Marta about the revolt. "What's the strategy?" he asked. "You've got everybody's attention, but where do you go with it? It seems really unlikely the administration will agree to any of your demands, and sooner or later they'll call in the cops to evict you."

"Either way, we win," she said. "If they agree to anything at all, it'll be a victory for us, and it'll fuel the movement. If they bring in the muscle to end it, we'll have unmasked the underlying brutality and arrogance of the system—and it'll fuel the movement. We can't lose."

"You can get an awful lot of people hurt, both physically and in other ways. Including yourself."

Marta shrugged. "I've become kind of a veteran at getting beat up by the pigs," she said. "I was out in the Bay Area last year for some actions. We were trying to shut down the Oakland transfer station where they ship guys out to 'Nam. We did it, too, for a while at least. But I've never seen cops go crazy like they did there. If I survived that, I'm not worried about anything here.

"And in any case, it's worth the price. Look at what's happening all over the world. The whole system is in crisis. We're on the verge of a classic revolutionary situation, and this is just part of it."

Marta's blend of pop Marxism and existentialist action-as-thought struck Michael as brave and heartfelt, but a bit naïve. He wasn't there to debate her, though, so he jotted down the quotes and asked if she could get him inside Low Library. The students in most of the occupied buildings were not letting members of the "bourgeois press" inside, just sending out emissaries periodically to talk to reporters.

"Well, I could try," she said hesitantly. "You might have to agree to keep it all off the record and clear the quotes and anecdotes through us before you use them."

Michael smiled at Marta's media savvy, for all her screw-the-system swagger. She knows how to play this game, he thought. "I can agree to use what I see and hear inside only as background, no names or direct quotes," he said. "But no pre-clearance of what I write. That's a no-go. And everything we talked about out here was on the record."

"I think that'll probably be okay. Follow me."

They walked through the door, Marta vouching for Michael, and climbed the stairs to the second-floor office of university president Grayson Kirk, which seemed to be the epicenter of the occupation. The wood-paneled, book-lined room was a mess, with file folders, loose documents and a good deal of trash strewn about. One student was leaning back in Kirk's big swivel chair, feet on the desk, peering out from behind sunglasses. He was puffing on a cigar filched from the president's private stash. He saw Michael gaping at him, turned in his direction and coolly blew a large quantity of smoke at him.

Marta told Michael to wait at the door and huddled with some fellow "facilitators." She came back, restated the rules of engagement, and told him to come in. He spent the next two hours circulating among the occupiers in Kirk's office and several other rooms, filling his notebook. The impressions and details from inside the occupation gave Michael's story a ring of authenticity that most of his competitors lacked.

He had less success at Hamilton Hall, which was occupied by black students who had a separate set of demands and had asked all white protesters to leave. He got one leader to come outside and give him a few turbocharged quotes condemning Columbia as a bastion of institutional racism that was exploiting the black community and quietly becoming one of Harlem's biggest slumlords. When he asked about coming in, though, the student just laughed and walked away.

What Michael took away from his day at Columbia was that the revolt typified the New Left, with all of its strengths and flaws. The occupiers were disorganized, faction-riven, prone to endless debates about everything from broad strategy to minor operational details. And there was a serious divide between the white SDSers, who had a broad agenda that encompassed ending the university's role in military research as well as fighting racism, and the black activists, who were focused on stopping Columbia's encroachment in Harlem.

Yet there was also an undeniable energy and commitment among these students, a seriousness of purpose, a passion, that transcended the divisions and personality clashes.

He got in touch with Marta and talked his impressions over with her, this time not for quotes but purely for his own understanding.

"It's true that we look like a mess from the outside," she said. "We've got anarchists, pacifists, Maoists, Trotskyists, black nationalists, even McCarthy supporters, and lots of people who couldn't care less about any ideology but just want to confront a system that they can't abide any longer. And that's the real point: it's happened. Despite all of that, it's happened. We've been trying to get something going here for months and months, without much success. And then we just decided to do it, to seize a building and ask people to join us. And they have."

"How long do you think you can keep this going?"

"I don't know. These kids are young, and maybe if the administration tries to wait us out, people will drift away and the whole thing will peter out. I've seen that happen before. But somehow I think they won't have the patience for that."

"Well, thank you for your time and your help. It's good seeing you again. Take care of yourself."

"Sure, glad to. Listen, when this is over, you wanna get together for something—coffee, a drink, whatever?"

Michael looked across the table and saw an attractive young woman with a great deal of passion for life. He didn't answer her immediately.

"That's really tempting, but I think it's too soon for me to do that," he said at last.

Was that a flicker of regret that flashed across Marta's face, just for a moment? "Yeah, I understand," she said. "Well, you take care, too."

Three days later, the university administration proved Marta right. They called in the cops, who charged into the occupied buildings through underground tunnels in the middle of the night. They routed the protesters with flailing truncheons, driving them out onto the central plaza and then into waiting police vans. When a crowd of students gathered to protest the police presence, a line of club-swinging cops charged and scattered them, trampling people underfoot. Plainclothes police, dressed to look like protesters, whipped out blackjacks and beat students. Some who tried to block police from entering one building were stomped and flung aside. The final tally read like a riot report: 1,000 police involved, 720 people arrested, 136 protesters and 12 cops injured.

When Michael got to Columbia a couple of hours after the police operation began, the center of campus was strewn with police cruisers, patrol wagons and ambulances. Injured students sat on curbs or steps, some with blood streaming down their faces, getting treatment from volunteer medical personnel. Knots of people gathered to shout angry slogans at cops, who chased them away with clubs and curses.

He tried to find out what might have happened to Marta, but without success. Later that day, she popped up on television, with a bandage on her head, but no lack of energy or vocal force for denouncing the police. Michael took that as a sign she was okay.

As he walked back across campus when he was done reporting, he passed the statue of Alma Mater in the plaza in front of Low Library. Someone had hung a hand-lettered placard on it: "Raped by the cops."

2: New Coalition

Working a story had agreed with Michael, had taken his mind off the breakup of his marriage, and he decided it was time to get back in the game full time. He got in touch with the Kennedy campaign and made arrangements to rejoin it in Indiana, where the first contested primary between Bobby and Gene McCarthy was now less than a week away.

It was not an easy test for Kennedy, Michael reported. The state was fundamentally conservative, and he was up against not only McCarthy but the governor, Roger Branigan, a stand-in for the still undeclared but obviously running Humphrey. The most heavily Democratic parts of the state, in Indianapolis and the industrial northwest, were dominated by two groups widely perceived to be at each other's throats: black voters and ethnic whites of Eastern European origins. The young people motivated by opposition to the war were mostly in McCarthy's camp. To make matters worse, the state's biggest newspapers, the Indianapolis Star and the News, were openly hostile to Bobby.

As he barnstormed around the state, Kennedy reacted to these multiple challenges with an exercise in needle-threading that struck many journalists as pandering. While not explicitly renouncing his views about the urgent need to address poverty and inequality, Bobby downplayed the federal government's role and emphasized the need for local communities and private businesses to take the lead. And he coupled that with denunciations of violence and lawlessness that were obvious overtures to fearful white voters.

Occasionally, the tactical persona slipped. At Indiana University, some white medical students challenged Kennedy about his call for a stronger federal health care program for the poor. One asked him where the money for such programs would come from. "From you," he answered, and proceeded to lay down a challenge.

"Let me say something about the tone of these questions. I look around this room and I don't see many black faces who will become doctors. ... You are the privileged ones here. It's easy to sit back and says it's the fault of the federal government, but it's our responsibility too. It's our society, not just our government, that spends twice as much on pets as on the poverty program. It's the poor who carry the major burden of the struggle in Vietnam. You sit here as white medical students, while black people carry the burden of the fighting."

When Michael and other reporters questioned whether his rhetoric about private enterprise and law and order was an exercise in opportunism, Bobby insisted he was simply saying what he had always said, just with a slightly different emphasis. He had an aide dig out the earlier quotes to prove it. And, in a late-night background session with Michael and a few other journalists, he laid out the overarching strategy that he thought would carry him to victory in Indiana and set him up for the primaries to follow.

"Everyone assumes that blacks and working-class whites are natural enemies," he said. "I don't believe that. I believe they're natural allies, because they share one characteristic that transcends race: They're on the bottom half of the economic ladder, and they're both slipping further and further down as automation eliminates blue-collar jobs and puts a premium on education and technical skills. They're also the ones bearing the brunt of the fighting and dying in Vietnam. You put those two groups together with the rural poor—and there's a lot of them in this state—and you've got a winning coalition."

It was a risky premise at a time when racial polarization was a dominant theme in the country, but Kennedy was betting his political future on it. And on the day before the May 7 primary, he put it to a test in the strangest campaign event Michael had ever witnessed: a 50-mile marathon of a motorcade through northern Indiana. It was the geographic heart of the coalition that Bobby was trying to assemble, and he was counting on his physical presence to provide the glue, as well as the motivation to vote.

For nine hours, from early afternoon to late evening, he wound his way west from Laporte to Whiting, passing from city to suburb to open country and then repeating the cycle. Enthusiastic crowds lined the entire route, even in the open stretches between communities. In the lunch-bucket cities of Gary, Hammond and East Chicago, the neighborhoods went by in a racial checkerboard, black, white, black, white, but in each there were crowds to greet him, some waiting hours for the experience.

Through it all, the candidate stood in the back of a slow-rolling convertible, shaking one hand after another while an aide held him around the waist to brace him. The hands reached for him with a kind of hunger that struck Michael, watching from the press bus, as visceral, even a little desperate, as if Bobby's mere physical presence could transform lives and communities and a country. As he watched the frenzy, Michael realized that the words Kennedy spoke mattered far less to these people than the bedrock hope he embodied and the emotions he aroused. It was elemental, Michael thought, and a little dangerous.

The payoff came 24 hours later, when the votes came in. In a three-way race, Kennedy led the field with 42 percent, followed by Branigan with 31 percent and McCarthy at 27 percent. Bobby had won black voters overwhelmingly, broken even among working-class whites and even done well in rural parts of the state. The coalition he envisioned had sprung to life and carried him to victory. "I've proved I can really be the leader of a broad spectrum," he said on election night. "I can be a bridge between blacks and whites without stepping back from my positions."

Many journalists had doubts about that last part; as the campaign moved on from Indiana to Nebraska, the "new, conservative Kennedy" became a media trope. Michael resisted this herd-driven consensus. He had seen something in the faces of the endless crowds in Indiana, and it told him Bobby represented something to those people that transcended the quotidian maneuvers of a campaign.

The conservative-sounding rhetoric was meant to reassure the power brokers Kennedy would need at the convention, signaling them that he wasn't the clenched-fist radical of his adversaries' caricatures. Most voters paid scant attention to such careful positioning. For them, Michael thought, it was what Bobby Kennedy symbolized that mattered, and they felt it in the heart and gut, not the mind. The world was changing, the country was changing, and it was hard to know what to make of it. What Bobby offered to those voters, at once frightened and hopeful, was the prospect that someone understood and was on their side and could channel the currents of change in ways that made their lives better. He crystallized it in a line he borrowed from George Bernard Shaw that became his standard closer on the stump: "Some men see things as they are and say, 'Why?' I dream things that never were and say, 'Why not?'"

Michael's analysis story for his Sunday paper, taking issue with the media pack's consensus, earned him some ribbing from his colleagues and mild pushback from his editors because he was breaking from the conventional wisdom. He thought it was one of his most perceptive stories from the campaign trail.

Those who fixate on Kennedy's "turn to the right," Michael wrote, are making the mistake of measuring him by the conventional rules of politics. But Kennedy was rewriting the rulebook, in ways that were just becoming apparent. His campaign apparatus might be slapdash, his positions on issues often improvised on the fly—but for many voters, the candidate was the message, and it was resonating.

The process by which this was happening, Michael continued, was an in-the-moment experiment in political alchemy. Kennedy's public persona was reserved, almost shy, his speaking style lacking the polish and pace of his late brother. Even his mannerisms were different, and revealing of personality, he wrote: Where John F. Kennedy habitually thrust his hand forward to punctuate a point, Bobby's reflexive gesture was shy, almost self-effacing: to reach up and brush aside his longish hair.

"The charisma is more indirect, more derived, but it is just as real. When Robert Kennedy talks about inequality and injustice and the need to attack these problems, his voice drops rather than rises, but his audience grows quiet and listens."

For Michael, that piece, and the thought process that attended it, marked something of a personal watershed. It brought to the surface internal tensions that he had long felt. He was a journalist to his core, committed to his craft's principles of skepticism and objectivity. He was also a citizen, with strongly held views about the world. A part of him was entirely with the young Columbia radicals who commandeered buildings to force society to confront racism and war. Another part of him doubted their vision of an impending revolutionary apocalypse. He thought the New Left was badly underestimating the system's capacity for blunting radical activism.

Bobby Kennedy, Michael believed, offered an exit from this conundrum. He walked in both worlds, a politician who understood how to acquire power and would use it to act on his empathy for those on the wrong side of society's ledger.

By the prevailing standards of his profession, Michael realized, it could be argued that he should not be covering Kennedy; he had "gone native," co-opted by the candidate he was supposed to be writing about dispassionately. Measured against another yardstick, he was the perfect reporter for this campaign, because he had an understanding of the broader political moment and how Kennedy was trying to address it.

The cascade of events in the turbulent world outside the campaign's bubble only strengthened this belief. The Columbia arrests had not ended the revolt; much of the campus was now on strike, and protests were spreading to other campuses. In France, the student revolt triggered a nationwide general strike, and the government was on the brink of collapse. In Czechoslovakia, the liberal communist regime of Alexander Dubcek junked press censorship and talked about a gradual transition to a multiparty political system. Historians began to write about 1968 as a modern analogue to 1848, a year in which revolutions had swept across Europe.

Michael sought some perspective on the campaign he was covering in a phone conversation with Anna. She had landed in the Kennedy camp, and she was staying put, but she was apprehensive about the emotions Bobby was unleashing.

"You see the adulation for him on the stump, but he scares a lot of other people," she told him. "There are plenty of Americans who are quite comfortable in their lives, and quite frightened by what's happening in the inner cities and the campuses. And there's an awful lot of pure hate out there. Look at the crowds George Wallace is drawing in his rallies. And Nixon too." For Anna, always there was Nixon, her great *bête noire*, lurking in the shadows, poised to profit from the Democrats' divisions and the spreading social discord.

Michael wanted to hear from someone else. He arranged to meet Marta for coffee. The story she had to tell was a complex one, and it told Michael a great deal about the Kennedy campaign and its multiple resonances.

As a deep-dyed radical, Marta viewed Bobby primarily as a threat. "He's the one establishment politician who can compete with us," she said. "McCarthy appeals mostly to the student government types, the goo-goo kids who still think you can change the system from within. There are fewer of them every day. But Bobby has this romantic aura, this rebel James Dean persona, and it hits people on a visceral level and draws them in, even if they know his positions are barely different from Humphrey's."

Michael smiled at this unprompted, backhand validation of his theory. "What about you, Marta? Is there a part of you that feels that pull? I know your New Left catechism would disdain it, but do you feel it?"

"You're not interviewing me, right? This is just us talking?"

"Yes. You're a friend, and I'm really curious about what you think. I'm not looking for a quick quote."

"What I think," Marta said, "is that Bobby Kennedy is sexy and calculating and cool as hell and manipulative and romantic and—dangerous."

"Wow. That's quite a string of adjectives to attach to one politician. Sexy?"

"Of course," she said. "You're around him all the time, you must sense it. I can feel it just watching him on TV. He projects this blend of vulnerability and force. It's an irresistible combination. Older women want to mother him, younger women want to screw him, guys want to be just like him. Watch him when you're out there with him, and see if you don't get what I'm talking about."

"And dangerous? How is he dangerous?"

"Dangerous in a lot of different ways, to a lot of different people," Marta said. "Dangerous to himself, too, maybe. You remember the story of the Gracchus brothers in ancient Rome?"

Michael shook his head. "I never took Ancient History."

"I started out as a Classics major before I switched to journalism," she said. "They were high-octane reformers during the Roman Republic who pushed hard for land reform. So the patricians murdered Tiberius Gracchus to put a stop to that bullshit. His younger brother, Gaius, came back later and tried to rekindle the movement.

"They killed him, too."

3: Nightmare

A few days later, Michael was back on the bucking bronco of the Kennedy campaign as it careened through the late primary states. The political calendar was highly compressed, and Bobby was still using his own presence as the campaign's main weapon. Nebraska voted one week after Indiana, and Kennedy beat McCarthy soundly there. Their next matchup was coming up soon in Oregon, and Michael sensed the Kennedy camp was increasingly wary about that state. Lowering expectations was a time-honored tactic, but this time, he was convinced they were genuinely worried. Oregon was prosperous, overwhelmingly white, full of middle-class voters who appreciated McCarthy's understated style. The coalition that had carried Kennedy to victory in Indiana was largely absent. "This state is like one giant suburb," Bobby remarked after a tepid reception at a campaign stop in Portland. "Let's face it, I appeal best to people who have problems."

The results justified his fears. McCarthy beat Bobby soundly, by 8 percentage points. Reporters, always looking for the superlative, found an easy one: it was the first electoral defeat any Kennedy had suffered, ever, anywhere. McCarthy, on the ropes before Oregon, was reborn as a political giant-killer. Kennedy's hopes of driving McCarthy out of the race to set up a head-to-head contest with Humphrey were dashed, and his argument that he alone had the ballot-box appeal to carry Democrats to victory was severely dented. Bobby didn't try to deny it. "I'm not the same candidate I was before Oregon," he said at a press conference.

That made California, coming up in just a week, absolutely vital. Kennedy increased the stakes by declaring that the loser in California should quit and let the winner concentrate on beating Humphrey—a statement that could be turned on him if he lost. And he agreed to debate McCarthy, something he had resisted until now.

For the most part, though, the Kennedy campaign in California was what it always had been: the candidate himself, trying through his physical presence to bring to life his cherished coalition of blacks, Hispanics, blue-collar whites and those young people who could be detached from McCarthy. Even in this huge state, it seemed Bobby was trying to be everywhere at once. As the clock ticked down, his pace picked up.

At times, the crowds were so thick that Kennedy's motorcade could barely make its way through them. During one such stalled street scene, Bobby got up on the back deck of the convertible for greater visibility. He looked down and discovered a young woman untying the laces on one shoe. Soon, both of his shoes were souvenirs. "I hope she's old enough to vote," Bobby said as he asked an aide to loan him some footwear.

Mostly, though, the crowd wanted to touch him, not pilfer his wardrobe. They reached up to him with the same raw yearning that Michael had first seen in Indiana. Kennedy was at the center of a maelstrom, turning this way and that, reaching for yet another hand, his own hands swollen and sometimes bleeding from the effort. Michael recalled what Anna and Marta had said about the feral passions Bobby aroused, and saw it borne out on the streets of Los Angeles.

The emotion was greatest in black and Hispanic areas, and Bobby fed off it, internalizing the crowd's energy. Campaigning in Watts and East Los Angeles with the midday sun beating down, he doffed his coat jacket, rolled his sleeves to the elbow, and reached for the next hand, drenched in sweat.

"If we make the effort, if we have that love and friendship and understanding for our fellow citizens, we will have a new America—and you here in Watts and you here in Los Angeles and in California, you will have made it possible. And I will work with all of you. Give me your help. Give me your hand." "You've got it!" people shouted back. Kennedy started to call L.A. his "resurrection city."

When the road show paused to allow Bobby to press the flesh in a barbecue eatery, Michael got off the press bus and started talking to some of the people crowding the street outside. Most of the other white reporters, apprehensive about Watts' reputation, either stayed on the bus or stuck close to the candidate. But Michael mingled, and found friendly people who were pleasantly surprised to see a presidential candidate in their neighborhood and happy to share their thoughts about him.

"I never would've imagined this," said one 30-year-old woman named Claudia Jackson, who had two young children, a girl named Ceci and a boy called Ron, with her. "I want them to see it. This man is about as famous as can be, and here he is, talking to us, talking about our problems."

"Do you think he truly cares about you and your problems, or does he just care about getting your vote?" Michael asked.

"How about both?" the woman replied. "That's the way politics is supposed to work, isn't it?"

"No argument about that," Michael said with a smile.

"I don't know if he cares about us, but I know one thing," put in a man in a gas station attendant's uniform, who had been listening to the conversation. "He's about the only big-time politician who's ever bothered to come down here and ask us to our face for our votes. That goes a long way with me."

"That's right," said the woman. "That's right."

During a swing through Northern California, Bobby took another gamble. He held a private meeting with a group of black militants, taking along only a few aides and reporters. He had been meeting with black activists for years, as far back as 1961 and as recently as the night before King's funeral; sometimes the sessions went well, sometimes not. On the way to this one, he warned his aides that they might hear some unpleasant things.

He was right. One activist dismissed him as just one more "white big shot" who feigned concern about black problems. Another asked Bobby what he thought about how to combat racism, and when the answer struck him as too limited in its scope, told him, "I don't need to listen to your shit." When one of his black aides tried to intercede, Bobby told him to let things take their course. "They needed to say it," he said on the drive back to the hotel. "I needed to hear it. And they needed to know someone will listen."

The final day before the primary was a long blur of crowds and noise and frenzied emotion, from one end of the state to the other: Los Angeles to San Francisco, back south to Long Beach, then San Diego and finally L.A. again, a total distance of 1,200 miles. Midway through the day, Bobby began to complain of feeling ill, and his stump speeches took on a disjointed quality. The crowds didn't seem to care much. At the final rally, he hurried through his remarks, walked to the steps leading off the stage, sat on one and buried his face in his hands, utterly drained.

What did it mean in the end? Was Michael witnessing the birth pangs of a new political ascendency that would transform the country, or the death throes of an old style of politics that was having its last hurrah before the impersonal forces of media and mass marketing took over altogether? Michael had time to ponder the question during the long wait for results on primary day. One of McCarthy's favorite jabs at Kennedy was to call his own campaign a quest for a "new politics" centered on issues rather than personalities, implying that Bobby was relying on old-school emotionalism and family connections. At the other end of the spectrum, Nixon was turning to tightly controlled events limited to friendly, carefully screened questioners to create a faux openness, a Potemkin Village campaign.

Certainly, Michael thought, Bobby's campaign looked backward to the New Deal coalition of blacks, working-class whites, big-city power brokers and what remained of the nation's small farmers. Yet that was only part of the story. In a country that was rapidly fracturing along demographic and ideological lines, he was trying to halt the fragmentation, at least long enough to win office and institute programs that evoked the common interests of his disparate base. Michael thought a President Robert Kennedy would have a decent chance of succeeding, especially if he could quickly remove the irritant of the war through an early peace settlement.

And then there was the private person, a man who had made an unlikely journey from his brother's single-minded enforcer to a public figure in his own right who sought out marginalized people and exuded empathy for them. Some observers found this transformation contrived. Those who knew Bobby well insisted it was genuine, that Jack's death had provoked a soul-shaking reappraisal of his life and the world. Another journalist related an exchange with Kennedy over the death penalty, which Bobby now opposed. When reminded that his position as attorney general had been quite different, he replied, "Well, I hadn't read Camus yet." How many politicians read, let alone quoted, French philosophers or Greek dramatists? Michael had met no others.

In early evening, Michael showed up at the Ambassador Hotel, a huge hodgepodge of Mediterranean and Art Deco architectural elements, a true tribute to California eclecticism. The hotel's main ballroom, the Embassy Room, where Bobby would claim victory or concede defeat, was filling up. A smaller venue called the Colonial Room, separated from the ballroom by a kitchen, had been converted into a press center. Here, amid the tables, typewriters and telephones, Kennedy would meet with reporters after talking to his supporters once the results were known.

The candidate, his family and senior staff waited in the fifth-floor Royal Suite. Small groups of reporters were invited up to sample the atmosphere and snag a few quotes. Michael was in the last group, which turned out to be fortunate, because by then the TV networks' projections were in, calling a Kennedy win.

The suite was crowded with supporters: John Lewis, farmworkers' union leader Dolores Huerta, newspaper columnists Pete Hammill and Jack Newfield, novelist Budd Schulberg. The mood was buoyant. The candidate was hesitant to say much until McCarthy conceded. But the trend was clear, and aides let it be known that Bobby was making phone calls to capitalize on his victory: to Dick Daley, the powerful Chicago mayor who had been a key Jack Kennedy ally, in a bid to move him off the fence, and to Al Lowenstein, the progenitor of the dump-Johnson effort, hoping to persuade him to lead a movement of McCarthy supporters into the Kennedy camp.

This is what victory looks like on the inside, Michael thought; you win at the polls and then you quickly exploit the momentum to consolidate your support with key people who have been wavering, while the glow is still fresh. He really could be president. It could really happen.

It was nearing midnight, and aides sent word from downstairs that the Embassy Room was packed and people were demanding the candidate. Kennedy did a quick round of interviews with the TV networks and then headed downstairs, trailed by a knot of aides and supporters and the small pack of journalists. They descended on a service elevator, walked through the kitchen and a corridor linking it to the ballroom, and emerged into a wall of heat and light and noise.

The room was indeed packed, and the combined heat from the bodies and the TV lights was intense. The crowd, mostly young, roared as Bobby emerged. The podium was small, and people pressed forward, once again eager to touch him. Kennedy flashed his shy smile, brushed his hair away from his face, and started by issuing shout-outs to key supporters.

He noted he had won this day not only in California but in South Dakota, a rural state. The twin victories in such different places, he said, showed his capacity to end the country's divisions.

"We can start to work together," he said. "We are a great country, an unselfish country, a compassionate country. ... The country wants to move in a different direction, we want to deal with our problems within our country, and we want peace in Vietnam."

The crowd was roaring again and flashing V-signs, with their double meaning, peace and victory. The heat in the room was now overwhelming. It was time to wrap it up, and he did so with an expression of gratitude to his volunteers. "So my thanks to all of you, and now it's on to Chicago and let's win there," he concluded, flashing a thumb's-up, then his own V sign, and one last brush of his hair.

More V-signs in response from the crowd, more hands reaching out to him, a thick circle of aides and supporters surrounding him as he turned away from the microphone. Bobby started to leave the podium in one direction, then was redirected through an open door at the rear of the ballroom that led to the kitchen and the press room beyond it.

Michael, standing at the rear of the platform with some other reporters, fell in behind the candidate as he went into the corridor leading to the kitchen. The passageway was narrow, constricted by an ice machine on the right and a long serving table on the left, and crowded with hotel workers who wanted to shake his hand. Bobby turned this way and that to accommodate them. Michael, at first trailing Kennedy, got shoved and pushed on ahead of him. He was accustomed to the controlled chaos of the campaign, but this movement seemed especially disorganized. Michael turned back for a moment, trying to catch Bobby's words to a radio reporter, then looked ahead to see how much farther to the kitchen. Very close now.

Behind him, a loud explosive sound. Michael had no doubt what it was. He wheeled around as more gunshots rang out. He saw two Kennedy supporters, pro football player Rosie Grier and Olympic athlete Rafer Johnson, pinning a small dark-haired man to the serving table, trying to wrest a gun from his hand. Screams echoed in the small corridor. And on the concrete floor, Bobby Kennedy lay on his back, eyes open but unfocused, a small pool of blood forming as it spilled from a wound just behind his right ear.

More screams: "No! No!" The radio reporter, Andy West, his tape recorder still running, was trying to narrate the nightmare in real time: "Senator Kennedy has been shot. Is that possible? It is possible. Oh my God. Senator Kennedy has been shot, and possibly shot in the head. Get the gun, Rafer. Get the gun."

Now it was complete madness. Grier and Johnson continued to grapple with the gunman for his pistol. There were shouts to kill the man, others to hold him for the police. A few feet away, a young kitchen worker knelt at Bobby's left side, trying to comfort him, pressing a set of rosary beads into his hand. Journalists from the press room, drawn by the gunshots, began to crowd into the corridor. One photographer raised her camera, then lowered it, unable to shoot, and told her colleagues to stop, too. They ignored her.

Others wounded by the ricocheting bullets were groaning and crying out in pain. "We need a doctor!" someone shouted. Michael's mind flashed back to the Central Highlands firefight and the calls for medical aid: "Corpsman! Corpsman!" Had the world become one vast combat zone? An image formed in his mind of a great spreading stain of violence, a slow-motion pandemic of insanity, from which there was no escape.

It seemed to take an eternity for medical workers to arrive, but by the clock, it was only six minutes from the time of the initial call. In the meantime, Kennedy aides tried desperately to push people away from the fallen candidate. His wife, Ethel, entered and knelt beside him, holding his hand and speaking to him softly. Michael was jostled and shoved against a wall, winding up back near the door leading to the ballroom. He could hear the joyful sounds of the victory party dissolve into cries of anguish as word spread about what had happened. Someone took the microphone and pleaded with people to leave. No one paid any attention.

Michael watched as Bobby was lifted onto a stretcher and carried away to a waiting ambulance. Then he pushed his way through the crowd into the press room. The place was a Babel of noise and confusion as every reporter simultaneously tried to reach his editors. The phone system became overloaded, and Michael had to wait several minutes for a dial tone, but he finally reached his paper. They had a TV on and had heard about the shooting. Michael dictated a long report of what he had witnessed, received the desk editor's terse praise, and hung up with a promise to file more when he could get it.

He sat down heavily, feeling the full weight of what had happened bearing down on him. He was back in Parkland Hospital in 1963, slumping against a wall in disbelief over JFK's murder. He was at the Muncie airport, just two months ago, learning about Dr. King. He realized with a shudder that he had become a veteran, a practiced hand, at reporting on assassinations; he knew the drill and did it by rote. He supposed some would call it a mark of his professionalism, but it left him feeling rather sick.

He looked around the room. Those who weren't on the phone or typing were slumped in their chairs with numb, distant expressions on their faces. Two photographers who had been in the corridor were weeping. He looked down at the notebook in his lap. It was wet with his own tears. The sight startled him. He hadn't realized he had shed them.

It was all surreal, a grotesque phantasmagoria with no awakening.

Chapter Eighteen
—Prague Spring—
July 1968

1: Fault Lines

For as long as Michael could remember, he had been coming with his family to the Delaware shore in the summer. As a boy, he learned to swim and body-surf in the Atlantic off Bethany Beach and spent evenings playing arcade games at Rehoboth. As a teenager, he flirted awkwardly with girls on the Ocean City boardwalk. As a young man, he arrived at his parents' summer house in Bethany with a stack of books and a battered portable typewriter.

Now, he showed up with a battered psyche and a deep melancholy, wanting only to sit on the beach and absorb the soothing sight of the rolling breakers.

He had covered Bobby Kennedy's emotion-wracked funeral in New York and the slow, sad train ride to Arlington Cemetery on autopilot, holding his feelings at bay through the narcotic of the next deadline. When he arrived at Bethany, nothing remained to buffer the shocks and traumas of the past two months, personal and political. A profound depression settled on him like the gray morning fog that crept in off the ocean. For three days, he barely got out of bed.

His parents had already opened the big, airy house for the season and were spending long weekends there. They tiptoed around him like he was a traumatized disaster victim. He had told them about his breakup with Riva in only the most fragmentary way, and in a manner that strongly discouraged any probing. He had openly shared with them the hopes he cherished for Kennedy, and now they ached for his loss—for both his losses.

Still, they were at their core a political family, and sooner or later, their political differences would resurface. For Kennedy's death had shattered an uneasy truce.

Before Los Angeles, Anna and Michael had been united in their feelings about Bobby—and Alan had evolved in his thinking about him, despite Bobby's opposition to the war. Alan deeply resented being marginalized in Washington because of his unrepentant hawkishness; he increasingly regarded Humphrey as a weak reed, and he remembered Bobby as an ally in the foreign policy debates of JFK's presidency over Cuba and Berlin. A new Kennedy administration, he felt, would hold opportunities for him to rebuild his access and influence. Even if Alan could not persuade Bobby to soldier on in Vietnam, there would always be new crises, new opportunities to have an impact. For his father, Michael realized, the game was always played on several levels. When he shared that insight with his mother, she smiled indulgently, as if to say she was glad he had finally awakened to that fact.

The assassination reopened all the old fault lines. Reluctantly but inevitably, Anna gravitated toward Humphrey as the only realistic Democratic nominee, however flawed. She had no illusions about his deficiencies, or the difficulties he would face in the fall campaign, but the imperative of keeping Nixon out of the White House was paramount for her.

Michael was done with that kind of thinking. The Democrats had forfeited their claim to power, in his view, by marching in lockstep with Lyndon on the war for so long, even when it was obvious he was leading them into a quagmire. A reckoning was inevitable, and if it took a season in the wilderness to bring it about, so be it. If he had a vote, it would go to McCarthy, but he understood how futile it would be. McCarthy would campaign on through the Chicago convention, but the outcome there was certain.

What was not certain was a path forward. Michael saw no one within the political system who could pick up Bobby Kennedy's mantle. He envied radicals like Marta their certitude that a revolutionary crisis was in the offing, but he doubted it. And he thought that if it did come, the right-wingers, unapologetically ruthless and often violent, were far more likely to prevail. He had no taste for that kind of dystopia. Politics had become a dead end for him. He returned to the beach and the breakers, which offered serenity and solace, but no solutions.

Alan was conflicted, for different reasons. He regarded McCarthy with contempt, of course, but his opinion of Humphrey was not much higher. He had heard rumors of some last-minute thunderclap: a bid by Ted Kennedy, Bobby's younger brother, to swoop in and take the nomination; a move by Johnson to shove Humphrey aside and reclaim the crown. He dismissed them as wishful thinking. The Democrats were stuck with Hubert, a weak and irresolute nominee at the head of a badly fractured party that would limp into the fall campaign with a divided soul, up against a confident, energized opposition led by a cunning, utterly shameless nominee.

Richard Nixon was working nonstop to reinvent himself, to shed his old image of an angry partisan hatchet man and offer himself as a unifying figure. Yet beneath the sunny smile and the two-handed wave, the old, calculating Nixon lurked. When asked about Vietnam, his stock answer was that he had a plan to end the war, but couldn't reveal it because to do so would aid the enemy. It was the most blatant dodge Alan had ever heard, which was saying something, but Nixon seemed to be getting away with it. Alan doubted Nixon had a plan of any kind, but he was curious. He knew one or two Republicans who had lines into the Nixon campaign. He would find out what that crafty con man had in mind, eventually.

After several evenings of desultory dinner-table talk, the subject of politics finally arose. Anna had been dreading the moment, but she was pleasantly surprised at the lack of fire in the conversation.

Michael, she thought, was just too played out, too emotionally spent, to rise to the bait. And Alan, uncharacteristically, wasn't offering any. At first, she ascribed it to her husband's empathy for their son's fragile state of mind. Then it occurred to her that Alan was as conflicted as anyone, still searching for his bearings in a political landscape that now had no more shape or solidity than the sands on their beach.

One political subject was safe ground: the amazing events taking place in Czechoslovakia. Dubcek had been in power since January, and was moving ahead with a reform program that included a commitment to end all censorship and a gradual transition to a multiparty political system. The great question was whether the Soviet leadership would tolerate such apostasy. For the moment, the answer seemed to be yes, but there was no certainty that would continue.

Michael regarded the "Prague Spring" as a solitary ray of hope in an otherwise dark political moment. He was heartened by the prospect of an often-victimized nation regaining its freedom, but he also saw much wider ramifications. The iron logic of the Cold War permitted no dissenters on either side; the Soviets had invaded Hungary in 1956 to crush a revolt, and just last year Washington had backed a brutal military coup in Greece that put an end to parliamentarians asking impertinent questions about the wisdom of Greek membership in NATO. The Vietnam catastrophe was born of this Manichaean mentality. But if the Czechs could loosen the bonds that held them in subservience to Moscow, it would call into question all the rigid assumptions that had accrued since 1945 on both sides of the divide.

"Did you see this?" Michael reached across the breakfast table to hand Alan the morning Washington Post, folded to an inside page. The story there recounted the publication of an essay by the writer Ludvik Vaculik, calling for the ouster of the remaining conservatives in the Czech government and urging the populace to back up this demand through demonstrations and strikes.

"This guy is openly calling for a mass movement to purge the opponents of reform, and half the newspapers in Prague have printed it," Michael said. "He's talking about the people as the motor force of politics, not the party. That notion undermines the entire system. This is how revolutions start."

"Yes, it's amazing, and heartening," Alan replied. "I'm not surprised that people like Vaculik are speaking out. I knew a number of Czech intellectuals in the days before the Soviets cracked the whip, and there wasn't a more vibrant political culture anywhere in Europe. The pent-up demand for change must be enormous.

"But it's ultimately up to the apparatchiks in the Kremlin how far this can go, and that's the problem. They frighten very easily, and when they're afraid, nasty things have a way of happening."

"But this turns everything upside down," Michael protested.

"Yes, and that's exactly the problem, from the Russians' point of view," Alan replied. "They don't want anything turned upside down, or even slightly sideways. Not on their side of the curtain."

They left it there for the moment. Anna thought it was the most agreement her son and husband had shared in a political discussion in years. It was also the most interest Michael had shown in anything since he arrived. For both reasons, she left the table smiling.

She was worried about her son, but uncertain how to act on her concern for him. She thought he would recover from the political trauma of the moment before long; he was a journalist to his core, and a story would come along and grab him. The breakup of his marriage was a much different matter. It was a deep wound, and she thought he compounded it by refusing to talk about it. Yet so long as that was the case, there was little she could do.

In the days immediately following the breakup, Anna had considered phoning Riva, but she rejected that idea as overly intrusive. Instead, she called Dorie, hoping that a mother-to-mother connection might yield some insight into the cause of the split and perhaps a way to heal it.

"How are you and Sam doing? I hope it's getting better, at least a little. Alan and I so wanted to come to Tommy's service, but we thought it would be very awkward under the circumstances."

"Yes, it would've made things even harder for Riva," Dorie said. "We know how you and Alan felt for us. Michael called me and asked if it was okay for him to come, but I had to tell him no. I hated doing that, but Riva was very clear that she wanted to make a clean break. I had to go with my child."

"Of course. I would have done the same thing."

"As for us, we're doing okay, just taking it a day at a time. Me and Sam, we've been through a fair lot in life. To be honest, we felt like we lost Tommy a long time ago. Didn't make the end any easier, though."

"Well, if there's ever anything we can do, please let us know."

"Of course. We will."

"I wanted to ask you about something else," Anna said. "It's a difficult subject, but—well, I thought as mothers we might put our heads together and see if there's some way to heal the break between Riva and Michael. He has no idea I'm talking to you about this, and he'd probably want to kill me if he knew, but I'm quite sure he wants to get back together with Riva if that's possible."

"I felt terrible for both of them when it happened," Dorie replied. "We love Michael, and we thought he was wonderful for Riva. But I know how she feels right now, and if there's one thing I know about Riva, it's that trying to change her mind about something once she's set on it is a waste of time. Believe me, I've tried before. Riva's going through something, and she just has to get through it in her own way. And we'll just have to hope that maybe when she has, they might get back together. I know that's not the answer you wanted to hear from me, but it's the truth."

"I understand. Tell me, how is Riva doing? Is she okay? Alan and I care about her a lot."

"I know you do. To be honest, we haven't had a lot of contact with her since—well, since the funeral. She's hurting from a lot of things, and that pains me, but it's something she's got to work out on her own right now. Sam and I are just trying to find the right balance, to let her know we love her, but not crowd her."

"I think you're a very wise mother, Dorie."

"Lord, I hope so. I couldn't help my son when he needed it. I hope this will work out better. But once a child is old enough to think for themselves, you never know for sure if you're doing the right thing by them. You just have to hope you are, but you never really know for sure."

• • •

A few days after Alan and Michael's conversation about the Czech events, Michael answered the telephone and found Jack Rothstein on the line. He was in the area and asked if he could come by for a talk. Michael had a good idea what his editor had to say, but Jack was not a man to put off.

He ushered Jack into the beach house's living room and, knowing him, offered him a drink, even though it was barely past midday. Jack was dapper as ever, in a white polo shirt and crisp khakis, but Michael noticed he was now graying at the temples. Working for a mercurial owner like Andy Franklin can't be easy, he thought.

"What brings you to these parts, Jack? I can't imagine it's just to celebrate July Fourth at the seaside and track me down."

"My daughter's in college now, God save me. Her ambition is to be a marine biologist, and she's doing a summer program with the University of Delaware up the road at Lewes. She wants to get into their master's program. But while I was dropping her off there, I thought I'd swing by and see you. I know you've been through a few things. How're you doing?"

Michael exhaled a long breath. "I'm okay. Taking it one step at a time. I appreciate your letting me take some time off."

"Well, you'd earned it, and you needed it. But now I think it's time for you to get back on the horse."

"Yeah, I understand. But I have to tell you, I don't have a lot of interest in the presidential campaign. I can't imagine three less appealing pols than Nixon, Humphrey, and Wallace."

"I've got a better idea. Have you been following Czechoslovakia?"

The question brought a smile to Michael's face. "Yeah, a bit."

"It's a hell of a story, and things are coming to a head," Jack said. "The last vestige of censorship was lifted last week. There's a big party congress coming up, where they're supposed to ratify the full reform program, including a commitment to move toward a multiparty democratic system. The Russians hate that, but the question is, how do they stuff this genie back in its lamp?"

"So, what are you proposing?"

"That you get over there and cover it. Our foreign desk is still rather undernourished, which is something I want to fix. Having you there knocking out stories will help generate some momentum for it, help me sell it to Andy. We have a stringer in Prague who's been giving us the basic running story, but you can do a lot more with it. The stringer is a cooperative fellow. He's more than willing to serve as your translator and legman."

"I'll need a visa. I hear they can be prickly about issuing them."

"I've already looked into that," Jack said. "I know a guy at State, who knows a guy in their embassy. The new government is actually getting eager to have western reporters there. They think it may provide some protection against you-know-who. You get your passport over to their consular section, and you'll have your visa in a couple of days."

2: Fulcrum

Prague's main airport would have been an embarrassment to any medium-sized American city, but Soviet-bloc countries did not bother to put up much of a front for visitors. The terminal was standard issue for the bloc, with all the homey touches Michael remembered from a student exchange visit to Russia: faded and peeling paint, dim fluorescent lighting, dirty linoleum floors, a long line for passport control and a longer one to clear customs. It took Michael almost two hours to get through the process. But at the exit gate, the paper's stringer, Janek Novotny, was waiting, holding a hand-lettered sign with Michael's name.

Janek turned out to be a sharp-witted 30-something former teacher with a mordant sense of humor, something Michael soon discovered was common among Czechs. Janek understood journalists' needs, having spent the past year working for various western news organizations. He was also a skilled translator, with two years' experience at the British embassy. And, miracle of miracles, he had a car: a patched-up East German Trabant that spewed noxious fumes, rattled like an ancient washing machine and bounced along Prague's rutted streets at a top speed of 30 miles an hour on a good day. Still, it ran.

Janek had been educated to be a high school history teacher and had taught for five years, until he grew sick of indoctrinating young Czechs with the regime-sanctioned version of their country's recent past. That version forced teachers to minimize or ignore the fundamental forces that had created the Czech nation in 1918: nationalism, and a powerful desire for democratic self-government. And it presented the Communist seizure of power in 1948 as the foundational event of the modern Czech state, a glorious triumph of the working class over its bourgeois oppressors.

Janek had parlayed his fluency in English into a job with the British, and his flair for journalism into work for Reuters, AP, and the Chronicle. He was candid about the old regime's demand that he inform on British diplomats as the price of permission to work at the embassy; he told Michael he had hated it, and kept the authorities at bay with a mixture of harmless gossip, things they already were certain to know, and a few spicy fictions. The new government didn't seem to care about snooping, and that suited him just fine.

Michael wondered whether Janek was worried about repercussions if the political weather changed. Janek responded with a fatalistic shrug, another common Czech tic. He was married with a young son, and he said his wife, an elementary school teacher, was less enthusiastic about the reform movement and frequently urged him to be more cautious.

"But I can't live like that anymore," Janek said. "If we all took that attitude, nothing would ever change. I have no idea how this will turn out, but I would like my son to have better choices in life than I had."

Janek gave Michael the unsanitized version of Czech history: nationalist and peasant rebellions running back to the 17th century; a thwarted revolution against Austrian rule in 1848; the rise of the Czech social democratic movement under Tomas Masaryk that linked the goals of independence and democracy; the fulfillment of Masaryk's vision at the end of World War I. Then came the tragic British-French sellout of Czechoslovakia at the 1938 Munich conference that paved the way for Nazi occupation, the equally tragic 1948 coup that turned the country into a Soviet satellite, the anti-Semitic Stalinist show trials of the early 1950s that ushered in a wave of intense repression.

An image formed in Michael's mind of Czechoslovakia as a fulcrum of modern European history, mirroring its broader currents. He shared that thought with Janek, who nodded in agreement. "I think it is our destiny," he said. "It is not such a happy destiny. But it seems we are fated to play that role again today."

Michael spent a couple of days walking around Prague's cobblestoned streets, immersing himself in the city's unique blend of baroque beauty and middle-European melancholy. He walked the length of Charles Bridge, with its rows of beautifully sculpted statues of saints, and found a shop that sold lovingly carved examples of Prague's famous wooden marionettes. He strolled along the Vltava River embankment, its vista dominated by the Gothic spires of Prague Castle. He walked through Wenceslas Square, where independence was proclaimed in 1918 and where Czech partisans battled German soldiers in a 1945 rebellion. He visited the Church of Saints Cyril and Methodius, its bullet-scarred walls bearing witness to the last stand made there by the resistance fighters who assassinated Nazi SS General Reinhard Heydrich in 1942.

On Prague's streets, he found a populace alive with the possibilities of the moment and full of opinions about the future. He quickly discovered that the western image of Dubcek as an unalloyed reformer was simplistic. To many young Czechs, Dubcek was a compromised figure, at best a transitional leader to a more radical transformation. His efforts to preserve some degree of Communist Party authority while steering the country toward pluralism were drawing attacks from both ends of the spectrum. Conservatives thought he was opening the door to "bourgeois counterrevolution," liberals called his program half-hearted and inadequate.

The end of censorship allowed these debates to be aired at a high decibel level in every possible medium. Writers and activists who once circulated their manifestos through sub rosa means were being published in widely read newspapers and magazines and appearing on radio and television. Playwrights who had satirized the regime through elliptical absurdist dramas suddenly could contemplate a more direct approach.

Michael discovered Prague had a thriving underground rock scene that was taking full advantage of the opening. Janek introduced him to a friend named Milan Hlavsa, a bass player and songwriter with a band called the Primitives Group, which took its inspiration from American groups like the Velvet Underground and the Mothers of Invention. Hlavsa proudly wore his dark brown hair at shoulder length, explaining that it identified him as part of the "máničky," a subculture that rattled the old regime by trying to live as independently of it as possible. Michael spent an evening in a basement club, drinking Pilsner Urquell beer with Janek and listening to Milan's band cover dark, subversive songs by the Doors:

Five to one, baby, one in five
No one here gets out alive
You get yours, baby, I'll get mine
Gonna make it, baby, if we try
The old get old and the young get stronger
May take a week and it may take longer
They got the guns but we got the numbers
Gonna win, yeah, we're takin' over!

As the song reached its crescendo, Michael looked around the cramped club. It was filled with young people swaying and nodding to the heavily syncopated beat, joining the band in shouting out that defiant last line. Michael had never quite bought into the belief of some young American radicals in an international youth culture that transcended ideology and would change the world through the power of a liberated consciousness. Now, amid these young Czech rebels, the idea seemed less far-fetched.

Looming over this heady atmosphere was the "great socialist motherland" to the east, keeping watch with a baleful eye. The current Soviet leadership had wrested control from Nikita Khrushchev four years earlier and quickly ended what remained of Khrushchev's cultural thaw of the early '60s. They had been sending conflicting signals about Dubcek's reforms, and divining Moscow's intentions was one of Prague's great guessing games. Yet in case anyone doubted Russian capabilities, several thousand Soviet troops were actually in Czechoslovakia, part of an elaborate Warsaw Pact war games exercise.

"What do you think the Soviets are playing at, with those war games?" Michael asked Janek.

"I learned about the English writer Samuel Johnson when I was in college," he answered. "I recall something he said about the prospect of being hanged. It concentrates the mind."

The possibility of Soviet intervention generated frequent demonstrations by students and other young people. The protesters were entirely peaceful, but Michael noticed a large police presence on the edges of the crowd, and he did not read friendship in the officers' faces. He wondered how they would react if in a crackdown. He wondered how many police spies were in the crowd.

On weekends, parents came to the demonstrations with their children, and at one gathering, Michael met Janek's wife, Katerina, and six-year-old son, Petka. Michael was a bit surprised to see Katerina there, given what Janek had told him about her state of mind. He struck up a conversation with her and learned that the presence of Soviet troops had driven her off the fence.

"We're supposed to still be grateful to the Russians for what they did during the war," she told him, as Petka looked up at his mother, wide-eyed and curious. "They drove the Germans out, that's fine, but that was 23 years ago. Now it's time for us to have our own country. We don't want anyone dictating to us, not East or West."

Once again, Michael was struck by the similarities between these demonstrators and the young people he had met at Columbia, the Pentagon, and McCarthy and Kennedy rallies. The young Czechs were perhaps more conservative in dress and appearance, but they shared a common impulse of discontent over being thrust into a world they hadn't made and didn't much like and yet were told they had to accept, even as it spun further and further out of control.

"I'm supposed to finish my economics degree and then write one paper after another, proving that a socialist economy is superior to capitalism," one student told him. "What kind of a life is that? How do I know that's true? West Germany is less than 200 kilometers away, but I can't go there to see what it's really like to live in a capitalist economy. They're afraid I'd never come back. Why, if capitalism is so oppressive?"

A young nursing student named Martina Vlacikova explained her presence at the demonstration with a rationale that was at once simpler and more profound. "I'm tired of being lied to," she said. "All my life, we've heard the same falsehoods and empty slogans. 'The socialist road,' 'unity of the working class,' 'fraternal socialist allies,' 'the party's leading role.' It's all meaningless. All you have to do is look around to see how false it all is. We knew it in our minds, but we couldn't express it. Now, we can."

Michael recalled something he had read in George Orwell's writings about how political language became debased: through words designed "to make lies sound truthful and murder respectable, and to give an appearance of solidity to pure wind." And Orwell's definition of freedom: the ability "to say that two plus two make four."

The nursing student told Michael she lived with her mother and aunt in a one-room apartment in a Prague suburb. Her aunt suffered from chronic asthma and often coughed all night, making it hard for everyone to sleep. When she became a nurse, the family would qualify for a larger apartment, but that was two years off. "Why do we have to live like this?" she asked. "We are not a poor country. But we live like we are."

The dramatic events taking place in Czechoslovakia had swelled the foreign press contingent to 10 times its normal size. Reporters for all the large western news organizations were on hand, rubbing elbows with the usual mix of collegiality and competition.

One of the journalists most in evidence was a flamboyant French correspondent named Edouard Radnovy. The son of a French mother and a Czech emigre father, Edouard had spent several years in Prague when he was younger and knew the scene well. Fluent in several languages, distinctive with his mane of long black hair and piercing brown eyes, dressed in jeans and silk ascot, he cut a striking figure. Edouard worked for a left-wing Paris daily called *Combat* and left no doubt that he, like his paper, strongly supported the reforms.

After one demonstration, Michael and Edouard spent a long evening over drinks—Edouard disdained Pilsner Urquell in favor of Georgian red wine—and struck up a friendship. Edouard was free with his opinions, and equally free about sharing his extensive contacts in the government and the various political factions. He even offered to introduce Michael to a key advisor to President Ludvik Svoboda, a Dubcek ally. Michael was pleasantly surprised by Edouard's professional generosity, but did not question the gift.

When he related the story to Janek, he was surprised by the reaction. "Be careful around fellows like that," Janek said. "You don't know what game they may be playing."

Michael wondered if Janek's warning might be born of professional jealousy, a desire to preserve his status as Michael's primary conduit to Czech sources. If so, it was a losing game, given Edouard's connections. Svoboda's advisor turned out to be cool and cautious, unwilling to say much of substance to an American journalist, but that certainly was not Edouard's fault.

It was now the end of July, and there was a growing sense that things were coming to a head. Most of the Soviet troops had withdrawn, but only to across the border. In one month, the Czech Communist Party Congress would convene, with formal adoption of Dubcek's complete program on the agenda. That would commit the party to support of full civil liberties, rapid economic liberalization, and a 10-year transition to a democratic political system. There was a widespread sense that there would be no turning back once the congress took that step.

With the clock ticking, all sides maneuvered for position. A bilateral meeting between Dubcek and Soviet leader Leonid

Brezhnev resolved nothing. As it ended, the Soviets and three allies announced they would stage military maneuvers just across the Czech borders.

Two days later, a formal Warsaw Pact meeting convened in the Czech city of Bratislava. Michael and the rest of the journalistic pack headed there and camped out through a long day and night at City Hall, where the talks were held. When they finally broke up, the result seemed to be a relaxation of tensions. The Soviets agreed to allow the Czech Party Congress to take place. The last remnants of Soviet troops were departing. The body language of Dubcek, Svoboda and other Czech leaders suggested that a compromise had been reached.

Yet the conference's formal declaration, released just before midnight, was puzzling. It made no mention of the Czech reforms, and bristled with language about American aggression and West German revanchism. And it was clear on one point: the sovereignty of all Warsaw Pact nations was limited by the principle of "the cohesion of the international Communist movement." It was a veiled threat, Michael thought, and he wrote it that way, despite all the soothing atmospherics.

Dubcek, back in Prague after the conference, was under siege. The demonstrations against Soviet intervention were now daily events. Dubcek became the reluctant host of East German leader Walter Ulbricht, a Moscow ally dispatched by Kremlin leaders to deliver a hard-line message. At a press conference after the meeting, the portly, goateed Stalinist blandly told journalists that East German citizens were quite puzzled by the fuss over Dubcek's lifting of press censorship. After all, he said with a straight face, no such censorship had never existed in his country.

Dubcek countered by inviting his own allies to Prague. Yugoslav leader Josip Broz Tito, who had broken free of Moscow's control two decades earlier, came and was greeted by cheering crowds as he rode with Dubcek to Prague Castle. Romanian leader Nicolae

Ceaușescu got an equally enthusiastic reception. Both leaders issued declarations of support for the Czech government.

Moscow responded with a long commentary in the party newspaper Pravda denouncing the Czech press for printing "a whole salvo of anti-Soviet articles" aimed at undermining the Bratislava declaration. It was the first anti-Czech broadside in the Soviet press since the Bratislava meeting, and it was widely interpreted as a signal that the Kremlin wanted to tighten the pressure. Pravda followed three days later with another article accusing Czech authorities of ignoring attacks on "socialist achievements."

3: Crackdown

The evening after the second Pravda commentary ran, Michael joined a large gang of correspondents in the Alcron Hotel bar just off Wenceslas Square to swap rumors, theories, and gossip. The level of tension was steadily rising, but the lack of hard information was maddening. In its absence, speculation abounded, most of it contradictory. The Soviets were about to intervene. The Soviets had decided to back off. Washington had warned Moscow it would regard a Soviet invasion as an act of war. Washington had assured Moscow it would do nothing besides utter loud protests. Dubcek was in the Castle preparing to lead the defense of the country. Dubcek was in the Kremlin preparing to negotiate a climbdown.

As usual, Edouard was a center of attention, hinting broadly but cryptically about his inside information. Edouard's basic take, presented with many conspiratorial flourishes, was that an invasion was possible but unlikely. When Michael thought about it, he realized Edouard had simply stated the obvious, and in a way that would allow him to claim vindication no matter how it turned out. He just did it in a manner that conferred great authority.

As the evening wore on, Michael pulled Janek aside. "What happens if the Soviets come in?" he asked.

"You'll probably be expelled. You'll have plenty of company. They won't want a lot of western journalists, especially Americans, around to witness what will happen, which won't be very pretty."

"And you?" Michael asked.

"Nothing, probably. I'll keep my head down and find work as a translator again."

"Really? If there's a crackdown, they won't care that you worked for the bourgeois foreign press?"

"They'll want to limit the damage," Janek said. "They'll go after people who played a big role in the reform movement, of course. And anyone who opposes them from now on will have an unpleasant time of it. But mostly they'll want us to quiet down and go back to sleep. That's what I'll do, if it comes to that. We have become rather adept at surviving in the face of superior power. We've had a lot of practice."

Early the next morning, Michael was awakened by loud noises outside his hotel. His head pounding from a first-class hangover, he squinted at his watch. Six a.m. He looked out the window and saw a large crowd carrying Czech flags and chanting: "Dubcek! Svoboda! Ivan go home!"

He heard the Russian armor a few minutes later, as he threw on some clothes. A Soviet T-55 tank, he discovered, makes a low rumbling sound, audible blocks away as it rolls over cobblestoned streets. It also tears up those streets, kicking loose many paving stones.

Michael thought about telephoning Janek, but decided to take his chances alone. When he picked up the phone to call the AP bureau, he discovered that the line was dead anyway. He hurried outside and followed the sound of the chanting.

It led him to the headquarters of the state broadcasting service on Vinohradska Street. It was still in the hands of the government, its broadcast emanating from several loudspeakers propped up on open second-floor windows. Its message was to obey only the lawful government, but not to resist the invading troops. A man in the crowd translated for Michael: "When you hear the Czechoslovak National Anthem, all will be over."

More than 100 people were in front of the building, constructing barricades from whatever material they could find. Several Soviet tanks and military trucks were arrayed in the street. Some people approached the tanks and pleaded with the troops perched on top. The soldiers appeared to be bewildered and a little frightened. Some of them looked like teenagers. Michael later learned that many did not even realize they were in Prague; they had been told they were headed for an exercise in East Germany.

The scene turned violent in an instant. Some soldiers fired in the air in an attempt to scatter the people behind the barricades. When that didn't work, they fired directly on them, then moved tanks forward to flatten the obstacles. A hail of paving stones, torn loose by the tank treads and turned into missiles by angry Czechs, rained down on the metal monsters.

Michael took cover behind a truck, then moved in search of a more secure vantage point. He was glad he did. A stray round hit the truck, which was filled with ammunition. It exploded with a deafening roar, spewing smoke and fire into the sky and leaving a large crater in the street. Several bodies were strewn about it. Ignoring the carnage, a detachment of soldiers rushed the front door and piled into the building. A few minutes later, the music of the national anthem played over the loudspeakers. Then they went silent.

Michael headed for Wenceslas Square, checking his watch and calculating the time difference. It was hours before his paper's first deadline. He had plenty to report, but no immediate way to report it. He pushed on to the square, hoping that he could file something from the AP bureau later.

Tanks were arrayed at either end of the long square and at various points within it. Hundreds of people were there, surrounding the tanks, chanting and trying to talk to the soldiers in and atop them. In the center, at the base of the statue of the nation's patron saint, King Wenceslas I, someone had placed a hand-lettered sign: "Svobody Narod"—"A Free People." Young people ringed the statue as if to protect it. Some looking grim, others in shock, still others impassive, they looked out at the soldiers.

Michael approached one young couple, who were holding hands as they watched the tanks maneuver. He asked them if they spoke English, then what they were feeling. "We had hoped so much for a different future," the young man said. "So many hopes we had. And now—now this—" He choked on his words and buried his face in his hands. His companion put her arms around him, and they wept together.

Michael spent the day moving around the city, keeping clear of the ever-present Soviet soldiers and piecing together the story. He did not know how much time he had before he was booted out, so every hour was precious. He knew very little Czech, but many people spoke enough English to make themselves understood or to translate for others. Several had transistor radios that provided news bulletins, sparse and full of spin, but still revealing. A few had short-wave radios that picked up the BBC and the Voice of America, which provided a fuller picture.

Czechoslovakia had been invaded overnight by hundreds of thousands of troops from the Soviet Union and three other Warsaw Pact countries. The Czech army had orders to stand down and let the invaders in, and had reluctantly done so. Dubcek and several other pro-reform leaders had been arrested, and their whereabouts were unknown. Later in the day, Soviet state radio reported that they were in Moscow. The Soviet government announced that it had intervened, with great reluctance, only after receiving a formal entreaty from a group of Czech party officials asking for help in saving their country from a counter-revolutionary plot. It cited the Bratislava declaration, with its language about the limits of state sovereignty, as legal sanction.

The Prague Spring was over, flattened as completely as the street barricades crushed under the tank treads. Everyone knew it, even those brave, angry Czechs who risked their lives to pepper Soviet forces with stones and Molotov cocktails. The Soviet troops might stay for a week or a year, but whenever they departed, they would leave behind a government that would end the reforms and dance to Moscow's tune.

Michael filled his notebook, hurriedly wrote his file and made his way to the AP bureau late in the afternoon. Miraculously, it still had a telex connection to London, although no one knew for how long. A considerable number of correspondents were lined up to send stories, and Michael waited for almost an hour. Halfway through his transmission, the telex went dead. He still counted himself fortunate. The eight journalists in line behind him were now out of luck. The phone system was working again, but international service was cut off.

Michael managed to call Janek and asked if he could come by. When he got there, he found Janek was upset because Michael had not reached him in the morning. Michael tried to explain that he hadn't felt justified in putting Janek in danger. There was a long pause. "Well, Katerina will thank you," he said.

He invited Michael into the kitchen for what was likely to be a farewell drink. His wife was there, looking exhausted, and so was Petka, despite the late hour, too keyed up to sleep. "I have something for you, to remember me by," Michael told the boy. He pulled from his bag one of the wooden marionettes he had bought on one of his first days in Prague and presented it to the child. Petka's round face lit up with an expression of joy that Michael knew he would never forget. He downed his shot, embraced Janek and Katerina, wished them good fortune, and took his leave.

When he got back to his hotel, he found a message waiting for him that he had half-expected: His visa was cancelled, and he was to show up at the Foreign Ministry press office at 8 a.m. for transport to the airport. He seriously considered ignoring the summons, but the Alcron bar consensus was against that course of action. "The authorities could get quite rough with you if they catch you in the country illegally," Edouard advised him.

"What will you do?" Michael asked.

Edouard looked uncharacteristically sheepish. "I believe it's only American correspondents who are being expelled," he said quietly.

This time, Edouard knew what he was talking about. When Michael arrived at the ministry, once again with a pounding headache, he discovered eight other journalists, all accredited to U.S. news organizations. "Badge of honor, I guess," muttered one colleague. "One I could do without," Michael replied.

The ride to the airport was on roads filled with military traffic. It was the same at the airport, which had been commandeered by the Soviets and closed to normal civilian flights. The bus bypassed the terminal, drove straight onto the tarmac and pulled up alongside a Russian Tupelov-154 airliner with Aeroflot markings. Under the eye of a police guard, Michael, his journalist colleagues and a random assortment of others now unwelcome in the new-old Czechoslovakia filed off the bus and climbed the jet stairs. At the top, a police officer handed Michael back his passport, with the Czech visa excised. There was even an exit stamp, he discovered. Bureaucracy prevails, he thought, even amid invasion.

As Michael settled into his stained, narrow seat for the flight to Vienna, the man next to him turned his way. "Well, at least we avoided going through passport control and customs," he said.

"I seem to recall a line from a Marx Brothers movie," Michael replied. "'I've been thrown out of better places than this.'"

The gallows humor took some of the edge off the moment, but not for long. As their plane started to taxi, they could see big-bellied military transports landing, one after another, bringing more troops and materiel. The Soviets were clearly settling in for a long stay.

A flight attendant tried to block their view of the scene by closing the frayed window curtain, but it was jammed open. Michael's smile prompted a glare from the attendant and a barked command: "Don't look! Forbidden!"

Michael's smile broadened into a grin.

"What're you gonna do to me? Kick me out?"

Chapter Nineteen
–The Whole World Is Watching–

August 1968

1: Welcome Home

Michael arrived home to a ringing telephone. Christ, I'm barely in the door, he thought, as he lurched toward the phone and picked it up just as it went silent.

Weighing the possibilities, he dialed his paper's national desk. The clerk put the phone down for a moment and came back on the line. "Jack was trying to call you. Hold on."

While the clerk transferred him to his executive editor, Michael kicked the door closed and tossed his bags onto a chair. He had spent the last 24 hours making his way back to New York from Prague by way of Vienna and London, the trip slowed by the many cancelled flights and stranded travelers strewn in the wake of the Soviet invasion of Czechoslovakia.

The long journey gave him plenty of time to read about the relentless success of the Russian operation. There were a few violent confrontations, more than 100 civilian casualties, but most Czechs limited themselves to peaceful protests that the occupiers easily shrugged off. Dubcek and the other government leaders were hauled to Moscow, browbeaten into signing a document renouncing their entire reform program, and dumped back in Prague like a pile of soiled laundry.

The trip also gave him ample time to reflect on another uncomfortable fact. This time, his father had been right. His warnings that Michael was too optimistic about the outcome of the Czech experiment, that the Soviets could not and would not allow it to succeed, had been borne out before Michael's eyes on the streets of Prague. Michael recalled the poet Thomas Gray's line about those who would "wade through slaughter to a throne." The men in Moscow had shown themselves ready, willing, and able.

Jack Rothstein's voice barked out of the receiver. "Michael? Welcome home. But don't get too comfortable. Like the old joke goes, I got good news and bad news."

"Comfortable? Now that's a joke. I just walked in the door. Well, give me the good news first."

"The good news is your Czech stories were big hits, especially that last one on the day of the invasion. It got picked up all over the place. And strange as it may seem, being one of the first reporters to get booted has only increased your stature, and the paper's. The fact that they thought you were important enough to kick out right away means they thought the Chronicle was important, too. Andy's thrilled. I think you just doubled my foreign desk budget."

"Glad to hear it," Michael said. "I'll help you spend it. Just remember all this when you get my expense report. So what's the bad news?"

"You're not gonna get any down-time. We want you here in Chicago, like, yesterday. Yes, I'm serious. The convention starts Monday. The town is already filling up with delegates and journalists, and with all the crazies, too. This is a big chance for the paper to really boost its stock, and we want you here as soon as possible to bat cleanup.

"So take today to catch your breath, and then catch a morning flight. The desk is already booking you, and the ticket will be waiting at National. We couldn't get you into the Hilton, but you've got a room at the Blackstone, right across the street."

Michael thought about disputing Jack's assumption that the anti-war demonstrators coming to Chicago were all deranged, but decided it wasn't worth it. Better to use his time and energy to catch up on what was likely to happen when the Democrats held their national convention next week.

He gleaned the political background from a quick round of phone calls, and it seemed straightforward enough. McCarthy would lead his forces in one final, futile charge up the hill, and then the delegates would nominate Humphrey, barring some last-minute thunderbolt. The most important question to be answered was how badly the party would be fractured, and that depended on the run of events.

The situation regarding the protests was a lot murkier. His best source for that would be Marta Hauser. He arranged to meet her that afternoon.

Marta's star turn in the Columbia strike had boosted her stock in the New Left. She had been elected to SDS's national board over the summer and headed its newly formed women's caucus. She was also SDS's representative on the coalition planning the Chicago protests, the National Mobilization Committee to End the War in Vietnam, a mouthful that was usually shortened to "the Mobe."

She was her usual self, dressed down in chambray and denims but with a bright red cotton scarf at her neck, full of energy and insouciance. The prospect of a Nixon-Humphrey-Wallace election, so depressing to Michael, filled her with delight. She was convinced it would drive millions of young people away from conventional politics and open them to radicalization.

Marta was also sanguine about Mayor Daley's bristling intransigence toward the protesters. The Mobe's discussions with city officials about permits to hold rallies and marches had gone nowhere. The message from the city was, don't come, and if you do, prepare for a hard time. Daley had announced that Chicago's entire 12,000-member police force would be fully mobilized, and the governor was putting the National Guard on standby. For good measure, a contingent of Army troops was being dispatched to the city.

"We had a meeting with one of our lawyers the other day," Marta said. "He told us, 'About six months from now, a judge is going to rule that everything that's about to happen to you is totally illegal. In the meantime, make sure you've got plenty of bail money lined up.'"

"You're smiling?"

"They'd be playing into our hands with a really harsh crackdown. It would expose the system for what it really is—a repressive engine of ruling class dominance."

"It could also get a lot of people hurt. You included, Marta. And I imagine it could also hold down the size of your turnout."

"You keep telling me that, and I keep telling you I can take care of myself. I really can, so let it alone. I don't think you're a male chauvinist, Michael, but you sound patronizing when you talk like that."

"Okay. Sorry."

"It's cool. And you're right about holding down the turnout. The other thing that's going to limit the numbers is a pretty serious split in the movement over whether this is worth it. A lot of groups aren't convinced it's a good idea. And most of the black organizations in Chicago don't see much point in provoking the cops over what they see as some pretty vague demands that don't serve their needs. To be honest with you, I was skeptical myself at first. But when it became clear that Daley and Johnson were going to turn Chicago into a police state for the week, it was a challenge we had to take on."

"How many people do you expect will show up?"

"On the record or off?"

"On the record first."

"We'll have as many people as we had in Washington last fall, hundreds of thousands."

"And off the record?"

"Far fewer than that, between Daley's threats and the internal dissension. If we get 10,000, I'll be pleased. The big unknown is how many McCarthy people come over and join us. But—and you can quote me on this—no matter how many people show up, we'll have made our point, which is that you can't declare the First Amendment null and void when it suits you and get away with it."

Not for the first time, Michael smiled at Marta's media sophistication. He also enjoyed the irony of a self-proclaimed revolutionary citing constitutional niceties. Well, we've all got our contradictions, he thought.

Michael genuinely liked Marta, and found that he enjoyed spending time with her. She was absolutely sincere in her political commitment, but also able to see the absurdity and humor in the most serious situation. He saw no sign that her head had been turned by her post-Columbia prominence. She did carry herself with a certain swagger, but he thought this was born of a genuine belief that she and her movement were riding the tide of history, not from any personal aggrandizement.

In addition, he admitted to himself, Marta was a very attractive young woman. His sexual side had been dormant since Riva left, but he realized Marta was causing it to stir again. He wasn't sure how he felt about that.

"Well, thanks for the intel. I guess I'll see you in Chicago. Take care of yourself, and keep your head down."

"You do the same," she replied. "I'm not sure the pigs see much difference between people like me and people like you."

2: Test of Wills

If Michael had any doubt about the mood of the city, the ride in from O'Hare Airport provided quick clarity. The Kennedy Expressway was dotted with cheery signs reading, "Welcome Democrats - Mayor Richard J. Daley." Yet as soon as the bus exited onto Ohio Street, Michael saw the clusters of police at every major intersection. Each carried a long truncheon—a "riot baton," in police parlance—and wore a battle-ready helmet, incongruously colored baby blue.

Chicago was a great metropolis, a visitor's delight, full of world-class museums and great restaurants and a pulsating big-city energy. But it was palpably on edge, still polarized over the April riots that followed the King assassination and Daley's shoot-to-kill order. Just a few weeks after King's death, an entirely peaceful anti-war demonstration had been violently broken up by the cops, a move widely interpreted as Daley's way of sending a message about what protesters could expect at the convention.

The city's instability was heightened by a wave of disruptive strikes: electrical and telephone workers, cabbies and bus drivers had all walked off the job, seeing the convention as an opportunity to leverage their pay demands. The transit workers' actions made taxis and buses scarce, and the electrical workers' strike disrupted phone service and restricted television coverage of the convention by severely limiting where the networks and local stations could do live remotes.

Michael had not been back to the Chronicle's home base in several months. Either the paper was prospering, he thought, or Andy Franklin was emptying his trust fund. The newsroom had been expanded and modernized, with rows of shiny new metal desks sporting push-button phones, and top-of-the-line IBM electric typewriters in place of the old manual Remingtons and Royals. The Chronicle was using convention week to launch a new a.m. edition designed to compete with the city's morning papers and open an escape path from the shrinking afternoon market. The paper had hired more reporters and editors, and the place buzzed with energy in anticipation of a big story. The new national editor, Ray Seccia, lured away from the rival Tribune, introduced Michael around, and Jack Rothstein emerged from his glass-walled lair to greet him and preside over a meeting of the convention coverage team.

The week ahead was going to proceed on two separate tracks that had the potential to collide in unpredictable and possibly violent ways. The first track was the convention itself. Prominent Democrats were already arriving and caucusing, and the rumors Michael was hearing about implausible scenarios were reaching a crescendo.

Much of the speculation centered on Johnson and his intentions. The politically hobbled president had been warned by party leaders to stay away, but would he heed them? Would his great vanity lead him to demand a tribute and a speaking role? Did he even harbor dreams of starting a stampede of delegates to snatch back the nomination? Trying it would be utter folly, in Michael's and many others' view, but that might not prevent LBJ from rolling the dice.

Then there were the delegates who had been pledged to Bobby Kennedy, a minority but a sizable one. George McGovern had stepped in as their nominal leader, but he was a placeholder and everyone knew it. Would Ted, the last remaining Kennedy brother, swoop in and try to unite the Kennedy and McCarthy delegates behind him? The Chronicle's city hall reporter said Mayor Daley was intrigued by the prospect.

Michael was very skeptical about that one, too. It would require a degree of cooperation with McCarthy that seemed unlikely, given the lingering ill will between the two camps. And several sources told Michael that Teddy had made a pledge to his family members, who feared another assassination, to stay out. Yet plenty of Democrats had a strong interest in tempting Teddy to break that pledge, so it could not be ruled out.

Finally, there was McCarthy himself, enigmatic as always. He had spent the summer campaigning hard, refusing to acknowledge the mounting odds against him, casting himself as the avatar of the bossless, issue-driven "new politics" and arguing that he alone could beat Nixon by winning the votes of independents and moderate Republicans. A large contingent of his loyal student volunteers, still staying clean for Gene, was coming to Chicago to join him in his last stand. He was publicly committed to a floor fight over the Vietnam platform plank and a doomed formal vote on his bid for the nomination, but what would he do after that? Grudgingly endorse the nominee? Break with the party and run as an independent? Or return to Minnesota, nurse his wounds in silence and allow his supporters to go their separate ways?

The common element in all these scenarios was Hubert Humphrey's political infirmity. Polls taken in mid-August showed him trailing the recently nominated Nixon by double-digit margins. Candidates usually rose in the polls immediately after their nomination, but a chaotic, divisive convention would not help Humphrey close the gap. The vice president's weakness provided a steady supply of grist for the rumor mill.

The second track was the protests. The "crazies," in Jack Rothstein's locution, filtering into town were of two distinct types. There were the New Left adherents like Marta, serious anti-war radicals who were determined to get in the Democrats' face. Daley's harsh threats of repression had scared off most of the moderate, older, middle-class opponents of the war who had swelled the size of the big national peace marches of recent years. That meant participation would probably be down, as Marta had acknowledged—but also that those who did show were the movement's most committed activists, unlikely to back down in a confrontation.

They had one opportunity to expand their base, and it rested with the McCarthy kids. Some movement leaders dreamed of a scenario in which Gene's student army, embittered and radicalized by their leader's ill treatment at the convention, took to the streets to make common cause with the Mobe's marchers. McCarthy was doing everything possible to keep his followers away from the protesters and out of harm's way, but the atmosphere was volatile.

The second group of protesters would not have minded Jack's epithet in the slightest. The Yippies—short for Youth International Party, if anyone was so unhip as to ask—were led by two professional provocateurs, Abbie Hoffman and Jerry Rubin, who viewed mockery and guerrilla theater as essential elements of any successful protest. They were there to mess with the Democrats, too, but they intended to do it through a series of mind bends designed to expose their targets less as repressive ogres than as empty-headed fools worthy only of ridicule.

The Yippies' opening move came three days before the convention began. About 50 of them showed up in front of the towering metal Picasso sculpture in Civic Center Plaza to unveil their nominee for president: a swine named Pigasus. The Yippies were media catnip; Michael and his fellow journalists almost outnumbered them. Jerry Rubin had just begun to read what purported to be Pigasus's announcement of candidacy when the cops swooped in, seized the pig and arrested Jerry and six other Yippies on charges of disorderly conduct. They could not have been more pleased with themselves.

The Yippies were off and running, and they moved quickly to their next gambit: a "Festival of Life" in Lincoln Park, a long strip of green along the lakefront north of downtown. The idea was to counter the Democrats' "convention of death" with a weeklong countercultural bash featuring nonstop live rock music, abundant psychotropic refreshment and a great deal of sex. "We will fuck on the beaches!" the festival announcement proclaimed. "We demand the Politics of Ecstasy!" And, somewhat more cryptically, "Abandon the Creeping Meatball!" As part of the fun, the Yippies started a rumor that they had injected LSD into the city's drinking water.

City officials most definitely didn't get the joke. They refused to issue even a single permit for the musical performances, which prompted most of the scheduled bands to pull out. The city also made it known that anyone trying to sleep in the park would be packed off to jail. This proved problematic for the Yippies, as sleeping in the park was their only strategy for housing the thousands they expected at the festival.

Although most outsiders lumped them together, the Yippies and the New Lefties had little in common, Michael learned. The city's hard line had thrown them together. In a different context, Michael thought, the Yippies' sendups of established authority would have been funny and politically effective. In a city whose leaders felt under siege and had turned their town into an armed camp, the Yippies were lighting firecrackers in an ammunition dump. And Daley was creating the very situation he said he was trying to prevent.

One of the few musical acts to show up at Lincoln Park was the MC5, a Detroit band that had memorialized the events in their hometown the previous year with an adaptation of a John Lee Hooker song. Whatever their intended message, it didn't sound like peace and love.

Ya know, the Motor City's burnin' baby
And there ain't a thing The Man can do
I may be a white boy, but I can dig that too.

Michael's thoughts flashed back to the basement club in Prague and the young Czech rockers wielding their guitars as weapons of defiance. What were those lines from their song? *"The old get older and the young get stronger."* East and West, it's the same message, he thought. Was that enough to sustain a movement? I guess we'll find out.

With no competition from other bands, the MC5 performed nonstop through Sunday afternoon on a makeshift stage before a crowd of about a thousand. The cops let them play for most of the day, but at dusk they moved in and broke up the gathering. And when it was fully dark, they made repeated sweeps through the park, rousting anyone they found and wielding their truncheons freely.

It was the first test of wills between police and protesters, and it soon spilled out onto the streets of the surrounding neighborhood, lined with carefully tended townhouses and upscale bars and restaurants. Residents out walking the dog or coming home from dinner stared in amazement and ran for cover as the club-swinging cops chased their prey through the streets.

3: Mobilization

The next day, the convention opened at the International Amphitheatre. It was a cramped, creaky arena on the South Side, next to the Union Stockyards, originally built to host livestock exhibitions—a history that generated countless jokes. The convention was originally planned to be staged in modern, spacious McCormick Place, but it had burned to the ground the previous year. Those looking for omens of Democratic disaster had an abundance of material.

For all the distance that McCarthy sought to maintain between his forces and the protesters, they were pursuing parallel strategies. Just as the protesters wanted to use their bodies to reveal the underlying brutality of the system, McCarthy aimed to force floor fights that would expose the party's rigged, undemocratic essence under the control of overlords like Daley and Johnson. He planned challenges to feudal procedures that allowed bosses to pick their state's delegates and then, through the "unit rule," bind them all to a single candidate. Most of all, he wanted a showdown over the platform plank on Vietnam.

Michael, swinging back and forth between the visible drama in the streets and the backstage maneuvering in the caucus rooms, had done enough reporting to know that McCarthy would lose most of the battles he waged. Yet his respect for McCarthy rose as he watched him leverage his position to wage principled fights over issues that were unsexy but held long-term importance. And he noticed that McCarthy won two significant concessions: an immediate end to the unit rule and a commitment to create a party commission that would reform the delegate selection process in time for the next convention.

In a clear sign of the times, the Democrats even managed to create controversy over the national anthem. The convention opened on Monday evening with the great soul singer Aretha Franklin belting out a heavily syncopated version of the Star-Spangled Banner in a style that melded gospel with R&B. Traditionalists sniffed their displeasure. The dissonance was increased by the fact that Aretha's instrumental backing came from a military brass band.

The chatter about a last-minute surprise that would upend the convention reached its peak on Monday night and Tuesday morning. The contradictory rumors reaching Michael's ears piled up on top of each other: Mayor Daley was pulling back on his support for Humphrey. A Johnson boom was starting among Southerners angry over Humphrey's agreement to end the unit rule. The Kennedy forces were on the verge of a deal with McCarthy that would give Teddy the nomination. Hold on, the Teddy boom had scared the Southerners back into the Humphrey camp. And Ted would accept the nomination only if it were "forced" on him by the delegates, but McCarthy would yield to him only if Teddy actively announced he was running. Because of this impasse, Daley was staying with Hubert after all. By Tuesday evening, the wheel had come full circle, and the state of play was where it had been 48 hours earlier: with Humphrey tenuously clinging to just enough support to defeat McCarthy's peace plank and claim the nomination.

Tuesday was also the day that the protesters and Yippies, now thrown together for better or worse, made a crucial tactical decision: to abandon Lincoln Park and take their battle downtown. They streamed down Michigan Avenue in the afternoon sunshine, staying on the sidewalks to avoid confrontations with the cops, and surged into Grant Park, directly across from the towering three-winged Conrad Hilton Hotel, where both Humphrey and McCarthy were based. Ringed by a double line of police, they settled in as night fell, alternately listening to passionate speeches by movement leaders and venting with angry chants—"Dump the Hump!"—and sarcastic banners: "Welcome to Prague West."

The street had come to the citadel, and the question was whether the McCarthy troops would heed the protesters' repeated chants to join them. The answer was not long in coming. By mid-evening, young people wearing the distinctive McCarthy daisy stickers were crossing Michigan Avenue in droves. As the crowd in the park swelled, nervous security officials pulled the cops and replaced them with National Guard troops, who reinforced the message to stay on the park side of the avenue by bringing up jeeps rigged with metal crowd barriers in front. But they made no attempt to dislodge the protesters, who were in one of the few spots where TV crews, hampered by the electrical workers' strike, could operate.

Tuesday night at the convention was only slightly less fevered. Kennedy supporters, still thinking a Teddy draft was possible, clustered in caucus rooms and corridors to swap stratagems. Out on the floor, an endless parade of challenges to several all-white Southern delegations ended in ill will and discontent on all sides. The cramped conditions on the floor, designed to accommodate far fewer people, contributed to countless shoving matches and squabbles over access to state delegation microphones.

Heavy-handed security guards made matters worse, manhandling anyone who incurred their capricious wrath. Journalist credentials didn't seem to matter to them; Michael, trying to interview an aide to Mayor Daley, was shoved and briefly clamped in a headlock by a security man. CBS television correspondent Dan Rather, trying to talk to a dissident Georgia delegate, was punched in the stomach and knocked to the floor, all on live TV. "This is the kind of thing that's been going on outside the hall. This is the first time we've had it happen inside the hall," Rather told his viewers, gasping for breath. "I think we've got a bunch of thugs here," CBS anchor Walter Cronkite told his viewers.

The chaotic proceedings careened toward the showdown over the Vietnam platform plank, as the clock edged past midnight— after 1 a.m. on the East Coast. Anti-war delegates complained that the party leaders had conspired to push the debate into the middle of the night, when most of the country would be asleep. Their calls for adjournment volleyed with convention chairman Carl Albert's futile appeals for order. The Democratic Party was unraveling on national television. Michael, watching from the press section, kept his eye on Daley, seated directly in front of the rostrum. Finally, as the cacophony swelled, the boss gave in to the inevitable. He rose, caught Albert's eye, and made a slashing motion across his throat. Albert dropped the gavel one last time to close the session.

As Michael made his way to his hotel, well past 2 a.m., he detoured through Grant Park. It was an eerie, otherworldly scene. Nearly a thousand people were still camped out there across from the Hilton, brilliantly illuminated by the banks of TV flood lights set up across the street. They were quiet now, so still that the hum of portable generators powering the lights and the wind off the lake rustling tree leaves were audible. The massive 29-story Hilton loomed over the scene, a dark fortress outlined against an even blacker night sky.

After a few hours of fitful sleep, Michael awakened and found a window that looked out onto Grant Park. Most of the protesters were still there, starting to stir. The Mobe had obtained a last-minute permit for a single event, a rally at the park's band shell that afternoon, with a long lineup of movement heavyweights to speak. The Mobe's strategy, Michael learned, was to attract a large crowd to this rally, then lead everyone willing to risk a confrontation out of the park and down Michigan Avenue on a march to the convention hall, five miles distant. It would be a long walk—but the chances of the cops letting them get anywhere near the Amphitheatre were virtually zero.

A round of phone calls to some sources—nobody got much sleep at a convention—reassured Michael that the Teddy scenario remained dead and buried. The surest sign of it was that people were starting to speculate about Humphrey's running mate. The convention would reopen in late afternoon, debate and reject the McCarthy peace plank, then move on to the formal roll call that would anoint Hubert as the nominee. There would be plenty of fireworks on the floor then, but not much action in the meantime. Michael decided to cover the rally in the park and see what developed.

He did not have long to wait. As he and a Chronicle photographer stood near the band shell listening to SDS leader Carl Oglesby orate, a group of scruffy-looking men ran up to the flagpole and pulled down the American flag. They replaced it on the halyard with a red banner—actually, it was more pinkish, to Michael's eye—and started to run it up the pole.

They did not get far. A line of cops ringing the rally charged forward, swinging their clubs to clear a path through the densely packed crowd seated on the grass, trampling anyone who didn't move fast enough. Several park benches that were in their path got overturned on top of people. Amid cries of pain and protest, the police reached the pole, restored Old Glory to its rightful place, and for good measure arrested several people unlucky enough to be standing nearby. People in the crowd began showering them with any missile they could find. The group that had started the trouble was long gone.

When the scene quieted down, the Chronicle's photographer, Ed Strelnik, pulled Michael aside. "Hey, I know one of those guys," he said. "I mean the guys who pulled the flag down. And you know what? He's a cop."

"C'mon. You're kidding."

"I'm not. His name's Ray O'Hara. I knew him a few years ago when I worked for a community paper in Marquette Park and he was in the station house there. He worked in uniform then. I ran into him a couple nights ago in Lincoln Park, and I recognized him right away, even with his biker clothes and long hair. He's hard to forget. He must weigh 250 pounds."

Michael shook his head and looked out over the crowd, now settling down after the incursion. He wondered how many others were undercover cops, and what other disruptive stunts might be on their agenda.

As the rally wound down, the Mobe's marshals led the move out of the park, which Michael and Ed trailed. The park was bisected lengthwise by the Illinois Central rail tracks, depressed below ground level and crossed by a series of bridges. Every span leading across the tracks to Michigan Avenue was blocked by cops or National Guardsmen. At the Congress Street bridge, protesters crowded forward and tried to persuade the Guardsmen to let them pass. The troops laid down a barrage of tear gas, sending the marchers reeling. They retreated to the ornate, triple-tiered Buckingham Fountain, splashing their faces with water to flush their reddened eyes. Michael caught a whiff of the gas and spent the next 10 minutes coughing and half-blinded.

The crowd kept moving north, searching for an exit from the park. At its northern edge, they found Randolph Street unguarded, and flowed out onto Michigan. They turned the corner just as a caravan from the Poor People's Campaign, the effort launched by Dr. King shortly before his death, came down the avenue. They had no permit either, but the cops appeared reluctant to interfere with a group of black demonstrators marching slowly and peacefully behind a symbolic farm wagon pulled by a team of mules. The protesters from the park fell in behind them and made their way south on Michigan, just as the afternoon sun dipped behind the tall buildings of the Loop.

By now, the convention was back in session and the Vietnam debate was heading toward a climax. Michael found a pay phone and called his office for guidance. "Stay with the protesters," Ray Seccia told him. "I think you and Ed are our only eyes on them, and we've got a full team at the Amphitheatre. But be careful, okay? What's wrong with your voice? You got a cold?"

"Tear gas works wonders. Turns a tenor into an instant baritone."

As the marchers flowed down Michigan, taking over most of the southbound traffic lanes, Michael matched their pace on the sidewalk. Curiously, he thought, few police were in evidence. It made little sense that they would throw up so many barriers to the marchers' exit from the park, yet allow them to pass unimpeded down the broad avenue. They traversed the nine blocks from Randolph to Balbo Drive, the intersection where the Conrad Hilton stood. Just south of Balbo, a double line of cops now blocked the way. More were in evidence on the park side of Michigan. It seemed that the cops wanted the marchers to get this far, and no farther. If so, they were creating a perfect set for TV to record whatever was about to happen.

Michael, keeping to the sidewalk, worked his way toward the front, winding up in front of the large plate-glass windows of the Hilton's Haymarket Lounge. He could see Ed on the other side of the street, snapping away. Michael watched as the marchers directly in front of the police lines sat down in the street, apparently offering themselves for arrest. Other protesters began to pile up behind them. Soon, all of Michigan Avenue in front of the hotel and for two blocks behind was packed tightly with demonstrators, brilliantly illuminated in the TV lights. An eerie stasis settled on the scene. Some demonstrators began to chant, "The whole world is watching." Apart from that, there was silence.

The police charge out of the side street caught everyone on Michigan by surprise. The cops came on a dead run, hitting the packed protesters broadside, swinging their clubs like scythes. Those who were able to escape the fury retreated into the park, but the people seated on the pavement were trapped, along with many others. Michael watched as they were beaten bloody, then pulled to their feet and frog-marched—or simply dragged—to patrol wagons that had pulled up behind the cops on Balbo. Still on the sidewalk in front of the hotel, Michael strained to look over the crowd at the chaotic scene. Suddenly, he had other things to worry about.

A squad of police formed a semicircle around the crowd Michael was in on the sidewalk, and began forcing them back toward the hotel, using their clubs like cross-checking hockey players. Then the sport switched to baseball, and they began swinging away.

Michael, in the middle of the crowd, heard the clubs thudding against people, then cries of pain. He could see nothing, because he was facing away from the cops and could not turn in the press of bodies. Then he felt the club blows on his shoulder, his neck, the back of his head. He felt his knees give way, and realized he would have fallen, if his body hadn't been held in suspension by the press of people. The cops pushed harder and harder. It was becoming difficult to breathe.

Then, the sound of breaking glass. The crowd had been compressed against one of the tall windows of the Haymarket Lounge, and it shattered under the intense pressure. The police paused in surprise. Stunned patrons backed away as glass showered the tables at the window. A few protesters climbed through the broken window and fled into the lounge. Others, including Michael, used the diversion to escape from the trap.

Michael shook his head to clear it. He reached a hand to the back of his head and felt some blood, but not too much. The park beckoned as a refuge on the other side of the avenue. As he stepped off the sidewalk, he stumbled on a prone figure. A young man was lying on his side, holding his hands to his face.

"What happened to you?" Michael asked.

"Cop maced me. I can't see."

"Can you sit up?"

"Think so."

"Can you walk?"

"I can try."

Michael got him upright and supported him with an arm around his waist. Someone else appeared on his other side and did the same. Together, they started across Michigan. The only route was through a gauntlet of police. The cops amused themselves by clubbing them as they passed.

Somehow, they made it to the other side and reached the park. The maced demonstrator slumped to his knees. The man who had helped him began calling for medical aid, shouting to be heard over the din. The scene on the street was still chaotic, with cops beating and arresting those who hadn't fled or been nabbed. From the park, people flung missiles at the cops, prompting periodic police charges into the crowd. Again and again, the chant: "The whole world is watching!"

A volunteer medical aid worker appeared, a young woman in a white jacket. She began bathing the injured man's face with a solution. He winced and cried out in pain at first, but gradually, his vision cleared.

"How many people have you treated?" Michael asked her.

"God, I've lost count now. Dozens. This is madness."

"What kinds of injuries? I'm a reporter. I'm not just being nosy."

"That's fine. Mostly head injuries, and people like this guy who've been maced. Some broken bones. A lot of people got trampled by the cops. I've never seen anything like this. The cops have just gone crazy. And they seem to be enjoying themselves."

"What brought you here?"

"I'm a nursing student at Chicago Circle. I canvassed for McCarthy during the primary. My boyfriend and I came down to help at the convention. He's back at the hotel, in the campaign operations center. When people started getting hurt, we turned part of the center into a medical aid station. And they asked for people who had some training to come down here. So here I am."

The operations center sounded like a potential story. When it was possible to cross Michigan without risking further injury, he darted over to the Hilton. Three times, cops turned him away from the hotel, ignoring his press credential, which seemed to mean nothing to them. He finally got in through a side door, found a phone, and emptied his notebook to a rewrite man. Then he joined a knot of people gathered around a television watching the convention. The McCarthy peace plank had been defeated, and the program had moved on to a filmed tribute to Bobby Kennedy. Now, as word filtered into the hall about what was happening in the streets, angry Kennedy and McCarthy delegates were registering their own protest by singing repeated choruses of the *Battle Hymn of the Republic* at the top of their lungs, ignoring the chairman's calls for order and bringing the formal proceedings to a halt.

At the elevator, a security guard looked askance at Michael's disheveled appearance, but honored his press credential and let him pass. The McCarthy operations center on the 15th floor looked like a field hospital. Many McCarthy supporters had been in the park and the streets and then swept up in the police violence. Now, dozens of injured, bloodied people sat in chairs or lay on sofas, tended by volunteer medical personnel. People were ripping up sheets and pillowcases to use as bandages on wounds. McCarthy himself was there, talking quietly with the injured. Michael approached and asked him for his reaction.

"This is the logical culmination of everything we've seen this week. The people who run the party decided to turn this city into a garrison state, and this is the result."

"Are you concerned that this will wind up helping Nixon?"

"Right now, my concern is not with politics. My concern is with these young people, who have been brutalized for no reason."

As Michael jotted down the quotes, a young man in a medical jacket tapped him on the shoulder. "You've got a little blood coming from the back of your head. Can I clean it up and bandage it?"

"Sure. Thank you very much."

4: Marta

Michael made the rounds, interviewing the injured and those tending to them. In a corner of the room, he saw a young woman, her shirt unbuttoned, a nurse winding an improvised bandage tightly around her midsection. When she turned her head, he recognized Marta.

As he approached, the nurse glared at him. "This isn't a peep show, buddy." Marta looked up, and said, "It's alright. I know him. He's a friend."

"Oh, okay. Sorry. I'm pretty much done here, actually. I think you've got a broken rib, maybe two, but they don't feel displaced. You should get x-rayed when you can, though. Basically, what we do for this is wrap you, like I've already done. But it's going to hurt for a good while, and you should rest, and definitely stay away from any activity that will aggravate it."

Michael knelt beside Marta. "How're you doing? What happened?"

"A cop decided to take batting practice on me. I had a helmet on, so he switched to my ribs." Marta gestured at a plastic football helmet on the floor next to her. A crack several inches long ran along the crown.

"He didn't arrest you?"

"That's the weird thing. I saw some people get dragged to vans, but a lot of those pigs seemed like they were more interested in hurting us than busting us. They just beat the shit out of us and then left us in the street and moved on to someone else. I tell you, I've never seen cops go so batshit. They were screaming insults as they were pounding us, really obscene stuff. 'Cocksucker' this and 'commie cunt' that."

"How're you feeling?"

"This hurts like hell, to be honest. They gave me something—I don't know what—but it hasn't kicked in yet."

"I'm sorry you got hurt. Anything I can do to help?"

"Yes." Marta reached out and grabbed his arm. He felt her hand shaking. "I think the pigs are looking for me. I think they're picking up everybody on the Mobe organizing committee. Tom Hayden's already been arrested, and they'll keep going. I'd really rather not be in jail right now, especially with these ribs. They might decide to have some more fun with me. Can you help me?"

Michael gave her a long look. Marta was a tough, battle-hardened radical. Yet what he read in her eyes was genuine fear, even a touch of panic. And he understood it, because he had felt the same emotions in the crush on the sidewalk in front of the Hilton. An uncontrolled fury had been unleashed in the cops, and it was not going to die out quickly.

Michael also understood exactly what Marta was asking of him. Doing it would break a lot of rules. Given what he had experienced, and what he was feeling for her, he didn't care.

"Can you walk?"

"I think so."

"Let's get out of here."

Marta buttoned her shirt, stood up gingerly, took a few steps, and nodded. They walked to the elevator and rode down to the lobby. Michael headed for a side door that opened on Balbo, keeping clear of the cops and security people who were crowding the hotel. Balbo had been turned into a police staging area, but the cops there were just lounging around, resting after their labors. Marta hesitated, but Michael locked arms with her and they crossed the street and were in the side door of the Blackstone before anyone could react.

More police were in the Blackstone lobby, but Michael flashed his press pass and room key, and it got them into the elevator. In his room, Michael suggested that Marta lie down and rest while he phoned his office. By the time the clerk answered the phone, she was asleep.

He dictated his notes from the McCarthy operations center, and then was told to hold on. Ray Seccia came on the line.

"How're you doing? Are you okay? The footage from Michigan Avenue has been playing on a continuous loop on TV for the last hour. Was it as bad out there as it looked?"

"It was worse, Ray. I've never seen cops so out of control. Read what I filed, you'll see."

"Did you see Senator Ribicoff?"

"No. What'd he do?"

"He was putting McGovern's name in nomination, and going on about what a great president he'd make, with George McGovern as president this would happen and that would happen, on and on. Then he looked straight down at Daley, right below him on the floor, and let him have it. 'And with George McGovern as president, we wouldn't have Gestapo tactics in the streets of Chicago.' The TV cut immediately to Daley, of course, and you didn't have to be a lipreader to see that he was shouting 'Fuck you' over and over at Ribicoff. One of our reporters was right next to Daley, and he says there was an anti-Semitic insult thrown in for good measure."

There was a pause. Then Ray said, "I think the Democrats are dead. They don't have a chance against Nixon after this."

"They deserve what they get," Michael said. "They handed the keys to the kingdom to a bunch of thugs." Another pause.

"Listen, Ray, I've got an idea. You want me to write a first-person about what it was like to be in the middle of it?"

"Sure, if you can do it, that'd be great. We're bending some deadlines for the a.m. paper, but can you write fast and call us back?"

Michael thought about writing it longhand to avoid waking Marta, but she was sleeping so soundly that he decided to risk it. She barely stirred as he banged out 800 words. It was an easy story to write, everything still fresh in his mind, no need to consult notes. He called back and dictated it, and held on while a desk editor read it. Then Ray was on the line again.

"Thanks, Michael. It'll really liven up our coverage. I'll pitch it for the front, although it may get pushed inside on one of the jumps. But it's a hell of a story."

"Wherever it runs, that's fine. Glad you liked it. You want me to come over to the hall?"

"No need. We got plenty of bodies there, and you must be pretty wiped out. Plus, who knows what tomorrow will bring? Get some rest."

As Michael was hanging up, Marta stirred.

"How do you feel?"

"Pretty shitty, but I don't feel nauseous. They said if I did, that could be a sign of trouble, like a ruptured spleen or some other internal injury."

"Hungry?"

"Well, I could eat something."

Michael rang room service and ordered a couple of sandwiches. "What about a drink? I stashed a bottle of Scotch for emergencies."

"Sure."

Michael went down the hall to get some ice, came back, and poured two drinks. They sipped the whiskey, feeling it burn down to their bellies, cauterizing the fear that still lingered there, Marta laying on the bed and Michael sitting in a chair next to her. The sandwiches arrived, and Marta sat up to eat, wincing as she did so.

"Thank you for this," she said. "I mean, all of this. I know you could get in a lot of trouble, harboring a dangerous radical fugitive and all. I'm sure your paper has rules about that."

"Screw the rules."

"I like your newfound embrace of anarchy. How far does it extend?"

"How far would you like it to extend?"

"I'd like it a lot if it extended to having you next to me here."

Michael edged onto the bed, gently slid his arm around her, stroked her cheek, and kissed her. She turned toward him, quickly grimaced in pain, and carefully slid down onto her uninjured side, trying to find a comfortable position. She kissed him, reached up with her free hand, unbuttoned his shirt, caressed his chest, and nuzzled it. He eased her shirt off, lightly stroked and kissed her broken ribs through the bandage, then looked up to see if it had hurt her.

"I like that. It feels good."

He did it again, then began moving up her body. He slowly unhooked her bra. She tried to roll onto her back, but it hurt too much, and she went back on her side. Now he had eased all their clothes off. As they lay side by side, Michael held her carefully in his arms, and they made love, very tentatively at first, but with gathering force, as they found a rhythm that didn't hurt her too much.

They did it again in the morning, just as carefully, and then lay together, joking about the constraints imposed by her condition. "Here's your first book," Marta whispered in his ear. "A sex manual for our times. 'The New Left Love Manual: Coitus After a Crackdown.'"

"I could ask Daley to do a blurb. 'A book that shows you how to fuck, after my cops have fucked with you.'"

"That'll sell it for sure."

"Daley's already a national punchline. One of my editors told me last night he's being booked on two Sunday news shows: Beat the Press and Mace the Nation."

"If you make me laugh again, I'm gonna slug you. Hurts too much, dammit."

Marta swallowed some pain pills with her breakfast and rose to make some phone calls. After the third one, she put the phone down and turned to Michael. Already, he could see, her natural confidence and hard-shell bravado were returning.

"It turned out to be a false alarm," she said. "Tom got sprung early this morning, and nobody else's been busted. I think I'm okay."

"You sure? You're welcome to stay here as long as you want."

"Yeah, I'll be fine."

"Okay, but remember what the nurse said about taking care of those ribs. Whatever happens today, stay out of it."

"Yeah, I'm on the sidelines. Plenty of other things to do."

They fell silent for a moment. Then she came to him and circled her arms around him. "Look, I really appreciate what you've done for me. Above and beyond, for sure. And I really enjoyed making it with you."

"I did, too. I'd like to see you when we get back to New York."

"I'd like that too. You're a very sweet man, Michael McMaster. You may not realize how unusual that makes you. Most men, and that includes my dear movement brothers, just want to fuck me, to get me in bed as quickly as they can. They certainly don't want to talk to me, to listen to my ideas, except as a way of humoring me until they can screw me. Then they're out the door as fast as they can be."

"Wow. That's depressing. It's that bad?"

"It's that bad, and worse. In bed, most guys are interested in what *they* like, and that's all. And some get turned on by freaky stuff. Sometimes it's benign, like wanting me to talk a certain way or wear a certain T-shirt. Sometimes—well, sometimes it's not so benign."

"All of a sudden, I'm thinking I've led a very sheltered life."

"You probably have. You were together with the same woman for, what, six, seven years? A stable relationship like that can be a very protected environment. It's a lot different when you're out there on your own, especially for a woman. Guys have it so damn easy. You don't realize, you just take it for granted. It's a battlefield, and men always hold the high ground.

"Incidentally, I think your wife is bonkers for leaving you. Guys like you don't come around very often. Take my word for it."

"Well, she had her reasons. She was hurting in a lot of different ways, and I couldn't help her. I couldn't ease her pain."

"Motherfuck, man, she flat-out left you, and now you're defending her? You're not pissed at her? She hurt you. I can tell she did."

"I'm sad about it. I'm incredibly sad. I'm not angry. She wasn't trying to hurt me. It just happened. A lot of things just happened. Neither of us wanted them to happen."

"Well, I don't know her, but I still think she's crazy."

"Actually, I think the two of you would like each other. You have a lot in common. You're both smart, and funny, and very proud, and very brave."

"I didn't feel brave last night. I was scared shitless."

"You had a lot of company. Me included."

They exchanged one more careful embrace, one more deep, warm kiss, and Marta headed out the door. Michael sat down, heavily, and tried to sort out his jumbled feelings. The conversation about Riva revived dormant memories that made him realize how much he still missed her, still longed for her. She cast a shadow across his life, a phantom lover who loomed, unseen but strongly sensed.

At the same time, he was glowing with the memory of Marta's presence. Their brief time together had filled a part of him that had been empty since Riva had gone, and maybe for some time before she left. He wanted to hang onto this fragile feeling, to replenish the emotional tinder that fed the fires. He was certain that he wanted to see Marta again. He was less certain about how much unconflicted ardor he could bring to this budding relationship.

5. Closing Doors

When Michael and Marta were back in New York, they met for dinner at a small French restaurant on the Upper West Side. It wasn't a particularly posh place, just a neighborhood bistro on a side street, but Marta still fired off a couple of gibes about Michael's emerging bourgeois tastes. At the same time, he could see that she enjoyed the meal. She was thinner than he remembered her from their student days, and she seemed to subsist mostly on coffee and cigarettes.

As they sipped Côtes du Rhône and sampled the pâté, their talk turned, inevitably, to politics. Marta was still on fire from the week before, convinced that the movement had won a signal victory by exposing the inherent brutality and intolerance of the established powers for the entire nation to see. She believed Chicago would be remembered as a pivotal moment on the road to revolution, an American equivalent of the 1905 Bloody Sunday massacre in Russia. As the wine put a glow in her cheeks, it fueled her revolutionary enthusiasm.

"They can't hide behind the pretense that this is a democracy. They dropped the mask. And they made a big mistake by going after reporters like you. Did you hear what the TV commentators were saying? My god, even Walter fucking Cronkite. When you've lost Uncle Walter, you've really lost the battle."

"I don't know, Marta. Did you see what happened when Nixon went to Chicago a few days ago? He rode through the Loop like a conquering hero. Hundreds of thousands of people turned out to cheer him. And you saw that Harris poll? Sixty-six percent thought Daley was right to turn the cops loose on you."

"That's just a stupid telephone poll. It means about as much as asking people whether they like Coke or Pepsi. It's how people act going forward that's important, and what happened in Chicago radicalized a lot of people who used to believe in the system."

"I hope you're right," Michael said. "But I guess we both have our historical reference points, and I can't shake the feeling that what we're replaying is 1848. There were revolutions all across Europe that year, from Paris to Prague, from Milan to Munich. The old order just waited them out and then cracked down very hard, and when it was over, the reactionaries were back in power and stronger than ever. I'm haunted by the prospect that we'll wind up with Nixon winning on a program of law and order, which are just code words for racism and repression."

"Well, nice alliteration, man. Paris to Prague, Milan to Munich. I can see why you're good at what you do. But it doesn't matter in the end, because Nixon can't resolve any of the system's contradictions. He'll just sharpen them. And we'll be the ultimate beneficiaries. It would be even better for us if Wallace somehow wins."

"Well, let me offer up another piece of history," Michael replied. "This one's a little more recent. The German left was convinced that Hitler's rise to power would be a boon to the revolution. Same logic; he can't solve the country's problems, he'll just make them worse, we'll pick up the pieces. They even had a slogan, *nach Hitler, uns*— 'after Hitler, us.' They kept repeating it right up to the day the Nazis rounded them up and marched them into Dachau."

"If you're trying to scare me, don't bother," Marta replied. "I'm not frightened by the prospect of a real showdown. I'm ready for it, however it turns out."

"I'm not trying to frighten you. You're one of the bravest people I know. I admire the hell out of your commitment. I'm just suggesting that you may be underestimating the resilience of the system, its ability to absorb shocks and co-opt dissent. And also underestimating the power of the right-wingers to exploit white working-class resentments and grievances, for a bad cause. That's why I saw Bobby Kennedy as such a seminal figure. He had a unique ability to appeal across racial and class boundaries.

"In any case, I'm a bit sick of politics right now, to tell you the truth. Chicago was the last straw for me, after everything else that's happened this year. The idea of having to cover a campaign between two poseurs like Humphrey and Nixon, with Wallace stirring up hate on the side, just fills me with disgust. I know my paper will expect me to, and I'm desperately looking for an excuse."

"We could run away to Paris together and foment the next French revolution," she said with a smile. "From a table on the terrace at Les Deux Magots. Like Sartre and Simone de Beauvoir. Except this time *I* get the first byline."

"I'll settle for some profiteroles for dessert, and then going back to my place. How does that sound?"

They went to Marta's one-room apartment instead, because it was closer.

With Marta's ribs on the mend, their lovemaking was more vigorous than in Chicago. Yet it was different, somehow. Less passionate. Less emotionally intimate.

Afterward, unable to sleep, Michael rose and sat at the window, staring out at the street. He had gone into this evening filled with expectation, but here, at what should be the culmination, it had felt almost mechanical.

No, that's not quite right, he thought. Not it. Me. There's nothing mechanical about Marta. It's all me. I feel like I'm going through the motions. And I know why.

He sat at the window for a long time, parsing the implications of his thoughts. When he turned, he found Marta was awake, silently looking at him, her cigarette glowing in the darkened room.

In the morning, they stirred, nuzzled, kissed, but made no move to make love. A process of withdrawal had begun. When he and Riva had lain together, the slightest touch, the lightest contact, had ignited their passion, as if their bodies possessed the power of spontaneous combustion. He didn't feel that now with Marta.

She got up, threw on a robe, lit another cigarette and sat down in the chair where Michael had brooded during the night.

"We should talk," she said.

"Yes, we should."

"I told you back in Chicago that you're a very sweet man. I still think that's true. But I'm starting to think that your heart isn't really in this."

"You're right. It's not. And, excuse the B-movie cliche, but it's not you. It's me. Entirely me. I think you probably understand why. And it's odd—like I said before, I think you and Riva would actually like each other a lot, if you ever met. You're a lot like her."

"Shit. The unkindest cut of all."

"No, I meant it as a compliment."

"I know you did," she said. "Look, here's the thing. We could go on like this for quite a while, getting together when we felt like it, enjoying being with each other, talking about politics, talking about our lives, quite pleasantly screwing from time to time, and probably not do each other much harm. To be honest, I've settled for less. But I don't think you're built for something like that. I don't think you'd be happy with it. And that would make me unhappy."

Michael emitted a long sigh and nodded in agreement. "So what the hell do we do? End it, now?"

"I think that's really the best thing. For both of us. Now I sound like a B-movie cliche."

Michael rose and hugged her. She was still so warm and inviting, he was tempted to try to change her mind. But it was really his own mind, or heart, that needed changing. Some part of him vibrated in harmony with Marta, and he knew that part of him would miss her. Yet her logic was inescapable. Sooner or later, they would come to an ending that would leave them both unhappy. Better to do it now.

One more embrace, and he left, closing her apartment door behind him. As he did, he was struck by a powerful feeling of *déjà vu*. A lot of doors seemed to be closing behind him. That isn't supposed to happen when you're young, he thought. Well, maybe I'm not so young anymore.

Chapter Twenty
—An American In Paris—

September 1968

1. Nuremberg in the Air

If there ever was a time when Michael felt less like celebrating, he could not recall it. Still, his birthday was at hand, and people insisted on marking the occasion. He appeased his New York friends with a convivial night at the Lion's Head tavern, a Village writers' hangout. But his mother wanted to organize a large dinner party. Michael bargained her down to a meal at Nanking Gate, a family favorite since his childhood.

The restaurant's Peking duck lived up to his expectations. So did his parents.

"We haven't really talked since Prague," Alan said as he sampled a dumpling. "I read your stories, and they were splendid. You captured the moment and the feel of the place wonderfully. But weren't you too optimistic in the days leading up to the invasion? All the signs were there that the Soviets would never allow the reforms to go forward. Liberal communism is an oxymoron."

Michael acknowledged, as gracefully as he could, the obvious: His father had been right about Czechoslovakia. The notion that Moscow might allow even a modest experiment in reform to take root within their empire now seemed hopelessly naïve. It made the world a colder and less hopeful place for him, and he said so.

"But I know where you're going with this, dad, and it doesn't change anything about the war. Southeast Asia isn't Eastern Europe.

And if we *are* doomed to keep facing off with the Russians, the sooner we get clear of Vietnam, the better our strategic position will be—to say nothing of the lives that'll be saved."

Alan started to reply, but Anna headed him off. "Michael, I'm very curious about what your sources say about the efforts to repair the damage in the party. Any sign that McCarthy will make his peace—pardon the expression—with Humphrey? It's the only chance we've got to save Hubert's campaign, and save the country from Nixon."

The waiter earned Michael's gratitude by arriving with the cart bearing their duck and carving it with many theatrical flourishes. It was a performance that demanded attention—and the interruption spared him from telling his mother that he couldn't care less about Hubert Humphrey's campaign and regarded him as the lowest form of political life imaginable. The widely reprinted photograph of Humphrey kissing the television screen at the moment of his nomination, oblivious to the carnage in the street outside or the injured demonstrators being treated in the same hotel just 10 floors below, captured the man perfectly for Michael.

He thought, mischievously, of a way to roil both his parents simultaneously by telling them of the "Welcome to Prague West" banners in Grant Park. Instead, he bit his tongue, and bit into a duck-filled pancake.

This was a season of discontent for each member of the family. Alan was still smarting from his loss of influence within the administration, and its flagging support for prosecuting the war. He was distressed by the start of negotiations between U.S. and North Vietnamese diplomats in Paris, but unsurprised—and privately encouraged—by the lack of progress. In his view, any peace deal at this point would lead inevitably to a communist takeover of the South. He picked up on an internal battle within the administration over whether to throw the Saigon government overboard in an effort to break the Paris stalemate, and quietly allied himself with the pro-Saigon faction. The fact that this group seemed to have won the argument filled him with some hope. It also got him invited to some meetings that allowed him to voice his views and gave him a better window into events.

That the talks continued anyway still filled him with angst. The lead U.S. negotiators, Averell Harriman and Cyrus Vance, were practiced diplomats who were more than capable of pulling off a deal. And Harriman was a veteran Democratic partisan with a strong interest in keeping Nixon out of power. If there was one thing that would revive Humphrey's flagging campaign, it would be a peace agreement, or even the strong possibility of one.

If a deal in Paris was Alan's worst nightmare, it was Anna's fondest dream. She had watched in near despair as the Democrats tore themselves apart in Chicago, and was determined to do everything she could to help patch up her party in the short time left before the November election. It seemed a hopeless task. Humphrey, trying to campaign, was dogged by demonstrators who disrupted his rallies with vitriolic heckling. McCarthy, the one figure who might coax anti-war Democrats back into the fold, showed no inclination to do so. Humphrey could help the healing process considerably by cutting himself loose from the administration with a call to halt the bombing of North Vietnam, but he could not seem to work up the courage to defy Johnson.

Anna helped achieve one step forward when the Americans for Democratic Action swallowed its misgivings and endorsed Hubert. And finally, on the last day of September, Humphrey took the plunge and announced he favored a unilateral halt to the bombing. Even that small step was fraught. The original line in the speech was tentative, conditional, typically Hubert-squishy: "I would be willing to stop the bombing." When Anna, tipped in advance, read that, she muttered a curse, got Humphrey aide Ted Van Dyke on the phone and argued that the line was far too weak and equivocal. When Humphrey delivered the speech that night in Salt Lake City, what came out of his mouth was more definitive: "As president, I would stop the bombing."

If we do manage to drag this guy across the finish line, Anna thought, it's going to be four years of constant spine-stiffening. Lyndon wasn't wrong when he said Hubert wasn't tough enough to be president. Well, better that than the alternative.

Michael was through with that kind of thinking. He had no illusions about Nixon; he would take the country backward on racial issues and fight on in Vietnam in search of an illusory military victory. He was running on a "southern strategy," promising to restore law and order and national pride—and crack down hard on those who stepped out of line. It was a thinly disguised appeal to racism, an effort to stoke white resentment of black assertiveness and white fear of urban crime.

Yes, a Nixon administration would be truly appalling, and Michael did not buy the New Left conceit that it would hasten a revolutionary crisis. Nixon would certainly increase the already palpable polarization in the country, because it was in his interest to demonize a long string of perceived enemies, from racial minorities to peace activists to Eastern intellectuals. Yet after watching Chicago and the national reaction to it, Michael believed that the forces on the right were ascendant. The latest Gallup poll attracted a lot of attention with its finding that Nixon was running 15 points ahead of Humphrey. Michael's eye was drawn to another metric: the combined support for Nixon and Wallace was now more than 50 percent.

His sense that the country was turning to the right was reinforced when he spent a few days covering a Wallace swing through the Midwest. The Alabama segregationist was supposed to be a purely sectional candidate, but his populist appeals were resonating with white working-class voters in northern cities riven by racial animosities. They were also stirring up strident opposition, which Wallace gleefully stoked and skillfully turned to his advantage to reinforce his us-versus-them message.

In Detroit, still on edge after last year's explosion, Wallace spoke at a downtown sports arena filled to capacity. His early-arriving supporters, all white, commandeered the hall's floor and main tier. The youthful anti-Wallace forces, a mix of white and black people, showing up later, were consigned to the balcony. As they waited for the candidate, the two sides volleyed chants at each other: "We want Wallace!" "Go home racist pig!"

Michael, curious about the nature of Wallace's appeal, circulated through the crowd talking with his supporters. He spent some time with a 35-year-old auto worker named Dave Kolczak, who lived in Detroit and drove 25 miles each way to his afternoon-shift job at Ford's Wixom plant. What Michael learned from the conversation told him a lot about the multiple sources of Wallace's appeal, and about the broader political moment.

Dave told him he had been trying to sell his small wood frame house on the city's west side for several months. He was sick of the long commute, he said, and his family needed more space. He had another reason, which he discussed with no reluctance or apologies: Last year's riot had frightened him badly, and he no longer felt his neighborhood was safe for his wife and two small children.

Dave insisted that he was not a racist, that he had gone to school with black kids and now worked next to them on the assembly line with no problems. But he also had no hesitation in saying that the violence in Detroit and other cities made him look differently at black people, made him fearful of them.

"I guess some folks would say that makes me prejudiced," Dave said. "Maybe they'd be right. That's not the way I think about myself. But I'd be lying if I told you that what happened hasn't changed the way I look at things."

Dave's house had been on the market since March, with no takers at a price that would allow him to capture his equity and buy a house in the suburbs. The neighborhood was "changing," he said; few whites wanted to move there, which made for a buyer's market and low offers. So he felt trapped.

When Michael asked about Dave's political attitudes, he got a surprise.

"I like it that Wallace isn't a typical politician, that he tells it like it is, that he wants to shake things up in Washington," Dave said. "But he wasn't my first choice."

Michael asked the obvious follow-up.

"Bobby Kennedy. That guy had something. He seemed like he understood what people like me go through, what we have to put up with. And he would've done something about it. So they killed him."

The conversation was cut short by Wallace's long-delayed entry. He strutted up to the podium like a cocky boxer trying to intimidate an opponent. And he wasted no time in spinning out his favorite attack lines, to the delight of his fans, Dave Kolczak included.

"There's not a dime's worth of difference between the two main parties!" Wallace thundered. Ordinary citizens, he said, were being bossed around by "pointy-headed bureaucrats" in Washington who looked down their noses at real Americans. "They ride to work on a bike in their three-piece suits with nothing but a peanut butter sandwich in their briefcase."

As boos and curses rained down from the balcony, Wallace looked up, hands on hips, mock-glaring at his antagonists. "The only four-letter words those folks up there don't know are s-o-a-p and w-o-r-k," he shouted. When the heckling persisted, his ridicule evolved into a threat. "After November the 5th, you anarchists are through in this country. I can tell you that."

It sounded to Michael like Wallace was rushing through his greatest-hits list, as if he didn't expect to have time for a long oration. If so, he was right. Less than 10 minutes into his speech, a contingent from the balcony charged the main floor, chanting and waving anti-Wallace signs. Wallace supporters met them with punches and kicks. The folding chairs on the arena floor became flying weapons. As the rally descended into a brawl, security agents hustled Wallace out.

When Michael emerged from the hall, he found that the confrontation had spilled into the streets. The plaza in front of the arena was filled with Wallace supporters, the sidewalks on the other side of the boulevard packed with his opponents. A double line of cops kept them apart—but Michael noticed they were all facing the protesters. Then they charged, and it felt like he was back in Chicago. As Wallace supporters roared their approval, the cops scattered the protesters like bowling pins, pounding any who could not move fast enough. When one group fled to a nearby hotel, the police chased them down and waded in, knocking one young man off a 10-foot wall and breaking his leg.

A short time later, with the protesters routed, Michael watched as police lined up in front of the arena for a Wallace campaign ritual. As the cops stood at attention, Wallace moved slowly down the line, personally thanking each one. The raucous chants of his supporters, now in full possession of the street, echoed off the buildings.

The night breeze carried a touch of the coming autumn chill, but Michael sensed something else in the air: a distinct whiff of Nuremberg.

2: Demimonde

More than anything, Michael felt emotionally exhausted—heartsick over his own personal life, heartsick over the year's blood-tinged events, weary of American politics in all its forms. He knew Ray Seccia would soon ask him to cover one of the candidates, or write analytical pieces on the state of the race. He had no appetite for any of it. So he decided to get out ahead of his editors with a memo proposing a different option.

The Vietnam peace talks, he wrote, were entering a potentially decisive phase. His sources told him the Johnson administration was likely to dangle an unconditional bombing halt in front of the North Vietnamese. If Hanoi bit, it could open the door to negotiation of a broad agreement entailing a step-by-step phase-out of U.S. military involvement in return for reciprocal confidence-building measures by Hanoi.

Besides being a big story in its own right, Michael added, it was also an important political story, because a peace deal could upend the campaign and put Humphrey back in the running. In fact, he said, part of the motivation for those administration officials pushing an agreement was its political impact.

"I propose that I head to Paris and dive into covering the talks. I have several well-informed sources in Washington and the U.S. delegation in Paris. While I don't know Harriman or Vance personally, I do know well one of their senior advisors, an academic named Richard Erlich. I'm sure he would be helpful."

The decision went all the way up to Jack Rothstein, who overruled his national editor and told Michael to go. Michael realized Ray probably resented the outcome, and might resent Michael as well. He concluded it was worth it. Ray would get over it, especially if the story panned out.

However, what Michael found in the French capital was anything but a clear narrative. The official meetings between the U.S. and North Vietnamese delegations, held at the grand double-winged Hotel Majestic on Avenue Kleber, just south of the Arc de Triomphe, drew flocks of journalists but yielded little news. The actual work was being done in private meetings at remote locations, such as the gritty southeastern suburb of Vitry-sur-Seine, where the North Vietnamese were based. Those sessions were usually over before any journalists even got wind of them, and reporting on them required hours of work after the fact to get someone to talk about what had happened.

This led journalists into a shadowy demimonde of unofficial sources who had some knowledge of the state of play and would talk about what they knew—or some part of it, the part that served their interests—but never for direct attribution.

It was an ideal environment for manipulation and misdirection, and all sides exploited it fully. Under the cover of vague, anonymous attribution, they floated a host of trial balloons and self-serving rumors that had the cumulative effect of confusing rather than clarifying matters. Perhaps the Americans would be willing to soften their demand that the North Vietnamese freeze all military activity in return for a total bombing halt. Hanoi might be prepared to seal such a compromise by offering informal assurances that it would not exploit a bombing halt by stepping up military operations in the South. That could be good enough for Washington. No, actually it wouldn't, the assurances would have to be explicit and include a commitment to halt infiltrations into the DMZ. Well, it didn't matter, because the North Vietnamese would refuse to sit at the same table with the Saigon "criminals," so the direct negotiations that were supposed to follow a bombing halt couldn't happen. The Soviets, eager to remove an irritant in East-West relations, were leaning on Hanoi to be more flexible. The Chinese, eager to frustrate their Russian rivals, were leaning on Hanoi to dig in.

After five years of reporting in Washington, Michael was well-prepared to operate in this netherworld. It did not take him long to develop connections and become competitive with his colleagues. His best entry point into the Americans was Erlich, a professor of international relations at Columbia. He was a family friend who had known Alan for years through international conferences and Erlich's consultant work for the government. In college, Michael had taken his legendary course in modern international politics, which routinely played to packed seminar rooms, and kept in touch with him in the years since then.

Erlich played the role of public intellectual to perfection. He was tall and lean, in his early 50s but looking younger, with just a bit of gray at the temples to lend gravitas. He eschewed academic tweeds in favor of well-tailored suits that highlighted his classic ectomorph frame; even his reading glasses were stylishly modern. He could be glib or taciturn, depending on the occasion, and here he was mostly buttoned up. But he agreed to renew acquaintances with Michael over a bottle of Sancerre at a wine bar near Michael's Left Bank hotel.

"I'm a little surprised to find you in Paris, Richard. The last I heard, you were advising Rockefeller."

"I was. I found it an unavailing venture. His views on foreign policy are quite sound"—Michael took that to mean Rocky had adopted Erlich's—"but it doesn't matter if he's never going to rise higher than governor of New York. By the time he decided once and for all to run for president, it was too late. That troglodyte Nixon had the nomination sewn up."

"No interest in working for him? You are a Republican, after all, at least nominally. And he's probably going to be president."

"May the gods proscribe it. He's certainly not *my* sort of Republican. I prefer the kind who eat with a knife and fork. And he wouldn't have much interest in what I have to offer. He regards anyone from an Ivy League school as the enemy."

In fact, Michael knew that Nixon, ever the insecure parvenu, would be glad to add some eastern-elite gloss to his gray retinue of former admen and bond lawyers. He let that pass for now. "So, what are you up to here?"

"Well, with Rocky on ice, pardon the expression, I'm back doing some consulting work for State. They thought I might be of some use to Av and Cy as they try to turn this sow's ear into a silk purse."

Erlich went on to offer only the vaguest hints on how this alchemy might be achieved, but that didn't bother Michael for now. By the end of the evening, he felt he had fulfilled his goal of establishing a line into the U.S. contingent.

The North Vietnamese were a tougher proposition. They held few official briefings and refused to talk to most western journalists on any basis. They communicated what they wanted reporters to know indirectly, often through a handful of sympathetic left-wing journalists whom they trusted to serve their interests. Michael discovered that one was Edouard Radnovy. Edouard was presenting a dressier front for Paris, swapping the jeans he'd worn in Prague for gray wool slacks and a mohair blazer, but with a silk scarf instead of a tie. He made Michael, in his workaday white button-down and striped tie, feel quite dowdy. Edouard was less voluble than he had been in Prague; Michael wondered if witnessing the Soviets crush the reform movement had been a chastening experience.

"I was a bit surprised they didn't kick you out with the rest of us," Michael said as he lunched with Edouard at a bistro off Avenue Kleber. "You were pretty free about your pro-Dubcek sympathies."

"Well, I think they mainly wanted you American journalists out of the way," Edouard replied. "They viewed you all as spies, either actual or potential. I guess they were less concerned about us Europeans. They even let that fellow from the Guardian stay for a while, and he was even more pro-reform than I was, in his repressed British way."

"So what are you doing here? Still writing for *Combat*?"

"Oh, I have some freelance clients," Edouard said. "They pay me to keep them up to date."

That was rather vague, but Michael didn't press the point. If Edouard was prepared to be a conduit for the secretive North Vietnamese, his interests and Michael's were aligned, no matter what game Edouard was ultimately playing. Nobody was showing their hand at this table.

"I appreciate your willingness to share your insights into the North Vietnamese thinking, Edouard. They must place a lot of trust in you."

"They know that I believe they are destined to unite all of Vietnam under their rule—and, just as important, that they have won the right to do so, many times over. The sacrifices they have made in the service of Vietnamese nationalism make them the true patriots. They may even surprise your Cold Warriors in Washington with their independence once they're in full control."

"Well, it's hard to argue your point, and I wouldn't try," Michael replied. The contrast between the North's single-minded commitment to victory and the endemic corruption and draft-dodging in the South could not be greater. "Of course, the North has made mistakes; they gambled that Tet would touch off a general uprising, and it didn't. And what we witnessed in Prague is a reminder that communist orthodoxy is still quite powerful."

"Every movement makes mistakes," Edouard said. "But this one is Vietnam's future. And your Americans are just the latest imperialists to try to prevent that future from coming into being. They won't be any more successful than the French or the Japanese who preceded them."

Michael thought Edouard was sounding more like a polemicist than a journalist. Still, he was voicing arguments that roughly reflected Michael's own thinking.

The wild card in Paris was the South Vietnamese delegation. It was not even officially a delegation; the nominal parties to the talks were the Americans and North Vietnamese, and Hanoi hadn't yet agreed to any form of participation by South Vietnam's representatives. Rumors periodically surfaced that the anti-Saigon faction in Washington had gained the upper hand, and that the U.S. was preparing to ram a peace deal down President Nguyen Van Thieu's throat.

Michael was convinced that this was just a bluff to make the South Vietnamese more pliant—but it made them even more paranoid than usual, and their small contingent in Paris holed up in a Right Bank hotel and talked to no one in the press. Michael discovered that they liked to drink in a small subterranean bar with the incongruously grandiose name of La Côte D'Or, and he spent some evenings hanging out there, but got only nods and terse pleasantries from them.

For all these intrigues and uncertainties, the potential stakes were enormous. If the immediate hurdles could be surmounted, a path to peace beckoned that would freeze the fighting, end American involvement in the war and create a coalition government for South Vietnam comprising all political forces, including the communists. How stable it would be once U.S. forces were gone was anyone's guess. But it was a way to stop the killing and extricate the United States from a war that was grinding up lives, degrading its military and poisoning its domestic political currents. As elusive as it seemed now, a deal might fall into place fairly quickly if the two sides could take the initial step.

The implications for U.S. politics were equally large. Humphrey's Salt Lake City speech had lifted Democrats' spirits and opened their wallets. More important, it had moved the needle of public opinion; Nixon was still ahead in the polls, but his margin was shrinking. The contrast between Humphrey's embrace of a bombing halt and Nixon's continued evasions about his Vietnam policy was changing voters' minds.

This meant the calendar was a factor. It was now October, less than a month to Election Day. For those in the U.S. government who wanted to help Humphrey, time was their enemy; they needed a deal as soon as possible, and no later than the weekend before the election. The North Vietnamese had come to Paris believing time was their ally; the longer the war ground on, the greater the toll on U.S. patience and resolve. They could afford to spurn a compromise and wait the Americans out. But what if they were dealing in three months with Nixon, the notorious hard-line anti-communist? Would they get a better deal now from a lame-duck Johnson who wanted to salvage his legacy and help his vice president? If so, November 5 loomed as a deadline for them as well. As for the South Vietnamese—well, their calculations were completely opaque, because they still were not talking, either in Paris or Saigon.

As the days before the election wound down, official comment became even scarcer, and the swirl of unofficial rumors grew more intense. The outstanding issues were separate but intertwined. If the U.S. took the first step by unilaterally announcing a bombing halt, how would Hanoi respond? A freeze on its military operations in the South? Something less than that? What would Washington find acceptable? What would be the minimum it could buy without appearing to be bargaining away South Vietnamese security for domestic political purposes? And once those questions were resolved, a host of new ones arose. How soon would formal negotiations to end the war begin? Who would take part? Even the shape of the negotiating table provoked a debate—round or square?

In late October, Nixon's lead in the polls fell to two percentage points—a statistical tie. On the ground in Vietnam, the level of fighting rose to its greatest intensity since the Tet offensive, as both sides tried to improve their positions before a cease-fire took hold. The upsurge in casualties made it certain that 1968 would be the bloodiest year of the conflict.

In Paris, the level of speculation rose to a fever pitch. The competition among journalists to land the big one, the story about the final breakthrough, rose as well. Michael warned his editors to be very cautious in this environment. He was convinced that the closer the two sides got to a deal, the greater the temptation to put out disinformation to keep others off balance.

Ten days before the election, Michael filed a long piece for his Sunday paper outlining the state of play and the prospects for a deal. His post-deadline adrenaline rush still coursing through him, he accepted Edouard's invitation for a drink. They sat in a corner of the bar, swapping rumors. At a certain point, somewhere after the third round, Edouard stopped offering theories and started asking questions.

"So what do the Americans really need to stop the bombing? What's their true bottom line?"

"Everything I know, I put in my stories," Michael said, growing a bit wary of the turn in the conversation.

"Of course, but we can never write everything we know."

"Actually, I do. If I can't source it well enough to write it, I don't really know it."

"Ah, you Americans. Such sticklers for sourcing. We have a more relaxed attitude here, and we're able to keep our readers better informed. So help me inform my readers. What will Washington really take for a bombing halt?"

Somewhere deep in Michael's mind, an alarm bell was sounding. "Just who are your readers, Edouard? Your real ones, I mean. Not the people who drop a franc or two at the kiosk for a copy of *Combat*."

"I'm not sure what you're getting at, *mon ami*."

"What I'm getting at is that for the last five or ten minutes, you've been trying to pump me for information on a rather crucial subject. And this makes me wonder if your interest in that subject is purely journalistic."

"Ah, Michael. Le Carre is *tres merveilleux*, but I fear you've read one too many spy novels."

"Maybe so, but give me a straight answer. I know you carry water for the North Vietnamese by passing information from them to people like me. Is it a two-way street? Do you also collect information for them?"

"Oh my, your imagination really is running wild tonight," Edouard said. "I shouldn't have ordered that last round of cognac."

"A straight answer, please. Are you a spy?"

Edouard started to reply, then stopped himself. He looked away, then leaned forward and met Michael's stare.

"And what if I am? Are you going to turn me in to your father's friends? Or are you going to start doing something about what you truly believe?"

"What the hell are you talking about?"

"We both have the same view of the war," Edouard replied. "We both know which side deserves to win. What passes for a government in South Vietnam is corrupt and brutal and not even close to democratic. It wouldn't last a month without its American sponsors, and we know what they are: a bunch of arrogant imperialists with a lot more money and weapons than brains. We both know this, you said it yourself just last week. The difference is that I'm acting on this knowledge. It's time for you to do as well."

"What the fuck are you getting at?"

"Keep your voice down. And I think you know, Michael. We are at a critical juncture, a turning point in this whole venture. Time is short. It is crucial for my friends to know what the Americans need, and the minimum that they need, to make the arrangement work. The whole negotiation may hinge on it. You are a very skillful journalist; I know this. I have been observing you for quite some time. You certainly have the sources to discover this; indeed, you may already know it. Will you help?"

"You're proposing that I betray my country and my profession."

"I'm proposing that you honor your true beliefs. It's not often that one faces such a crisis of conscience. They are difficult moments, but they are privileged moments. You've told me about your father, back in the days before he became a Cold Warrior, working as a diplomat in Europe and also gathering intelligence against the fascists. He's on the other side now, and he would no doubt be horrified that we are even having this conversation. He would tell you to walk away. But his younger self would see things very differently."

"I'm not sure I can do what you're asking," Michael said.

"Don't give me an answer now. Think about it—but not for too long. You know where I'm staying. Call my hotel and leave a message, asking me to lend you the new novel by John Updike. Remember that—Updike. I will meet you that same evening at 8 at the bar on Avenue Kleber across the street from the bistro where we lunched. Remember—Updike, and Avenue Kleber."

"That's rather close to the Majestic."

"If you are suggesting that someone will notice us, nothing will seem more natural than two journalists having a drink. We'll be hiding in plain sight."

It was not until later that Michael realized what he had done at the end of the encounter. He had begun discussing operational details.

3: The Test

Michael slept very little that night. Well before dawn, he gave up the attempt, dressed, and went for a long walk, out the St. Germain to the Seine and then back along the embankment toward Saint-Michel, with Notre Dame aglow on his right across the narrow channel of the river. Paris was at its most alluring, silent and glittering, but his mental state could not have been more at odds with the city's tranquil beauty.

A part of him could not believe he was even thinking about what Edouard was asking. And yet, he was. It would be, as he had told Edouard, a betrayal, both of his country and his journalist's code. But—had he not thought many times, and told close friends, that the leaders who dragged the nation into Vietnam had betrayed America's best sense of itself? Does a government that lies to its citizens and flings its young men into a senseless, unwinnable, immoral war merit any loyalty? And what is the ultimate aim of journalism? He had wanted to become a reporter to help hold those in power accountable. Accountable to whom, or to what? Only to those who, as he had put it to Edouard, tossed some coins on the newsstand counter? Or to some higher standard of history?

By the time he got back to his hotel, the cafes were opening. He went into one, drank two café au laits, and resumed walking. The city was coming to life on a Saturday morning, but he was oblivious to it.

Where was his ultimate loyalty? It came down to that. The North Vietnamese were no angels, no Jeffersonian democrats. He knew that without ever setting foot in their country. He had interviewed too many Vietnamese who had fled south after the French defeat in

1954 to have any illusions about the hard men running the show in Hanoi. Yet they had paid the price in blood many times over for the right to rule their country. Their adversaries in Saigon were an unsavory collection of ruthless warlords and venal bureaucrats, ruling by brute force over people who mostly had no interest in fighting for what was supposed to be their country. Michael had seen that for himself. As for the Americans, they were stand-ins for the French colonialists who had been run out of Vietnam 14 years ago, no matter how much they pretended otherwise.

So what was stopping him? He had spent this long morning slowly talking himself into saying yes, and Edouard was just a phone call away. But he hadn't picked up the phone. Was he too conventional, too enmeshed in what Edouard would call "bourgeois morality," too bound up in his precious professional ethics? Was he too stubbornly independent, too much of a loner to take the first step on a path that he instinctively knew would lead to deeper involvement? Or was he just scared, afraid of the consequences of exposure? That last possibility was the most unsettling to him, because his courage had been tested many times and he did not think of himself as a coward.

Something else was preying on his mind. He realized that part of his motivation for even considering Edouard's overture was personal, and illegitimate: the opportunity to strike out at his father. Had Edouard skillfully planted this idea in his mind with that curious riff about Alan in his younger years? For that matter, how did he know about all that? Michael had no memory of sharing this story, although he couldn't be certain what might have come out of his mouth under the influence. And what was it Edouard had said? "I have been observing you for quite some time." No doubt he had been—as a talent scout.

When he finished his second circuit, it was late morning. Using the phone in the lobby, he called Edouard's hotel.

"Bonjour. I would like to leave a message for—pour Monsieur Radnovy, chambre trois cent quinze. Oui—parlez-vous anglais, peut être? Oui, j'attendrai, merci. Yes, a message. For Mr. Radnovy in 315. I would like to borrow his copy of the new John Updike novel, *Couples.* Yes, Updike. U-p-d-i-k-e. Thank you."

Michael arrived at the bar early. Edouard was already there. No eagerness here, Michael thought. Either of us. Well, best to get straight to the point.

"I can't do it," Michael said. "I won't walk the road you're beckoning me onto. I won't debate the ins and outs of it with you, but that's the bottom line—my bottom line."

"I have no idea what great decision you are talking about, *mon vieux,* but if you are comfortable with it, whatever it is, I am pleased for you."

Michael looked puzzled for a moment, then chuckled. "Don't worry, Edouard. I have no intention of playing the informer against you, either. But I do think it's best that we avoid each other from now on."

"Yes, I agree. And, in any event, it's all quite academic now. We have the information we need."

"Yes, of course you do," Michael said with a smile as he rose from the table. "That's why you came tonight."

4. Back Channel

The big bang came five days later. And it broke in Washington, not Paris, to Michael's considerable annoyance. That evening, President Johnson went on national television to confirm the breakthrough. All air, naval and artillery bombardment of the North would cease. Hanoi agreed to sit at the same table with the South Vietnamese and dropped its demand that the Viet Cong be given separate official status; it would participate as part of the North Vietnamese delegation. The formal talks would begin in six days. While nothing explicit was said about further concessions from the North, Johnson strongly implied that it had given private assurances of a slowdown in its military activities, including a halt to rocket attacks on South Vietnamese cities and incursions into the DMZ. The long-rumored deal had come together.

Johnson spoke on the evening of Thursday, Oct. 31. It was already early Friday morning in Paris. The U.S. presidential election was five days away.

Humphrey, unsurprisingly, strongly supported Johnson's decision. Nixon, having no choice, endorsed it as well, although Michael could easily imagine his private thoughts. Eight years ago, he had lost the presidency to John Kennedy by the smallest of margins; he must be wondering if it was about to happen again. It would take two or three days for new polls to measure the impact of the breakthrough, but many political analysts were not waiting. The news columns and airwaves filled with speculation that Johnson's announcement would push Humphrey over the top.

The president's speech fell in mid-morning in Asia on Friday. The North Vietnamese quickly announced their confirmation of the terms. From Saigon, curiously, there was only silence.

What was going on? Could Johnson, desperate for a pre-election coup, have announced the deal without getting the South Vietnamese on board? Was he gambling that a pre-emptive declaration would force them to fall in line? If so, was a countermove afoot? Throughout the fall, there had been low-intensity chatter about the Nixon camp's efforts to establish a back channel to Saigon, using Anna Chennault, the Chinese-American widow of a World War II air hero, as a conduit. Was this card now being played?

The South Vietnamese were not saying anything in Washington or Paris, either. Their elusive spokesman in the French capital issued a one-sentence statement saying he was awaiting clarification from his government, and then went silent. This was probably nothing more than ruffled feathers in Saigon, Michael thought, but as the hours went by, the mystery grew.

As the day wound down, Michael headed for La Côte D'Or, the South Vietnamese watering hole, hoping to find someone who could provide some clarity. He stumbled down the steep stairs into the subterranean gloom, his eyes taking a couple of minutes to adjust. The bar was filling up with Friday evening drinkers, but none of the faces looked familiar. He looked around a second time, and off in a dimly lit corner, he spotted his quarry.

Three South Vietnamese officials were huddled around a small table. They were deep in conference with a fourth man, whose back was turned to the rest of the bar. As Michael walked up, waving a greeting, the man turned to see who was approaching. It was Richard Erlich.

Before Michael could speak, all four men pushed back their chairs and rose. The South Vietnamese glared at him and left without a word. Erlich, looking rather sheepish, dropped some money on the table and murmured a few words that Michael couldn't catch over the buzz of the bar. Then he, too, was gone.

What the hell was going on? When Michael got back to his hotel, he tried several times to phone Erlich. No luck. He went to Erlich's hotel, phoned his room from the lobby, then went up and knocked on the door. No answer. Radio silence apparently was contagious.

It was broken the next day by President Thieu, who went before the National Assembly in Saigon to announce his rejection of the accord and declare that South Vietnam would not take part in the new talks. The presence of Viet Cong representatives at the table was a deal-breaker. Their participation in the negotiations "would just be another trick toward a coalition government with the Communists," Thieu said, and this he would never accept.

The great October Surprise had vanished like a mirage in the desert, and so had Hubert Humphrey's momentum. Three days after Thieu torpedoed the talks, Nixon was elected president by a narrow margin. The next afternoon, basking in victory, Nixon announced his transition team. Most of these people would be in line for a job in the new administration, if they wanted one—and most would want one. One name on the foreign affairs group jumped out at Michael: Richard Erlich.

What had derailed the peace breakthrough? Michael cornered several U.S. officials, and they all told the same story. Thieu and the rest of his government had known exactly what Johnson was going to announce and had signed off on it in advance. There had been full coordination between Washington and Saigon, they insisted. So what had happened between Thursday night and Saturday? "I suggest you put that question to Mr. Nixon," one American diplomat said. Michael wanted to put it to Erlich, but he was no longer in Paris. He had checked out of his hotel the morning after Thieu's speech.

In Michael's mind, the signs pointed to one conclusion: a deal had gone down between the Nixon campaign and the Saigon government. Nixon's motivation for such a bargain was obvious, and he had some juicy bait for the hook: a promise to demand tougher terms from Hanoi once he was in office. Yet if Nixon had really gone there, he was taking a desperate gamble. He had sabotaged a promising peace initiative that could have saved innumerable lives for the sake of his narrow political interests. Some people might view that as close to treason—if it were ever exposed.

Michael was eager to expose it. Could it be proven? He sat down and drafted a long memo to his editors, outlining what he knew, what he suspected, and what reporting lines should be pursued. This would need to be a coordinated, large-scale effort. The fact that Michael had stumbled upon that nocturnal conference between Erlich and the Saigon crew provided one lead, but Erlich was probably just one of several conduits Nixon might have used. That was common enough tradecraft, because multiple channels meant multiple opportunities to communicate. Yet it also meant multiple chances of a leak.

By the time Michael finished his memo, it was late at night, and he decided to give it another read in the morning before sending it.

He was awakened from a restless sleep by the ringing telephone. The room was still dark. The bedside clock read 4 a.m.

"Michael? Can you hear me? This is a terrible connection."

"Yes, mom. What's going on?"

"It's your father. We're at the hospital. He's had a heart attack."

"Shit. How bad?"

"I don't know for certain yet, but it's serious," Anna said, a catch in her voice. "He passed out in the ambulance, and I thought for a moment he was gone. He's still unconscious."

Chapter Twenty-One
—The End of the Trail—

November 1968

1: ICU

The international arrivals hall at Dulles Airport was the usual teeming mess, and all the working pay phones were on the other side of passport control. After a full day of traveling, it took another hour for Michael to navigate the line, phone the hospital and connect with his mother.

"He's still unconscious. He's in intensive care. His doctor would prefer that he be at Georgetown Hospital instead of here, but he says it's not possible to move him now."

Michael grabbed his bags, tossed them into a cab, and headed straight for Sibley Hospital. Forty minutes later, he was at the boxy seven-story building in northwest D.C., asking for directions to the intensive care unit. After several false turns, he found his mother, napping on a cot in the foyer outside his father's room. She stirred as he entered, rose and hugged him, then rubbed the sleep from her eyes. He perched on the edge of the cot, and she sat in a straight-backed chair next to it.

"It's not good," she said. "He hasn't been fully conscious since we got here last night. I think his heart actually stopped once, and they had to restore a rhythm, although they won't confirm that. They're not great about giving information."

"You said on the phone that his cardiologist—what's his name? Dr. Rathman?—would like him to be at Georgetown?"

"Yes, because he says it's a better cardiology hospital, but he doesn't want to move him in his present condition. They ran some tests to determine how much damage his heart sustained, and we're waiting for the results. There's also the question of whether he suffered any brain damage, because the blood flow to his brain was constricted."

"How'd it happen?"

"We were having dinner in Spring Valley. You know, that Italian restaurant he likes because of the veal." Anna stopped and covered her face with her hands. Michael thought he heard a stifled sob, but he couldn't be certain. "He was halfway through his martini. And he just passed out. Nothing more dramatic than that. No clutching at his chest, no cry of pain or anything. His eyes just got very wide for a moment, like something had startled him, and then he slumped over on the banquette.

"He was in and out while we waited for the ambulance. I thought it might be a stroke, but when he still could talk, he said it felt like there was an enormous weight pressing down on his chest. So it was clear he was having a heart attack. Once we got in the ambulance, he squeezed my hand a couple of times, and then passed out again. That's when I thought we'd lost him. But he's a tough old guy, we both know that."

Michael hugged his mother again, then looked into his father's room. One nurse was inside, attaching a new IV bag. "Is it okay to go in and see him?"

"Sure, as soon as the nurse is finished."

"You must be exhausted. Were you here all night?"

"Yes. I didn't want to leave," Anna said, "in case he came to, or the doctors had some news, or—I made a quick trip home this morning to grab some of his things, then came right back."

The nurse finished her work and left the room, nodding to them. "Why don't you lie down again and sleep for a while," Michael said. "I'll go in and sit with him."

Michael found that easier to say than to do. As he stood and took a step toward the door, he felt as if an invisible force was pushing against him. He was reluctant to enter his father's room, so reluctant that his body slowed to a standstill. It took all his will to overcome his inertia.

His father was pale and motionless, tethered to a tangle of tubes and wires. His face held some residual tension around the mouth, but was otherwise expressionless. His breathing, aided by oxygen through a nose tube, was labored and shallow. The only other sound in the room was the beep of the monitor recording his heartbeats.

Michael sat down in the chair next to the bed and held his father's limp, pallid hand. There was no obvious sign of life in it. With his other hand, Michael brushed his father's gray, tangled hair away from his face and stroked his forehead. Michael leaned forward, close to Alan's ear. "I'm here, dad. I know you can't hear me, but—I'm here. I love you."

Michael leaned back in the narrow chair. A flood of memories washed over him. His father had not been a large presence in his early life. Work came first, and during the war and the years immediately after, Alan had traveled a great deal and was extremely busy when he was in Washington. Yet as Michael entered his teenage years, the change of administration gave Alan more free time, and he began to view his son less like a small, mysterious alien and more as a potential sidekick. He made time for some Senators and Redskins games, picnics and canoe trips. When Michael, at age 16, abruptly decided it was the height of cool to cut school and hole up in the Cleveland Park library listening to progressive jazz and reading Baudelaire, it was Alan who took him for a long drive and talked him out of his destructive self-indulgence.

Michael owed his interest in the world and his generally serious mien to both parents. But his father had been the larger role model—and the figure he rebelled against more strongly: insisting on Columbia for his college years instead of Alan's alma mater of Georgetown, embracing first the Beats and then the folkie-hipster milieu of Greenwich Village, rejecting his father's Manichaean Cold War worldview.

As Michael sat there reliving their many arguments, he felt no regret, only a sad inevitability about them. Are we always destined to commit patricide, in word if not deed, as a rite of passage? Would the children that Michael hoped to have someday perform the same ritual sacrifice?

He realized now why he had been so reluctant to enter this room. He was confronting many things here, thoughts and emotions and phantoms, the memories of lives spent together and apart, but there was something else present. In the face and form of his stricken father, he was glimpsing his own mortality.

Michael sat there for a long time. The outside light faded, swallowed up in the November gloom. His father was now shrouded in shadow. He switched on the bedside lamp, kissed him on his pale forehead, squeezed his hand, rose, and quietly left the room.

He left his mother sleeping on the cot and walked down the hall for some coffee. When he returned, Anna was awake. They embraced again and went downstairs to the cafeteria. Neither felt very hungry, but they shared a sandwich and some milk. When they returned, Dr. Rathman was in the room, giving some instructions to the night nurse. Then he turned to Michael and Anna.

"My suggestion is that you go home and get some proper sleep," he said. "We won't get the test results back until tomorrow morning. He's stable enough right now, and if there's any change, we can call you."

Anna reluctantly agreed, and after she went in and spent a few minutes with Alan, they drove to the family home. Michael assumed his father's role as bartender, and they sat up for a while, sipping some of his favorite Scotch and swapping memories of him. Anna was a small woman, and it seemed to Michael that in her fear for Alan she was shrinking into herself, swallowed up in the armchair, as she talked about their life together.

What she chose to remember, not surprisingly, were the positive memories; how they had met and fallen in love amid the political and social convulsions of the Thirties, how Alan had recognized and encouraged her blossoming talent as a writer, respected her political views and the activism they spawned, and accepted her as a serious person, as his equal in the world. Michael had heard many of these stories, but it seemed appropriate to retell them.

They talked until almost midnight, when their weariness overtook them. They were sleeping so soundly that the phone rang several times before they heard it. Michael got to it first. He listened for a few moments, put the receiver down and turned to his mother. "It's the hospital. He's gone."

2: Private Line

Alan McMaster's memorial service filled the Copley Hall Lounge at Georgetown University, the school where he had studied decades earlier and lectured about international affairs intermittently from the 1950s on. The guests were a parade of characters from his long, eventful life: surviving colleagues from his diplomat days in prewar Europe; fellow veterans of his wartime work, both overt and covert; Truman administration cronies who had worked with him to harden U.S. foreign policy as the Cold War began; colleagues from the Kennedy and Johnson administrations. A panoply of national security mandarins was present, and old disputes were set aside for the day; Michael spotted Dean Acheson and Allen Dulles, who shared Alan's hawkish views, but also George Kennan, who had become an apostate over the implications of his own policy of containing the Soviets.

With another change of administration about to take place, more than one journalist chronicling the service saw a broader meaning. "There was a palpable sense that these were the obsequies not only for a man, but for an era, for a milieu of foreign policy

Brahmins who guided the country up into the heights of international pre-eminence but also down into the fever swamps of Southeast Asia," the Washington Star wrote. Michael thought the story itself was a bit fevered, but he still clipped it for his mother's collection of memorabilia.

Assembling that collection involved sorting through Alan's voluminous files of papers, a trove that went back decades. Some would go to Georgetown's School of Foreign Service, his designated repository for documents with any scholarly significance; others were to be filed away for private use, or discarded. It was a daunting task, for Alan was something of a pack rat. Once the service was over, Anna and Michael settled in and divided up the material. The need to focus on a concrete task was a welcome respite from shock and sorrow. Michael sat at his father's desk in his study, Anna in the overstuffed armchair across the room.

Michael's first batch of papers was from the Thirties, and they made fascinating reading. Alan had kept his notes from his diplomatic work in Germany, as well as carbon copies of the cables he had filed—and private reports prepared for a readership of one. Michael knew his father had served President Roosevelt as a back-channel informant about events in Europe during the continent's descent toward the cataclysm, but seeing the tangible evidence of Alan's prescient warnings about the Nazis was chilling.

Michael had moved on to some files from the war years when his mother rose and walked across the room, holding some papers. "Do you remember Richard Erlich?" she asked.

"Of course. In fact, I ran into him in Paris last month. Why do you ask?"

"Well, this is curious. He and Alan knew each other for years, so there's a lot of correspondence between them. I think at one point Alan regarded him as something of a protégé, and they worked together on some joint projects, in and out of government. But there are some other things, more recent, that are rather odd."

"Odd in what sense?"

"Well, it's hard to say," Anna said. "Just different, out of the ordinary. Look at these, for example."

Anna handed him two typewritten letters from Erlich to Alan, both dated in early September. One was written on the stationery of Erlich's Paris hotel; it announced his arrival, some comments about his pleasure in renewing his acquaintance with the beautiful city, and a detailed description of the *haute cuisine* dinner he had enjoyed the previous night. The second letter, dated two days later, was on plain stationery, and unsigned, but also was from Erlich; the postmark and typescript made that clear. It was brief and cryptic. "The tourist sights here are as beautiful as ever. I will send postcards as I visit them."

"You're right, this is curious," Michael said. "He'd already written about how lovely Paris looked. And why in the world would he send letters describing the city to someone who knew the city as well or better than he did?"

"Yes, that's what I thought. It makes no sense." She paused. "Unless it does." She paused again, looked down at the letter, then back at Michael. "Could it have some sort of hidden meaning?"

"Someone recently told me that I was reading too many spy novels. But that guy, it turned out, really was a spook. I don't know what to make of this. Are there others? Where did this come from?"

"It's from his most recent batch of papers. He saved everything, and he was very diligent about keeping them organized chronologically. Here, let's look."

They found more letters from Erlich, and they fell into the same pattern. Some, written on hotel stationery, were innocuous and chatty, filled with the kinds of things a traveler would share with a friend back home. Others, on plain paper and always unsigned, were much briefer; each focused on one specific tourist attraction, describing some detail of it. "The Jeu de Paume has a lovely Degas," one read. "The dancers' limbs beckon toward an unseen audience."

Michael put down the file and told Anna in some detail about the murky milieu surrounding the Paris talks and the questionable characters who inhabited it: about Radnovy's attempt to turn him into an intelligence asset, his encounters with Erlich, the strange scene he stumbled upon at the bar the night before Thieu blew up the peace talks, the U.S. negotiators' suspicions of a Nixon hand in Thieu's decision, and Erlich's surprise appointment to Nixon's transition team.

They both sat silently for several moments, puzzling over the implications of what they had found. A thought was forming in both their minds, but they were reluctant to voice it.

"Have you gotten your phone bill for October?" Michael asked.

"Yes, it came last week. Or, rather, both of them. We have two lines, one for the house, and one that was for Alan and his work. That one's private, and unlisted."

"Have you looked at them?"

"No, not really. But I know where they are. I'll get them."

She left the room and returned with the bills. The one for Alan's line was several pages long. It showed several international calls to the same number in Paris. Michael compared it to the telephone number on Erlich's hotel stationery. They matched. The last one was made on Oct. 30—the day before Johnson announced the peace breakthrough.

The bill also showed a series of calls to a number in the Virginia suburbs of Washington, including calls on both Oct. 30 and 31.

"Do you recognize this number?" Michael asked.

"No. I never saw it before."

"Do you know where dad's telephone book is?"

"He usually kept it right here, in the top right-hand drawer of the desk. Yes, here it is."

Michael started leafing through the book, not sure what he was looking for. Most of the names were familiar to him, some were not, but none of the numbers matched the one on the phone bill. Then, on one of the spare pages in the back, Michael found that Alan had scrawled "B. Haldeman" and a phone number next to it. It matched the Virginia number on the bill.

"B for Bob. Bob Haldeman. One of Nixon's closest aides. Do you know him? Do you know if dad knew him?"

"I don't, and I never heard Alan speak of him. I've heard of him, of course, especially since the election. Why would Alan be making calls to one of Nixon's top people?"

"I can put together a hypothesis that explains all of this," Michael said. "But it's not a very pleasant one."

"What exactly are you saying, son?"

"I'm saying that Richard Erlich earned his spot on Nixon's transition team by leaking information about the Paris talks and the likelihood of a peace deal. To give everyone some deniability, he was doing it indirectly, through a conduit—a cutout, in the parlance of the spy trade. And the cutout was dad."

Anna passed a hand over her face. She shook her head, as if to ward off the effects of a blow.

"I can't believe he would do that," she said. "He despised Nixon. He loathed him as much as I did. It was one point we were never in disagreement on. And this is—if someone did this, it was dishonorable and unpatriotic. That's not the Alan McMaster I've known and lived with for 30 years."

"He was very fixated on the war, and on the need to fight it to a conclusion," Michael replied. "He thought Johnson's turn toward negotiations was a huge mistake. And he never trusted Humphrey. We heard him say so many times. He thought Hubert was weak and unreliable, even before he called for a bombing halt. Alan may have decided that Nixon was a better vehicle for achieving the policy outcome he wanted. I can't quite believe it, either, but it would explain all this curious evidence we've found."

"It might explain it, but that's not the same thing as proving it."

Michael stood and folded his arms around his mother. God, she doesn't need this, he thought. This would be like losing him twice. But we've found what we've found, and we can't walk away from it now. If we do, she'll always wonder if it was true, and she'll have no peace. Neither of us will.

"You're right, this doesn't prove it," Michael said. "But we can't ignore what we've discovered. I don't think you want to spend the rest of your life in uncertainty about this. Let's begin at the beginning."

Michael picked up the phone on the desk and dialed the Virginia number on the bill. It rang three times, and then a female voice answered.

"Is Mr. Haldeman there?"

There was a long pause. "Who's calling, please?"

"This is Michael McMaster. I'm Alan McMaster's son. I believe he and Mr. Haldeman knew each other."

Another pause. "Mr. Haldeman isn't available. May I take a message?"

"No, that's alright. I'll call back later. Sorry to disturb you."

He hung up the receiver and turned back to Anna. "Well, that's clearly Haldeman's number, probably his home number. The woman who answered might have been his wife, or maybe a housekeeper. And it may have been a private number, not the main one; whoever answered seemed a bit hesitant."

"Okay, so where do we go from here?"

"Let's look at what we know. We know Alan was in contact with Richard Erlich. We know Alan was in contact with Haldeman. We know Erlich was in contact with the South Vietnamese. And we know he's been named to play a significant role on the Nixon team, despite a history of working for Nixon's rivals."

"That doesn't connect the dots, Michael. We may have good reason to suspect that Erlich was leaking to the Nixon gang, but we don't know it for a fact. And we certainly don't know that's what Alan was talking to either Erlich or Haldeman about."

"No, we don't. We need something more to go on. I might be able to turn it up."

3: Fishing Expedition

Michael had first met J.D. Harris in Vietnam, where he was attached to Army intelligence. J.D. had known Alan for years, from the days when they were young wartime operatives helping the United States develop an intelligence capability commensurate with its newfound power in the world. When Michael learned he was headed for Vietnam, Alan recommended he look J.D. up, and asked his old friend to help his son as he could. In his sardonic, screw-it-all way, J.D. had done just that.

J.D.'s specialty was signals intelligence. He had spent years working for the National Security Agency, the super-secret government organization that coordinated all U.S. signals surveillance and cryptology from its isolated headquarters in rural Maryland. When Vietnam heated up, the NSA dispatched him to Saigon to work with the Army. When he returned stateside last year, he was loaned out to the FBI for the last few years before he reached retirement.

He agreed to meet Michael, but only at an out-of-the-way restaurant near Great Falls, the Old Angler's Inn.

"Very sorry about your father," he said as he slid into his chair. "He was quite a man. Washington won't be the same place without him. And sorry to make you come all the way out here, but these days I can't afford to be seen consorting with you newsie types. I'd like to keep my job long enough to collect my full pension, and that seems to get harder each year."

"Thank you for your thoughts. I spotted you at the service, but there were so many people there, I didn't get a chance to come over and say hello. But I appreciate your coming to it. My mother and I have taken great comfort from all the support of Alan's friends."

Michael paused while J.D. put in his drink order, then looked back at Michael with an utterly blank expression. Michael had an inkling that J.D. knew what Michael wanted to talk about. But he wasn't offering any points of entry into the conversation.

"Actually, my father is the subject I wanted to talk to you about."

"On what basis? As a journalist, or as a son?"

"Does it matter?

"It matters a great deal. If you're a journalist tonight, we have nothing to talk about."

"And if I'm a son tonight?"

"Then you can ask me questions, and maybe I'll answer them— but absolutely off the record. And that doesn't mean sort of off the record, or deep background, or any of the other weaselly little dodges you news guys have come up with. That means you can't share what I tell you with anyone else, for any reason. Except for your mother, who I have had the pleasure of meeting and is a thoroughly admirable woman. But it goes no farther than her, and she has to understand that, too. The only reason I even agreed to meet you is because you're Alan's son."

"Okay, I understand."

"Really? Do you really understand? Do you understand that if any of this gets into print, I am going to come looking for you and cut your goddamn balls off?"

"You have such a lovely persuasive touch. Yes, I understand how serious you are about keeping this quiet, and I'll respect it completely. But I can't be held responsible for what some other journalist writes."

"I'm not talking about what the New York Times digs up on its own and prints, or the Washington Post, or the West Bumfuck Banner, for that matter. Unless I find out that you were whispering in their ear. And I will find out. Then I'll—"

"Yes, then you'll cut my goddamn balls off. I get that. I like them right where they are, so I think we'll be okay."

"Alright, Alan's son, what would you like to know?"

Michael narrated what had gone down in Paris right before the election, the suspicions about Nixon's role, and what he and Anna had discovered about Alan's contacts with Erlich and Haldeman.

"All very interesting. Suspicious, but not conclusive, as you say. What would you like me to tell you?"

You're really not going to make this easy, are you, Michael thought. Well, you're an intelligence man, so I suppose that's standard procedure. That's how you're trained to operate. Okay, here we go.

"I think you can help me fill in the blanks, connect the dots, if there are dots to be connected," Michael said.

"Ask me specific questions."

"As I see it, there are three. One, did Nixon, or any of his people, play a role in persuading the South Vietnamese to scuttle the peace talks? Two, was Richard Erlich gathering intel for the Nixon crowd about the talks, to help guide them in their dealings with Saigon? And three, was my father the link, receiving Erlich's information and passing it on to Nixon? I think that about covers it."

"Yes, I would say it does." Harris paused and reflexively looked around. The restaurant was half empty on this rainy weekday night, and none of the other diners were paying any attention to them.

"Okay, first question. Yes, the Nixon people were neck deep in trying to screw up the peace talks—to monkey-wrench them, as Nixon himself put it. They had established a couple of very private channels to the South Vietnamese, one through Anna Chennault— you know who she is, right?—and the other through the South Vietnamese ambassador in Washington. Their message to the Saigon boys was very simple: hold out until after the election, because you'll get a better deal from us."

"Shit. It's true, then. How definitively do you know this?"

"Very definitively. First-hand. We were listening in on the conversations."

"And the second question? Erlich?"

"Yes. He wasn't alone; they had multiple sources, because this was of vital importance to them, and they wanted to be sure they had a window into the talks so they could act in a timely manner. They didn't want to get blind-sided. But, yes, Erlich was one of their informants, and from what I read, he's collected his reward."

"And question three?"

"Michael, are you sure you want to know the answer to that one? Are you sure your mother does?"

"C'mon, J.D. I'd like to be almost anywhere else than here, asking you these questions. But here I am."

"Okay, then. The answer is yes. Your father was the go-between. Erlich was feeding him the information, and he was passing it on. His main Nixon contact was Haldeman, as you seem to have discovered."

Michael sat silently, absorbing the moment, the knowledge, the sense of having crossed a frontier after a long approach. "And your knowledge on this point is also definitive?"

"There's no room for doubt. As I said, we were listening."

"And you couldn't stop it?"

"There was an attempt. At a very high level. Nixon simply didn't care. The stakes for him were too high."

"So who takes the fall for this? Who's going to jail?" Michael asked.

"Nobody's going to jail."

"How can that be? This sounds utterly illegal—maybe treasonous."

"Because the boss has decided that this will never come out publicly," J.D. said. "The boss, as in the president of the United States. I suppose he has his reasons. For one thing, the legality of the surveillance was, well, questionable. For another, the knowledge that the president was bugging the other party's candidate would be, let's say, a trifle sensitive politically. So he's made a decision to bury it."

"And you're okay with this? You were in Vietnam, so was I. How many lives would be saved by a peace agreement? And Richard Nixon sabotaged it so he could win an election?"

"There's no way to know for certain whether there would have been a peace deal, even if Nixon had kept his hands off it," J.D. said.

"Fine, true enough, but Nixon made sure it wouldn't happen. What do you think about that?"

"I think your question is above my pay grade. I report, ultimately, to the president, and until January 20th, that's Lyndon Johnson. And he's made his decision about what to do with this information, and I'm going to respect it. And you are, too."

Chapter Twenty-Two
—The Reckoning—

November 1968

1: A Winter's Tale

The aftermath of Michael's dinner with Harris was extraordinarily painful. As Michael had foreseen, it was like a second death, a second grieving. Anna sank into a melancholy deeper than her sorrow immediately after Alan died, one prolonged by the absence of any pressing tasks this time. And Michael was hardly immune. Working might have helped, but only one story was on his mind, and it was off limits. He was thankful he had never finished his memo to his editors about the possibility that Nixon sabotaged the peace talks. Had he sent it, he had no idea how he would have explained why he suddenly could not work on the story. As things stood, he would have to forget about it, and hope no one else put all the pieces together. Anna's private sadness was deep enough; a public exposure would be far worse.

Michael felt a responsibility to try to bring his mother out of this new trauma, but he was uncertain how to approach her. He hadn't been in his own home since before Paris, but he was reluctant to leave her in her present state of mind. So he stayed on in Washington, both of them padding around the big house like ghosts, their matching moods as gray and washed out as the weather. He proposed a drive out to Great Falls, one of their favorite haunts since his childhood, but Anna just sat wordlessly looking out the car window, her face devoid of expression.

Finally, after a week of this purgatory, Michael decided to try a more direct approach. He came into the living room with a couple of generous drinks, snapped off the TV, and took a seat next to Anna on the sofa.

"We've got to come to terms with this," he said, turning to face her. "Or at least begin to. It's not going to go away, but we have the rest of our lives to lead, and we can't let this consume us."

Anna looked away and said nothing. She hadn't touched her drink.

"Mom, this isn't like you. You're the most resilient person I know. You've never let anything knock you flat for long."

"This isn't like anything else. At least nothing I've ever experienced. Or ever hoped to."

"Of course it isn't. I understand that. But I think we have to try to find our way out of this—I don't even know what to call it. Maybe if we could try to understand what was going through dad's mind, it would help us."

Anna still said nothing, but finally picked up her drink and took a sip. Then another. Then a large one, and soon the drink was gone. She set the empty glass on the table, still looking straight ahead rather than at him.

"I've thought about it," she said at last. "Or rather, I've started to think about it. Just in the last day or two. Before that, I couldn't bear to. The taste of betrayal was too strong."

"I think we have to try to move past that," Michael said. "It's not easy, because we both feel it so strongly. But we have to try. When you were a novelist, you used to step outside your own persona and inhabit your character's. We have to try to do the same thing here."

"As if my husband were a character in one of my books?" As Anna said this, she turned to look at Michael for the first time, and he noticed the faintest of smiles, for just a moment. He took it as a sign of progress.

"Well, why not, if it works?"

"Life is strange, son. Very, very strange."

"You're telling me."

"Yes, I suppose you've learned that yourself, especially this past year."

Once again, Anna fell silent. She gestured at her empty glass, and Michael rose and refilled it. His own drink was still two-thirds full.

"I don't know if you'll understand this, because I barely understand it myself."

"Well, try me."

"One thing you have to try to understand is the trauma of the McCarthy years. Especially for people like Alan. I got tarred by the red-scare brush, too, but I wasn't in government, and I wasn't as vulnerable. Anyone who *was* in the government, anyone who had a security clearance, could suddenly find themselves in the spotlight, presumed guilty, forced to prove their innocence, often forced to prove a negative. Forced to defend themselves against the vaguest of anonymous accusations. And in Alan's case, it wasn't anonymous, and it wasn't vague."

Michael looked puzzled for a moment. Then he nodded. "You mean Spain."

"I mean Spain, and a lot more than Spain. He spent a lot of time and effort trying to convince President Roosevelt, or anyone who would listen, that it was a terrible mistake to stand by idly while Franco destroyed the Spanish republic. That wasn't a popular position in Washington in the late 1930s, to put it mildly. But Alan also put it in a broader context, which was even less popular. He saw Spain for what it was—a proving ground for Hitler and Mussolini, a way for them to test their military power, and, even more important, to test whether the western democracies had any will to resist them. And when it became clear that the answer was no, it made a broader war inevitable."

"He was right about all of it."

"Of course he was. But at the time, very few people wanted to hear it. Roosevelt understood, but he was hamstrung politically. It took years before most people grasped the threat. And then, after the war, when the Soviets turned from an ally to an enemy, people started looking with great suspicion at that small group who'd sounded the early warnings. They even had a name for them: premature anti-fascists."

"That's crazy. And sick."

"Yes, of course it was. And you can't imagine how crazy, and how sick, unless you lived through it. People turned on each other. Lifelong friendships ended. The Republicans had been out of power for years, and suddenly they saw this great opportunity—smear the Democrats with the accusation of being soft on communism. And if you'd been sounding a warning against Hitler back before it was fashionable, that was prima facie evidence that you'd done it because you were secretly a Soviet sympathizer. And that made you a security risk."

"Okay, but how does this connect with the here and now? Wasn't Nixon one of the worst of the red-baiters back in the late '40s?"

"Yes, he certainly was. You've never quite grasped the depths of my horror at the prospect of him becoming president. But if you'd seen him playing the Grand Inquisitor in congressional hearings, or smearing his opponent in his Senate race by calling her the Pink Lady, you'd have understood."

"So how does this explain—"

"I'm getting to it. For someone with Alan's background, one way to fight off suspicions about your loyalty was to sign up as a true-believer cold warrior. It wouldn't silence all the doubters, but it certainly helped. And there was the undeniable fact that the Soviets were fulfilling the worst stereotypes of the anti-communists. The hopes we cherished during the war that, once Hitler was defeated, Stalin could afford to relax his grip, all that turned out to be a foolish illusion. He cracked down even harder domestically. He broke all the promises he made to Roosevelt at Yalta. He turned Eastern Europe into a bunch of vassal states. He had the world's most powerful army, and a few years later he had the Bomb, too. You didn't have to be a right-winger to reach the conclusion that he had to be resisted. And there was only one country that could do it. The British were broke, the French were weak and divided. Tag, we're it."

"So what does this all add up to?"

"It adds up to the fact that Alan came by his anti-communism, which you have always found so distasteful and crude and gauche, quite honestly. Yes, it may have served his personal interest for political self-preservation. But it also fit his worldview, which was entirely consistent from the day I met him to the day he died. Democracy is preferable to autocracy. Aggressive dictators have to be resisted. Give them an inch, and they'll take a continent. And anyone who doesn't understand that is objectively helping the aggressor, whether they realize it or not. In fact, it's even worse if they don't, because that just makes them fools, and there's nothing more dangerous than a well-intentioned fool."

"I seem to recall him applying that label to me."

"Yes, he probably did. I suspect he thought it about me, too, although he never said it, at least not to my face. You and I see Vietnam as a grotesque mistake. He saw it as a necessary war, one front in a much larger conflict. That meant politicians like Johnson and Humphrey, who were backing away from it because they found it politically untenable, were not only wrong, they had put themselves on the other side of a very bright line. And it made someone like Nixon, who offered the possibility of staying the course, acceptable, even preferable, no matter what his history was."

Michael turned it all over in his mind. He could see the internal logic of it, how it could be used to justify such a massive betrayal of trust, even if it seemed twisted and blinkered when viewed from the outside. He recalled how Edouard had tried to talk him into a similar betrayal, using the same logic, of service to a higher cause. And he recalled how he'd been tempted, how he'd spent considerable time trying to talk himself into accepting that logic.

He decided that he, too, needed another drink.

2. Exiles

When he returned to the living room, Anna had her feet propped up on a pillow on the coffee table and her eyes closed, as if the effort to explore and explain Alan's motivations had left her utterly drained. Michael sat silently beside her for a time. He thought she might have fallen asleep. Then she opened her eyes and reached for her glass.

"So where does this leave you?" he asked her. "I assume you don't buy his logic, even if you've read his motivations correctly. And there may have been something else here, too, something much less elevated than pursuing the Holy Grail of vanquishing the communists. We know how much he resented being frozen out by Johnson this past year, and that wasn't likely to change if Humphrey won. He took it very personally. He may have seen what he did as his ticket of entry into the Nixon crowd, just like Erlich."

"Of course I don't buy his logic. When it comes to Vietnam, I'm a fool, a useful idiot, just like you. And you may be right about him hoping for a place in the sun under Nixon, although I suspect he would've been disappointed. But there's a logic to that, too, and it's not nearly as base or selfish as you're making it out to be. And it's one I happen to share."

"Let's keep in mind what really happened here," Michael replied. "If I'm right about this, dad helped sabotage a peace deal that might have saved thousands of lives so he could wangle a chance to stay on the inside, to be within the charmed circle when the big decisions are made. If that isn't base or selfish, I don't know what is."

Anna rose from the sofa and walked to the big window that looked onto their front yard and the street beyond. Some wet snow had fallen that morning, but now the sun was out, and most of the snowfall had melted. She turned and sat down in an armchair facing Michael.

"I told you once—it seems like a long, long time ago—about how I'd spent years in the political wilderness, pure but powerless, and that I'd never regretted deciding to come inside and try to accomplish something. To come in from the cold, to use Le Carre's turn of phrase. I don't think you really understood what I was talking about, and perhaps you couldn't have, because you hadn't had the same experiences. Maybe that's changed now. I don't know.

"I do know what it was like to be on the outside looking in when I was young. I remember how it felt to spend weeks and weeks picketing and leafleting to try to stop the state of Massachusetts from murdering two labor activists, and in the end they just brushed us off like pesky gnats and went ahead and pulled the switch to electrocute them. I remember the rage I felt, and the heartbreak.

"I remember what it was like to watch Hitler amassing power and turning Germany into a militarized madhouse, seeing it up close, and most of the world either heedless to the danger, or else enabling him because they thought that suited their own interests.

"And I remember seeing up close what real deprivation and poverty were like, what it did to people, how it warped lives and stunted children, and how the efforts of social reformers to ease that suffering seemed so hopelessly inadequate to the task.

"And then I had an opportunity to have some real influence. It was quite by chance, you know. I happened to write something about a school in New York that was preparing girls for college and serious careers instead of debutante balls. One of the people running the school was the wife of the governor. That's how I met Eleanor Roosevelt. And one thing led to another."

Michael had remained motionless and silent during this recitation, but now he shifted and shook his head. "I'm not sure where you're going with this, but I don't recall you spilling any state secrets to stay in Eleanor's good graces."

"No, but there were other things over the years. There are always things. Small compromises. At least you tell yourself they're small. You don't push your organization to take a strong stand against a bill that grossly violates the First Amendment, because that would embarrass some liberals who are co-sponsoring the bill to insulate themselves against McCarthy. Yes, that really happened. Or you pretend not to notice when a senator has too much to drink at a party and makes a pass at you, instead of telling him where to go, because he's an important ally on a campaign you're running.

"You tell yourself it's worth it, because it keeps you on the inside, and on the inside is where you want to be. Where it's happening. Where power is wielded. And you tell yourself it's better to be on the inside, where you can do some good, than back in the wilderness, where all you can do is rage at the injustices. Even if you have to cut some corners, swallow some things. Because you can't really imagine not being on the inside anymore."

The sun had gone back behind some clouds, and the room was growing dim as the short December day slipped away. Michael switched on a lamp, walked over to Anna, and hugged her.

"I'm not sitting in judgment of you, or your generation, or anyone else. If this year has taught me anything, it's how flawed we all are, how much we're at the mercy of the gods' capriciousness, how we're all hostages to fortune."

"Well, that's good, son. That's a start. A start at understanding me, and your father too, and the choices we both made, and maybe our entire generation and what we experienced. We didn't do everything right, that's for certain. There are times—especially now, when I'm alone—when I lie in bed at night recalling things that happened, sometimes years ago, and I cringe in embarrassment. Maybe that always happens when you get old—now, don't bother to flatter me by telling me I'm not, we're telling the truth today—or maybe it's just a sign of an uneasy conscience.

"And the truth is, the joke's on me, because after all my efforts, it's back in the wilderness for me after all. This Nixon gang that's coming to Washington will have no use for me, or anyone like me. I think Alan would have found that out, too. My whole tribe is going into a kind of exile, and we may be wandering in the desert for a long time."

"I know some people who'd say that's not the worst thing in the world," Michael replied. "That it might even be a kind of blessing. That being too close to power for too long tames you, dulls your capacity to be outraged over things that should inspire outrage. I guess that's my tribe speaking from our experience. We had to fight for years to get people in power to do anything about civil rights, even if they called themselves liberals. We were even more out in the cold over the war, until events on the ground finally made a reckoning inevitable. The whole political system seemed completely dysfunctional. That seemed to change this spring, but in the end it didn't. Now we're left with Nixon in power, and millions of people alienated and angry."

"Yes, and if anyone knows how to exploit alienation and anger, it's Tricky Dick Nixon," Anna said. "But here's one silver lining. Vietnam will soon become his war, and he'll be on the receiving end of all the hostility over it. And the fact that it's Nixon's war will free up a lot of Democrats to oppose it. A lot of opinion-shapers, too."

Now darkness had fallen, and the streetlights winked on outside. Neither of them felt much like cooking or going out. Michael found some leftovers in the back of the refrigerator and warmed them in the oven. They sat at the kitchen table, chewing on the reheated stew and the long day's conversation.

"So where does this leave you?" Michael asked again. "In your work, and in your mind?"

"As for work, I suspect Nixon will keep us very busy. He'll try to undo just about everything that was accomplished over the last eight years, and it's a long list. We still control Congress, which gives us some solid ground to stand on. It's a poor substitute for the White House, but it'll have to do for now."

"And in your mind? Can you live with what we know? Can you accept it?"

"I have no choice but to live with it. It happened, we know it happened, and I think we've figured out why it happened, as best we can.

"As for accepting it, that's another matter. No, I don't think I'll ever be able to, not fully. My feelings about Nixon are too strong. I can talk about his motivations, and at great length, as we've seen today, I can even have some empathy for them—but in the end, I still think it was a betrayal. I don't think I'll ever get over that feeling. And I'm not sure I want to, as much as it leaves me feeling conflicted. I don't want to spend the rest of my life with bitter memories of my husband—we shared too many good things, and I want to hang onto them—but I can't pretend this didn't happen. And in the end, I can't excuse it."

Michael kept silent and let her thoughts hang in the air. He foresaw a long road ahead for Anna, a difficult one, filled with unpleasant realizations. She had spoken about being banished to the wilderness again for a time, but Michael thought she might never fully escape this new exile, because events were conspiring to undermine the foundations of her life. The old Democratic coalition she had helped build and sustain over so many years had cracked apart, and Michael did not think it could be put back together. Those who tried, and Anna would surely be one, were destined to fail. And she would have to face that failure alone, without a partner, and with the bitter knowledge that her husband's last political act helped bring about the crackup.

As he turned these thoughts over in his mind, he felt an overwhelming surge of sorrow and sympathy for her well up, a sense of grief for all the losses his mother had suffered and would suffer. It was all he could do to keep from breaking down and bawling into the beef stew.

She had spoken of her generation as a tribe. Was it now a lost tribe, like the Israelites, doomed to wander in perpetual exile, far from its homeland? And what of him and his tribe? He had always felt something of an exile himself, an outsider admitted to the more distant circles of power on a temporary visa that could be revoked at will. He realized that was not entirely true, that his background and education conferred privileges that few people enjoyed, but it still defined his mindset, his inner image of himself. In that sense, at least, he and Anna were now alike.

Another image formed in his mind, another kind of loss that Anna was experiencing. She had lived fully in the world. But the world was now beginning to rush past her, to leave her behind, puzzling over its sudden strangeness and lamenting her disconnection from it. Was this our common fate? Was Michael glimpsing his own future, just as he had glimpsed his own mortality in his father's hospital room? Would he, in some distant year, experience this same unmooring, this slow slide into insignificance? He would have to find out, in his own time.

Chapter Twenty-Three
–The Castaways–
November 1968

Michael stayed on with his mother until she began to show signs of emerging from her penumbra of sorrow. He arranged for some of her friends to keep an eye on her, then headed home to New York for a few days.

The day after he returned, the ringing phone jarred him out of a deep reverie.

"Michael? Hello. It's me."

"Riva. It's good to hear your voice. How are you?

"Michael, I'm so sorry. I wasn't sure if I should call you. I finally decided to phone Anna, and she said it would be okay."

"Of course it's okay," Michael said. "I'm glad you called. I've—I've missed you. A lot."

"I'm so sorry about your father. I know you two had your problems, but it can't be easy losing him."

"How much did my mother tell you? Beyond what was in the papers, I mean."

"Well, not much, actually. She was a bit mysterious. She said I should talk to you."

"There's more. A lot more." Michael paused. "Could I tell you about it in person?"

An even longer pause. "Okay. Yes."

Half an hour later, Riva was at the door. Michael was struck by how thin she looked, how her face seemed drawn and burdened. He noticed that she walked as if she were in some pain.

They embraced, tentatively, then more firmly, and sat down on the sofa. Riva positioned herself carefully, not at the far end, but leaving some distance between them.

"I'm so glad you reached out," Michael said. "I've missed you, missed you a great deal."

"I wasn't sure if I should. But now I'm glad I did. You mentioned there was more to the story about your father?"

Michael narrated what had happened in Paris, and what he'd learned about Alan after his death. Riva listened with a growing sense of anguish, her eyes moistening. When Michael was done, she reached out and embraced him tightly.

"I can't imagine what this has been like for you and your mother."

"It's been surreal," Michael said. "He got this hero's funeral, lion of the establishment and all, lots of bigwigs there, and all the while there was this secret life he was leading right at the end. And now I think about all the people who were there and wonder if any of them knew. I think some of them must have, but they live by this goddamn code of silence.

"And I also can't help but wonder what other secrets he was keeping, ones we haven't tripped across, maybe never will. In fact, he was so habitually secretive, it's made me think that perhaps he left behind that paper trail about Paris because a part of him wanted it to be discovered. I don't know, maybe I'm overthinking it, playing armchair shrink."

"He always struck me as a complicated man," Riva replied.

They fell silent for a moment. "Riva, how are you? Tell me what's going on with you. You look—rather troubled."

She leaned back and sighed wearily. "When was the last time we talked? Not since right after—not since April, I guess. It's hard to believe that was just seven months ago. A lot's happened, and most of it hasn't been good.

"After I left, I got a lot more involved with the Black Panthers, and then with a group called the New Nation. It started out as a faction within the Panthers, then split off. Their rap was that the Panthers talked a good game but never did anything, just play-acted like revolutionaries. We were going to do it for real. All 15 of us. It sounds so crazy now, I'm embarrassed to even tell you about it."

"Riva, don't worry about that. We all do crazy shit. I've done my share, that's for sure. But I think I know something about the New Nation. Anyway, tell me what happened to you."

Riva looked at him curiously, then picked up her story. "Well, I guess I was flattered that a bunch of real revolutionaries were interested in me. But it was so fucked up. They were just a bunch of posers. The Panthers actually did something, ran some programs that did some good, like feeding breakfast to schoolkids. And they were honest people for the most part, when I look back on it, sincere about trying to build a movement that could help the community. The New Nation guys—and they were mostly guys—didn't really do a goddamn thing. They just wanted to cause trouble, which they were quite good at.

"It took me a while to realize how screwed up this whole scene was. When I did, I started to edge away. But that didn't go down well. The leader, a guy named Malik, told me I needed to be a fully committed revolutionary, or there was no place for me in the New Nation. And he also made it clear that leaving the group was not an option, as far as he was concerned. He hinted pretty strongly that there would be consequences for doing that, painful consequences.

"That scared the shit out of me, because I didn't doubt that he was serious. It got me back in line for a while, just out of sheer fear. But I kept noticing more things that bothered me, like the fact that we never tried to do anything positive, we just wanted to fuck with the Panthers. That we weren't doing anything to build the organization, we weren't trying to recruit new members from the community. And that Malik would disappear for stretches at a time, and then pop up again, and not tell me or anybody where he'd been. The whole scene just began to give me the creeps. I thought about going back to the Panthers, but by that time, there was so much hostility and suspicion built up that I didn't think they'd accept me.

"So I decided to just split. But somehow Malik found out about it. I'm not sure how, but he did. He cornered me, called me a traitor, called me quite a few other names, and said he knew how to deal with people like me.

"And then he hit me. A lot. He was really good at it, too, like he'd had a lot of practice. He did it in a way that didn't leave many bruises or blood, but still caused a lot of pain. I really thought he was going to kill me that night. But maybe he thought he didn't need to, that he'd terrorized me badly enough that I'd stay, or at least keep my mouth shut. Anyway, he stopped after a while. His parting shot was to kick me hard in the knee. Tore some cartilage. I might have to have surgery. I don't know yet.

"He was wrong about my being too afraid to leave, though. As soon as I could, I got the hell away. Far away."

Now it was Michael's turn to draw her close and hug her. They were both weeping softly.

"My god, Riva. I'm so sorry. When did all this happen?"

"It came to a head about two months ago. I crashed with some old theater friends for a while, got a place, then moved again. I was afraid he'd come looking for me. But he's left me alone. So far, anyway. But tell me—you said you knew something about the New Nation?"

"I don't know for sure, but I think they're a fake, an FBI creation. Hoover really hates the Panthers, thinks they're public enemy number one. I've heard that one of his tactics is to disrupt them by causing internal conflict. They send in an undercover agent. He builds up a little credibility, then he recruits some people into a faction and starts to stir up divisions. The line about the Panthers being faux revolutionaries is a classic part of the play."

Riva shook her head and cursed under her breath. "I thought about that. I knew there was something off about him, and how it would explain a lot if he was really a cop. Like why he was so devious. Why he turned out to be such a motherfucker. And why the group never really did anything real. But then I wondered if I was just being paranoid. Being in that group was like being in a hall of mirrors. Are you sure about this?"

"No, not a hundred percent. Earlier this year, I was doing some reporting for a story on the FBI and the black movement, but I wasn't able to get anyone to go on the record. I never got enough to write it. But several sources told me about what the FBI was doing to screw with the Panthers, totally off the record or on very deep background. And the New Nation was one name I heard."

Riva looked so angry and distraught, Michael half-regretted telling her what he knew. Yet it was rather late for any illusions, he thought. And our stories mirror each other. Hoover and Nixon were a perfect match, two products of the paranoid style of politics that had flourished in the Red Scare era and never fully died, two devious men who spun webs of deceit to trap the unwary.

"Do you still like Cinzano?" She nodded slowly. He poured out a couple of drinks and sat down next to her. They clinked glasses, wordlessly.

"What now? What are you planning to do?" he asked.

"I'm just trying to get my bearings again, get back some sense of myself, get rid of the taste of feeling used and dirty."

"I'd like to help you do that."

"I don't know if you can, Michael. I don't know if anyone can. I may have to do it by myself. If I can. I'm not sure I can."

"It's easier with some help," he said. "From someone who loves you. And I've never stopped loving you."

Riva gave him a searching look. "Have you—have you been with anyone?"

"Yes," he said. "Once. It didn't last long. I missed you too much."

"Thank you for being straight with me about that." She reached out and touched his hand. "Michael, I'm not sure I can be with you. I'm not sure I'm ready for that."

"I understand."

"And I certainly can't live with you," she said. "Not now. Not yet, anyway. I can barely live with myself right now."

They looked at each other, silently, for a long time, sitting very close. Slowly, gradually, they drew together, then held each other.

They felt a sense of peace settle over them. They felt the possibility—the possibility—of becoming whole again after being broken. They barely dared trust these feelings. They had no idea how long they would last. But at this moment, it was the best thing that had happened to either of them in quite a while.

"Do you remember our honeymoon?" Michael asked.

"Ye-es. That seems very long ago."

"It was right after Kennedy was killed. The first one. I still can't believe I have to say that. We were on this tropical island, it was all beauty and serenity, and the world around us had gone mad.

"We felt like we were castaways. I have the same feeling now."

"Two shipwrecks in one lifetime?" Riva replied, touching his cheek and laying her head on his shoulder. "We might be pushing our luck."

Author's Note

Thank you for spending some time with the McMasters and their era. If you enjoyed the experience, please consider leaving a review or a comment online. Even a brief one can make a great deal of difference. If you would like to contact me directly with a comment or question, please do, at khfireman@verizon.net or on Twitter (@kfireman1).

A note on sources: This is, of course, a work of fiction, but it includes several real people and actual events. I witnessed some of these events myself, including the 1967 march on the Pentagon, the disorders in Detroit that same year, the protests at the 1968 Democratic convention in Chicago, and the chaotic George Wallace campaign rally in Detroit.

For other events that I wrote about, I relied for factual background on the accounts of journalists, scholars, and participants. The attack on the freedom riders in Montgomery and the events at the First Baptist Church have been recounted in several books, including Howell Raines' oral history of the civil rights movement, *My Soul is Rested* (Putnam, 1977). Martin Luther King Jr.'s meeting with the cab drivers was described by Bernard Lafayette Jr., a participant in the freedom rides, in an article published in the New York Times on May 19, 2011. Taylor Branch's history of the civil rights movement, *Parting the Waters* (Simon & Schuster, 1988), contains a detailed account of the 1963 Birmingham campaign.

The events of the Cuban missile crisis and Robert Kennedy's role in it have been recounted in several books, including Kennedy's own memoir, *Thirteen Days* (Norton, 1969).

The events in Dallas on Nov. 22, 1963, have been chronicled many times; especially detailed accounts can be found in William Manchester's book *The Death of a President* (Harper & Row, 1967), and in Robert Caro's *The Passage of Power* (Knopf, 2012). Caro also detailed Lyndon Johnson's early priorities as president, especially his commitment to the civil rights bill, and events at the Johnson ranch in late 1963, including the president's mistreatment of Pierre Salinger.

The events of Robert Kennedy's presidential campaign, including his Press Club breakfast, his campaigning in Indiana and California, and the scene of his assassination, were vividly reported by journalist Jules Witcover in his book *85 Days: The Last Campaign of Robert Kennedy* (Putnam, 1969).

Richard Nixon's attempts to block a Vietnam peace deal shortly before the 1968 election, and the Johnson administration's knowledge of it through FBI surveillance of Nixon, came into public view through the release in 2013 of tapes of Johnson's conversations with aides. More details came to light when notes taken in 1968 by Nixon's senior aide, H. R. Haldeman, became public. Biographer John A. Farrell wrote about the Haldeman notes in an article published in the New York Times on Dec. 31, 2016.

While all these writings were of invaluable assistance in helping me understand what happened during some critical junctures in the 1960s, the final product is, of course, my own—and any errors are mine, as well.

About the Author

As a young activist, Ken Fireman participated in many of the events narrated in *The Unmooring*, from civil rights picket lines to the 1967 march on the Pentagon and the street protests at the 1968 Democratic convention. He went on to a career as a journalist, covering wars and upheaval in Russia and the Persian Gulf, and the inner workings of Washington as a White House and Pentagon correspondent. (Photo: Matt Mendelsohn)

Note from the Publisher

Word-of-mouth is crucial for any author to succeed. If you enjoyed *The Unmooring*, please leave a review online—anywhere you are able. Even if it's just a sentence or two. It would make all the difference and would be very much appreciated.

Thanks!

We hope you enjoyed reading this title from:

BLACK ROSE
writing™

Subscribe to our mailing list – *The Rosevine* – and receive **FREE** books, daily deals, and stay current with news about upcoming releases and our hottest authors.
Scan the QR code below to sign up.

Already a subscriber? Please accept a sincere thank you for being a fan of Black Rose Writing authors.

View other Black Rose Writing titles at
www.blackrosewriting.com/books and use promo code
PRINT to receive a **20% discount** when purchasing.

9 781685 130589